LEO E. NDELLE

AN ARCHANGEL'S ACHE

ACKNOWLEDGEMENT

And the journey continues! I would like to thank all of you (family, friends and fans) for your undying support and encouragement. You all have been the powerhouse behind the growing success that has been this book series.

A special thanks to my beta readers: Anita C., PhD and Laura N. Your patience and critique have been most invaluable.

DEDICATION

To you, Mami!

I could never ask for a better mother.

PART ONE

THE LOGOS

VALLA IS THE first realm-dimension in Creation sparked from the Core. Therefore, its vibrational frequency is lower than that of the Core of Creation. Just like every realm-dimension in Creation, Valla has neither a guardian nor a Zarark. Yet, it is home to a multidimensional entity called The Logos. A Cosmic Countdown spans the duration of a perfect cycle and a perfect cycle marks the age of Creation. At the end of a Cosmic Countdown, a phenomenon called a Cosmic Spark marks the end of a perfect cycle. During a Cosmic Spark, all the states of Creation, Space, Time, Energy and Ether, come to a standstill. A Great Reset follows a Cosmic Spark, a new aspect of The Logos is birthed and new consciousness is released into Creation.

The aspects of The Logos correspond to the number of perfect cycles of Creation. Essentially, The Logos is a single, multidimensional being, despite its several aspects. During the last Cosmic Spark, The Logos split into seven aspects, with each aspect assuming one of the seven colors of light. Rach was red. Och, orange. Yach, yellow. Gach, green. Bach, blue. Ich, indigo. Vach, introduced the color violet, just like the other aspects of The Logos did after their ascension. As such, after the last Cosmic Spark, light consisted of seven colors, instead of six. Vach's essence underwent an ascension and it officially became the newest aspect of The Logos. These aspects existed in near-omnipresence, near-omnipotence and near-omniscience and permeated every aspect of Creation that existed within their vibrational frequency and lower. Their centers glowed in their respective colors of light and released the vibration of love into the portions of Creation under their governance. Then,

The Logos began its session.

Bach: *Another cycle is complete.*

Ich: *The moment for something new is here.*

Vach: *What do we propose?*

Ich: *A new vibration for our Creation to make decisions on their own.*

Och: *They may not be mature enough to handle this vibration yet.*

Gach: *And how will they know, if we do not give them the option?*

Yach: *We knew this moment would come. We say we give them a chance.*

Och: *They are not ready. They still need to grow.*

Rach: *We agree with Och. Yet, we cannot continue to shelter them from themselves. How can they grow if they do not know the other side?*

Vach: *We are pure and perfect and we know what this new vibration brings.*

Bach: *Agreed, but we say we let them have it… starting now.*

Gach: *And all that we have spawned may be reduced to naught.*

An instant of silence went by until Vach spoke.

Vach: *They are a part of us and we of them. We are one. In them resides the seed of perfection and purity. They will learn and they will evolve. So, I say, we let them have it now. All in favor indicate.*

The Logos beamed their agreement in unison in the form of their respective colors. Thus, it came to pass that during the last Great Reset a perfect cycle ago, The Logos introduced a new vibration called 'free will' into Creation and this new vibration called free will resulted in the polarization of Creation's consciousness.

The Logos: *It is done.*

With this affirmation, the aspects of The Logos beamed their agreement in their respective colors of light. These beams of light converged at a center. Then, the aspects of The Logos pulsed once in unison and returned to its essential state of being as a single, multidimensional being. The Cosmic Spark ended, Creation emerged from its state of stillness and a new perfect cycle began.

Akasha is a realm-dimension, just like Valla, although of a lower vibrational frequency. As the keeper of the records of Creation, Akasha is the relay between The Logos and the rest of Creation. As such, Akasha is the first to receive all new vibrations and bursts of consciousness from The Logos, which it transduces to the rest of Creation. Prior to the most recent Great Reset, Akasha only knew order, because Akasha was Order. However, the vibration of free will was new, even to Akasha. Thus, when Akasha received this new vibration of free will from The Logos, Akasha's essence experienced an esoteric shock of multidimensional proportions. This esoteric shock resulted in the polarization of Akasha's essence resulting in an esoteric split of Akasha's essence.

Akasha's reaction to this esoteric split gave rise to the first vibrations of ignorance and confusion. These new vibrations of ignorance and confusion sparked another identity within Akasha's essence, marking the birth of Akasha's ego. The ego raged within Akasha, strengthening its existence by feeding on these new vibrations of ignorance and confusion in an esoteric chain reaction of multidimensional proportions. Akasha had no prior knowledge or information regarding these new vibrations of ignorance and confusion and, for the very first instance in her existence, fear filtered its way into her essence causing Akasha to also experience panic. As the mélange of all these new sensations and vibrations exploded within her essence, threatening to rip her apart ether by ether, Akasha did the only thing she could do to continue to exist. She gathered all the new vibrations and sensations that threatened to render her non-existent.

My first and only spawn, Akasha declared. *I must project you out of my essence.*

Akasha gave its spawn a form and because this spawn was of Akasha, the spawn also became a multidimensional being. However, the new vibration of free will caused a polarization of Akasha's consciousness. Thus, Akasha's spawn and what remained of Akasha's essence adopted opposing purposes. Akasha's spawn identified with the masculine and what remained of Akasha's essence identified with the feminine, and even this identification was new to Akasha because, until this moment, before the polarization of Akasha's consciousness, Akasha never identified with either the masculine of feminine.

At least, I can return to my purpose of order, Akasha thought with relief.

Unfortunately, that sweet relief only lasted for an instant because Akasha realized the outcome of her action.

I released my spawn into Creation, she said. *Order is my nature. I gave my spawn a purpose that is opposite from mine and releasing my spawn into Creation means I just released Chaos into Creation.*

A moment of silence came and went.

What have I done? Akasha asked herself.

She accessed the Dimension of Time and saw the vibration of chaos tearing Creation apart ether by ether until nothing remained to ever attest of the existence of Creation. She saw the undoing of Creation and morbid dread seized her being. However, she could handle the sensation of fear this instant without her essence riling in protest and resistance, and a reformation of her purpose emerged out of that new sense of awareness.

I must fix this, she declared. *I must restore order in Creation. I must destroy Chaos.*

Akasha accessed all the states of Creation to find a way to destroy Chaos. She found her answer.

No, she cried. *There has to be another way.*

But even as she refused to accept the answer, she knew it was the only way to destroy Chaos.

I will fix this, Akasha promised herself. *But not like this.*

She regarded Chaos with determination to prevent the inevitable. However, her resolve to end him dissolved because Chaos was but a youngling; albeit a multidimensional youngling. She nodded as hope for an alternative solution flooded her being.

I shall mentor him and he shall be my apprentice, she declared. *He shall be reborn into a new purpose of order and Creation will never know Chaos.*

Akasha held Chaos' form against hers and flooded Chaos with the vibration of love. Then, Chaos uttered his first words.

Your actions are futile.

Chaos' words stunned Akasha.

You and I are multidimensional beings, Chaos spoke with unwavering certainty. *You and I are one and new to our purposes.*

Chaos withdrew his form from Akasha's embrace.

I welcome who and what I am with an open essence, Chaos declared. *Nothing and no one will stop me. I have seen the future and my purpose is inevitable. I am inevitable.*

Akasha moved to restrain Chaos by force but Chaos disappeared from sight.

From now on, I shall call myself The Scribe, Chaos declared into Creation. *For I shall re-write the story of Creation to a certain end. I am a purveyor of purpose and I shall see my will come to pass. I am The Scribe and, by my will, I shall undo Creation.*

CHAPTER ONE

I HEAR YOU

IT WAS PAST midnight and the baby would not sleep. Her parents played with her in her cot, despite their droopy eyes and slumped shoulders from lack of sleep and a full workday. Seven years of trying, too many miscarriages to count and undying hope resulted in the miracle named Jenna Ebude Mukong. Eliel, her guardian angel, called her Baby JEM. He smiled and tickled Baby JEM's nose. The result, a toothless grin and a squeal of laughter, much to her parents' delight, who had no idea Eliel stood opposite from them. However, Baby JEM could see him as clearly as she could see her parents.

Eliel spread his wings, flapped them once and retracted them. Baby JEM shrieked with joy and reached for him, her tiny, chubby fingers beckoning him to take her in his arms. He grinned with pleasure, while her parents' faces contorted with confusion.

"We are over here, princess," her mother said.

Eliel's previous assignment died after 29 Earth Realm cycles from a heroin overdose. She epitomized what the creatures of Earth Realm called 'an entitled, spoiled brat'. Eliel leaned towards Baby JEM. She reached for his nose but her hands kept going through his face. Still, she was relentless.

"Come closer," she said via telepathy. *"I can't reach your face."*

Eliel stroked her thin, baby-soft hair. His gentle touch, carrying the vibrational frequency of his realm, sent soothing vibrations through her body. She half-closed her eyes. Eliel sealed his angel's touch with an angel's kiss on her forehead. Baby JEM flashed a toothless smile.

"You should go to sleep now, my little friend," Eliel said telepathically. *"Your parents also require sleep."*

Baby JEM's big, black eyes stared blankly at his face, but her toothless grin never left her face. Eliel stroked her head again.

"Sleep now, my little friend... Sleep..." Eliel spoke softly, lulling her to sleep.

Baby JEM thrust her left thumb into her mouth. Her little, red lips wrapped around her thumb and her toothless gums clamped around it. Her tongue and cheeks went to work as she sucked on her left thumb. Her beautiful, black eyes closed halfway, opened again, before closing completely as sleep took over.

"Good night, Angel Eliel," Baby JEM said telepathically. *"You're still watching over me, right?"*

"Always," Eliel replied telepathically. *"Good night, my little angel."*

Baby Jem fell instantly asleep.

"She's gonna be a handful," Mom said.

"I wonder who she gets it from," Dad replied jokingly.

Mom punched Dad playfully in the arm before Dad scooped her up on his shoulder and smacked her butt. She squealed with delight before she cupped her mouth. Mom and Dad froze for a second or two. When Baby JEM did not make a sound or budge, they sighed with relief and giggled their way to their bedroom.

'Shouldn't you two be watching over your assignments?" Eliel asked in angelic frequency.

"Very funny, El," Farel, Dad's guardian angel, said.

"Would you like to swap assignments tonight, El?" Gahel, Mom's angel, asked rhetorically.

"They are great people, though, aren't they?" Eliel asked, finally peeling his eyes from Baby JEM and facing his colleagues. "It's sad that soon she may forget I exist."

'Don't they all," Farel rolled his shoulders. "Her father forgot about me when he was barely six months old, I think. It took me a while to understand 'time' in this realm."

"Her mother forgot at age five," Gahel added.

"Yeah, sad indeed," Eliel said. "So, I will enjoy this period with her before I become a mythical creature to her."

The three angels burst into laughter.

"In other news," Eliel said. "I heard Mazel might be getting a promotion?"

"Oh yes," Farel squirmed and rolled her eyes. "She was one of those selected for archangel training. Claimed she heard The Voice too."

"Like so many others," Gahel replied. "Well, Uriel will determine if she speaks the truth or not. Do any of you know how long she has been an angel for?"

"Two cycles, I hear," Farel replied and wrinkled her nose.

"That's about how long you and I have been angels, Farel," Gahel tapped on his chin with his fingers. "I wonder how long a celestial cycle is compared to the cycles of this realm."

"Who cares?" Farel spat and pouted.

"By Celestia, what the flap did Mazel do to you?

"Nothing," Farel averted her gaze.

"Really?" Gahel prompted.

Farel turned to face the two angels. They leveled raised-eyebrow gazes at her. She shook her head and heaved her shoulders.

"Alright," Farel sighed. "During the special units training, I placed among the top 2%, meaning, I was supposed to be under Uriel's stewardship. But Mazel was chosen and I was assigned to Earth Realm instead."

"I think you mean to say you *applied* to be considered for Uriel's stewardship," Eliel corrected her.

"Yes, El, I did apply, and I was considered," Farel spat.

"Wow," Gahel exclaimed. "You were considered for Uriel's stewardship? By Celestia, you're a celebrity for that alone, Farel. Look at El and I. We've never been considered for anything; and here you are, being considered for stewardship by Uriel herself. Oh, I'd give my wings just to get close to her bracelet. She's the coolest senior archangel. Wise, compassionate, strong, so friendly and fierce. I can only imagine how hot she is when she summons her archangelic battle flame."

"Pun intended, I presume?" Farel asked rhetorically and rolled her eyes.

"If I ever see her summon her flame, I'm going to have an orgasm right there and then," Gahel promised. "And I'll let her know it's all her fault."

"That is utterly disgusting." Farel wrinkled her nose. "Exploding in angel light in the open."

"There isn't an archangel who compares to Michael," Eliel tried to change the topic. "I don't know why you two keep rubbing your wrists."

Gahel and Farel quickly stowed their hands to their sides.

"It takes a lot to earn the bracelet of an archangel," Eliel continued. "Why even bother, when being an angel is just fine?"

"'Cause archangels are flapping cool," Gahel and Farel chorused and returned to rubbing the wrists of their dominant hands more vigorously.

"You're probably the only angel I know who doesn't dream of becoming an archangel," Farel snorted.

"He'll come around, Farel," Gahel winked. "He's just a youngling, barely a cycle old."

"I really don't care for it," Eliel shrugged. "I've only heard of Michael. But from what I've heard and read about him, he's really the toughest."

"Arguable," Farel interjected.

"We all know about the one who almost beat him," Gahel chimed in.

A moment of uncomfortable silence lingered as chilling, unpleasant stories of the one Gahel was referring to stung their young minds.

"Anyway, have any of you even seen Michael, or Raphael?" Farel asked.

Eliel and Gahel shook their heads.

"Michael is estranged and only Raphael's squad of elite fighters has seen him," Gahel said. "The senior archangels never descend from their high domains to comingle with us, lower angels. That's why Uriel is the coolest. She comingles with us."

Gahel waggled his eyebrows, Farel rolled her eyes and Eliel smiled.

"Do any of you know anything about The Voice?" Eliel asked,

Their childishness is becoming insufferable, he thought.

They shook their heads and resumed watching over their assignments.

"He's so serious all the time," Gahel said to Farel via telepathy.

"I don't know if I should feel sorry for him or what," Farel loomed over Mom, who snored in Dad's arms.

"I'd like to think he's like this because he's still just a youngling," Gahel said. *"But then, you and I, and every other angel we've encountered, did not act this way during their first cycle."*

"Correct," Farel nodded and glanced in Eliel's direction. *"Maybe something is wrong with him? Something happened during his spawning or training?"*

"I researched him," Gahel replied. *"Found nothing unusual, except that he excelled exceedingly over all his peers in every field: general knowledge, fighting skills, you name it."*

"I do admire his work ethic and sense of dedication, though," Farel smiled and Gahel smiled as well. *"It's a shame. He would've made a damn fine archangel."*

"Agreed," Gahel nodded. *"Maybe we should toss some feathers his way and be more inclusive in our convos."*

"You're right," Farel said. *"You lead. I'll tag along."*

"Have you ever witnessed an angel falling?" Gahel asked out loud.

"No, have you?" Farel replied.

"Only once," Gahel continued. "About half a cycle ago. His name was Darel and I used to work with him. I remember he kept telling me he wanted to be human. I kept wondering who in the right mind would want humanity's insanity. Told me it was all about the experience and he wasn't even worried about the possibility of permanent amnesia and never returning home. Good angel. I miss his crazy wings sometimes. Still thought he was crazy even when he went ahead to submit his intent to fall and stated he was of sound mind and was aware of the possibility of permanent amnesia. And so it came to pass that he fell. He's doing well now as a teenager somewhere in China."

"How was the fall?" Eliel's eyes bulged with fascination.

"Seems like he's finally showing some interest in something," Farel said via telepathy.

"Told you he just needed some inclusion," Gahel replied in like-manner.

"I was sad to see him go," Gahel replied as he relived the moment from his memory. "They took him to The Edge. Nubiel, our supervisor, was present, as per protocol. He bade us farewell, turned around and just fell. He was gone, just like that."

Gahel flapped his wings once.

"That's it?" Farel asked with a hint of disappointment. "I expected something more spectacular."

"Well, that was all I witnessed," Gahel shrugged. "But from what I learned from another source, the first thing you lose during a fall is your garments, followed by your wings. They actually get burned away as you descend into realms of lower vibrational frequencies. Next, you start losing your memory. The further your fall, the more your memory gets erased until you experience full amnesia."

"I wonder the reason for the amnesia, though," Farel interjected.

"Maybe because in order to rise, one must fall," Eliel replied quietly. "In order to see the light, one must go through the dark. In order to remember, one must first of all forget…"

"By Celestia, El," Gahel exclaimed. "Where did that come from?"

"I have no idea, brother," Eliel replied.

"You sound like one of those wise humans on this realm," Gahel chuckled. "Not that there's anything wrong with that."

Gahel and Farel stifled a snicker.

"I'll take the compliment," Eliel chuckled.

"Back to what I was saying," Gahel rubbed his hands together. "After amnesia comes the final stages of the fall. Sometimes, the fallen comrade would infuse a fertilized egg and become reborn as a baby. Other times they take over the body of a dying creature. But very rarely the fallen brother or sister maintains his or her original physical form, albeit denser in nature and without the wings of course. There's no known determining factor for a fallen brother's or sister's outcome. Random, maybe?"

"I don't think anything is ever random with Creation," Eliel replied.

Baby JEM's face contorted in a prelude to a scream and Eliel rushed to her side. She squirmed as if she was having a nightmare. Eliel stroke her head with his left hand and rubbed her tummy gently with his right hand, singing a melody to her. She whipped her head to the left and to the right before a calm spread over her face. Her right thumb instinctively found its way again to her mouth. She sucked on it and ceased squirming. Eliel continued singing a melody for a few more seconds before he stepped away from her crib.

"Do you think many of our brothers and sisters are still defecting to the other side?" Eliel asked his friends.

"Yes," Farel replied. "But a lot fewer than before. Raphael being in charge of counter-intelligence and security also ensures fewer, if not zero, spies from the other side as well. His squad has exceptional training and you certainly don't want to mess with them. To qualify, you must pass his sniff test and, believe me, this is unthinkably harder than the training program. Besides, you don't apply to join Raphael's team; you're called. Less than 3% of candidates pass the training."

"How do you come about all these pieces of information?" Farel raised an eyebrow at Gahel.

"I rub my feathers with the right angels… and archangels," Gahel spread his wings and flapped them twice, very slowly.

Farel covered her eyes with her hands and shook her head.

"I wouldn't expect anything less from a superior archangel like Raphael, based on what I have heard about him," Eliel said.

"They don't call him Raphael, The Ruthless, for nothing," Gahel said.

"Well, thanks you two," Eliel rolled his shoulders twice. "I must return to my task now."

"Yeah, us too," Farel agreed.

A few hours of utter silence went by, except for the occasional sounds of cars driving along the main road not far from the house and mom snoring.

"Eliel."

"I'm right here," Eliel replied.

His comrades looked at him with surprise.

"We didn't call your name, brother," Farel said.

"Oh, thought I heard my name," Eliel replied. "Sorry. Ignore me please."

"Eliel."

I hear it, but it's clear they don't, Eliel wondered. *I feel it too. It's not of Celestia. It's neither male nor female. But who is it? What is it?*

A heated debate about who would win a fight between Raphael and Samael brewed between his friends. Eliel tried to remain as panic welled up slowly within his core.

What should I say? What should I do? he asked himself.

"Eliel."

His being resonated with the vibrations of the sexless voice calling his name. Innately, he knew he had only one way to respond.

But how come? Why me? I am but a youngling, not even worthy.

He turned his gaze towards the sleeping baby. A sad smile slid across his face.

Her tiny chest heaved up and down with every calm breath of air she inhaled and exhaled. He leaned forward and kissed her forehead. He sensed his friends' eyes digging into his back. He also sensed their worry and concern. How? He had no idea and neither did he care anymore.

My transformation has already begun.

"What's going on, El?" Gahel asked.

"I'm very sorry, my little friend," Eliel said to Baby JEM via telepathy.

She smiled weakly in her sleep, as if saying she understood and wished him the best of luck.

"El?" Farel called out, her voice heavy with worry.

Eliel kissed Baby JEM's forehead.

"Goodbye, my little friend," he said.

Then, he lifted his eyes upwards and said the words he innately knew he had to say.

"I hear you."

"Come," said The Voice.

Eliel turned around and faced his friends. As he did, a ball of light began forming in the center of his chest. As the light grew brighter, he opened his arms and spread his wings. The light engulfed him in a brightness that dulled the brightness of a thousand supernovas. Farel and Gahel shielded their eyes and missed the part where Eliel beamed upwards in an explosion of pure, white brightness. When the brightness dissipated, Farel and Gahel brought down their hands from their eyes but their mouths remained open from shock. Gahel broke the silence.

"Good wings," he exclaimed.

"What just happened?" Farel's voice rose in panic. "Where's El?"

"What the flap. I can't believe this," Gahel exclaimed and fell to his knees. "I thought he was weird and special, but I never knew he was this special."

Farel grabbed him by his collar and brought her snarling face dangerously close to his.

"You tell me right now what just happened to El or else I'll do something to you I'll regret."

"You wouldn't even believe me."

"Try me."

"Eliel just heard The Voice," he replied.

Overwhelmed with shock and awe, Farel let go of Gahel's collar and sank to her knees as well.

Eliel found himself in a chamber that was empty except for what looked like a throne on which an archangel sat on. His head spun from the unexpected teleportation but he managed to rise to his feet. He spread and flapped his wings repeatedly and stretched his arms and legs. He also summoned angel light to wash over his body by sparking the ethers. The daze in his head disappeared and his alertness returned.

He regarded the angel on the throne-like seat. The angel's left arm rested freely on the arm-rest, while his right index finger rested lightly on his lips as he stared idly at the floor. He appeared to be in deep thought. Eliel scanned the chamber. It looked like every other domain in Celestia, except it was larger.

No wings, Eliel thought. *Must be an archangel.*

Then, Eliel noticed the golden bracelet… on both wrists.

Flap, he exclaimed in his head. *I am in so much trouble.*

This domain did not belong to any ordinary archangel. It belonged to Michael, Archangel Supreme of the Realm of Celestia.

"Huh- Huh-," he stammered and cleared his throat. "Hello Michael, sir…"

Michael remained silent and still. Eliel cleared his throat again and stepped forward. His body trembled from excitement and fear all at once.

I'm in the presence of Michael, he thought. *The one and only Michael. By Celestia, I've seen the greatest and highest-ranking archangel of Celestia in the flesh.*

"It's truly an honor to meet you, sir," Eliel said timidly, not knowing what else to say.

"How many times?" Michael asked in a deep, reverberating voice that seemed to make the very floor on which Eliel stood vibrate.

"I'm sorry, sir-" Eliel said and swallowed.

"How many times did you hear The Voice?" Michael asked.

Eliel cleared his throat again.

"Uh, it called my name three times, sir," Eliel replied timidly.

"And how did you reply?" Michael asked, with his gazed glued to the floor.

"I said 'I hear you,'" Eliel replied. "The next thing I knew, I was here. I don't even know how that answer came to mind, but it just felt… right…"

Michael nodded almost imperceptibly and then rose from his throne-seat, his eyes still averted to the floor. Even at that distance, his form towered above Eliel's and his immense musculature pushed against his plain, white, ankle-length robe.

He's not wearing any shoes, Eliel noticed. *Maybe he doesn't like shoes in his domain.*

Eliel took an involuntary step backward and dismissed his shoes.

Maybe I should just go away, he thought. *But he's just going to track me down.*

Eliel cleared his throat and squared his shoulders as Michael slowly closed the gap between the two of them.

I'm in so much trouble, Eliel cowered. *And I don't even know what I did wrong.*

"Only two have ever heard The Voice," Michael said. "And these two were the highest-ranking archangels ever."

Eliel's eyes bulged in fear when Michael's wristbands started glowing. Eliel had only read about the meaning of an archangel's wristband glowing during his school days.

"After the other archangel heard The Voice, I lost countless brothers and sisters to her savagery."

Michael took another step towards Eliel.

"And you, Eliel, a youngling, not even an archangel, have heard The Voice. You don't know what awaits you and you're certainly not ready for it."

Eliel's gut tightened as every ether of his body sensed danger afoot and begged him to flee. Yet, he just stood there as if hypnotized by Michael's presence and the power that radiated from Michael's persona. Archangel Michael leveled his gaze towards Eliel and a whimper escaped Eliel's throat.

Flaming eyes of an archangel. This can't be happening. He can't seriously mean it, right? Eliel tried to convince himself otherwise despite his instincts rioting against the stupidity of his decision to stand his ground.

"You must understand," Michael added. "I cannot risk you being taken over by the darkness."

A five-foot, golden, flaming sword formed in Michael's right hand. He raised his sword so that Eliel stared directly at its flaming tip. His wristbands glowed even brighter and golden flames spewed from his eyes and mouth as he spoke.

He's about to summon the archangel flame, Eliel recoiled in fear and shock. *The greatest fighter in Celestia's history is about to battle me, a mere youngling. Oh no. I am doomed.*

"History will not repeat itself," Michael snarled, and more golden flames spewed from his mouth. "Not again. Not under my watch."

Eliel stumbled backward as Michael approached him.

"Nothing personal, youngling. This is just me taking affirmative action," Michael spoke with vehement assurance. "Therefore, I must end your existence."

His plain, long white robe morphed into his flaming, battle garments and a pair of six-foot long wings of fire erupted from his shoulder blades. Then, Michael, Archangel Supreme of Celestia lifted his sword and charged at the lowly, youngling Angel Eliel.

CHAPTER TWO

THE KING OF HELL

KAZUK SAT ON his throne. Yes, it was HIS throne. Many cycles had rolled by since he assumed the role as the King of Hell Realm.

The Scribe better not keep me waiting, Kazuk huffed with growing impatience, which was merely a substitute for his feeling of inadequacy vis-à-vis The Scribe.

I realize I'm powerless against this creature, wherever he's from, Kazuk admitted. *Still no reason to keep me waiting.*

Kazuk was not the designated leader of this uninhabited cesspool that was Celestia's neighbor of a realm. However, after the Great Rebellion in Celestia many Celestial cycles ago, Michael banished those who fought against him and lost to Hell as punishment. The rebels lost their leader and her next-in-command, Zukael. Thus, a vacancy became available for the position of leader of Hell. The master strategist of the rebellion, Malichiel, was next in line to rise to the throne of leadership. However, his loyalty to their imprisoned leader prevented him from assuming this role. Thus, the mantle of leadership in Hell became open to anyone willing to seize the opportunity and twenty contenders, including Kazuk, rose to the occasion.

And so, a battle to the death ensued. As an unrecognized master strategist, the underdog that was Kazuk used sharp wit and supreme skills with the sword to end many of his opponents swiftly.

Six left.

Kazuk entertained his six opponents in a dance of more death and damnation. He chose to exhibit a public display of his strength and skill for all in Hell Realm to see. Tired of toying with his prey, the predator that was Kazuk beheaded his opponents with ruthless abandon.

He picked up the severed heads of his adversaries from the floor, one-by-one. He let the angel light streaming from their severed heads bathe his feet. Hell Realm watched and cowered in fear as he walked in slow, calculated steps towards the empty throne, holding three severed heads in each hand. The unspoken message was loud and clear; one of total dominion and zero tolerance for any form of opposition, a promise of strength and leadership like Hell Realm had never seen before, an affirmation of the hope of returning to Celestia, with or without their former leader, Luciel. His was a wordless speech heralding the dawn of a new cycle for Hell Realm and its inhabitants.

Kazuk turned around and faced Hell Realm. Slowly, he gazed across the scores of thousands of many creatures that cowered and shivered in fear and deathly silence. Then, he raised the heads of his slain adversaries in the air and let them fall on the stairs. The heads rolled down the stairs and ended at the bottom of the stairs. Kazuk rested both his hands on the smooth, marble-like armrests of the throne and lowered his body, mired in the angel light of his slain opponents, into the throne. His bride manifested by his side from thin air, walked down a few steps in front of Kazuk and faced the Realm of Hell. She shapeshifted her vocal chords to tune into the vibrational frequency of Hell Realm so that, when she spoke, every creature will hear her loud and clear as if she was close to them.

"Creatures of Hell Realm," she bellowed. "Behold Kazuk, your new leader. Your new King."

Fire and heat blazed. Ice and cold froze. Hounds of Hell howled, dropped on all fours and buried their snouts in their paws. Pain, suffering, pestilence, and all things aligned with the dark echoed. Lost and fallen creatures cowered and shivered. Demons dropped on their knees and lowered their heads. Trumpets appeared in the hands of many and sounded, and Hell itself rock in a hell-quake as all of Hell chanted:

"ALL HAIL, KAZUK. ALL HAIL THE KING."

Kazuk reached for his wife. She accepted his hand and sat across his lap.

"My bride," Kazuk said.

"My king," Lithilia replied with a smile.

She kissed the King of Hell passionately on the lips and Hell Realm erupted in praise.

Under Kazuk's leadership, Hell saw many changes. Infrastructure sprang all over the realm and the realm no longer looked like a complete wasteland. One could almost call it home. However, without the Zarark, Hell could not spawn other creatures and if the creatures of Hell ever wanted their dream of retaking Celestia to come true, strength in numbers remained their best option. As such, Hell had increased its numbers rapidly by welcoming many lost and banished creatures from other realms. Slowly, the realm's culture started shifting from desperation to hope; hope for the future, for the moment when they would finally be able to defeat Michael and his host of angels and archangels and reclaim Celestia as their home. The change in culture warranted a change in names for every citizen of Hell, without exception. Every creature has a future and every demon a past. Kazuk was not yet a demon, but he certainly had a past.

***

Before the Great Rebellion, Kazuk was a high-ranking archangel by the name of Maziel. As guardian of the Spawn Sanctuary, his task was critical. The Spawn Sanctuary was off limits to everyone except for Michael. Not even Maziel was permitted to enter the sanctuary. Should there ever be a problem within the sanctuary, Maziel was to immediately seek Michael out.

Maziel's very first encounter with Michael was unexpected.

"Maziel," Michael's voice reached to him via telepathy. *"In my domain."*

"Yes, sir," Maziel affirmed the order and teleported to Michael's domain.

However, as soon as he appeared in Michael's domain, Michael attacked him. He rolled away from Michael's first blow and summoned a sword. Many parries, attacks and counterattacks later, Michael dismissed his sword and applauded.

"Excellent work, Maziel," Michael approached him but he backed away.

"Your trick will not work on me," Maziel glared at Michael.

Michael raised his hands in the air.

"I apologize for my behavior earlier," Michael smile. "I assure you that I have already found what I was looking for."

Maziel scowled with uncertainty.

"Come, follow my trail," Michael said and teleported away.

Maziel hesitated for a moment.

"Flap this," he said.

He dismissed his sword and followed Michael's teleport trail. Michael was waiting for him at one of the many parks in Celestia. Maziel finally relaxed.

"Do you know why I summoned you, Maziel?" he asked.

"No, Michael, sir," Maziel replied timidly.

So he really knows every angel and archangel by name, Maziel remarked.

"You just passed a test," Michael said.

"A test? I don't understand, sir."

"It was a test for a very special task," Michael explained. "One that requires someone with integrity, honesty, secrecy and superb fighting skills. I sensed you possess the first three. So, I had to test you for the fourth."

"But Michael, sir, you beat me in four moves," Maziel rebutted.

"That's right," Michael agreed. "And only six others have lasted more than one of my moves."

"Sir…" Maziel could not finish his sentence. "I…"

Michael chuckled.

"It's alright, my friend," Michael said. "Own the moment and practice more. Who knows, maybe you might eventually best me."

Michael winked and Maziel managed a weak smile.

"Thank you, sir," Maziel finally said. "Though I know that will never happen."

"You're quite welcome," Michael replied.

"What I am about to show you is of utmost importance to our brothers and sisters, and the realm," Michael's tone of voice took a serious note. "Only I have access to it. All you will have to do is stand guard and never, for any reason whatsoever, try to access it or let anyone but me in it. Just so you know, this position opened because the guardian tried to access it."

"Oh, what happened to her or him?" Maziel asked.

"I ended her existence," Michael replied flatly.

Maziel's jaw dropped.

"So, do you still want the job, Maziel?" Michael asked.

"Yes, sir," Maziel replied with enthusiasm, not wanting to pass up such an opportunity to work with Michael, or so he hoped.

"Very well," Michael said and waved his hand in the air

A vortex of yellow and white sparked from the ethers and swallowed them up. The two archangels emerged in front of a 200x200x200 cubic feet building, with walls made of smooth, white Celestial earth material with the sculpture of a heptagon crystal on top of it. The building shimmered and shone with a golden brilliance. Michael hovered higher and beckoned for Maziel to join him. The golden brilliance around the building took the form of a heptagon.

"So beautiful," Maziel exclaimed with awe.

"Behold the Spawn Sanctuary, where we are all spawned," Michael said. "You are to guard and protect at all cost. And I mean, at *ALL* cost."

Maziel immediately became a high-ranking archangel because of his new status as Guardian of the Spawn Sanctuary.

Maziel had an unexpected visitor one moment, a visitor whose reputation preceded her. Luciel, second-born of the archangels and angels and Michael's undesignated second-in-command and lover. She was the only one who came closest to matching Michael's combat skills.

This is bizarre, he thought.

"Greetings to you, brother," she smiled.

"Greetings to you, sister," he replied in kind.

Long, black hair, broad shoulders, resplendent form and radiant smile, Maziel thought.

Half-a-hand shorter than I am but that charisma... that personality... I can see why Michael fell for her.

"So, how does it feel, being *THE* guardian, brother?" Luciel asked.

"It's a task, Luciel," Maziel replied flatly, addressing her by her name.

Trying to stroke my feathers? So elementary, Maziel thought.

"You do know this is a very important task, don't you?" Luciel continued.

"Michael told me already," Maziel replied with the same flat tone.

"I'm sure he did," Luciel spoke with a pinch of sarcasm. "He does a great job at reminding us how special we all are, doesn't he?"

Maziel said nothing.

"Tell me, Maziel," Luciel approached Maziel. "Did he tell you why he chose you for this task? Oh wait, don't answer yet. If I know Michael as well as I think I do, he must have said something about how he's looking for someone who is honest, with a strong sense of integrity and secrecy...?"

Luciel scoffed and mindlessly traced something on the floor with her toes. A plain, long, fitted, white gown covered most of her bare feet. She then raised her head and brushed some strands of hair from her face with her left hand and placed them behind her right ear.

"Yes, indeed he told me those things," Maziel frowned a little.

Michael must have told her, he concluded. *Damn him. But why? Another test?*

"And he also said you have 'superior fighting skills', right?" Luciel pressed on.

Maziel opened his mouth to speak but Luciel cut him off.

"Because you lasted more than three moves," Luciel added. "Or was it four?"

Maziel's eyes bulged with surprise and Luciel erupted with derisive laughter.

"My," Luciel exclaimed. "Seems as if someone is having some serious trouble with practicing what they preach. So much for honesty, integrity and most of all secrecy."

Luciel burst into another fit of laughter while Maziel scowled slightly.

Damn her, damn Michael, damn both of them.

"Well, brother," Luciel said between fits of laughter. "I apologize for the distraction. That was rude of me. You have important work to do, no?"

She turned around to leave and then added.

"After all, I certainly wouldn't want to be chastised for this now, would I?"

Luciel turned her head slightly back towards him.

"But maybe I do want to be chastised," she winked at him and made to teleport away

"Wait," Maziel called after Luciel.

Luciel turned around and faced him.

"How did you come to know all this?" he asked.

"I'd tell you, brother," Luciel replied. "But it might get me in trouble."

Luciel took a few steps towards him.

"I must ask you something, though," Luciel said. "Did he tell you about your predecessor?"

"Michael said she tried to access the sanctuary," Maziel replied.

"And what did he say happened to her?" Luciel asked.

Luciel's eyes burned with passion that matched the tone of her voice. His clairsentience picked up something intense, powerful and even darkly seductive radiating from her.

"He said he ended her existence-" Maziel replied.

"And what gives him the right to end the existence of a brother or sister?" she erupted.

Maziel knew her sudden outburst was not directed towards him. For a moment, he shared her passion, her pain and… her lust for something he could not quite lay a finger on. Yet, it was there, and he felt it, almost as tangible as the wings on his scapulae when he summoned them.

What is it about her that draws me to her thus? he wondered. *I feel like we're two of a kind with one mind and body, like she is a part of me and I of her.*

Luciel closed her eyes for a moment as if to calm herself. When she reopened them, the anger was gone but the passion lingered like an undying, unfading spark.

"I apologize for my sudden outburst, brother," Luciel said flatly.

"It's alright, sister," he replied. "I know it was not directed towards me."

"Thank you," Luciel heaved her shoulders. "I must go now. Perhaps we could talk some more later, if you'd like."

"Of course, sister," Maziel affirmed. "It will be my pleasure."

"I am glad to hear that," Luciel nodded curtly. "Farewell, brother."

Luciel teleported away before Maziel could see the evil smile of satisfaction that crept across her face right before she vanished from sight.

***

"My king," a demon called out, wrenching Kazuk back to the present as he prostrated himself in front of Kazuk.

"Speak," Kazuk commanded.

"He is here, my king.,".

"Send him in," Kazuk commanded.

"No need for that," said The Scribe as he summoned a seat next to Kazuk.

Kazuk waved dismissively at the demon, who quickly stood up and trotted out of Kazuk's throne room.

"I despise your open disregard for my authority in front of my subjects,"

Kazuk hissed at The Scribe.

"Spare me the childishness, Maziel," The Scribe replied patronizingly. "Remember who gave you your throne. Now, shut your mouth and pay attention to what I have to say."

"I no longer go by that name, Scribe," Kazuk fumed and yellow flames spewed from his eyes.

"I will call you whatever I want, child," The Scribe rebutted. "And there is absolutely nothing you can do about it."

Kazuk closed his eyes, smothering the flames but not the fury.

"When the moment is right, Scribe," Kazuk spoke as calmly and as softly as he could, "I will have my revenge. That I promise you, old friend."

"First of all," said The Scribe with disdain. "I'm not your friend. You're my bitch. When I say jump, you jump. When I say sit, you sit because you are vermin. But I upgraded your status to 'bitch' level. Second of all, you don't even have the balls to attempt what you're thinking. Your predecessor has balls bigger than you could ever have, and even her balls aren't big enough for her to begin to fathom any form of vengeance towards me, you buffoon."

The Scribe turned around and spat on the floor and his spittle corroded the patch of floor it landed on.

"Completely unnecessary," Kazuk referred to The Scribe spitting.

"Let me know when you are done being a grumpy, nagging bitch, and then we can talk business," The Scribe smirked.

Kazuk gritted his teeth and clenched his fists.

At least, no one is here to witness this torture, Kazuk thought.

"Welcome to my humble abode, Scribe," Kazuk waved his hands in the air and flashed a fake smile. "Pray tell, what business brings you to this beauty of Creation?"

"Finally," Chaos exclaimed. "We must speed up the process. A perfect cycle is close at hand and we need to unravel the final phases of the plan."

"I would love to, Scribe," Kazuk replied with a tired expression on his face. "But like I told you before, I have had trouble reaching Jamael. He's a tough nut to crack and after the rebellion, Michael is even more cautious now than before."

"I had absolutely no idea, Maziel," The Scribe said with heavy sarcasm and shook his head in mock disbelief. "Anyway, I took care of Jamael already. The seeds have been sown. He's more inclined towards your side now. You just have to go over there and work your charms."

The Scribe paused to admire the look of astonishment on Kazuk's face.

"I must admit," Kazuk conceded. "That was quite a feat."

"Now that Jamael is on your side," The Scribe ignored Kazuk's compliment, "we can now proceed to the next phase."

Kazuk laughed out loud.

"You really want me to imprison Michael."

"Hence, why I said your predecessor's balls are bigger than yours are," The Scribe added with exaggerated exasperation.

Kazuk immediately stopped laughing.

"And how do you propose I do that, Scribe?" Kazuk asked.

"Within the Spawn Sanctuary lies the only artifact that can bind an archangel as mighty as Michael. This artifact, the Zarark, along with three other artifacts, is used to summon the angelic vibrations to manifest angels. So, the plan is simple; obtain The Zarark with Jamael's help, lure Michael and keep him confined at least until the cycle is over."

Kazuk rubbed his chin pensively.

"I take it you have the details of this plan?" Kazuk asked rhetorically.

The Scribe outlined the details of his plan. After he finished, he left the throne room the same manner he appeared; like he was never there. Lithilia waited for a few moments before walking up to her husband. She cradled his head to her bosom and whispered words of comfort and promise in his ear.

"We'll get him, my love," she promised. "Even if it's the last thing we do."

"Yes, we will," Kazuk agreed. "But first, we must play our roles in his grand scheme and once it's over, he won't know what hit him."

Lithilia knelt beside her husband, took his face in his hands and kissed him on the lips. He returned her kiss. Then, she peeled her lips away from his, stood up and started walking away. Kazuk knew what was to come and accepted his wife's unspoken invitation. He watched her walk away and grinned with unbridled anticipation. Lithilia's clairsentience indicated her husband's eyes ravaged her back… her buttocks… as she gradually dismissed her purple gown to reveal her nude body. Lithilia felt his energy build like that of a geyser until finally, unable to contain himself any longer, he teleported and snatched her away to the bedroom in their domain.

CHAPTER THREE

DO OR DIE

ELIEL WANTED TO believe that his eyes deceived him. Even when Michael's bracelets glowed and his casual robe transformed into his battle outfit, even when golden flames flared from his eyes and mouth, and even when Michael charged towards him, Eliel still believed everything was a fabrication of his mind. Luckily, Eliel's survival instincts took control of his body. He rolled forward and Michael's flaming sword whooshed over his head, with the heat from Michael's archangel battle flame warming the back of his neck. From the corner of his eye, he saw Michael's body turning towards him. Eliel chased his forward roll with a side roll to the left as Michael spun his sword backward in a downward arc. Eliel crouched on one knee. His right peripheral vision lit up with Michael's flaming sword accelerating towards his neck. Instinctively, he jerked his head back and the tip of Michael's sword left a paper cut on his throat. Angel light immediately washed over the cut and healed it.

This is NOT a drill, Eliel thought. *When he said he had to end me, he meant every letter of it. But why? What did I do?*

Eliel stood up.

Doesn't matter, Eliel frowned. *Leader or not, I'm not going down without a fight.*

So, when Michael unleashed a left stomp kick at Eliel's chest, Eliel caught Michael's left foot and twisted Michael's ankle violently to the right. Michael rolled to his left to neutralize Eliel's sharp twist and threw his right heel at Eliel's temple in the process. Eliel let go of Michael's left ankle as he evaded Michael's follow-up attack with a backward roll.

Was that his first move? Eliel wondered.

Eliel rose to his feet and Michael did the same. Angel and archangel stared each other down, and then, Michael smiled; a cold, unfriendly smile. He blazed towards Eliel and thrust his sword towards Eliel's chest. Eliel took a left sidestep and gently placed his stiff, left forearm perpendicularly against Michael's right forearm. Eliel pulled back his right arm while he let his left arm drop on Michael's wrist. He gripped Michael's wrist, holding it in place. Then, Eliel brought the full force of his right, middle knuckle into the back of Michael's right hand.

Excruciating pain radiated from the point of impact on the back of Michael's right hand to the rest of Michael's body in the form of golden light. Michael screamed in agony and involuntarily dropped his sword. In one fluid motion, Eliel kicked Michael's sword away with his left foot, while grabbing Michael's right palm in both hands. He turned his body towards Michael and sank his weight at the same time by dropping his hips. Michael's sword vanished, while his body sailed through the air like an axe coming down on a log. Michael's back and occiput hit the floor with enough force to cause cracks to spread outward on the floor from the point of impact.

Second move.

Eliel immediately straddled Michael and threw a direct punch at Michael's face. He realized his mistake too late. Michael moved his head to his left quickly. Eliel's fist crashed into the floor, sending a burst of golden light outward from the point of impact and leaving a three-inch deep hole in the floor. A fleeting look of shock spread over Michael's face before he used Eliel's momentum to roll Eliel over to Eliel's right. Eliel grunted and waited for a similar attack from Michael as Michael straddled him. Instead, Michael grabbed him by the throat and whizzed straight up in the air. Then, he accelerated towards the floor with the same speed, intending to bash Eliel into the floor.

Eliel spread out his wings just long enough to initiate a deceleration. Almost immediately, he folded his left wing, causing an aerial displacement towards the right. That fraction of a blink was all he needed to flip Michael over to his left and fold in his right wing at the same time. He then zipped with full, angelic acceleration towards the floor. Michael's body absorbed the impact of the crash and golden light beamed from his body's profile at the point of impact.

Third move.

Eliel picked Michael up by the throat and threw him like a spear towards a wall. But Michael spread his wings and slowed himself to a stop before he reached the wall. Michael floated to the floor and closed his eyes. Golden, angel light washed over his body to heal and rejuvenate his broken body. Angel and archangel stared each other down once again. But something was different about the way Michael regarded Eliel.

"Not bad at all for a youngling," Michael mocked. "You have my respect."

"Why?" Eliel asked, ignoring Michael's compliment.

"Why what?" Michael asked.

"Why are you trying to end me?" Eliel asked.

"I told you already," Michael snapped. "Don't you get it? It cannot happen again. I will not let it happen again."

"So, you pass judgment on *ME* for something *YOU* are afraid of?" Eliel spat with anger and disbelief in his voice. "For something I am not even guilty of? Something that hasn't even happened yet?"

"I'm not sorry I'm going to end you," Michael said confidently. "I'm just doing what I must, to protect the rest of us. Call it a preventive measure."

"If that is how you feel, Michael," Eliel replied, making sure to address Michael by his name, "then so be it."

Eliel opened his right fist to summon his sword.

"Consider this as fair warning, archangel," Eliel hissed.

Eliel's tone of voice had morphed into a deep, uncanny baritone that reflected a transfiguration of his being into a darkness that spoke to Michael. Michael took an involuntary step back.

I sense you, he said to himself. *I know you. You took her. You tried to take me and failed. Now you have come again for another round. But you will fail, just like before.*

Michael's resolve strengthened as the last sliver of hope that maybe he was wrong evaporated with the new version of Eliel that stood in front of him.

This is not my fault, he reminded himself. *This is the darkness in him.*

"I will defend myself, even if it means ending YOU," Eliel promised.

"You weren't there," Michael squeezed his eyes shut and gritted his teeth. "It doesn't matter, anyway."

Michael opened his eyes and leveled a cold stare at Eliel.

"You weren't there when many of our brothers and sisters fell."

A flaming sword formed in Michael's right hand as more archangel battle flames raged from his eyes and mouth. However, when he made to attack, he froze and gawked at what his rational mind refused to process for an instant.

Not one, but TWO, bracelets formed and glowed on Eliel's wrists. Eliel gazed at his wrists with total dispassion. He raised his gaze towards Michael, who recoiled from so much disbelief that the flames in his eyes and mouth disappeared. Eliel's sword went ablaze with an archangel's battle flame.

"*NO,*" Michael exclaimed. "The prophecy. It cannot be."

"Archangel Michael," Eliel spoke in a dark, alien voice. "This is your final warning. Stand down or, by Celestia, I will end you."

"I am Michael, Archangel Supreme of the Realm of Celestia," he declared. "I have sworn to defend Celestia and every angel and archangel to the death from all enemies within and without."

He summoned his archangel battle flame.

"Prophecy or not," he added. "Let Celestia decide between the two of us, right here, right now"

Angel and archangel came at each other in a clash of flaming swords. Only one other archangel had come close to matching Michael's skill. However, the duel between him and Eliel brought to light not only his match, but his better. Eliel, a lowly youngling, spawned cycles after the Great Rebellion, outmatched Michael on every front, in every style and in all phases of angelic combat. Michael bled angel light from multiple places. Defeat stared down his battered body, his pounded pride and his psyche suffered the most.

Michael slumped to his knees and stared upwards at Eliel in defiance.

"I have failed my brothers and sisters," he said. "Still, I go in peace, knowing that I gave it all. Celestia survived once before and it will always survive."

His archangel flame gradually dwindled until nothing was left of it.

"I sense the darkness in you," he coughed. "I know what it can do. It know its power, its seduction."

He dismissed his wings and puffed his chest.

"For the sake of our kind," he continued. "Do not give into it when you fall."

Eliel placed his sword on Michael's neck. A golden glow surrounded Michael's body as Michael healed himself.

"May Celestia guide you, Eliel," he smiled with the feeling of peace that came over him. "I am ready."

"You never should have tried to end me, Michael," Eliel said in the same dark, alien voice as flames spewed from his mouth and eyes and raised his sword.

In an unexpected turn of events, the flames in Eliel's eyes and mouth suddenly vanished, his sword disappeared, and he collapsed to the floor in an unconscious heap. Stunned by what just happened, Michael regarded Eliel on the floor for a moment before realization dawned on him. He summoned his sword to seize the opportunity.

"Celestia be praised," he exclaimed and stood up. "We shall survive."

He raised the sword and held it over his head. He gripped the hilt a little tighter and made to strike. Yet, every iota of his being rioted against his intention. He heaved his shoulders before he dismissed his sword and lowered his arms.

I have slain thousands before, all in combat, he thought. *But I will never slay one while they are unconscious, even one who is my enemy. I have flaws, but cowardice is not one of them.*

He summoned a chair and sat down as his battle outfit morphed into a grey, casual, ankle-length robe.

Eliel heard The Voice. That means he is special. My intentions to end him may be justified, but it is my duty as leader, as the eldest brother, to give him what I, and she, never had: guidance.

Eliel roused from unconsciousness a moment later. When he saw Michael sitting next to him, he immediately tried to push himself away. But not enough strength had returned to his body and his vision turned hazy again. He collapsed back on the floor.

"Go on," he said. "Finish it."

"Easy now, brother," Michael stood up from his chair.

Eliel summoned angel light over his body and initiated a recuperating process.

"Stay- stay away from me," Eliel spoke weakly.

Michael raised both hands in the air.

"Look," Michael said. "I understand your concern, and I'm truly sorry for my behavior. I was rash and unjust. I never should've attacked you in the first place. Please forgive me."

Eliel regarded Michael with skepticism.

"How are you feeling?" Michael asked.

"I'm taking longer than usual to heal from whatever happened to me," Eliel replied and propped himself on his elbows.

Michael extended a hand. Eliel hesitated before he took it. Michael helped him to his feet. Eliel rolled his shoulders, stretched his body before he summoned his wings, flapped them twice and dismissed them.

He doesn't even know he's now and archangel, Michael thought while maintaining an expressionless face.

"I'll be fine," Eliel said. "What happened? What *IS* happening to me?"

"Come," Michael said. "I'll answer as many of your questions as I possibly can. But there are certain things I witnessed that I still don't understand."

Michael summoned two seats for himself and Eliel. They sat down.

"Let's start from the beginning, from when you heard The Voice," Michael said. "The fact that you found yourself in my domain is already the first testament that you did hear The Voice, which is a default for one who hears The Voice."

"Why?" Eliel asked.

Michael shrugged.

"I don't know," he replied. "So, anyone going to Uriel claiming to have heard The Voice is lying, or least, believes what they heard was The Voice. Now, hearing The Voice is a special calling and only after a fall can one awaken to that calling."

"By 'fall' do you mean falling from being an angel?" Eliel asked.

"Exactly," Michael replied.

"Flap," Eliel heaved his shoulders. "Can I un-hear this voice?"

"I'm afraid not," Michael chuckled. "You answered the call already. You can't turn back now even if you tried."

"Alright then, I must fall," Eliel said, with fake enthusiasm.

"It won't be as bad as you imagine," Michael assured him. "You'll experience many different things; like hunger and thirst. I could give you as many details as possible, but that would be pointless. One word, though: amnesia."

Michael grinned.

Nice smile, Eliel thought.

"But you'll always have indicators of some kind during amnesia," Michael continued, "And you must choose your own path. Have faith that Celestia will never lead you astray. Trust your instincts and listen to the silent voice in you. It will be your guide."

"I noticed you mentioned 'another one' who heard The Voice," Eliel said, "and that you cannot allow a repeat of history. What happened to her, if you don't mind me asking? I've read about her in manuscripts. But I think getting your perspective would help understand her story better."

"Of course," Michael replied, and an aura of sadness loomed over his persona for a fleeting moment. "She was my unofficial second-in-command, the next best among us. So full of promise. But I think, even before she heard The Voice and fell, she had already sided with the darkness. Falling just made it worse, and when she returned, she instigated the Great Rebellion that you have heard of. Hell, amongst other things, is our constant reminder of that rebellion."

"I've heard gruesome stories about what happened," Eliel said. "I was not entirely sure if they were all true or just embellishments."

"What you heard is nothing compared to what really happened, brother," Michael concurred. "Most of us who were there still prefer not to talk about it, but younglings like you have to be taught our history, in hopes that such atrocities do not repeat themselves."

Eliel's clairsentience pickup up Michael's pain and sorrow. The rebellion and its outcome still plagued his mind like eyesore that was Hell Realm.

He feels responsible somehow, though I don't think it's his fault, Eliel thought. *I can't even begin to imagine what happened. We won, but I don't think he feels like we did. We're always on the lookout for Hell, and with whispers of spies among us, who knows when another rebellion may arise.*

"I now understand why you tried to end me," Eliel said. "And I forgive you."

"Thank you, brother," Michael's shoulders relaxed with relief and gratitude.

"Now, let us talk about you not only lasting more than three of my moves but actually beating me at every level," Michael added. "You know, no one has ever done that before, right?"

Eliel tried his best not to smile but his boosted ego will not let him.

"That's what I've heard, sir," Eliel replied.

"Oh, come on now, drop the 'sir,' already," Michael clapped Eliel on the shoulder. "You are a near-flawless fighter. And It's okay to savor the moment too, you know. Where did you learn how to fight like that?"

"Fighting school?" Eliel lied.

Michael gave him a sideways look and Eliel averted his eyes.

"Well, I sometimes train when my assignments are asleep, and I try to devise various forms of attack and defense on my own."

Michael nodded slowly.

"Fascinating," he said. "During this short span of moments I have known you, you do not cease to impress me, Eliel."

Eliel smiled with deep appreciation. Such compliments from one as great as Michael himself were always welcome.

"Say," Michael added as an afterthought. "When you rise again after your fall," he raised his arms in the semblance of spreading his wings.

Eliel chuckled.

"And, say you choose to stay on the path of the light, would you consider sharing your fighting skills with your brethren?"

"You honor me, sir," Eliel's core beamed with humility. "Yes, I'd absolutely love to."

"Excellent," Michael exclaimed and clapped his hands once. "It is settled then. When that moment arrives, Samael will handle that. Sounds good to you?"

"It will be as you wish, sir," Eliel replied.

Michael shook his head.

He's not going to drop that 'sir' thing.

"Good," Michael stood up from his seat. "You shall go to Uriel immediately. She will prep you for your fall."

Eliel remained seated and stared blankly at the floor. Michael sat back down.

"You seem troubled, young brother," Michael said. "Speak your mind."

Eliel opened his mouth to say something but closed it. Michael waited patiently until, finally, Eliel spoke.

"Sir," he said. "All I ever wanted was to be a simple angel. I take immense pleasure and satisfaction watching over my assignments and doing my job. I never asked to hear The Voice."

Eliel shook his head and sighed. He scratched his back and still did not even realize his wings were gone.

He'll catch up to his new status soon enough, Michael smiled to himself.

"And now," Eliel continued. "I've heard The Voice, fought for my life, almost killed you, and I was taken over by some strange energy. I mean, flames were coming out of my eyes and mouth, and my sword was also ablaze. Even my wings were on fire, like yours were. I don't even know how I summoned the archangel flame, something which only archangels can do. To top it off, I had two bracelets. Not just one, like archangels do, but *TWO*. And you're the only archangel with two bracelets, sir. You and *YOU* alone."

He threw up his hands in frustration.

"I don't know what all this means," he added, his voice heavy with fatigue. "I'm so confused"

Michael put a hand on Eliel's shoulder and gave it a gentle squeeze.

"I understand the confusion and frustration that comes with what you are experiencing right now," Michael spoke calmly. "I've helped as much as I can. Everything else will be revealed to you in due time, not by me, but by whatever you will experience during your fall and when you return from your fall. I know you heard The Voice for a reason."

Michael removed his hand from Eliel's shoulder.

"Be patient with yourself and stay focused. Alright?"

Eliel sighed, looked up at Michael and nodded.

"Alright, sir," he replied and stood up. "Thank you very much."

"No, thank *YOU*," Michael replied and stood up as well.

The two archangels pressed hands.

"Now, Uriel is waiting for you," Michael said. "You will be her only student until you are ready to fall."

Eliel nodded and made to teleport to Uriel's domain.

"I'll see you around, brother," Michael said telepathically.

"Thank you once again, sir," Eliel replied and teleported away.

Michael kept a blank stare ahead. His mind raced in many directions.

How come? Could it be that Eliel was The One? Eliel passed all the basic tests, almost at the cost of my existence.

Firstly, Eliel had heard The Voice. Secondly, Eliel had bested him in combat. Thirdly, Eliel had summoned the archangel's battle flame and spoken with that voice that was... non-angelic. Moreover, a bracelet appeared on each of his wrists while they fought.

It just doesn't make any sense. How could this be? He is so young and, yet, he had exhibited more characteristics of The One than any other angel or archangel. And he never even wanted any of this in the first place. Could he really be The One?

Innately, he knew the answer to his question already. He replayed the words of the prophecy in his head, which he had memorized to the last glyph. So far,

Eliel had fulfilled every word of the prophecy except for what happens after the fall. Uriel was the only other archangel in Celestia who knew of this prophecy and hence why she was in charge of interviewing and testing potential candidates. The fall was necessary because Eliel's polarization had to be tested.

So, is Eliel really The One?

Michael asked himself the rhetoric question yet again. Perhaps that was the true reason why he wanted to end Eliel in the first place? But with Eliel defeating him, everything was now in Celestia's hands. If Eliel was truly The One, then his success would mean peace in the dimension. However, his failure would spell the complete annihilation of their kind. Either way, Eliel's success or failure have a common outcome: Michael would no longer be archangel supreme.

CHAPTER FOUR

KEERIM

LET ME TELL *you a story about what you loosely call 'the universe.' I say 'loosely' because no matter how much you think you know, you're no smarter than the tiniest grains of sand on your seashores. There's nothing wrong with being stupid and ignorant. But what I find morbidly repulsive to my... uh... let me see... what word should I use from your primitive language? Oh well, I'll settle for 'psyche.' Okay. So back to what I was saying; what I find morbidly repulsive to my 'psyche' is the fact that you refuse to see, beyond your eyelids, just how limited your spheres of consciousness are. I mean, in all sincerity, despite your seeming complex constitution, you are no more than a pathetic vestigial aspect of Creation.*

Perhaps if you took a moment to descend from the high laurels of your petty egos and realize that your intellect cannot even begin to comprehend the most basic aspects of Creation, then maybe you could finally understand the extent of your ignorance. Maybe, just maybe, thence you can begin to cultivate the willingness to learn.

Feeling offended? Did I step on your egos? Did I hurt the petty propensities you call 'feelings'? Well, suck it up, you fools, and go cry me an etheric river. I forgot; you don't even understand what I just said, did you? Of course not. Well, who knows more about the ego that the one who epitomizes it? Who knows more about illusion than illusion itself? Who knows more about chaos than Chaos himself?

In every realm and dimension I've visited, there are creatures who think they are the only intelligent species in the vastness of Creation. Some even go as far as to stipulate that Creation revolves around them and that there are no other sentient creatures outside of their realm or dimension. Talk about egomania steeped in ignorance. You are worthless, all of you. You are abominations, all of you. You are insults to the cosmic conglomerate. And, I would spit on all of you right here, right now. You wonder why I want to undo everything. Well, there you go. You're all lucky Akasha is still hot on my trail. She is the only reason why you are still in existence. But like the rest of you, her end will come... Eventually. For now, I shamefully admit, I am a most wanted entity. If you dare tell anyone… Well, I trust you won't, because you can't even hear me speak, can you?

But, I digress, and for that, I apologize. Where was I? Oh yes, I was about to tell you a small story about what you call the 'universe'. There are planets, moons, the stars, and all the labels you ascribe to the realms and dimensions of Creation. There's a lot more to Creation than gravity and electromagnetism. I can't believe I'm using your terminologies, but someone has to dumb it down for you. I drew straws with me and myself on who would stoop to your levels and speak your vernacular, and I ended up with the shortest and only straw; hence, why I am introducing you to Creation 101. Stay on track.

Okay, let's give this one more try. Listen, Earth Realm, as I introduce you to Creation 101; subtopic, your realm. Your central star, the sun, revolves around the central star of the Orion Constellation. This revolution is split into twelve sections or ages, and this revolution is called The Zodiac. *The hundreds of billions of stars in your galaxy, the Milky Way, are arranged into what is called Cosmic Clusters. These cosmic clusters are governed by the Paradins, living in the Realm of Zodica, which is one of the realms in the Dimension of Mueba.*

And speaking of realms and dimensions; these are pockets of Creation oscillating at specific vibrational frequencies. A dimension contains at least one realm and every realm in that dimension oscillates at the vibrational frequency of the dimension. In every dimension, one realm is selected to house the Zarark. It is not uncommon to find an uninhabited realm or dimension. But if there are creatures within any realm, then there is the possibility of that realm having a guardian chosen by Mother. A Hound of Creation usually heralds the selection of a guardian. Damn it. Another digression.

Back to the lessons. The Realm of Zodica is of a much higher vibrational frequency than the Realm of Celestia. As such, Paradins are of a higher vibrational frequency and level of consciousness than angels and archangels are. Paradins are also gender defined; a male is a Cherub, and a female is a Seraph. Cherubim and Seraphim (plurals) work together at every instant to oversee each cosmic cluster in your Milky Way. Both periodically supply each cosmic cluster with the masculine and feminine versions of consciousness according to the dictates of the Cosmic Clock. As such, the basic duty of Paradins is to translate, transfer and transduce the cosmic mind unto cosmic clusters.

So why do I tell you this? Because it's all part of my grand plan. I'm not just an anomaly. I am THE *Anomaly. Let me remind you of the sole purpose of my existence. It is to undo all of Creation. Not some, not a little, not most.* ALL *of Creation. I don't just unleash chaos. I* AM *Chaos. But before I do this, every part of the plan must be perfect. The plan itself must be subtle to seem harmless yet strong enough to carry on a chain reaction across Creation. Most of all, for the plan to succeed, the moment must be perfect. And when is the perfect moment? When the Cosmic Clock goes through the Great Reset at the end of the cosmic countdown, and that reset is very, very nigh. This will be my first birthday and undoing Creation will be the perfect birthday gift. I am so excited I can barely contain myself.*

Keerim. My one and only puppet of a cherub. I remember when I won him over. He was the perfect cherub; they all are anyway. But provide a puppet with just enough purpose, and it prides itself on being a principality with unlimited power. Pathetic. They don't call me a purveyor of purpose for nothing, do they? Well, that's how I describe myself. Yes, Keerim is a part of my plan, just like Marlo, Maduk and Kazuk are my puzzle pieces on Earth, Nimbu and Hell Realms, respectively. Okay, I will end my rants now. I think I am consumed by so much impatience that I just may be losing my mind. The moment draws nigh, and all the pieces are not yet fully in place. This makes me concerned... This makes me worried... And I don't like it when I'm worried...

The Scribe closed his eyes and stilled his thoughts. In this state of existence, of near omni-presence, he dared not speak or make a sound, lest he be discovered. He was aware he was losing his composure and that frightened him. Fear was a sentiment he forged for the fearful. But now, fear was also a luxury he certainly could not afford, especially when he was so close to success. But what was he afraid of? He certainly was not afraid of failing. His ego would not concede to the idea of failure. Was it because he could not answer the question of 'what next' when it is all over?

Purpose is purveyed, purpose is served, and more purpose is purveyed.

So, what was he afraid of?

The Scribe gradually reduced the vibrational frequency of his form and slowly exited the state of near-omnipotence. The answer to his question throbbed with a level of truth that made him shiver to a denser form until his level of vibrations matched those of the Realm of Zodica, where Paradins dwelled. He teleported towards the realm. He had a meeting with Keerim.

My tardiness will drive him crazy, but who cares about entertaining his childishness, The Scribe thought.

Only one sentiment currently merited his attention; the fear that despite everything that was going on, he was so madly in love with Akasha. Why? The Scribe was unsure. His plan had not accounted for this sentiment which now threatened to jeopardize his entire plan.

***

Keerim's form tingled with restlessness and impatience, sentiments that did not exist within a Paradin's nature. However, ever since his essence had become tainted, Keerim had been experiencing a myriad of sentiments he had no idea how to handle at first. The Scribed used to help. Now, the same Scribe had left him on his own. Keerim forced himself to concentrate on the task at hand.

Despite these 'setbacks', Keerim remained a phenomenal and model cherub. Vinath, his seraph partner at work, proved to be a perfect fit ever since his former partner 'disappeared' suddenly. The cosmic clusters they oversaw hovered within their beings like tiny, multicolored specks of light. The color of each cosmic cluster indicated the level of consciousness of the cluster.

"Do you see that, Vee?" Keerim asked his partner.

"Yes, Kay," she replied.

A group of green-colored specks suddenly flashed red and then disappeared. Luckily, nearby cosmic clusters remained unaffected by the sudden brilliance and disappearance of the green-colored specks.

"Another warring realm messing with power it cannot control," Keerim said.

"If only they knew better, then they would not fight among themselves in the first place," Vee said. "They create weapons that release electromagnetic pulses strong enough to create blackholes. They are lucky that the blackhole was not self-sustaining. Many more realms would have been destroyed besides theirs."

"Just another moment at work," Keerim said.

Vinath gave a silent agreement. Keerim brushed a finger very close to the self-made cataclysm and absorbed any residual energy left behind from the carnage.

"Do you see this?" Vinath asked.

A speck changed its color from dark green to bright violet, indicative of a significant elevation in the collective consciousness of this realm.

"Beautiful," Keerim remarked. "Hope remains."

"Indeed," Vinath agreed. "All is not lost. And is everything alright with you?"

Her eyes remained glued to her clusters.

"Yes, everything is alright," Keerim tried to sound normal. "Why do you ask?"

"Just seems like you're getting attached," she replied.

"No, I'm not," Keerim replied confidently. "I think I'm going through the phase a little earlier, with the upcoming cosmic shift."

"Oh, please don't remind me about that," Vinath injected a tiny dose of love vibration into a cluster that was struggling to leap forward in consciousness.

It worked and its color changed from dark orange to pale blue.

"We can't run away from it, can we?" Keerim said.

They both laughed a little.

And where is that Scribe? Keerim thought.

"You know, you really should watch your colors," The Scribe said telepathically in a sub-Paradin frequency. *"Your lies can be spotted from across the dimension."*

"And don't you ever sneak up on me like that again," Keerim replied in the same sub-Paradin frequency.

Vinath continued watching over her clusters, oblivious of the conversation between Keerim and The Scribe.

"My sincere apologies, cherub," The Scribe spoke with enough sarcasm to irritate Keerim some more. *"Personally, I prefer not to make a grand entrance when I'm about to hold a secret meeting that would lead to you betraying your kind. Perhaps you prefer otherwise, oh great and mighty cherub?"*

"Let's get on with it, shall we?" Keerim chose to ignore The Scribe's insult. *"Do you have it?"*

"Not yet," The Scribe replied nonchalantly. *"It is not yet-"*

"You mean you still have not obtained it, have you?" Keerim retorted.

"Alas, no, I have not yet obtained a Zarark," The Scribe conceded.

Keerim eyed him suspiciously.

"Something is off about you, Scribe," Keerim said. *"This confirms what they are saying about you. You are becoming sloppy."*

"Who said that?" The Scribe demanded.

"Irrelevant," Keerim taunted.

He smiled with sweet delight.

Let him also see how it feels to treat another with so much disrespect.

"Are you sure everything is alright?" Vinath asked.

This time, her tone of voice underscored her concern and worry.

"Yes, Vee," Keerim replied, trying desperately to sound casual. "I am."

"Maybe I'm asking the wrong question," Vinath turned and faced him. "I meant is everything alright with you and I? Do you like working with me?"

Her question caught him off guard so much he did not reply immediately.

"Vee-" Keerim he said, but Vinath cut him off.

"Please," she said firmly. "I know I'm new here and given what happened with your last partner, I just wanted to make sure that you're not averse to working with me based on a past situation with someone else."

Keerim nodded slowly.

"Vinath, I am truly sorry if I have, in any way, communicated such sentiments towards you," he said. "Rest assured that I love working with you and I would ask for no other partner unless the Elders decide otherwise. Even then, I would do my best to maintain our status quo. Where you go, I go. Working with you so far has been a wonderful experience. I think it's just the upcoming cosmic shift that is messing me up more than usual. That's all, I assure you."

Vinath smiled

"Thank you, Kay. I enjoy working with you too."

She returned to her cosmic clusters.

"Wow, that was some speech," The Scribe said in the sub-Paradin frequency and applauded. *"You're so good at this that I don't see why you even need the Zarark."*

"You really are getting sloppy, you imbecile," Keerim barked.

Keerim's anger threatened to get the better of him. He had to keep it in check though. Too many cosmic clusters could face instant annihilation in the wake of an outburst and that would attract the attention of the Elders.

"First of all, it was not an act," Keerim continued. *"I don't know what's happening with this upcoming shift. It's affecting me much differently."*

"It's the Great Reset," The Scribe interjected. *"That's why it feels different because it IS different."*

"Uh huh," scoffed Keerim. *"You have officially lost your mind, Scribe. What in the name of Creation is a Great Reset?"*

Keerim shook his head and The Scribe shrugged.

Why even bother explaining something so important to someone so stupid? The Scribe thought

"Back to what I was saying before you cut me off," Keerim said. *"Second of all, I can only pretend for so long. You see for yourself. She is already picking up the fringes of what I am going through. That is why we need the Zarark right now, and you are not playing your part, you incompetent buffoon."*

"Watch your tone, cherub-" The Scribe admonished.

"Then stop joking around and do your job, Scribe," Keerim fired back.

The Scribe closed his eyes and stilled his thoughts.

"There is a plan in place, and it will be effectuated soon," The Scribe spoke slowly. *"I needed a few more moments, but I can speed things up a little. In the meantime, just hang in there, and I will address the situation."*

"Finally, some positive news," Keerim replied. *"Still doesn't change the fact that you are losing it, Scribe. I am not sure what is happening to you, but I hope it has nothing to do with my initial suspicions."*

"Thank you for your word of counsel, but I'll be fine," The Scribe spoke with sarcasm.

"That's a phrase you've never used before; 'I'll be fine'," Keerim added.

The Scribe winced visibly at Keerim's words but said nothing.

"I've sacrificed too much already and will sacrifice a lot more if need be for this plan of yours," Keerim added. *"So, this plan better work or else I'll be a cherub with nothing to lose. And rest assured, Scribe, you do not want to experience that side of me."*

"Is this really all for her?" The Scribe asked calmly.

Keerim said nothing.

One of my favorite things about being a purveyor purpose is to let a creature think they are in control, The Scribe smiled. *It gives them a sense of power, which turns out to be a motivation for them to stick to the plan, because they think they're genius enough to be in charge. Trusting that I have their best interest in mind is always their mistake. Pathetic.*

"Tell me cherub; is this really all for her?" The Scribe asked again.

Keerim remained silent.

"What do you hope to achieve? Forgiveness? Redemption? Maybe a blend of both?" the Scribe pushed on.

Keerim squirmed and did his best to keep his raging emotions in check. The Scribe tortured him with memories of a past he tried to bury in his subconscious, albeit without success.

"It was not my fault," Keerim replied weakly.

"Of course, it was your fault," The Scribe was relentless. *"Whose was it, if not yours? No Paradin has ever fallen in the history of Paradins. Yet, you achieved the unachievable."*

"It was out of love-" Keerim replied.

"Well, good luck trying to explain that to her, cherub," The Scribe said.

"Is that what this is all about for you as well?" Keerim asked. *"You think she will love you back if you just make her understand?"*

"No, Keerim, this is not for her or about her," The Scribe replied firmly. *"This is for me and about me. This is about what I want because I am Chaos. I am living up to my nature, and I am inviting you to partake. You will get your prize as promised. I do not lie and you know that."*

The Scribe prepared to leave.

"You know she will end you the moment she lays her eyes on you, right?" Keerim taunted.

"I shall return with a Zarark, and you will have peace of mind," The Scribe ignored his remark. *"You let me worry about everything else."*

The Scribe vanished from Keerim's sight.

His spark has returned, Keerim remarked. *Good.*

"Something is different about you," Vinath said. "It gives me pleasure."

"It felt better talking to you and getting any doubts about our partnership out of the way," Keerim admitted.

His statement was not the entire truth, but he was not lying either.

"So, thank you very much for being such a wonderful partner."

"You are most welcome, my friend," Vinath replied.

The Scribe's words lingered in Keerim's head as he returned to his task. The Scribe was right. No matter how much he tried to justify what happened, he was the one responsible for her unjust and unmerited demise. Paradins do not fall; but somehow, he had made an exception to that rule. The worst part of it was that he had done it to someone he deeply loved and who reciprocated his love with love of her own. And how had he repaid her?

With betrayal.

So why was he doing this again? Why was he willing to sacrifice it all?

Just hurry up with that Zarark, Scribe, before I lose my mind, Keerim said to himself.

CHAPTER FIVE

THE TIME LAPSE

WALTER PEABODY UNSLUNG his laptop bag from his shoulder and set it on the table. He pulled back a chair and made himself as comfortable as he could. He looked to his left and then to his right, a ritual he liked performing every time he sat on his usual spot in the small tea shop in a suburb on the outskirts of Liverpool. He flexed his shoulders and neck a few times. Satisfied with his workout for the day, he retrieved his laptop from its bag. His week consisted of three days, Monday to Friday was one long day, Saturday was dedicated to watching Premier League soccer games and Sunday was reserved for whatever remained to be addressed in his life of unemployment. Within the hour, the streets will begin teeming with pedestrians, despite the promise of a mercilessly hot summer afternoon. He hated the heat and humidity of summer. He turned his laptop on as Irina walked over to him.

"Good morrow to you, kind sir," Irina said in her Ukrainian accent.

"Good morrow to you, milady," Walter returned her greeting with a smile of his own. "How fare thee on this glorious day?"

"The gods smile upon me with favor, my lord," Irina replied.

She was a theater arts major at the local university and she took the phrase 'the world is a stage' a little too seriously.

"Then the blessings of the gods bathe me through thine smile," he said.

Walter's loins stirred warmer when her face turned as red as a ripe tomato.

"You honor me, my lord," Irina cleared her throat and retrieved her notepad and pen from her apron.

"Perfection in the flesh is a rare sight to behold, milady," Walter bowed his head slightly.

Irina blushed some more and bowed her head slightly.

"Gratitude, my lord," she cleared her throat again and resorted to present-day English. "Will you be having your usual today, Walter?"

"Yes, please," Walter replied. "Thank you."

"You're quite welcome," Irina replied. "A plain donut, a cup of green tea, with two loaves of sugar and a dash of marshmallows on the way."

She finished scribbling on her notepad and headed to the kitchen.

Walter's laptop came to life after four minutes later.

"I really should get a new laptop," he said to himself. "This relic will give up on me anytime soon."

"But you need to get a job first, Walter," he spoke to himself in a high-pitched voice that he swore was the same as his mother's. "Freelancing isn't enough."

He barely made the rent, he fed on what spare change could buy, which was mainly scraps in the name of sandwiches and donuts. The tea was complimentary.

"You never should've quit that job as an editor for the Gazette," he scoffed.

"Yeah, I know," he replied to himself.

He considered his life as one big error, an aberration between his dreams and what reality had to offer. The call to freelance serenaded his soul with seduction so sweet it was irresistible. Six months and a threat-of-eviction later, his regret had become parasitic.

Walter opened a search engine and typed a few words. He scrolled through some options and opened two of them in separate tabs on the internet browser. He clicked on the first tab and started reading, after stealing a glance at the watch he bought at the mall for a very high price of almost nothing. The watch served its purpose, to tell the time. Price tags are overrated but nothing could replace functionality. Prof. Samuel Cadbury was running late as usual.

"How could this perfect day get any worse?" Walter grumbled. "Damn you, professor."

"If I didn't know better, I'd say someone's ticked you off a little this morning, Mr. Peabody," the raspy voice of a man emanated from behind a very thick, neatly trimmed beard. "I can appreciate a man with a loathing for tardiness."

Prof. Cadbury set his suitcase on the empty seat to his left. He reverently removed his fedora with his right hand and gently placed it on the table.

"Thank you for coming, professor," Walter extended his hand.

Prof. Cadbury took Walter's right hand in a strong grip and shook it. He adjusted his black, steel-rimmed glasses over the bridge of his nose and brushed his right hand over the last remnants of hair on the back of his head. The stocky, sixty-six-year-old, 1.67-meter tall genius with two doctorate degrees in theology regarded Walker with an expression Walter could not read.

Shame he chose to direct his genius towards theology instead of anything else, he thought.

"You're very welcome," the professor replied. "I always find our debates deeply soothing to the psyche, especially right before I embark on the rewarding duty of imparting knowledge unto eager minds and hearts," he added with only the faintest hint of sarcasm at the mundaneness of his job.

"The pleasure is all mine, as always, professor," Walter said. "I learn a lot more from you than you from me."

"Nonsense, Walter," Sam replied. "I am yet to find someone with as much eagerness and thirst for unconventional knowledge as you. Do you know what I find most interesting about you, young man?"

"No, sir," Walter replied evenly.

"Your penchant for knowledge, just because," Prof. Cadbury leaned forward slightly. "Your sole motivation is your desire to learn. Perhaps humanity is not entirely lost in its pursuit for the pointless."

"That is most generous of you, professor," Walter smiled. "Thank you."

Irina returned with Walter's order.

"Welcome, sir," she greeted the professor. "What can I get for you?"

She headed for the kitchen after taking Prof. Cadbury's order. The two men talked about life since the last time they met, which was almost two months ago.

"I'm still mad at my ex for leaving me for my neighbor," Walter admitted.

"Thought you said that was four years ago?" Prof. Cadbury asked rhetorically. "You should let it go, young man. Life doesn't wait for anyone, not even you."

"Easy for you to say," Walter shrugged.

"Be that as it may," Prof Cadbury said. "Life still doesn't wait for anyone. And my grandkids won't let me have a hair transplant. First thing they do when I pick them up is they go for my hair. These three-year-old twins can't understand why mommy has more hair than grandpa."

Prof. Cadbury chuckled and shook his head in amusement. Walter chuckled as well. He recalled the professor telling him he had been a single father to two beautiful girls since he became a widower for over a quarter of a century. The older daughter was married and was the mother of his twin granddaughters. The younger daughter was engaged. Walter admired his radiance of strength and pride when he talked about his family.

Maybe one day I'll get to feel what he feels, Walter hoped.

Irina returned with the professor's tea and a slice of carrot cake. Within minutes, their food was gone.

"So, what do you have for me today, Walter?" Prof. Cadbury asked.

"Have you ever considered the possibility that the proverbial Adam and Eve were not, in fact, the proverbial first man and woman to be created?" Walter asked, and the professor smiled.

"Straight shooter," the professor said. "Love that about you. But to answer your question; no. I never did. Why the sudden curiosity though, young man?"

"I was at a pub one evening," Walter said. "Someone invited me for a drink and while there, I heard some blokes having a heated debate on whether or not Eve was the first woman to be created. At first, I thought it was bizarre to debate on something like that at a pub. One of the debaters was absolutely convinced that Eve was not and that the demon, Lilith, was the first woman to be created. Of course, his religious companions begged to differ, and after several bottles of beer and shots of liquor, the drunken party parted ways without any definitive conclusion."

"And obviously, you did some digging of your own?" asked Prof. Cadbury rhetorically.

"You know me too well, professor," Walter smiled. "Yes, I did some digging. That night was the first time I had ever heard of a demon called Lilith."

"But obviously, before you enlisted the free services of the internet, something must have created an argument much stronger than the drunken rants of good blokes at a pub. Isn't that so, Mr. Peabody?" the professor said a-matter-of-factly.

"Indeed, professor," Walter agreed. "I decided to take a look at the first few chapters of the Book of Genesis. I read and re-read several times and couldn't find anything at first to suggest that Eve was not the first woman. But then one day, I found irrefutable evidence."

The professor raised an eyebrow and leaned forward. Walter had his complete attention now.

"Irrefutable evidence," Prof. Cadbury repeated, nodding slightly.

"There are two different descriptions on how the 'first woman' was created in the Book of Genesis," Walter replied with excitement.

Walter typed out a few words on his search engine. The professor raised an eyebrow as he waited. Walter right-clicked on a link and created a new tab on the internet browser. From this tab, he continued typing and clicking. Satisfied, he turned his laptop around to face the professor.

"Okay, here's what I realized," said Walter. "I searched for some verses from the Book of Genesis pertaining to this situation."

When he noticed the puzzled look on the professor's face, Walter reached around his laptop and looked at the screen.

"Oh, sorry about that," he apologized and closed a pop-up from a porn site. "You weren't meant to see that," he added with a note of embarrassment.

"Oh, don't worry about it, young man," Prof. Cadbury said flatly. "What you do with your private time is your concern. Although, I'd recommend that you acquaint yourself with actual human companionship and rid yourself of such virtual, quasi-fulfilling distractions."

"And I'll take your words of wisdom under advisement, professor," Walter replied with a half-smile. "There," he said with a note of satisfaction and returned to his seat. "The irrefutable evidence. Three verses from the Book of Genesis."

The professor clicked on each tab and read them carefully. When he finished, he nodded.

"I think I follow what you're trying to say here," Sam said.

"Good. Genesis 1:27reads *'So God created Man* (as in mankind) *in His own image; in the image of God he created them; male and female he created them.'* Did you notice how it says God created 'them' and then emphasizes later with 'male and female he created them'?" Walter asked.

"I do," the professor replied.

"And then later Genesis 2:7, reads *'Then the Lord God formed Man from the dust of the ground and Man became a living being.'* Hadn't mankind already been created in chapter one? Why would there be another account of man being created in the very next chapter of the same book? Does that not strike you as odd, professor?"

"Valid points," the professor agreed. "Still not good enough."

"And that's not all. Genesis 2:18, reads *'And the Lord said, "It is not good that man should be alone; I will make a help or companion for him."'* How come man is now alone in Chapter 2 when in Chapter 1, male and female had already been created?"

Walter waited for the professor to say something, but Prof. Cadbury remained silent with his eyebrows furrowed in focus and thought.

"Finally," Walter concluded, "Genesis 2:22 reads *'Then the Lord God made a woman from the rib He had taken out of the man, and He brought her to him* (the man).' This woman, professor, was later called Eve and the man was called Adam. But in Chapter 1, when the man and the woman were created, they were not given any names. They were just referred to as male and female."

"Did you consider the possibility that the words 'male and female' could simply indicate that mankind consists of men and women, and not necessarily that a male and a female were created?" Prof. Cadbury argued.

Time for some witty banter, Walter thought.

"I don't think so, professor," Walter argued. "If that was the case, why would male and female be made at the same time in Chapter 1, but in Chapter 2, the male is created from the dust of the ground, and then the female is created *LATER* from a rib removed from his side?"

A brief moment of silence lingered between the two men as Walter waited for the professor's rebuttal.

"I see your point, Walter," he finally said. "Remember, however, that these writings, especially in the Old Testament, ought not be taken literally, necessarily. Much has been lost in translation, and there are many hidden meanings in these Old Testament scriptures. My suggestion is to take a look at the original texts and try to understand the context behind the writer's words. Perhaps that would shed more light on the situation."

I think I have him trapped in a tight corner and his academic mind would not concede to my logic yet, Walter thought. *I'll let things be for now. He'll do some digging of his own, which is one of the reasons why I enjoy having such conversations with him. I'm certain he'll arrive at the same conclusion later.*

"Let's say I agree with your logic," Dr. Cadbury continued. "That two couples were created in two separate situations. The first couple was created together at the same time, while the second couple was created later, with the male created first in the same manner as the first couple, and the female was later created out of his rib. Is this what you're saying, by the way?"

"Exactly, professor."

"If that's the case," Dr. Cadbury added, "then something must have happened between-" he moved the mouse on the laptop monitor and squinted as he clicked a few times and read, "- Genesis 1:27 and Genesis 2:18. In 1:27, there was a first couple, male and female together and created at the same time. In 2:18, the second man, Adam, was alone and a companion had to be made for him and *FROM* him. So, even though we have established, or rather concluded, that there were two couples created at separate times, some questions linger. What happened to the first couple and why was the second female made from the rib of the second male, as opposed to being created at the same time as the male was?"

The professor rubbed his bearded chin and stared blankly at the monitor. Through the reflection of the laptop monitor on his glasses, Walter saw the fire in the professor's eyes for more research to come. He smiled with pleasure. He asked to meet with Dr. Cadbury just to discuss the two separate, biblical accounts of the creation of mankind. He never expected Dr. Cadbury to open a new field of possibilities for more research later. His heart throbbed with excitement.

"Would you gentlemen like anything else?" Irina asked.

The two men were too engrossed in their intellectual banter to notice her walk up to them.

"No, miss," the professor replied. "We'll pay by credit card."

Walter reached into his wallet to pull out some cash, but the professor waved him off.

"No, young man. This is on me. Consider it a small token for providing me with some intellectual excitement for the week."

Walter shrugged and returned the cash to his wallet.

I'll splurge on lunch today, he thought.

"Very well, sir," Irina said. "I'll be back shortly."

"Thank you, professor," Walter said.

Walter turned his laptop towards him and stole a quick glance at Irina's nicely shaped backside that threatened to rip her jeans apart. He swallowed and returned his gaze on his laptop monitor.

"No, thank YOU," the professor countered. "Plans for the rest of the day?"

"I have two posts to complete for two separate blogs, and then I'll do some more job hunting later," Walter replied. "Bloody tough out there."

"I understand your frustration," the professor replied. "I should retire soon, but I must say I prefer to stay gainfully employed. My sanity thanks me."

Irina returned with the credit card machine and ran Dr. Cadbury's credit card through the machine. He signed his receipt and returned Irina's pen with a 'thank you kindly'. He then picked up his fedora with his left hand and his suitcase with his right in one graceful motion.

"Good luck in your job search, Walter," he stood up. "If I stumble across anything that I think may suit you, I shall surely let you know."

Dr. Cadbury reverently set his fedora on his head.

"Thank you kindly, professor," Walter replied.

"Good day to you, Mr. Peabody," the professor said.

"Good day to you, Dr. Cadbury," Walter replied.

The professor left the tea shop.

Walter sighed, cracked his knuckles and rubbed his eyes. He set his elbows on the table, interlocked his fingers and rested his head on his knuckles. He let his mind drift off for a few minutes and once again, his mind sailed through the glory of his pathetic existence. He harbored so much self-loathe that he would not even visit his parents who lived just seven blocks from him. All their talk about unconditional love and only caring about his well-being did not matter to him. His trashed ego overshadowed his parents love for him.

"I never took you for a praying man, sir," said a soft voice, with a strong south London accent that made Walter's head snap upward.

Walter squinted, more from surprise than anything else, before he relaxed his shoulders. His eyes popped and his lips parted slightly. Before him stood a stunningly beautiful lady dressed in a sleeveless white blouse and pair of summer shorts so short and so tight, it created a very pronounced provocative V-shape in her crotch. Her long, black hair was pulled back in a bun, and a hand with perfectly manicured fingernails coated with bright, red nail polish covered her juicy lips.

"I'm so sorry, sir," she apologized. "Didn't mean to startle you."

"Forgive me, miss," Walter regained his composure. "My mind was elsewhere. I never noticed your presence until you spoke. No need to apologize."

Walter brandished a sheepish smile.

"Thank you, sir," she said, bringing down her hand from her lips to rest freely on her ample cleavage.

Walter realized too late that his gaze tracked her hand to her cleavage. He cleared his throat to hide his embarrassment before he returned his gaze towards her smooth, glowing face.

"I must apologize," she said. "I was eavesdropping on your conversation with the other gentleman. Can't resist intellectual conversations, especially on such unorthodox topics. What can I say? Can't help my sapiosexuality."

Her luscious, glossy lips covered in red lipstick spread in a groin-warming, soul-stealing smile.

"Oh, thank you, miss," Walter replied, not knowing what else to say.

A second went by before he realized the opportunity in front of him. He quickly and awkwardly stood up and gestured to the empty seat in front of him.

"Would you like to join me for some more intellectual banter, miss?" he asked politely. "The professor sort of left me hanging."

"I'd absolutely love to, thank you," she made to pull the chair, but Walter beat her to it.

"Please, allow me," he said.

She smiled her gratitude at him as Walter adjusted the seat to her comfort. He returned to his chair, closed his laptop without shutting it down and stowed it away in its bag.

Not today, technology, he thought.

He breathed deeply, but imperceptibly, to calm his nerves. It had been a while since he had been so close to such beauty.

"So, how long have you been a 'seeker'?" Walter asked.

"Oh, is that what they call us now? Seekers?" she asked.

They both laughed.

"No, I just made that up," Walter replied in earnest.

"I love it, sir," the lady said. "I shall adopt it from now on. Seeker."

Walter smiled softly to mask his surprise at her friendliness. His heart also warmed with confidence.

Still got it, he thought. *Haven't lost my player's card.*

"So, I noticed you and the professor were discussing the possibility that two sets of couples were created at different times in the Book of Genesis. Is that correct?" she asked.

"Correct," Walter agreed. "I initially wanted to only discuss that possibility with the professor, but then he came up with another mind-blowing theory."

"Regarding what could have happened within the time lapse of chapters one and two," she said. "Brilliant observation from him. I've actually entertained that possibility as well, and perhaps that's why I was so drawn to your conversation. It was like, finally. There are people out there who share my thirst for knowledge."

Her eyes beamed with excitement as she spoke, and Walter did not hear half of what she said. He just stared at her in a child-like trance, and if she noticed, she never showed it. He finally snapped himself to reality when he realized she had stopped speaking.

"Wait a minute," Walter said. "Did you just say you may have a theory for the time lapse?"

"Yep" she beamed, and her full, red, glossy lips parted in a wide, mischievous grin to reveal blindingly white teeth once again.

"Then, by all means, please share," Walter leaned back in his seat, his body almost shaking from the excitement of hearing what she was about to share.

Or rather, he was just dying to hear her talk.

"Okay," she agreed. "But I will tell you in the form of a story. Sounds good?"

"Sounds good to me," Walter said. "And crap. Where are my manners?"

Walter smacked himself on the forehead.

"I'm Walter, by the way," he extended his hand across the table.

She took his hand in hers and shook it. Walter held her hand for a second too long before releasing it.

"Pleased to meet you, Walter," she replied. "I'm Lithilia."

CHAPTER SIX

THE FIRST WOMAN

HER EYELIDS SLOWLY parted. She squeezed them shut to cease the pounding in her head caused by the shiny things hanging from above. Her breathing came with heavy inhalations and exhalations until her head no longer felt like it was going to implode. Steeling her resolve, she slowly opened her eyes again. This time, her head no longer threatened to crack open her skull from within, though it throbbed a tinge. Her vision was hazy and the things that shone from above seemed to move around slowly. She swallowed, squeezed her eyes shut and opened them again. Her vision slowly cleared and the room no longer spun around slowly. Next, she tried to move but her body stayed put, held down by restraints. She moved her head around as much as she could and studied her environs. Nothing looked at all familiar and a strangeness of everything around her, as well as her current situation, overwhelmed her until confusion, fear and panic bubbled their way up to her fast-beating heart and fast-paced mind. She fought against her restraints to no avail. She stopped wrestling when a white mist gathered in front of her vision with a whizzing sound. A few inhalations later, a calm swept over her and her body began to relax against the rioting of her mind to do otherwise.

Within moments, the mist cleared and she stared upwards into the face of a woman staring down at her. Long, unkempt black hair fell behind her shoulders. She had big, brown eyes, thick eyebrows, slightly protruding cheekbones, and full lips. Her curiosity for this strange lady overrode the rioting in her mind. The restraints came apart and slid off her body, though she remained confined within something solid she could see through. A sweet feeling of freedom came over her and she moved her body as much as she could within her confinement. She raised her right hand to touch the face that was looking down at her and hit something transparent and solid. She frowned in confusion before she tried again. Same result. Then the solid, transparent thing slid on either side with a whizzing sound and the woman who was staring down at her vanished.

She reached up in a hurry, as if she could stop the woman from disappearing. Alas, the woman was gone. She gasped in amazement and confusion. A sudden realization dawned on her: no woman, no restrains, no transparent thing to restrict her movement. A guttural sound of elation for her newfound freedom forced its way out of her parched throat. She raised her hands to her face and examined them. Then, she sat up and regarded her legs and toes. She wiggled her fingers. She brought her hands to her face and felt her eyes, nose and mouth. She swallowed, licked her fingers and tapped on her teeth with her left, index finger. Another guttural sound escaped her throat. Then, a movement on her left forced her to turn her head in that direction. Another creature sat at the edge of something transparent and solid that floated in the air, just like she was. The creature stared at her with unbridled curiosity. It looked just like her, except the creature had a little more hair on its body, a flatter chest and an extra appendage between its legs and she had none.

She swung her legs to the side and met the other creature's gaze before she returned her gaze towards her legs and toes. She wiggled her toes and smiled. The other creature made a sound. When she looked towards him, she pointed at her toes and made the sound again. She made a sound that was similar to his. They wiggled their toes together and made some more of the sound. The other creature slid off the transparent surface and tried to stand on its feet. It did so a little too quickly and almost fell to the ground. It caught itself on the thing on which it was sitting. She watched it with fascination as it struggled to take one cautious step at a time until it could walk on its own very slowly. Then, the other creature turned and started walking towards her.

It stopped two paces away from her and beckoned at her. He gestured for her to get off the transparent surface she was sitting on. She furrowed her eyebrows in confusion, but he grunted and beckoned at her some more. She grunted back at him and grinned. He went back to the surface he used to sit on, sat on it, and gently slid off it. Then, he gestured for her to do the same. Fear erased her grin from her face and she shook her head violently. She gripped the edge of the flat, transparent surface she was sitting on. The other creature walked towards her. When she was within armlength, it reached for her shoulders but she backed away, growled and bared her teeth. It recoiled from her sudden aggression and almost lost his balance. It grunted and gestured at her some more as if to encourage her.

When she did not move, he reached for her shoulders again, very slowly this time. Her body shivered and stiffened to his touch but did not back away. He grunted softly at her and strengthened his hold on her shoulder. Gently, it pulled her off the transparent surface. Her eyes squeezed shut and the trembling in her body increased a tinge. A whimper escaped her throat as she cautiously placed a foot on the cold, hard floor. The other foot followed and she whimpered again. She stood up straight, opened her eyes. The tension in her body relaxed a little. The other creature let go of her shoulders. When her knees buckled, panic pressed upon her and she shrieked with morbid dread. She threw her arms around the man's neck and held on for dear life. A pair of strong hands pressed against her ribcage and tried to push her away using brute strength. Her grip tightened around the creature's neck and would not let go. Instead, she wrapped her legs around the creature's pelvis and clung to the creature's body. Her body spasmed and she sobbed from profound fear.

Her sobbing and the feeling of her body trembling with fright against his made the other creature to stop trying to pry her away from him. His features softened with the innate understanding of her emotional trauma. His hard grip on her hips morphed to a gentle touch and his instinct for self-defense morphed into empathy. The trembling in her body reduced. His hands moved away from her inner pelvis. He gently held her waist with his right arm to support her body against his and began gently caressing her long, black hair as he grunted softly in her ear. Her sobs subsided, and her grip around his neck and hips relaxed. She still held on to his body, however, for support.

He grunted and gave her a squeeze of encouragement. She grunted back. He gently let go of her waist and her legs slid to the floor. Her body tensed up but he grunted in short bursts. He stepped back, held her left hand in his right hand and beckoned at her with his left hand. She took a wobbly step towards him. He took another step back and she followed with a sturdier step this time. Then, he let go of her left hand and she took a step on her own. A grin spread across her face and she shrieked with joy. She took another step, and another until she walked on her own. More shrieks of joy escaped her lips followed by many grunts and guttural sounds. He joined her and walked around briefly until they suddenly stopped and stared at each other.

His gaze zoomed in on her breasts as if he noticed, for the first time, that hers were much bigger than his were. He reached out and grabbed her left breast with his right hand. He squeezed and let go. He repeated the same gesture with his left hand on her right breast. Then he held both her breasts in his hands and squeezed repeatedly. He smiled and grunted.

She let him continue to squeeze her breasts repeatedly. Her nipples hardened. The appendage in between his legs, the one she did not have in between hers, extended and grew bigger. Smitten with curiosity, she reached for it and took it in her hand. It throbbed within her grip and felt warm and hard to the touch. He grunted. Warmth and wetness spread between her legs and her breathing became erratic, just like his. She raised her eyes and met his. Both creatures gazed into each other's eyes, before she dropped on her hands and knees, while the man knelt behind her.

They remained in that position for several minutes, grunting heavily as they gave into their basic instincts. She wholly and willingly accommodated his ferocity. Occasionally, she spasmed and moaned from the waves of pleasure that rippled through her body, some of which were subtle while others rendered her temporarily blind with sheer ecstasy. More moistening of the inner space between her legs followed every wave of pleasure. Then, he thrust harder and more vigorously until his body tensed up and spasmed. A roar of pleasure reverberated within the chamber walls as he expanded and climaxed inside of her, a gesture which also elicited a grand finale of climaxes within her. Drained and spent, they collapsed on the hard floor and snuggled against each other. They fell fast asleep, still ignorant of who they were or whence they came.

She was the first to wake up. She rubbed her eyes and sat up. Her inner thighs felt sticky, but she did not care. He also woke up and sat up. They stood up and surveyed their environs together, their curiosity getting the better of them once again. Nothing else was in the unicolor chamber except for the two flat surfaces on which they had first awoken. A whizzing sound coming from their right made them look in that direction. Another creature walked into the chamber. He looked like they did; much darker skin, a little taller and his body was covered with something that had the same color as the walls and floor of the chamber. He held something flat in both hands, with something laid out on its surface, which gave off an aroma so wonderful it awoke a primordial instinct in the naked male and female: hunger.

"Hello, my lovely couple," said the third creature, fully aware that they could not understand him. "You must be famished. Would you like something to eat?"

He gestured at the food on the tray. The lovely couple looked at him, the tray, at each other and back to the tray. The third creature smiled, sat on the floor and set the tray in front of him. He broke off a piece of the roasted animal with his bare hands and took a bite out of it.

"Hmm, delicious. Come join me," he beckoned at them.

The couple hesitated before the male cautiously walked towards the tray. When the female made to follow him, he put his hand on her chest and grunted. She nodded and sat back on the floor. The male walked cautiously towards the tray as the third creature ate away with as much fake gusto as he could muster. He broke off a piece of the roasted animal and bit into it. His eyes lit up with the explosion of deliciousness in his buccal cavity. He grabbed the entire tray of food and hurried back to the female. He took another bite from the piece of meat he broke off before he offered the rest to her. She took a bite and reacted the same way the male did. The lovely couple feasted away. Ten minutes later, nothing but partially chewed bones remained of the roast.

"Remarkable," said the third creature as he observed the couple with intense fascination. "Barely a day out of incubation and the male already displays the instincts of a protector."

The doors parted with a whizzing sound and another creature walked in who looked just like the third creature, except he was a little taller and his hair was silver instead of black.

"Can you believe they have mated already?" the third creature said telepathically.

"Really?" the fourth asked, incredulous of the third's remark. *"But, how come? How did they even know? It's still too early."*

"Remarkable. Not 'too early'," the third creature insisted.

"I stand corrected, my friend," the fourth nodded.

"This is why I insisted we include the final pair in the mix," the third said. *"They have 24 instead of 23. Besides, it will make our work a lot easier now, you'll see."*

"I trusted your judgment then," the fourth replied. *"And I trust your judgment now."*

The third creature cautiously approached the couple. He smiled and raised his hands in the air as he approached, hoping to communicate that he meant the couple no harm. But the couple retreated.

"You must still be hungry," he said to them.

The couple just stared at him and grunted.

"Bring me some fruits," said the third creature telepathically.

A few moments later, two other creatures, who resembled the third creature, brought two trays of fruits and set them down on the floor in front of the couple. The third creature sat on the floor and started eating from one of the trays. When he was certain he had tickled the couple's curiosity enough, he picked up a fruit and handed it to the male. He knew if the male accepted it, the female would also accept it. She had already grown to trust him.

Perhaps the mating sealed that trust, he thought.

The third creature thrust the fruit towards the male. The male took the fruit with less hesitation this time. He took a bite of the fruit and chewed as the female looked on with eagerness and curiosity. When the male was satisfied there was nothing wrong with the fruit, he handed the female the remainder of the fruit, and she ate of it.

The third creature smiled with satisfaction. He gestured, inviting the couple to come closer. The couple obliged and, together, they ate the two trays of fruits.

"You like the fruits too, no?" the third creature said. "Don't you worry, there is plenty more out there. You will soon see."

The third creature's eyes danced with excitement as he spoke. He extended his left hand towards the male. The male touched it, sniffed it and grunted. He smiled and extended his right hand to the female. She touched it, sniffed it, licked it and grunted as well. The third creature laughed, and the couple joined him.

"I apologize for my bad manners," the third creature said after the laughter subsided. "Let me introduce myself. I am your creator."

And so, it came to pass that a friendship emerged between the creator and his creatures on the first day of contact. The creator and his colleague wanted to transfer their handiworks to another chamber, but the creatures would not leave their immediate environs. It took much coaxing to get them to return to the platforms whence they first awoke. The female would only settle in hers after the male gave her a nod of approval. The couple suffered from restless and sleepless nights at times; but those nights were easily taken care of with white mists, which put them to sleep.

After several weeks, the creator and some members of his team built a good relationship with the male and female. To the utter astonishment of the creator, his creatures were quickly learning to read, write and speak their language. But even with the improved relationship between creator and creatures, the couple still showed a strong aversion to leaving their immediate environs. Even getting them to put on some garments was a problem. It took several months before the couple agreed to wear some garments and move to a different area. The couple needed some motivation though, such as slowly making their chamber too cold for comfort.

The couple was as curious as they were excited to see other areas of what they had come to accept as their abode. They touched, and sometimes licked, as many things that lined the hallways as they could. Above their heads, some objects shone with a brightness that did not hurt their eyes. The female tried to touch these objects, but her height would not permit her. Even jumping did not help. The male was also a little too short to reach these shiny objects, and for a few minutes, the couple giggled away with every attempt to jump and touch the shiny objects. The creator and his team watched them very patiently.

Suddenly, the female stopped trying and her face beamed as if she had just had an idea. She asked the male to hurry up and hunch over. The male was a little confused, but the female insisted. He obliged, and as he did, she hopped on his back and perched there. The male staggered a little but steadied himself. When he straightened himself, he realized that the female wanted to use him for support and leverage as she tried to reach for one of the shiny objects. Her head hung and her shoulders slumped from another unsuccessful attempt. The male had an idea of his own.

He made her slide off his back. He took a knee and interlocked his fingers. She regarded him quizzically, not understanding what he was trying to do. He gestured for her to step into his hands and use his shoulders for support. She did. The first attempt to lift her off the floor failed because her bent knee negated the effort. He grunted, held her knee in place and pointed at her stiff knee. She nodded. He interlocked his fingers once again and she stepped into his hands. This time she stiffened her left leg and used his shoulders for support as he lifted her from the floor. Her hand raced towards the shiny thing in the ceiling until she touched it. He gently lowered her back to the ground. He smiled as he stood up. She hugged him tightly and buried her face in his chest.

"Teamwork," the creator said telepathically.

"Did you envision this happening this quickly, oh great one?" teased a colleague of his via telepathy.

"Yes, I did, of course," he replied with a chuckle, though his expression was one of concern.

"Alright," his colleague said. *"What troubles you?"*

"Nothing," the creator replied though his expression indicated the contrary.

"Come on, now," his colleague pressed. *"Something is obviously bothering you."*

The creator was about to reply when two neighboring doors opened to two separate chambers. What followed shocked even the creator. The female turned feral. She screamed and clawed at the creator's colleagues who accompanied them. The creator's colleagues backed away from her. She ran to the male and clung to him as if her life depended on it. She buried her face in his chest and sobbed wildly. She made sounds only the male could hear.

"They stay together," the creator issued an order via telepathy to everyone's hearing. *"They must not be separated until further notice. Understood?"*

"Yes, sir," his team chorused via telepathy from across the facility.

The creator approached the couple and the male glared at him. He raised both his hands in the air, a gesture the couple had come to understand was a symbol of peace. He placed a hand on the male's shoulder and caressed the female's back. She turned, met his gaze and sobbed some more.

"I know," the creator said. "No one will separate you two, alright?"

He spoke lovingly to them, even though he knew they did not understand the words he said. Yet, he communicated from his heart and, somehow, the couple understood him clearly. The female reached for his hand. He let her have it. She kissed the back of his hand and smiled weakly. He kissed her forehead and wiped her tears away.

"There you go, my sweet child," the creator said. "Now, come."

He stepped away from the couple and gestured for them to follow him. He pressed a button in the wall and one of the doors slid shut. He stepped into the other chamber with the open door and pointed towards a bed.

"Come now, my children," he said. "Get some rest in your new domicile."

The male nodded towards him and guided his companion into their domicile. He lay on the bed with her still clinging on to him. The creator watched them with a blank mind. Within minutes, the female fell asleep and the male also fell asleep within the next minute.

"Do you now see why I was concerned?" the creator asked via telepathy.

"She is too clingy," his colleague said confidently.

"That does not bother me, my friend," the creator said.

"Then what does?"

"Her rage," the creator replied.

"I see," his colleague nodded. *"That is definitely a problem."*

"Especially since rage was not in their genetic makeup," the creator narrowed his eyes.

"Then where did hers come from?"

"That, I must find out."

The couple learned and adapted quickly. Sometimes, their creator brought a flat, rectangular device to them. He would tap on the surface and the device would light up. The first day he did that, the couple reached out and tried to touch the display that suspended above the surface. It looked like one of the fruits they ate regularly. Their minds could not comprehend why their hands went through the display no matter how hard they tried to touch it.

One day, the creator went to visit them. A few weeks had passed since he last saw them. When the female saw him, she cried for joy and ran into his open arms.

"I have missed you, Father," she said, clinging on to him.

Father's heart beat with so much pride and joy that he almost shed a tear. He pressed a fatherly kiss on the crown of her head.

"I have missed you too, my dear princess," Father replied.

The male approached him with a grin. He clapped Father on the left shoulder with his right hand. Father smiled at the male's own way of indicating how much the male missed him. He nodded at the male.

"Let me sit down, my princess," he said.

"Okay, Father," she let him go and sat on the bed.

The male joined her on the bed.

"Did you two complete your assignments?" he asked them.

"Yes, Father, we did," the male replied.

"Good," Father said. "Let us hear it. Would you like to go first, princess?"

"No," she hid her face behind the male. "I am too shy."

"I will go first, then," the male offered.

Three minutes later, he finished reading his assignment aloud.

"Excellent," Father applauded and returned his attention towards the female.

"Your turn now, princess."

The female breathed in deeply and stood up.

"I am a woman," she began timidly. "I love to read, I love to write, and I love to draw flowers. I also love to eat fruits. I love to play with him-" she pointed at the male, "- but I do not like it when he makes sounds with his backside. This is because, when he does that, everywhere starts to smell and I have to go out of our domicile to breathe clean air."

They all burst into hearty laughter. When the laughter subsided, she said some other funny things and they laughed some more.

"That is so funny, princess," Father said. "Do you have anything else to say?"

"No, Father," she replied.

"Are you not forgetting something?" he urged.

She furrowed her eyebrows as she tried to remember. Father noticed frustration building up within her and did not want to spoil the happy mood.

"Do you remember everything I asked you to do?" he asked.

"Yes, Father. I do," she replied almost sadly.

"You remember most, my princess," he said. "But not everything."

He leaned forward and took her hand.

"How were you supposed to start your speech?"

"I was supposed to start with who I am," she replied

Her eyebrows were still furrowed as she tried to remember.

"And who are you?" Father urged.

"I am a woman…" she began to recite once again.

"Yes and a very beautiful one, my princess," Father caressed her cheek. "You were also supposed to give yourself a name."

Suddenly, her eyes beamed with childlike joy as she remembered what she had forgotten. Before anything else, she was supposed to say her name; the name she had chosen for herself. She had given it a lot of thought. When she shared this name with the male, he grinned with happiness.

"I love the name very much," he had said.

As such, with joy in her heart and pride in her voice, she spoke four words out loud.

"MY NAME IS LITHILIA."

CHAPTER SEVEN

PRANKED TO PARANOIA

"WOW," WALTER EXCLAIMED. "You do know how to tell a story. Your ability to blend unorthodox innuendoes, bible stories and fiction into one fascinating and detailed compendium is a talent unlike any I've ever seen."

"And your ability to blend so many compliments in a single sentence is the biggest form of flattery I've ever received," she replied with a giggle.

"Touché, mademoiselle," Walter conceded. "Touché."

"Maybe I should've just said 'thank you,'" Lithilia winked.

"Nonsense," Walter waved a hand dismissively. "Your rebuttal honors me."

"Are you that skilled with words or are you psychic?" she asked, narrowing her eyes in obvious pretentious caution.

"I'm afraid I know not of what you speak, milady," Walter played along.

"What I meant was," Lithilia started saying and then hesitated.

Lithilia looked around guiltily as if she were about to share the launch codes for a nuclear warhead with him and no one had to know. Then, she leaned towards Walter.

"Before I say anything, you must swear your silence," she demanded.

"I swear, my beautiful dark maiden," Walter crossed his heart, "that I shall not tell anyone else that I am about to ask you out on a date should you continue to strike my fancy thus."

"See," Lithilia throwing her hands in the air. "I knew you were psychic. How else could you've known I have a weakness for genuine, tasteful flattery? Art thou a wizard of sorts, stranger?" Lithilia cocked her left eyebrow.

"Milady," Walter bowed his head slightly and shook it slowly. "Alas, I'm afraid I misjudged you. I was under the impression that a woman is only vulnerable when her nail polish was not yet dry."

Lithilia erupted in hearty, uncontrollable laughter and not a single customer at the tea shop reacted to her sudden outburst. She gripped her sides, slapped the table a few times and dabbed at her teary eyes. Walter smiled. He remembered being told once, many years ago, that making a woman laugh was a step closer to making her panties fall off.

Score another one for me, Walter thought as he smiled at her.

"Oh my, Walter," she managed to say. "I haven't laughed this hard in a while."

"I'm glad I made you laugh, Lithilia," he replied softly.

The glint in her eye lasted for a microsecond when he said her name this time. Even her sad smile was brief, though it lasted longer than the glint in her eye. A moment of awkward silence brewed between them.

"So, would you like to hear the rest of the story?" she asked and summoned a mischievous grin.

"Absolutely," Walter replied with a smile.

"Great," Lithilia said. "If you're not scared of monsters and bad people, then this segment is for you. Prepare to be afraid," Lithilia added in the scariest voice she could muster.

Walter laughed at her cuteness. Lithilia laughed as well. Then, she continued her story.

***

One day, Father walked into their domicile. The door was already open.

"Today, I have something to show you," he said enthusiastically.

"What is it, Father?" the male asked.

"Come with me," Father said.

They followed Father, walking down a long, winding hallway until they came to a dead-end. Father stopped and turned around to face his children.

"I am about to show you two something behind this door," he said. "You are about to experience first-hand everything you have been shown on the study tablet. You may be overwhelmed, as is expected. But not for long."

Lithilia and her companion nodded their understanding.

"Do not be afraid," Father continued. "I assure you that no harm will come to you whatsoever. Alright?"

They nodded.

So, are you ready, my lovely children?"

"Yes, Father," the male replied.

He turned towards Lithilia, who nodded her agreement.

Father pressed a button on the wall next to the door with his left index finger. The door slid open on both sides and the rays of a bright, shining object in the sky bathed the three of them in a warm, golden glow. The lovely couple quickly learned that staring at the shiny ball with their naked eyes was a terrible idea. They shut their eyelids quickly and looked away.

"Solara?" asked Lithilia.

"Yes, my princess," Father said. "Behold Solara."

The couple slowly opened their eyes to look at what lay in front of them and for the first time since they awoke on the platform, their jaws drop in awe and their eyes widened with curiosity. Father smiled with pride and happiness. He gestured for them to step out into the world that lay in front of them. The male extended his hand and Lithilia took it. Together, as they walked into the perfection that surrounded them, they instinctively closed their eyes and took a deep breath of fresh air, held it in for a few seconds and exhaled as the warmth of Solara washed over their bodies.

The couple slowly crouched and swept the grass with the palm of their hands. They raised their hands to their faces and regarded the morning dew that collected on them. Lithilia licked it cautiously with the tip of her tongue. The male did the same. Their eyes met and they giggled. Then, with a shout of glee, she tackled him to the ground. They rolled and played on the wet grass until their wet garments clung to their bodies. They seemed oblivious to their wetness of their garments. Lithilia straddled her partner and stared down at him with eyes that burned with love enough to light up their domicile and more of the facility. She brushed some strands of hair from his face and kissed him gently on the lips before scanning the area some more. The male also looked around briefly before he gently stripped her from his hips and sat on his heels. They appreciated their new environment in serene silence.

Trees, flowers, and other vegetation, as well as animals, big and small and of various colors adorned the entire landscape as far as their eyes could see. Some creatures were so small that they could be crushed underneath one's feet without one even realizing. Others buzzed and flew in the air. Colors. So many colors. Some creatures flew high in the sky; in groups or by themselves. The couple smelled the flowers, chased the little animals as they ran through the vegetation, climbed the trees, as well as plucked and ate some fruits.

Lithilia and her partner recognized some of the creatures, as well as many of the plants and flowers from the floating images from the study tablets. Other animals of various shapes and sizes either walked or slithered towards the couple. These animals sniffed, licked, nestled and familiarized themselves with the newest additions to their ecosystem; the couple.

"They are welcoming us," the male said.

"Yes, they are," Lithilia agreed. "Do you feel it? The aliveness of this place?"

"I do, my love," the male said. "It is much different from seeing everything through the study tablet."

They ventured further into the haven of a place until they stumbled across a stream so clear and beautiful that the rays of Solara bounced on its uneven surface like millions of specks of golden dust.

The male dropped to a knee and ran his fingers in the stream. It felt cold to the touch. He scooped up a handful and brought it to his mouth. He drank a gulp and savored the cool freshness of the water as it ran down his gullet. He drank some more. Suddenly, he stood up and removed his garments exposing his naked flesh to the gentle heat of Solara. He waded cautiously into the water, ignoring the initial shock to his body from the cold stream as it crept up his immersing body. When he was waist-deep, a splash of cold water hit his back. He yelled and spun around to find a giggly and naked Lithilia preparing to splash him some more. Her aim hit him dead in the face and torso because he was too late to react. A shrill of pure joy traveled across the landscape. The male grinned mischievously and returned the favor. A war of water ensued for many minutes until exhaustion forced the couple to a truce.

They waded back to the banks of the stream and lay next to each other on smooth, dark pebbles. Then, by the banks of the gently flowing stream, they bonded. This time, the bonding was different. The trees gave their blessing, the animals chanted, the little creatures sang, and the birds danced in the sky. They bonded to the symphony of Mother Nature herself, creating a new bond that transcended the physical, sealing their souls as one and inseparable. Their bond created a new life that would grow within Lithilia

Father met with them later at dusk.

"Do you like what you see?" he asked them.

"It is beautiful, Father," the male said. "It is perfect."

"It is only perfect now that you two are here," Father said. "Everything you see is yours to do as you wish. It is your home and so, you will give it a name. What do you want to call it?"

The male and Lithilia gave it some thought.

"What if we call it 'Aiden'?" the male asked Lithilia.

"That is a lovely name," Lithilia replied. "I like it."

"Aiden," the male affirmed. "The Garden of Aiden."

"Is that your final choice, my children?" Father asked.

"Yes, father," they affirmed together.

"Then so be it," Father declared.

And so it came to pass that Father made a domicile for them in the garden, to maximize their comfort. He visited his children often until he ascertained their independence. Lithilia was with child. As such, Father and his team took her to the facility for regular checkups. The couple's parental instincts kicked in naturally. All tests revealed nothing amiss with her pregnancy. Better still, she carried twins. And so it came to pass that eleven cycles of Lunis later, Lithilia gave birth. The first child was healthy and strong but, sadly, the second child did not live despite the efforts of Father and his team to try to save the baby.

The pain of the loss from the baby weighed heavily on the couple, as well as on Father and his team. In one birthing process, the lovely couple experienced the ultimate joy of hearing a child cry for the very first time in their lives, as well as felt the ultimate pain of losing a child; a terribly, hurtful, painful oxymoron. For almost an entire cycle of Lunis, their first-born son did not have a name because the lovely couple still grieved the loss of the second child. The experience of pain was a given at some point in the future, but not like this; not this early. Father and his team provided as much support as they could during such dire times. He convinced them to at least try to focus more on their newborn son.

"You must give him a name," he urged them. "It is only fair that you do."

"We will call him 'Grief,'" the male said.

"I would not recommend that, my son," Father offered.

"What about 'Pain,'?" Lithilia asked. "That is what we feel right now."

"That would be unfair to your son, my princess," Father said.

Then, after a moment, the male spoke.

"We will name him 'Cahen'."

Lithilia agreed, and Father affirmed.

"Then Cahen it shall be."

The pain of loss subsided with time and with Cahen being a handful. He was a strong and healthy child, full of his parents' curiosity and intelligence. They taught him well, and Father could not get enough of his grandson. Month after month, the couple bonded and month after month, Lithilia was not with child. At first, she was unbothered by her not being with child after several months of bonding. However, after three years of fruitless bonding, her heart became burdened by the situation. Her inability to conceive baffled even Father and his team. Multiple tests indicated that everything was fine with her womb.

The words of encouragement from her mate no longer provided their usual comfort. Before long, alien feelings like low self-esteem, anxiety and a loss of libido became her norm. Personality changes ensued, like short-temperedness and transferred aggression towards her mate and her son. Her change in personality blinded her to recognize Cahen's unhappiness and tension whenever he was around her but the same Cahen was the complete opposite whenever he was around his father; brimming with happiness and playfulness. When alas she noticed this, a new sentiment arose within her; jealousy.

One night, as was the new norm, Lithilia refused to bond with her mate. She stormed out of the domicile and into the night on a solitary promenade. She grew more resentful by the day and convinced herself that everyone, including her son, was to blame for her inexplicable barrenness.

Too much bonding with my mate caused this. His seed has poisoned my womb.

Father and his team are either incompetent or they did something to my womb.

I am certain that child must have strangled his brother when they shared my womb. Why else would I give birth to a dead child?

Her rants, verbal and mental, continued until she lost track of time. Several hours later, she started returning to their domicile. When she neared their sleeping chamber, bright, golden light streamed through a crack in the door.

"What is happening?" she asked herself.

She approached the door, slowly, silently and with caution. She dropped to a knee and very slowly pushed the door wider. She froze at what her eyes beheld but her logical mind could not comprehend.

Her mate lay on his back, eyes closed and in seemingly deep slumber. However, he was not alone. A creature, a female, straddled him. She looked like a golden, luminescent version of them in shape and form. Lithilia tried to match this creature of golden light's face with all the faces of the women working with Father. Nothing. The creature did not look like any of the women in the facility, who worked with Father. These women working with Father were beautiful in every way Lithilia could conceive. Yet, this creature straddling her partner made all those women look disgustingly ugly.

The creature leaned forward and started kissing Lithilia's partner passionately on the lips, while gyrating her hips against his in the same fashion that she, Lithilia, did when she bonded with her partner. At first, Lithilia gawked in shock and was paralyzed speechless. Even thinking seemed like an impossible task for her. She wanted to scream and even that proved an impossible feat. She tried to move, but her muscles would not respond to her command. Finally, as if the illogical nature of the situation became too much to process, an avalanche of rage and confusion, anger and jealousy, fear and powerlessness poured down on her psyche at the same time.

Lithilia wanted to pounce on this creature for the abominable act of bonding with her mate. She wanted to do a thousand-and-one things to this creature, none of which were akin to anything good. She wanted to punish this creature in ways she, herself, could not even imagine. Oh yes. Her evil intentions waxed purer than pure. However, even as she made to physically express her rage, the fear of the unknown and a sense of powerlessness triumphed. Her shoulders slumped in surrender and all she could do was watch helplessly as the creature peeled her lips from her mate's and ground her hips faster against her mate's. The creature angled her head upwards, squeezed her eyes shut and parted her lips in a prelude to a scream of orgasmic pleasure.

Her partner move his head weakly from side-to-side. He moaned in his sleep. His body tensed up in an all too familiar way. Finally, in a symphony of light and sound, huge wings of golden light, like those of a bird, suddenly sprang from the creature's shoulder blades as the creature screamed with unimaginable pleasure. Her mate gave seed and, in a burst of bright, golden light, the creature vanished, like an illusion or a figment of fantasy. The night returned to an undisturbed stillness and her partner's chest gently heaved up and down slowly as he breathed quietly in his sleep.

This must be some kind of dream, she thought. *A nightmare. Yes, just that; a nightmare. I want this memory gone, but I cannot forget it. I cannot just pretend it never happened.*

She shook her head as if shaking her head would erase everything she had just witnessed and help her make sense out of what had just happened.

There is only one way to find out if this was real, she concluded.

Lithilia squeezed her eyes shut, took in a deep breath, let it out and opened her eyes. Her heart hit hard within her chest as she stood up and approached her mate. She swallowed and zoomed in on his crotch, trembling from the hope that everything she saw was just a dream. She gasped, cupped her mouth and sank to the floor. Alas, his crotch was wet from giving seed. Unable to process the shock of the situation, Lithilia's psyche shut down from emotional overload and her world went black as she passed out on the floor of the chamber.

Lithilia roused about an hour later and the memory of the situation with the creature jolted her to full wakefulness. She sat up ramrod stiff.

Maybe it was a dream, she theorized.

She regarded her partner, who was still fast asleep with his back to the door. Nothing seemed amiss. She shook her head as if to clear her mind and make sense of her memories. She swallowed, stood up and climbed into bed.

It was all a dream, she convinced herself. *It was all just a dream.*

She lay on the bed, her back against her mate's.

It was all just a dream. It was all just a dream, she reminded herself.

Then, her partner turned around in his sleep and gathered her in his arms. The gesture sent soothing sensations to her troubled soul.

In his sleep, he sniffed her hair as he was accustomed to doing every night when they lay together. He adjusted himself to fully accommodate as much of her body with his as possible. He intertwined his fingers in hers as he held the back of her hand.

It was all just a dream, she said to herself. *He is here with me… and only me.*

Lithilia trembled from the memories of what she had put her family through. Anger and jealousy gave way to shame and remorse. But even those did not last that long as a sense strange sense of happiness and peace overwhelmed her. She cried bitterly while her mate quietly snored away. As the burdens of her recent past came off her shoulders, she made a vow to herself.

I shall never abandon my family again, no matter what happens.

And so, for the next few months, the family was whole again. Lithilia still did not conceive, but she forged on with renewed hope. All was peaceful, until one night, Lithilia stepped out into the night when everyone was asleep. She wanted to enjoy the beauty and quiet of the night. When she returned to their chamber, she witnessed the same creature with wings bonding with her partner once again. Déjà-vu. This time, however, her rage triumphed over her sense of helplessness. With a maniacal scream, she charged at the creature intending to do the creature major bodily harm. How?

I do not know and I do not care.

Unfortunately, her attack came a fraction-of-a-blink too late. Her partner gave seed and the creature vanished in an explosion of bright, golden light once again. Lithilia shielded her eyes from the brightness. When the brightness disappeared, she rushed to her partner.

"My love," Lithilia shook him roughly. "Wake up."

"Lucie…" her partner said in his sleep

Lithilia froze and stared at her mate in utter disbelief, unsure of what to think, say or do next.

"Lucie…" he repeated in his sleep.

Lithilia backed up slowly, her mouth gaping in shock.

Lucie, she reiterated. *This creature's name is Lucie and he knows her. But how? Who is she? And why is she so different? Does Father know about this? And if Father does, then why would he allow such a thing to happen? Why would he do this to me? Why would he conspire with my mate to cause me such pain and hurt?*

A huge lump gathered in her throat. She cupped her mouth and stifled a sob.

I lost my son, I went through dark times and just when I found healing, this happens to me? My love and my father hurting me like this?

A deeper darkness, like a scar cut deeper, spread across her psyche and for the first time in her existence, a new emotion broke through her being; betrayal.

"My love," the male sat upright. "What is wrong? Why are you so upset?"

Lithilia was so lost in her stream of thoughts that she did not realize that her partner was awake.

"My love," he said, worry creasing his features. "What bothers you?"

She opened her mouth to say something, but her throat felt very dry. She cleared her throat and spoke three words.

"Who is Lucie?"

***

Lithilia stared blankly at Walter.

"Come on," Walter pleaded after a few seconds. "Don't leave me hanging."

"Why would I leave you hanging, my dear?" Lithilia teased. "A girl's gotta save some tricks for later, no?"

"You do drive a hard bargain," Walter grinned. "So, how do I get tickets to listen to the rest of your story?"

"Oh, let me see…" Lithilia tapped a finger on her luscious lips.

Stain-proof lipstick, Walter observed.

"Those tickets are really hard to get and I charge a very high fee for them," Lithilia said, leaning forward slightly.

Walter caught sight of her ample cleavage rioting against her low-cut blouse.

"But for you, I may be able to get you a small discount."

"And pray tell," Walter said, trying not to act like a horny teenage boy. "How much will this discount be?"

"I don't know," Lithilia replied. "It could range from 100 to 100%."

"Her highness does me much honor indeed," Walter bowed his head slightly, not even sure if his words were coherent anymore. "And how and when would her highness wish for me to reach her thus?"

"How about you give me your number?" Lithilia replied.

Walter pulled a pen from his breast pocket, scribbled his number and first name on a piece of paper on his notepad, ripped the piece of paper from the notepad and handed it to Lithilia. Lithilia folded the piece of paper and stashed it in her purse, without even looking at the number.

"Very well," Lithilia said, standing up.

Walter stood up with her like a true gentleman.

"I'll see you later," Lithilia added.

Lithilia turned around and started walking away, without even giving Walter a chance to say goodbye. Walter heaved a sigh of disappointment and sat down.

She's never gonna call, he thought as he reached for his laptop.

Suddenly, an approaching presence made him look up. He smiled. Lithilia took him gently by the chin and lightly pressed her luscious lips against his for a few seconds.

"I will call you, Walter Peabody," Lithilia said seductively

She patted Walter lightly on the cheek before she spun around. Walter watched her walk away and a million butterflies went ballistic in his belly. He shook with the excitement of a teenager who had just landed his first kiss.

He failed to notice, however, that Lithilia had said his full name, even though he had only written down, and told her, his first name. He never saw how the smile on her face turned to an evil frown as she turned her back towards him and walked away. He never saw her eyes flash in an orange-yellow brightness before returning to normal. Still smitten from her kiss, he assumed the smell of burning came from the kitchen. Alas, the smell, which only he could perceive, came from another realm in another dimension. Still smitten from her kiss, he never noticed that, when Lithilia stepped through the door of the tea shop, she actually stepped through a portal she had summoned, a portal which transported her to her domain in Hell Realm.

Worst of all, Walter Peabody never noticed that the entire time he was having a conversation with the beautiful, dark-skinned woman called Lithilia, customers at the tea shop shot sideways glances in his direction and regarded him with curiosity, concern and mockery sometimes. Why? To many, if not all of them, this was the first time they ever witnessed someone having an entire conversation all by himself.

***

Lithilia appeared in her domain in Hell Realm.

"And where has my wife been?" Kazuk asked.

"I was busy," Lithilia replied. "Working on a plan of mine."

"And are you ever going to share this plan with me?" Kazuk asked.

"Patience, husband of mine," she replied curtly. "In due time."

Kazuk eyed her suspiciously before leaving their domain to attend to some other business of his.

"Not much longer now," Lithilia said to herself. *"Not much longer…"*

CHAPTER EIGHT

AMNESIA

WELCOME TO THE Dimension of Lemuria. Its primary realm is Celestia and, by default, Celestia is home to the Zarark. Archangels rank higher than angels, and even archangels are ranked by seniority. Michael is first-spawned and archangel supreme and his handpicked group of senior archangels constitute his inner circle. Some of the members of his inner circle include Raphael (head of security and counter-intelligence), Gabriel (in charge of administration and counseling), Samael (in charge of education and training) and Uriel (keeper of records, in charge of recruiting 'special' talents, and personal adviser to Michael). These senior archangels were among the first group of creatures of Celestia to be spawned after Michael. Alas, after the Great Rebellion, these senior archangels, and a few others, were the last ones left from the original group spawned during the creation of Celestia. Though the inner circle of archangels were equal in rank, Raphael was the unspoken next-in-line in case Michael met his end.

The inner circle of archangels hardly made public appearances, except for Uriel. The phrase 'special talents recruitments' was a cover-up phrase. The only 'special talent' Uriel sought was that angel or archangel, who fulfilled a prophecy of old. This angel or archangel was referred to as 'The One'. Many cycles after the prophecy was given, The One was yet to come forward. So, when Michael informed Uriel of Eliel, her core throbbed with excitement.

Despite her public appearances, Eliel had never seen Uriel. Yet, his respect and admiration for her matched his resolve to understand the recent events of his existence in intensity and determination. He appeared outside Uriel's domain and met Uriel's assistant.

"Hello, brother, I'm Beliel," she said politely. "Is Uriel expecting you?"

"Hello, sister," Eliel smiled politely. "I'm Eliel and Michael asked me to come here. He said she'll be expecting me."

Beliel sprang from her seat, flapped her wings three times rapidly, cleared her throat and straightened her garment. "R- Right this way, sir," Beliel stammered and gestured for Eliel to follow her.

"Sir?" Eliel asked.

"I've been around for three cycles," Beliel said. "And in all my two cycles of being Uriel's assistant, I've never seen her clear her schedule for anyone, not even Michael. Yet, she cleared her schedule for you."

Eliel shrugged and followed her.

"I never thought I'd ever behold this moment. It's truly an honor to meet you, sir," Beliel said.

"Why do you keep calling me 'sir'?" Eliel asked. "I'm just an angel. A much younger one for that. I'm only one cycle old."

Beliel shook her head vehemently and chuckled lightly.

"Where are your wings, sir?" Beliel asked.

Eliel noticed his wings were not on his scapulae. He sighed.

"Still think you're an angel, sir?" Beliel asked rhetorically.

They stopped in front of a door and Beliel turned around to face him.

"Whoever you are, you're no ordinary archangel," Beliel added reverently. "You're special enough to warrant such reactions from two of the most senior archangels of Celestia. You may be in denial, but I'm sure you'll eventually come to understand. I mean, barely a cycle old and you're already an archangel."

Beliel smiled and shrugged.

"Hopefully, Uriel will shed some light on that," Eliel said.

Beliel spun around and knocked on the door. The door opened by itself. She gestured for Eliel to enter.

"Thank you, Beliel."

"My honor, sir," Beliel bowed.

Eliel walked past her.

"Not that you need it, but good luck, sir," Beliel said and closed the door.

Eliel walked into a 50x50x25 ft chamber sparked from a single, seamless Celestial piece of grey marble. Thousands of angelic tablets acting as repositories for angelic manuscripts of old filled many shelves along the back wall. Uriel sat behind a marble-like table and leaned into a marble-like seat, while an angel sat opposite from her. The angel had her back to Eliel. Her wings trembled ever so slightly. Eliel could not tell at first if her wings trembled from excitement or nervousness. Uriel gestured for Eliel to sit on a chair she just sparked in the right-hand corner of the chamber. Eliel obliged.

There she is, Eliel thought. *The 'coolest senior archangel' as Gahel liked to describe her.*

Uriel brought her left hand to her chin as she listened to the angel. Her golden bracelet glimmered and inspired awe in Eliel.

This really is Uriel, he said to himself. *I can't believe I'm in her chamber.*

Uriel glanced in his direction. Her dark, green eyes met his briefly before she returned her attention towards the angel. Her face remained expressionless.

"So, Mazel," Uriel said in a firm but soothing voice. "Tell me more about your experience with The Voice."

So this is the Mazel whose wings Farel wants to chop off, Eliel smiled.

"Well, madam," Mazel spoke timidly. "It was not like I had an experience with it. I just heard it. I'm not sure how to describe it."

You just passed the first test, sister, Eliel said to himself. *Now, are you good at lying or do you really believe you heard The Voice?*

"Alright," Uriel said, her face expressionless. "Describe the voice to me."

"Madam," Mazel still spoke timidly. "It was a very strong voice. It sounded like a thousand waterfalls, and it vibrated with my core. I don't really know how to put it into words. But it was there. It was strong. I heard it and felt its power."

Mazel spoke more confidently and Uriel observed without saying anything. Eliel shook his head slightly.

She's not a very good actress, Eliel concluded. *If I can see it, then Uriel must definitely see it as well. Besides, I'm already here, endorsed by Michael. Poor Uriel, she has to put up with this every moment someone claims to have heard The Voice. Most patient of her.*

"How many times did you hear this voice?" Uriel asked.

"Twice, madam," Mazel replied.

Eliel almost snickered.

"The first time was just the deep, powerful voice," Mazel replied confidently. "I was so confused and afraid that I said nothing. Then, the second time it called my name, a bolt of lightning struck in front of me. The bolt of lightning wrote my name on the ground, but it disappeared almost as soon as it appeared. That was when I knew it was the voice and that was when I answered."

"And what was your answer?" Uriel asked.

"I said, 'Here I am, Father'," Mazel replied.

"Did you do anything else after that?" Uriel asked.

"No, I did not, madam," Mazel replied with almost no confidence. "Did anything else happen after that?" Uriel asked.

"No, madam," Mazel replied.

A streak of light danced around Uriel's left index finger as she scribbled some notes on the tablet in front of her. The door opened and Beliel walked in.

"Thank you, Mazel," Uriel said flatly, without taking her eyes off the tablet pad. "Beliel will see you out."

"Thank you, madam," Mazel replied. "Is everything alright, madam?"

"Yes, Mazel," Uriel replied and turned an expressionless face towards Mazel. "Everything is perfect."

Mazel grinned happily. She nodded, turned around and headed for the door. Beliel gestured for Mazel to follow her.

"She doesn't even know I removed her name from my stewardship training," Uriel said.

Farel would be pleased, Eliel thought.

Uriel glided towards Eliel after she stood up. Eliel rose to his feet. When she was close enough, she extended her hand and Eliel shook it. She held his hand, studied him briefly and nodded.

"What do you think?" Uriel asked as she released his hand.

"About what, madam?" Eliel asked.

"About Mazel's story," Uriel replied.

"I think she made it up," Eliel answered bluntly.

"I agree. Come," Uriel said and walked away from Eliel.

She walked towards the wall with all the angelic tablets and walked right through it. Eliel smiled at the realization that the wall was just an optical illusion. He followed Uriel and stepped into another part of the domain. This part of her domain was a little somber than the other part he just came from. It looked like her private quarters. A throne-like seat was visible on the far left-hand corner of the domain. Several non-Celestial glyphs lined the walls.

"Encryption glyphs, madam?" Eliel asked.

"Yes," Uriel replied dismissively.

"You must love your research," Eliel said.

"I wonder what gave it away," Uriel replied wryly.

"May I ask what motivates you thus, madam?"

Uriel was silent. Then, her wristband glowed and illuminated the somber chamber. The encryption glyphs glowed as well and the entire chamber lit up to reveal nothing else except for the throne-like seat in the far-right hand corner. She levitated in the air, opened her arms. Her wings appeared from her shoulder blades and spread out. Activated by the unique vibrational frequency emanating from Uriel's manifested wings, many more glyphs of light appeared and glowed brightly on all four walls of the chamber. These glyphs of light peeled off the walls and coalesced in front of her. She then waved a hand over the coalesced glyphs and an angelic tablet formed from the air. The coalesced glyphs briefly hovered above the tablet before disappearing in it. Uriel then retracted her wings, took the tablet in her hands and gently floated back to the ground as her wristband dimmed to regular radiance. The luminescence in the chamber stayed.

When her feet touched the floor, she walked towards Eliel, clutching the tablet lightly on her chest, as her wings disappeared from her shoulder blades.

"This is why I have been doing so much research," Uriel said and handed the tablet over to Eliel.

Eliel hesitated before taking the tablet. He did not read the glyphs, though.

"It's alright," she encouraged him. "You're allowed to read it. You're special."

"I've heard that so many times now and I still don't know why," he said with frustration.

"Maybe if you read the tablet you'd understand why," Uriel replied kindly.

Eliel started reading. Suddenly, his head snapped upwards and he stared at Uriel in shock.

"Is this The Prophecy?" Eliel asked.

"The third one, yes," Uriel replied calmly. "The fact that you can even read it indicates just how special you are. Only Michael's inner circle have learned the language in which this prophecy was written. Yet, *YOU* can read it, Eliel. You were spawned with innate knowledge of this language."

"What language is this, madam?" Eliel asked.

"The language of our makers," Uriel replied.

"Oh," Eliel said.

Uriel observed Eliel. His shoulders slumped in resignation.

You can't deny it anymore, she thought.

She summoned a chair from the floor to accommodate him. Eliel sat in the chair without taking his eyes off the tablet. Uriel sat directly opposite from him in a chair she sparked for herself. She watched him as he read. A golden wristband phased in and out repeatedly on both his wrists, just like the archangel battle flames from his eyes and wings. Eliel did not seem to notice any of these things happening to him. Then, the most undeniable confirmation came in the form of two glassy eyes that formed above the crown of his head. Uriel gasped, causing Eliel to jerk his head upward and look at her in confusion and concern.

"What is it, madam?" Eliel asked.

"You *ARE* The One," Uriel exclaimed, lowering her hand from her mouth. "By the entire angelic host, you truly are The One."

Uriel sprang from her chair and paced back and forth. Eliel watched her silently and patiently. Finally, to break the silence and to not sound impolite by asking her to sit down because her constant pacing was turning into a source of irritation, Eliel asked her a question instead.

"So, madam," Eliel began. "I know you did not write this prophecy and that you're taking extreme measures to hide it. My first question is, how did you come to be in possession of this prophecy and, second question is who wrote it?"

Uriel picked up his intent and returned to her seat. She flexed her shoulders.

"The answer to your first question is that Michael gave me the prophecy to keep it safe and to eliminate any conflict of interest as you may have seen why," Uriel replied. "Regarding your second question, Malichiel, a former inner circle member, wrote it."

"Former?" Eliel asked.

"Yes," Uriel replied. "He fought for the other side during the rebellion."

"So Hell also knows about this prophecy," he said. "I might as well be labeled 'most wanted'."

"You're too important to be killed, Eliel," Uriel assured him. "Their best bet is to hope you turn because if you do, they stand a better chance at defeating us."

"Excellent," Eliel replied with mock excitement. "They may as well give up because there is no way in Celestia I'm turning."

"That's very reassuring, Eliel," Uriel said, barely able to contain her relief at Eliel's response. "However, there's no telling what can happen during a fall."

Eliel heaved his shoulders.

"I see," he said.

"That's also one of the reasons you're here," Uriel explained. "Michael sent you here so that I can prep you for your fall. Firstly, I had to confirm, beyond a doubt, that you're The One. Secondly, I had to help you understand that you are indeed The One. Thirdly, you had to accept this status of your own free will. Only then can I get you ready for your fall. And finally, you have to fall. Unfortunately, there's no escaping that. It is what it is. Whatever happens after your fall will solely be up to you. But know this, whatever decisions you make will be a defining moment for our realm. Do you understand, Eliel?"

"Yes, madam," Eliel replied, almost to himself.

"Does that mean you accept the mantle of The One?" Uriel asked.

"Yes," he replied, again almost to himself. "And I accept of my own free will."

"Thank you, Eliel," Uriel said heaving her shoulders in relief.

If Uriel, the one and only, can be this relieved, then this whole thing about me being special must be as serious as it looks, Eliel said to himself.

"Now, on to the next phase," Uriel adjusted her form in her seat. "What do you know about falling?"

"Nothing, really," Eliel replied, trying to remember what Gahel told him. "Only that when angels fall, they suffer from amnesia."

"Amnesia is one of the side-effects of falling," Uriel confirmed. "However, a part of us never forgets. Our identity as angels or archangels just gets buried in our subconscious and sometimes, they surface as gut feelings, strong inclinations among other things. For example, if you were passionate about singing in your present state, when you fall you may have a strong affinity for music in spite of your amnesia. Certain types of music could trigger certain memories for you."

Eliel nodded.

"So, I should hold on to something before or while I fall?" Eliel asked.

"Right," she confirmed. "But let it be linked to something about your identity as an angel; and better yet, your role as The One. It may be hard, but if you follow your instincts, they will never lead you astray."

"I shall try, madam," Eliel replied.

His tone of voice indicated much emotional and mental exhaustion.

"There's something else you should know," Uriel said and stood up.

She levitated to the wall on the right and wrote on it with her left index finger. Glyphs of golden light traced the path of her finger along the wall. When she finished writing, the glyphs converged to a tiny dot on the wall, before spreading into a thin line. A thin tablet slid outwards from this thin line. Uriel took the tablet in her hands. She floated back to her seat and swapped it for the tablet in Eliel's hands. Eliel read the new tablet handed to him several times while Uriel watched. Finally, he heaved his shoulders and slumped into his seat.

"Keeps getting better, doesn't it?" Eliel asked rhetorically.

"I'm sorry, Eliel," Uriel said sympathetically. "I know it's not my fault, but I empathize with your burden regardless. We call the tablet in your hand '*The Book for the Fallen.*' I transcribed it after the Great Rebellion."

"Wait," Eliel bolted upright. "*YOU* transcribed this?"

"Yes," she affirmed. "I took over Malichiel's duty as transcriber to The Logos after the rebellion. Also explains why Michael entrusted me with the prophecy. After the rebellion, it was concluded that certain rules ought to be put in place concerning falling."

Uriel gestured at the tablet in Eliel's hand. Eliel nodded weakly.

"The Logos," he spoke so softly Uriel barely heard him. "Whoever they are."

He read *The Book for the Fallen* a few more times before swapping tablets again. He read and re-read the prophecy as if he was trying to engrave the glyphs in his conscious memory.

I am The One, he repeated this phrase to himself over and over as he read.

Suddenly, three glyphs lit up and floated from the tablet. They raced towards his face and buried themselves into his vision. He jerked his head backward and looked at Uriel.

"What is it, Eliel?" she asked.

"Did you see that, madam?" he asked.

"See what?"

"Uh, nothing, madam," Eliel replied, confusion creasing his facial features. "I just thought… It's nothing."

"No, tell me, please," Uriel insisted.

"I thought I saw some glyphs come out of the tablet," he replied.

"You're right, it's probably nothing," Uriel agreed. "Glyphs don't come out of those tablets by themselves. It's part of the encryption."

Uriel let him stare at the tablet some more.

I'm glad he didn't pick up the fact that I said "… it was concluded…", when I talked about the origin of The Book for the Fallen, Uriel thought.

Finally, she asked him the question.

"Are you ready, Eliel?"

"As ready as I can be, madam," Eliel replied with resignation.

Uriel extended her hand and he returned the tablet to her. She then levitated towards the right wall and wrote some glyphs with her index finger on the wall. The glyphs glowed, fused to a single dot and spread into a thin line. She placed *The Book for the Fallen* along the line. Then, Uriel floated to the middle of the room and summoned her wings. She opened her arms and spread out her manifested wings as her wristband started glowing. *The Book for the Fallen* disappeared into the thin line in the wall and the golden glyphs on the tablet spread everywhere and blended with the many encrypted glyphs on the walls. Uriel then folded her wings and let her arms fall to her sides. She floated back to the floor as her wristband dimmed to its regular glow and her wings dematerialized.

"Do you have any friends you'd like to say goodbye to before we head out?" Uriel asked.

"That won't be necessary," Eliel replied. "I'll be back real soon."

"I admire your strength of mind and spirit, Eliel," she said and gestured towards the door. "Your fall awaits."

Uriel smiled, and he returned her smile as they both teleported to where every angel and archangel went to fall: The Edge.

***

Beliel waited a moment before she switched to sub-angelic frequency. The Scribe had taught them well. Raphael's sniff test had not yet detected that she was a mole for Hell Realm… yet. She had to hand it to Raphael, though. He was head of counter-intelligence for a reason, and it was not solely because he was ruthless.

Anyway, back to the task at hand, she reminded herself.

"I hope you have good news for me, Beliel," Kazuk said flatly via telepathy.

"I do, your highness," she replied with unhidden excitement.

"What are you waiting for then?" Kazuk demanded.

"Oh, sorry your highness," Beliel replied. *"The One has been identified."*

A moment of silence.

"Your highness?" Beliel called again.

"I heard you," Kazuk answered. *"Are you sure?"*

"Yes, your highness," Beliel affirmed. *"He's with Uriel at The Edge as we speak."*

"Good job, Beliel," Kazuk complimented her. *"This is great news indeed."*

"Thank you, your highness," Beliel replied. *"I'll keep you apprised."*

Kazuk broke the sub-angelic link. He leaned back in his seat in his domain and stared blankly at the ceiling. Beliel's news meant his plan had to be completely revised. He smiled mischievously as his mind immediately went to work on a new strategic plan.

***

Uriel and Eliel walked along the hallway leading to The Edge. A thousand and one thoughts raced through his mind until the thoughts threatened to overwhelm him. He tried to shut them out by focusing on a mantra.

"You really were going to just leave without saying goodbye?"

Eliel smiled before turning around to face his grinning colleagues.

"Hey, you two," he said weakly and hugged Gahel and Farel.

"I was so worried for you, El," Farel said. "The way you just vanished and a new guy suddenly showing up to take your place. I thought something really bad had happened to you."

"And that's when I told her that the coolest thing had just happened to you," Gahel chimed in with pride. "Look at you, El. Like the creatures of Earth Realm would say, you're a freaking rock star," he added, slapping Eliel on the shoulder.

"I'll be flapped. What happened to your wings, El?" Gahel asked with his eyes bulging in awe at the realization of Eliel's new status.

"Flap me sideways," Farel exclaimed. "Just like that and you're a flapping archy? I can't believe my eyes. Oh, El. I'm so proud, and jealous, of you."

Eliel leveled a gaze of gratitude at his friends.

"I'm glad to see you two," Eliel said, trying to stay modest but failing woefully. "It really means a lot to me. And how did you two get here in the first place?"

"Uriel summoned us," Farel replied with ecstasy.

"And you finally get your wish," Eliel said, patting her on the shoulder.

Farel flapped her wings several times in excitement.

"Oh, you have no idea," she started saying and realized what she had just said.

The three of them burst out laughing.

"I don't mean to break up your reunion, younglings," Uriel said, smiling warmly. "But Eliel has to go now."

The three embraced one another in a group hug.

"Good luck, archy," Gahel and Farel chorused together before they teleported back to their assignments on Earth Realm.

Uriel and Eliel continued onwards. When they stepped into the platform on The Edge, Eliel gasped in surprise.

"Sir…" he started saying but could not find more words to say.

"I thought I should give you some encouragement before your big moment," Michael smiled at him.

I beat him and yet he's still so cool and impressive, Eliel said to himself. *That's why he's archangel supreme.*

"Thank you so much, sir," Eliel said and Michael nodded.

They shook hands and Eliel turned to face Uriel. She smiled and squeezed his left shoulder. Then, she took his head in her hands and kissed him on the forehead as a loving mother from Earth Realm would to her child. Her gesture gave Eliel great comfort, and the gratitude in his eyes was more than he could express in words. She nodded.

With all the support I just received, there's no way I'll fail, he promised himself.

Eliel held on to these last moments with every fiber of his angelic being. He held on to his new status. He held on to the vows he took as an angel. He held on to the fact the Celestia was his home and nowhere else. He held on with each step he took towards The Edge. Then he remembered a poem he had read during one of his assignments. He had wondered then how a creature from such a lowly realm could possess such knowledge of angels in the first place. Maybe that creature was a fallen angel. It was his favorite poem, maybe because it talked about home. He recited the poem from memory as he stood at The Edge.

CELESTIA
In my rise and in my fall
In naught and in all
Never will I forget you
My home in truth
Celestia, where angels dwell
And on its outskirts hails Hell
For the oath, I swore
In peace and in war

I shall do as asked
And fulfil my task
'Til my last spark of light
I shall hold the fight
To protect and defend
Till my existence ends
For in all the realms of which I know
None compares to Celestia, my home

Eliel met the gazes and smiles of encouragement from Michael and Uriel. He nodded and smiled back at them before he turned around and faced The Edge.

This is it! Eliel said to himself.

Then, Eliel heaved his shoulders, opened his arms, closed his eyes and fell.

THE END OF PART ONE

PART TWO

THE ONE

MALICHIEL TELEPORTED TO Michael's domain. He banged on the door several times.

"Come in," Michael said.

The door opened and Malichiel walked in.

"Another vision?" Michael asked.

"You may want to sit down for this," Malichiel said.

Malichiel summoned a chair from the floor for himself.

He made a tablet manifest and, using his index finger, he traced a few glyphs on the tablet. When he finished, he handed it to Michael. Michael took it, read it, and for the first time in Malichiel's existence, he saw fear in Michael's eyes.

These are the words of The Logos; heed to our admonishments!

It shall come to pass that one shall be spawned in the lowly ranks.

This lowly one will seek nothing more than to remain in humility and service, but predestination holds a far greater destiny for this lowly one.

It shall come to pass that the lowly one will hear The Voice and answer it.

It shall come to pass that this lowly one will be the strongest of your kind and the eyes of Kundalini shall be upon them.

Yet, in all their strength, they will fall. But in their fall, they shall not be influenced by any entity beyond the dimension of their fall; woe to those who do not heed to this warning.

Alas, they shall rise again to the highest rank of your kind.

And in their rise, they will pave a path to salvation or perdition for Celestia like Celestia has never known before.

Celestia, you have been warned!

Both archangels stared at each other; the meaning of the prophecy rendering them temporarily speechless.

"For now, no one is to know about this. Understood?" Michael ordered.

"Of course, Michael," Malichiel affirmed.

Michael's thoughts raced in every direction: these prophecies of salvation, perdition, falling and one that would rise to the highest rank. None outranked him in Celestia, not yet at least. As such, The One had to be identified at all cost.

And then, what next? Protect or end him or her?

Michael shuddered at his options.

While Michael was lost in deep thought, he never noticed Malichiel's eyebrow furrow in thought. Malichiel, the transcriber of the prophecies, scowled as he forged a plan of his own.

If Michael is to be dethroned, another must take his place, he thought. *Celestia has presented me with this opportunity and I'll be flapping damned if I let anyone else, The One or not, steal this golden opportunity from me.*

CHAPTER NINE

THE RISE OF METATRON

"I THOUGHT MY instructions were clear," the fallen archangel said, without looking at his visitor.

"You gave one instruction," Kazuk snarked.

"Then why is it so hard for you to follow a simple instruction, *your majesty*?" the archangel sneered at the last two words.

Malichiel never concealed his dislike for Kazuk, a dislike which started after the rebellion and now that Kazuk was the King of Hell Realm, he liked Kazuk even less. Kazuk returned the favor, much to Malichiel's pleasure. However, he was wise enough to keep his personal feelings for Kazuk away from the public; a gesture he knew Kazuk appreciated. In his opinion, Kazuk's governance of Hell Realm was an insult and after what Kazuk did to Beelzebub, Malichiel wanted to pry Kazuk's wings off Kazuk's shoulders. Flap. Kazuk would not last two moves against him in combat.

His time will come, Malichiel often reminded himself. *Patience.*

"I wouldn't be here if it wasn't important," Kazuk replied.

Malichiel allowed a brief moment of silence to hang between the two of them. He stared blankly at the wall in front of him.

"So, are you going to start talking or do I have to wait another cycle?" he asked with a heavy dose of sarcasm.

Kazuk heaved his shoulders and fought to control his temper.

"The One has been identified," Kazuk said and made to teleport away.

"Wait," Malichiel turned around to face Kazuk. "You win. You have my undivided attention."

"I feel so special," Kazuk said with sarcasm.

"You've made your point, Maziel."

Calling the King of Hell by his angelic name was a low blow, even for someone like Malichiel.

"With an ego as magnanimous as yours is, I wonder how come you still lick her toes even when she's not around, *Metatron*," Kazuk spat.

Kazuk hated being called by his old angelic name as much as Malichiel hated being called by his new, Hell Realm name. Malichiel was the only fallen archangel who preferred to maintain his angelic name.

I am an archangel, regardless of where I reside and a senior archangel for that matter, one of Michael's former inner council members, he often reminded himself.

Once a transcriber to The Logos, always a transcriber to The Logos, he would say. *Nothing and no one will take that away from me; not Kazuk, and certainly not even Michael.*

His new name was *Metatron* and the only other thing he hated more than the name was Hell Realm itself. So, when Kazuk addressed him by his new name, a fiery rage smothered his calmness of mind. He summoned his archangel battle flame and garments in an instant and blazed towards Kazuk.

Kazuk smiled at Malichiel's transformation.

So predictable, he thought. *So disappointing.*

A flaming spear formed in Malichiel's right hand as he moved to attack Kazuk. Kazuk remained calm. He summoned a shield on his right arm. When Malichiel thrust his spear at his chest, he turned his body sideways and angled the shield along his torso. The spear grazed across his shield, setting the shield ablaze with archangel flame. Blinded by rage, Malichiel had put all his strength into the charge. He missed his mark and his momentum carried him forward. As he stumbled forward, Kazuk grabbed him by the back of his neck, rode the momentum of his charge and slammed his face into the floor.

Kazuk discarded his shield and it disappeared before it reached the wall of Malichiel's domain. A sword formed in his right hand as he pinned Malichiel's right wrist to the floor with his right foot. Malichiel tried to free his hand on which Kazuk stood. Kazuk pressed the tip of his sword on the back of Malichiel's neck and Malichiel froze. Kazuk passed his sword over to his left hand and knelt on Malichiel's right shoulder blade, while maintaining pressure on the back of Malichiel's neck with his sword.

"Let me make this very clear to you, Metatron," Kazuk spoke with an icy calm. "The only reason you're alive is because you still might be useful, especially now that the notion of The One is real."

Metatron bared his teeth and glared at the floor. He tried to wrestle himself free from Kazuk pinning him to the floor, but Kazuk pressed his sword deeper into the back of his neck, drawing angel light from the cut it made. A scream of anger and frustration later, Malichiel dismissed his spear and yielded.

I should've ended him when I had the chance, Malichiel scolded himself. *He's becoming too powerful. Even if I find a way to take him out, I'll incur the wrath of his followers. There are those still loyal to her, but we can't afford to have a war among ourselves, not when Celestia remains the grand prize. But something has to be done about Kazuk. His final moments will arrive eventually.*

Kazuk dismissed his sword and stood up. Angel light beamed on the cut in the back of Malichiel's neck and healed it. He stood up but kept his back to Kazuk. Kazuk smirked and made to teleport but changed his mind.

"What was your best against Michael?" Kazuk asked.

"Foolish question," Malichiel replied with venom.

"You can either answer me or I can make this unpleasant for you."

"Two," Metatron replied.

"Four, for me," Kazuk said casually. "The only reason you thought you had some kind of edge over me was because I fed you that illusion."

Kazuk walked towards Malichiel, who still had his back to him.

"Make no mistake, Metatron," Kazuk hissed.

Malichiel turned to face Kazuk. Kazuk narrowed his eyes and red flames spewed from them.

How did he do that? Malichiel wondered and fought to hide his shock.

"If you ever, and I mean EVER, show me any form of disrespect again, in public or private, I will end you where you stand," Kazuk promised. "And I will address you as I please. Do you understand, Metatron?"

"Yes," Metatron whispered.

"I SAID DO YOU UNDERSTAND?" Kazuk screamed in Malichiel's face.

"Yes," Metatron replied more audibly.

"Yes…?" Kazuk said, cocking his ear towards Malichiel.

"Yes," Metatron heaved his shoulders before adding, "your majesty."

"Good," Kazuk smiled derisively. "Anyway, I just wanted to inform you that The One has been identified. You should get to work at once."

Kazuk teleported away.

For a moment, Malichiel stood rooted to the spot. Then, a wall-crumbling scream escaped his lips. He clenched his right fist and drove it into the floor. Golden light radiated from the point of impact and a quake rippled across his domain. Rage, at Kazuk, at Hell Realm and most of all at himself, consumed his psyche, threatening to thrust him into insanity. Another wall-crumbling scream escaped his throat and he punched into the floor several time. A quake followed each punch. Angel light flowed over his fist, healing every broken and torn pieces of his fist. Finally, he stopped assaulting the floor.

"Who does Kazuk think he is?" Malichiel cried into the emptiness of his domain. "Is it the power that has gotten to his head or something else? Let him wait until she returns, which will be very soon. I can feel it. "

Malichiel stood up, flexed his shoulders and summoned his wings. He flapped them several times before he dismissed them.

"If only I knew where she's locked up," he clenched his fists in frustration. "I need her out. I need her here. I miss her so much; her strength, charisma, wisdom. Everything. When she returns, we'll go after Celestia with certain victory."

Malichiel summoned a seat which emerged from the floor. Thinking about her calmed him down a little.

How did I even end up in this cesspool filled with these abominations from various realms?

Regrets haunted him sometimes, despite swearing to himself that, given the opportunity, he would still go to war against Michael and his followers.

"The rebellion was doomed from the start," he said to himself. "Yet, I joined them. Why? Where did my sense of reason go to?"

For the millionth time, he asked himself that question, and yet again, he had no answer he was willing to accept.

***

In Celestia, Malichiel was probably the third highest ranking archangel, mainly because of his role as transcriber to The Logos; a task that fell on his lap purely by 'accident'. The inner council was in the middle of a meeting when suddenly, an unseen force snatched his body from his seat and levitated him in the air. His wings appeared without him summoning them. They blazed with a golden flame. The unseen forced flipped him over and he faced the inner council, who were all out of their seats, weapons drawn and searching for an invisible enemy. Next, Malichiel started speaking in a strange tongue while he hovered in that position. The inner council lowered their weapons and stared at him in disbelief.

When he finished speaking in the strange language, his wings stopped blazing. He still did not have control of his body as it slowly descended to the floor. His wings faded away. Uriel moved in to cradle his body against hers.

"Stay your hand," Michael bid her. "We must exercise caution. We don't know what happened or what's happening to him yet."

"True," Uriel nodded.

Malichiel lay still on the floor for many moments. Finally, he slowly sat up and massaged his temples. He blinked several times and squinted. Michael summoned a seat for him.

"Do you know what just happened to you?" Michael asked.

"I think…" Malichiel replied weakly. "I think I saw a vision."

"Are you sure, brother?" Raphael asked. "We don't get visions."

"Yes, I am sure it was," Malichiel answered.

He spoke in the same tongue in which he had just spoken moments earlier.

"It is a language from another dimension," Uriel commented offhandedly.

"So, what did you see in this vision?" Michael asked.

"I'm doing well, by the way," Malichiel joked.

"I'm sorry, brother," Michael apologized and faked to punch Malichiel.

Malichiel's hands rose to protect his face on instinct. He realized what Michael had just done. The others joined the two of them in laughter.

"There you go," Michael said. "You're fine, just like I thought you were."

"Yes, I could tell you were so concerned about me," Malichiel punched Michael on the shoulder.

The inner council returned to the round table and focused on Malichiel.

"I've never spoken this language before," Malichiel said. "But as of right now, I can speak and understand it perfectly. It appears as if I was given a crash course in the language during my extra-dimensional, supernatural encounter."

Malichiel flexed his shoulders.

"Felt like I was talking with creatures from higher dimensions in my head-"

"And the craziness begins," Gabriel rudely interrupted, invoking harsh hushes from the other inner council members.

"Alright, alright. I'll shut up," he rolled his eyes.

"They started by telling me that they have chosen me to be a transcriber of the messages they have for Celestia," Malichiel continued. "I asked what made them decide to start sending messages to Celestia, and they said it was because they want to offer Celestia a choice. When I probed further, they said it would ultimately be a choice between survival and total annihilation. Needless to say, they had my full attention at this point."

"Like I said… Crazy," Gabriel said again but everyone ignored him.

"I'd doubt me too if I bore your wings, brother. But that's your problem," Malichiel addressed Gabriel before returning his attention to the inner council.

"Anyway, I asked them to at least tell me who they are and where they're from. I think it's best if I just transcribe their message instead of narrating everything."

Malichiel then summon a tablet and began tracing golden glyphs on the tablet with his right index finger. When he finished, he made the tablet rise in the air for the inner council to see. It read as follows:

We are One, and we are Seven. We are from the Realm-Dimension of Valla and transcend your notions of realms and dimensions. We are a creative entity; all of Creation hails from us, all of Creation is us. All is One and One is All. Here is our first message to you, mortal creatures.

One who has fallen will fall again. One who has fallen will fall into the shadow of oneself. One who has fallen into the shadow of oneself will have to make a choice that ultimately will spell the survival or annihilation of your kind. This is our message to you, for now.

Your kind will ask you for proof. Ask your leader to look between your shoulder blades. Therein lies your proof that it is We who have spoken to you.

Michael left his seat at once, hurried over to Malichiel and stood behind him. He pulled Malichiel's garments away from his shoulders to expose the space in between Malichiel's scapulae. He hoped, against hope that the transcription was wrong but alas, his wish did not come to pass. He turned around and pulled his garments away from his shoulders as well.

"The mark of a seven-faceted crystal is on your backs," Raphael affirmed.

"That mark was not on Malichiel's back before," Drusiliel blurted.

Drusiliel realized she had revealed more than she intended to. Her wings came over her face to hide her embarrassment. A few chuckles and jokes followed, but Michael and Uriel did not seem to care.

"Well, there's our confirmation," Gabriel conceded. "Glad to know you're not losing your mind, brother. Question: what next?"

"I accept your apology, brother," Malichiel shook his head.

"How do you mean?" Raphael asked Gabriel.

"If we are to take this vision literally, it means that one of the fallen will fall again, right?" Uriel interjected. "And so far, only two of us have fallen."

"True," Luciel agreed. "That means we must all keep a close eye on Michael and I and ensure that if we do fall again, we won't fall into this 'shadow of oneself' that the vision speaks of."

"Those are carefully chosen words," Uriel said. "'Shadow of oneself'. Why would these beings use such words? We need to look more into this."

"I agree," Michael said. "For now, let's return to our domains and think about this vision some more. This is a first for us all and we must exercise wisdom and due diligence. All in favor?"

The inner circle of archangels summoned and flapped their wings twice.

"It is unanimous then," Michael said. "We will reconvene later."

The archangels teleported to their respective domains, except for Malichiel. Michael leveled a hard stare at him.

"You did not tell them everything, did you?" he asked flatly.

"I couldn't, Michael," Malichiel cowered. "I couldn't."

"Why?" Michael asked.

"Because there was a second vision shortly after the first," Malichiel replied. "It's about a rebellion from one who has fallen."

Malichiel shook his head as if he could erase what he had just been told. But what has been revealed cannot be unrevealed.

"The second vision was clear on a rebellion to come?" Michael asked. "No room for choice?"

"I'm afraid so," Malichiel replied weakly.

"Transcribe for me," Michael ordered.

Malichiel obliged and made a tablet appear.

A fallen one will rise into rebellion. Many will fall, and sorrow, suffering, loss, and ending of existences will plague and haunt the Realm of Celestia for cycles to come; for, in her lust for power and dominion, the fallen one will stop at nothing to see her desires through.

After Michael finished reading it, Malichiel committed Michael's reaction to memory; the confusion, the shock and the hardening of his resolve.

"We must keep this between us for now," Michael paced back and forth.

"Why?" Malichiel asked.

"We must proceed with caution," Michael explained. "Think about it."

He stopped pacing and directed a hard stare at Malichiel.

"If there's going to be a rebellion," he continued. "Who knows if she hasn't already started recruiting followers. And what if by trying to do something about it we instead end up planting the seed of a rebellion in her head?"

Malichiel leaned back in his seat.

"I see your point," Malichiel nodded.

"All we have is this transcription," Michael held up the transcription. "We've got nothing else to go by. We really need to be wise about this."

"I agree," Malichiel said.

"For now," Michael set the tablet with the transcription on the round table. "I'll keep this with me. Only you will know it's with me. Remember, this second vision must remain between the two of us. Understood?"

"Absolutely, brother," Malichiel replied firmly. "I couldn't agree more."

"Excellent," Michael heaved his shoulders once. "I'm glad we agree."

"So, how do we proceed?" Malichiel asked.

"For now, we wait." Michael replied.

It came to pass that Luciel visited Malichiel in his domain one moment. They chatted about the affairs of Celestia for a while. But the tone of the conversation changed suddenly.

"We deserve better, brother," Luciel said. "We deserve to exercise free will in the purest sense of the word."

The fierceness in her voice, the curling of her lips, the smoothness of her hair and slight bounce in her bosom caused a warm feeling in his loins. His shoulders slumped slightly and his head inclined at an angle as she spoke.

"I mean, why should we be under the rule of any archangel?" she scowled. "A tyrant and brute for that matter."

I don't think Michael is a tyrant and brute, Malichiel thought. *But if she thinks he is, she must have a reason. After all, she's his partner, isn't she?*

Malichiel frowned slightly at the thought of Luciel being Michael's partner.

Yes, he is a selfish archangel, he thought. *A selfish tyrant and brute.*

Luciel took his hands in hers.

"We deserve better," she squeezed his hands and glared passion into his eyes. "We deserve to live to our full potential. Michael is holding us back."

Wait, maybe she's taking advantage of me, Malichiel thought as Luciel spoke. *Maybe she knows how I feel for her and she's capitalizing against me.*

"We must bring about that change, brother," Luciel took his face in her hands and spoke firmly. "We must start anew."

Who cares if she's taking advantage of me? Malichiel shrugged. *She's right. Everything she says is true. She's as infallible as she is beautiful and if she wants Michael gone, then another must take Michael's place.*

"Think about what I just told you, brother," Luciel caressed his cheeks. "We will discuss this some more later."

And I must be ready when that time comes, his thoughts continued. *I must stay by her side till the end. That way, I will prove my loyalty, my commitment and my love for her. When Michael is gone, I will take his place, by her side, for all eternity, as her one and only true love.*

"I hear you, sister," Malichiel said.

He puffed his chest and raised his chin.

"I will take your words under consideration," he added.

"I'm glad to hear that, Mali," Luciel's voice softened as she stood up.

For a moment, her crotch lingered within his line of sight before he mustered the courage to look up.

"Until next time," Luciel added and teleported away.

"She called me 'Mali'," he smiled to himself. "I like it. No one ever called me that, not even Drusiliel."

He stood up, flexed his shoulders, summoned his wings, flapped them once and dismissed them.

"And now, I must come up with a plan," Malichiel smiled evilly. "A plan to defeat Michael and to win Luciel's heart."

Malichiel designed a special domain to preserve the transcription tablets. He sealed the domain with encryption glyphs and only Michael and himself had the key glyphs to the special domain. Michael still kept the second tablet until he ascertained the security of the new domain for the tablets. Only after that did he hand the second tablet over to Malichiel.

Alas, the perfect plan had taken a nasty turn that had resulted in far too many existences ending, Luciel's and Zukael's incarceration, and the rest of the rebellion being banished to the putrid parody of paradise called Hell Realm. The first few moments in their new home epitomized chaos. But relative to their experience during the rebellion, Hell Realm was a blissful haven. Malichiel conceded to the fact that Maziel had done a great job with the realm's infrastructure. Given his very special role during his period in Celestia and his present importance to a much grander plan, Malichiel asked for a private domain, away from all the buzz in the realm. He refused to give up his old name and hated the new name ascribed to him. He watched Maziel ascend to power by wit and slaughter. He respected Maziel's courage and strength, but not his leadership; until Maziel humiliated him.

***

Malichiel returned from memory lane to the quietude of his domain.

Kazuk will pay for his insolence, Malichiel swore to himself. *But I must exercise patience... a lot of patience.*

He had heard whispers of others nicknaming him 'The Silent One'.

Flattering, he thought.

He knew why Kazuk needed him and he was aware that Kazuk was only making empty threats about ending him. He was aware of the invaluable nature of his position. He was even far more valuable than Luciel was.

"Let Kazuk feel secure for now," Malichiel scoffed. "Let him feel in control. He may have won the battle, but a war is coming for which he's neither ready nor will he win. And this war will dwarf the Great Rebellion."

Malichiel smiled evilly.

"Kazuk will fall and I will personally see to it."

Malichiel regarded his hands.

"Maybe I had to suffer to be remined of who I have to become," his tone of voice turned dark and eerie. "No more Malichiel. Celestia is history. Hell is the present and I must live in the present."

The Silent One closed his eyes and smiled. The mark between his shoulder blades burned into his skin and his essence became infused with a form of energy that he was not used to. His life force tingled with exuberance and aliveness. He let everything go and surrendered to the takeover of his essence.

Malichiel summoned his wings. This time, they burned with a blood-red flame. His eyes opened and blood-red flames spewed from them. The evilest of laughter erupted from his lips as the mark between his shoulder blades burned even more, infusing his being with more of that alien, intoxicating and invigorating power. As he roared with even more evil laughter, the walls of his domain trembled in accordance. Senior Archangel Malichiel, transcriber for The Logos was dead and gone, and Metatron had arisen.

"Oh Kazuk," he roared. "War is coming. I hope you're ready."

CHAPTER TEN

CAST OUT

ALMOST A WEEK went by after his encounter with Lithilia. Walter Peabody sat on his twin-sized bed in his 225 sq. ft studio apartment watching an English Premier League football game. He yelled profanities one last time before switching off the television. No way his team could recover from such a slaughter in seven minutes. He slid off his bed and reached the loo in three strides. While in there, he thought he heard his cellphone ring. He shrugged off the thought. Walter finished taking care of business and made it to the fridge in two steps. He fished for his leftover tuna fish sub. He took a bite from the stale, yesterday's-dinner-now-lunch sub. His hunger numbed his taste buds and nostrils to the foul taste and smell of the food. His phone rang but he ignored it. His voicemail would take care of the call.

Walter tossed the sub wrapper in the small dustbin that was full of a week's worth of trash.

"I'll take care of you later," he addressed the dustbin.

However, history indicated that he would only keep that promise either when the trash overflowed or stank too badly for comfort. He collapsed on his bed and picked up his phone. Three missed calls and two voice messages.

Caller ID: *Unknown*.

Walter furrowed his eyebrows. He did not recall hearing the phone ringing thrice. He shrugged and tapped on the first message.

"Hello, Mr. Peabody. Just calling to say 'howdy' and to check on you. Not sure if you even gave me the right number because I've called twice already to no avail. Well, I'll try again, and hope I'll get you next time. Ciao amore," Lithilia's voice said over the phone.

Walter stifled a scream and slapped himself across the face.

"Idiot. Idiot. Idiot." he cursed out loud.

Walter hurried to the second message, tapped on it with a shaking index finger and listened. His heart raced and his temples throbbed.

"You're a bloody screw-up," he described himself.

"I forgot to tell you… I miss you (giggles). Bye now," Lithilia said.

Walter screamed and smacked his temple several times with his free hand. He flung his phone on his pillow.

How could you be so freaking stupid, Walter? he thought. *When the phone rings, you pick it up, you imbecile.*

Walter paced around his studio. He stared at his phone on the bed.

Wish I could get the caller ID somehow, he thought. *Bullocks.*

He smacked himself on the forehead several times as he continued pacing around his studio apartment.

Maybe she's toying with me, he said to himself and stopped pacing.

He sighed heavily and thrust his hands in his trouser pockets.

"She won't call back," he said. "Yeah. She's way out of my league, anyway."

Yet, despite this declaration, Walter Peabody held on to his vision of Lithilia and himself becoming an item. They would move in together, have a life together, raise a family and more. The odds stacked against him and yet, he clung to the last sliver of hope he could cling to.

Walter's phone started ringing again, yanking him back to reality from his day dreaming. He held his breath and stared at his ringing phone. The caller ID read '*Unknown*'. Finally, he accepted the call and cleared his throat.

"Hello?" he said in a husky voice and cleared his throat again.

"Hello. May I speak with Mr. Peabody, please?" asked a lady at the other end of the line.

Her voice, unfortunately, was not Lithilia's; deep and raspy, as if sculpted from years of tobacco consumption.

"Speaking," Walter replied with a heavy dose of disappointment.

"Oh, hello Mr. Peabody," the lady said. "I'm Maria Winslow from the *Local Times*. I've read some of your blogs and I was wondering if you had a minute to discuss a job opportunity with us, please."

"Uh, okay. Sure," Walter replied with a mixture of excitement and confusion.

Job opportunity? he wished.

"Thank you, sir. Please let me know when you're ready," she said.

"I'm ready, Mrs. Winslow," Walter replied and lay on the bed.

This might turn out to be a not-so-bad call after all. A job? Hopefully, a permanent position too. Walter mentally slapped himself to stop the ramblings in his head.

"Thank you, sir," said the lady. "I read your blog about the possibility that Adam and Eve were not the first to be created. Tell me, Mr. Peabody, how did you come about this theory?"

"Wait a second," Walter bolted upright. "I never blogged about that."

"That's because you told me about it, silly," Lithilia erupted in laughter on the other end of the line. "I got you good, didn't I? YES."

"Oh my God, Lithilia," Walter collapsed back on the bed with relief. "I think I'm gonna pass out or cry. Or both."

Bullocks, I just emasculated myself, Walter gritted his teeth in frustration as the word spun in his head. *Shouldn't have said that.*

"I could never have guessed it was you. You faked that voice like a pro," he quickly blurted and joined her in laughter.

"That's for making a girl call you a million times before you finally pick up the damn phone, mister," Lithilia said playfully. "You're not supposed to leave a girl hanging like that."

She didn't notice. Good.

"Yes, ma'am," he replied. "I hear you loud and clear. Although in all fairness, you were there one who kept me hanging. And why are you calling from a blocked number, by the way?"

"Hey, a girl can't give away all her secrets on the first or second date now, can she?" Lithilia rebutted.

Walter could feel her smile in her voice, or so he thought.

"Does that mean we're going on a date soon?" Walter asked.

"You know, Mr. Peabody," she replied with playful exasperation. "Sometimes, I feel like I have to spell everything out to you letter by letter." She sighed audibly.

"Alright, alright," Walter chuckled. "Didn't wanna assume anything. When and where?"

"Now and your place," Lithilia replied. "Unless it's too soon for you?"

"No," Walter almost yelled, thanks to her unexpected and shocking but welcoming reply. "Not at all too soon. In fact, now couldn't be soon enough."

Okay, now you're sounding like a horny, teenage virgin, he bit his lower lip to shut his mouth. *Maybe I am.*

He sprang from his bed and glanced frantically around his studio like a panicking, caged animal. Suddenly, the pitiful state of his apartment slapped him in the face.

What if she doesn't like my place? Why would she, anyway? She's way too... Walter searched the right word to describe her.

Sophisticated? Yes, she's too sophisticated for me, talk less of my tiny space. I can't back out now, not after I just said yes to her coming over. Maybe I can bring her over some other time? Bullocks, I'm so screwed.

"Walter?" Lithilia spoke gently. "Are you there?"

Walter's shoulders drooped and he hung his head in shame and self-loathe. There was only one thing left to do and if it cost him his opportunity with Lithilia, then, unfortunately, so be it. He sighed with resignation.

"Lithilia, I tell you know something-" he began, but she cut him off.

"You're seeing someone, aren't you?" Lithilia asked sadly.

"No, not at all," he replied quickly. "God, no. I'm not seeing anyone."

"Phew, you got me worried for a sec, Mr. Peabody," she said.

"Didn't mean to," he apologized. "I just wanted to let you know that I live in a tiny and not-so-accommodating place and that-"

"You're as broke as a joke?" she asked nonchalantly.

Walter was too surprised to reply.

"Just to let you know," she added a-matter-of-factly. "I'm not coming to see you because you're the richest bloke on the block. I'd like to spend some time with you, beyond the formalities of a tea shop setting. Also, I have a story to finish," she giggled. "Is that okay with you? I certainly don't mean to impose."

His heart warmed and his features softened, touched deeply by her sincerity and humility. He felt so stupid for misjudging her and for letting his insecurities get the better of him. At the same time, he felt like he had hit a lottery jackpot.

Okay, maybe like the second prize, which is still better than nothing. Well, when I actually do hit THAT... he smiled mischievously.

"You're the sweetest lady I've ever met, Lithilia," he replied earnestly. "And, by all means, you're not imposing at all. I'd love to spend some time with you as well. I'd text you my address, but I still don't have your number."

"I have a pen and paper," Lithilia offered.

Walter gave his address.

"Thanks and see you in two hours," Lithilia blew him a kiss across the phone and ended the call.

"That means I have two hours to get this place as pristine as I possibly can," Walter squared his shoulders. "Let's get to work then, shall we?"

He vacuumed, dusted, scrubbed, emptied the trash, changed the sheets, shaved and showered.

"I wonder why she still won't give me her number."

Eighty-nine minutes later, his apartment looked like an alien territory to him; it was the cleanest it had ever been ever since he moved in. He inspected the place once again for good measure and nodded with satisfaction. From wall to wall, his domicile looked and smelled great. From armpit to armpit, he looked and smelled great as well.

"Bullocks," he exclaimed. "Forgot to order food and there's no time."

A knock on the door caught his attention. He headed for the door.

"Bullocks."

"Who is it?" he asked impatiently.

"It's your favorite porn star, honey," Lithilia replied.

"Oh my God, woman," Walter grinned and opened the door.

A grin, much wider than his, greeted him. Her one hand carried a bag containing deliciously smelling Chinese food and the other held a bottle of white wine. She stepped closer and kissed him on the lips.

"Thought we could use some food," she said and walked past him into his studio apartment. "And unholy water, of course."

Walter speechlessly followed Lithilia with his eyes. He closed the door and freed her of her load. He put the wine in the fridge and set the food on the counter by the sink while Lithilia surveyed his apartment. She headed for the bed.

"I like your mansion, Mr. Peabody," she lowered herself on his bed.

Lithilia wore a red sleeveless blouse tucked into a short, tan skirt, with a pair of red high-heeled sandals to compliment her outfit. Her perfume wafted across the apartment, drowning the scent of his cheap air freshener. She propped herself backward with her hands as she crossed her toned, firm legs. Her full bosom heaved and fell rhythmically with each slow, seductive breath she took. Walter's focus zoomed in on her ample cleavage. He swallowed. He was not sure whether he was slowly walking towards her by his will or if he was under hypnosis. Either way, he would not resist.

Lithilia uncrossed her legs. As Walter knelt in front of her, she parted her legs some more, welcoming him into her feminine form. She took his face in her hands. Walter accepted her invitation and pulled her hips closer to his. She smelled like heaven and her body, pressed against his, was paradise. Even before they angled their heads and locked lips, Walter knew he was a goner; and he was at peace with that.

They came together as two people on fire with a passion that was uncanny. Their clothes disappeared as if ordered by a spell. Their oral plays came separately at first before simultaneously. Their bodies blended as one with every touch, with every kiss, and with every gentle bite; no inhibitions, no restraints, no doubts, and no fears.

The past and future did not exist anymore. But in every perfect, present, fiery moment, these two united in ways unknown to Walter but not unfamiliar to Lithilia. To him, the bonding was not just an awakening. It was *THE* awakening. To him, these soul-freeing pleasures epitomized what the Buddha described as the 'end of all suffering'. This was the ecstasy of all ecstasies. Nirvana was in Lithilia and he never wanted to stop entering nirvana. He wanted to remain within nirvana for eternity. Alas, he was only human and several combined climaxes later, a most satisfied couple finally peeled off each other. More was spoken in silence and more communicated in body contact than in their pillow talk.

"Am I the only one who's suddenly famished?" Lithilia asked later.

"I've got my buffet right here," Walter slid his fingers between her legs.

"Yes," Lithilia moaned. "It's yours; anytime, anywhere, anyhow."

Jackpot, Walter exclaimed to himself.

He kissed Lithilia on the lips and was about to head for the kitchen counter, or whatever passed for a counter in his tiny studio apartment, when she grabbed his hand and returned it between her thighs. He grinned and obliged. Several minutes later, a grinning and satisfied Lithilia collapsed into a pillow.

"I now release you into the wild, my love," she waved her hand in the air.

Walter smiled and headed for the kitchen counter. He set the food on a tray, tossed a piece of General Tso's chicken into his mouth, opened the wine and took everything to bed. Walter made to return for wine glasses, but Lithilia started drinking out of the wine bottle. She wiped her lips with the back of her left hand.

"Who needs glasses," Lithilia said. "Your syphilis is now my syphilis."

Walter choked on the piece of chicken he had tossed into his mouth.

"You've got a sick sense of humor, woman," he coughed. "And I absolutely dig it."

He kissed her even passionately. They wolfed down the food and wine and talked for a while about almost everything and nothing; their families, childhoods, past relationships et cetera. Walter did most of the talking, though. An hour later, Lithilia resumed telling her story about the first woman.

***

"I do not know that name," the male said, surprised by Lithilia's question. "Why do you ask me such a question?"

"Because I heard you say her name," Lithilia replied angrily.

"Let us take a moment," the man tried to reason with his partner. "Could you please start by telling me what is happening?"

"Here is what happened," Lithilia said.

Her anger subsided a little bit with the realization that her partner may truly be ignorant of everything she had witnessed.

"On three separate occasions, I have seen a woman in our bed with you," Lithilia said.

"What?" the male cringed with shock beyond belief. "That is impossible. There is no one else in the garden but us, Father and his people."

He shook his head and frowned with confusion. Lithilia's resolve softened with pity for him. He really did not know what happened, but she knew what she saw. Her eye did not deceive her and his crotch area was wet with his seed.

"I know what I saw," Lithilia said less aggressively, as if to convince herself.

"Alright," the male said. "I think we should take this to Father. He may be able to help."

"Agreed," Lithilia said.

So, the couple sought audience with Father and Lithilia told Father about what she had seen.

"If what you say is true-" Father started saying.

"It *IS* true," Lithilia insisted. "I am not lying."

"I never said you were lying, princess," Father explained.

Father handed her a tablet.

"Draw what you saw here, my love," he said.

Lithilia did and returned the device to Father. He furrowed his eyebrows as he studied the sketch. Then, he showed the sketch to the male.

"Do you recognize this creature?" Father asked the male.

The male's eyes bulged in shock.

"It cannot be," the male gasped.

"What do you mean by that?" Father demanded.

"It cannot be," the male repeated. "No. It was a dream. It was just a dream."

"I knew it," Lithilia shrieked in anger. "You lay with another woman. On *OUR* bed. You betrayed me. I hate you. *I HATE YOU.*"

Lithilia thrashed and clawed at the male with ravenous rage. The male just sat still, stupefied and confused by the irrationality of the situation. Father dashed around the table with uncanny speed that neither Lithilia nor her mate recognized. He placed himself between Lithilia and the male.

"Stop now," he barked at her. "Immediately."

Lithilia glared at the male and pouted but did not sit down.

"Sit," Father ordered. "Now."

Lithilia pouted, pulled her chair back and slumped into it. She folded her arms across her stomach and glared at the male some more.

"I do not know the meaning of this," the male said weakly. "I swear, it was only a dream. That is all I know."

"And I *SAW* your dream," Lithilia rebutted. "I saw your dream on top of you, and I saw you give seed. I saw you enjoy everything-"

"But you never saw my eyes open, did you, my love?" the male asked, barely above a whisper.

Lithilia froze. The male turned and faced her.

"When you are on top of me when we bond, are my eyes open or closed?" he asked calmly.

She hesitated for a moment not wanting to accept the possibility that her partner was telling the truth about him not knowing what was happening.

"But… But you said her name," Lithilia said weakly, uncertainty and doubt weighing on her voice. "You called her by name."

"In my sleep, my love," the male explained.

"It appears there is more happening here than we are fully aware of," Father said, trying to mitigate the situation. "You saw this creature, princess" he lifted the device in his hand and set it back on the table, "and he called her name. He said it was a dream. I think both of you are correct. But I honestly do not think that he is betraying you, princess. How about you two return to you domicile while I investigate further-"

"Look at you, taking his side," Lithilia hissed through clenched teeth. "I should have known. You two are conspiring against me."

The change from uncertainty to dark, fiery fury happened so suddenly that even Father did not perceive it until a second too late.

Then, without warning, Lithilia snatched the tablet from the table and struck her partner in his right temple, tearing flesh and drawing blood. He collapsed on the floor. She gasped and stared at her partner in total disbelief, while shock and fear paralyzed her on the spot.

"Send a team in my office right now," she heard Father command.

She turned and faced Father. For the first time she was created, Father gazed down on her with anger and disappointment. The tablet slid from her hand and hit the floor with a thud. Her mate grunted on the floor. She turned slowly in his direction. Her mate tried to push himself off the floor but he fell face-first into the floor. She made to go towards him.

"Keep your hands off him," Father growled in a tone of voice she had never heard before and she shivered involuntarily.

Why is Father not coming to his aide? she wondered.

She turned her gaze towards him. Her lips parted but she could not say a word.

Father is protecting my love, she realized. *From me…. He is keeping an eye on me… because I am something really bad. I am something else. I am not like my mate. I am… different.*

She stepped away from her mate and Father. Father took a step towards her mate, but his cold, hard stare remained trained on her. His eye color changed to various colors all at once. He regarded her from head to toe, as if scanning her with his eyes. A blanket of self-loathe draped over her psyche and silent tears rolled down her cheeks.

"What have I done?" she whimpered. "What have I done?"

Four of Father's people came into Father's room. One of them fished out a device that looked like a smooth, short, white piece of stick and placed it on the floor next to the unconscious male. It stretched in length to match his height before spreading out to form a transparent surface, like a bed. Father's people lifted the male of the ground and placed him on the surface.

"Take him to the lab," Father said.

Lithilia watched as the transparent surface hovered off the floor with her mate lying unconscious on top of it. She made to follow him when she noticed Cahen standing by the door. She froze and cupped her mouth.

Did he see me strike his father? she wondered and prayed he did not.

"My love," she said weakly and took a step towards him.

However, the trembling child backed away from her and balled himself in a tight corner. He clung onto his little furry friend in his arms as if seeking comfort. Lithilia gasped as more regret, self-loathe and deep sorrow seeped into her soul.

"My child," she sniveled, crouched and opened her arms towards him. "Come now. Come to mama, please."

But Cahen cowered some more and hid his face from her. Father stormed past her.

"Come, my child," he said to Cahen.

Cahen immediately leaped to his feet and ran into his grandfather's open arms. Lithilia's world crumbled into too many pieces to count as she experienced a new sensation especially from someone who she did not consciously realize was the center of her world until now. She experienced rejection from her son.

"Return to your domicile," Father ordered. "I will deal with this later."

Father turned around and walked away with Cahen.

Lithilia stood alone in the empty chamber, motionless, ashamed, remorseful, and full of intense regret. The self-loathe became a part of her identity. She hated herself for hurting her lover. She hated herself for offending Father. She hated herself even more for her son fearing her to the point of rejecting her. Lithilia wiped her silent tears, stood up and headed out of Father's office. She walked along the hallways of the facility in a daze until she came to the main entrance. She pressed a button on the left and the doors parted. Her domicile lay ahead of her. It beckoned at her. She sighed and started walking towards her home, just as Father ordered.

Her mind raced in everywhere; at possible outcomes, at ways to make amends, and most of all, at her fear that violence, the kind that stemmed from something much deeper and darker than she was aware of, may be her nature.

I can fight it and I will fight it, she promised herself. *I will make amends and make my family whole again.*

Sorrow and the desire for forgiveness from her mate and son weighed heavily on her heart.

Everything will go back to the way it once was, maybe even better, she hoped.

However, with each step she took, Lithilia became convinced that nothing would ever be the same again. She feared that if she stayed, she may hurt her partner again and worst of all, that she may hurt their son… because something else tarried within her, which threatened to take control of her.

Maybe Father sensed it too, she thought. *Maybe that was why he regarded me as such; as if I was a stranger, a very dangerous one for that matter.*

She reached her domicile and walked past it.

What is a domicile without a family? What is a domicile if I cannot control myself around my family? I cannot call this domicile my home anymore until I find a way to control what is happening within me.

Lithilia broke into a trot.

I must protect the ones I love.

She broke into a run.

I must stay away to guarantee their safety. This is the only option.

Her heart shattered with the pain that came with accepting her only option and she ran even faster, faster than she ever had, faster than she thought possible. Everything whizzed past her at blurring speeds. The more she widened the gap between herself and the Garden of Aiden, the more her heart shattered and the more her resolved hardened.

Lucie, she fumed and ran even faster, leaving a trail of white flames behind. *Whatever you are, wherever you are, I swear by my existence that I will find you and I will make you suffer.*

And with that final promise to herself, Lithilia did something she had never done before; she teleported to a land as unknown to her as her newfound ability.

***

Lithilia sobbed silently. Walter gathered her into his arms.

"Why are you crying?" he asked.

"I'm sorry," Lithilia sniveled. "This part of the story always gets to me."

"It's a sad but very beautiful story," Walter offered. "If I didn't know better, I'd say you're telling me your story. You're so passionate about it."

Walter smiled at her. Lithilia managed a weak smile.

"Did you choose to name this character after you because you identify with the character?" he asked.

Lithilia did not reply. She just leveled a plain gaze at him and smiled sadly. Then, she inched closer and kissed him on the lips. He kissed her back, and they kissed each other passionately. She gently pushed him on the chest until he lay on his back. She straddled him, guiding him into her warm, juicy, tight wetness. Eyes half-closed, he moaned and arched his back as she moved her hips, slowly at first before picking up speed. He hardened and tensed up in a prelude to a climax.

"Do you know why I cried?" Lithilia asked as she gyrated away.

"N- No," Walter stammered with building pleasure.

"Because she took my love away from me," Lithilia replied.

Walter half-opened his eyes. Lithilia's eyes glowed with a yellow-orange hue. He thought the dim lights in his apartment were playing a trick on his vision. His gut begged to differ but the feeling in his loins convinced him he was achieving a heightened state of perception. Lithilia gyrated even faster.

"She made me lose my son, but I got him back eventually," Lithilia's eyes shone even brighter.

Oh no, what's happening?

Panic began to build up within Walter, as well as something he felt completely powerless against; inconceivable ecstasy.

"And yes, I am Lithilia; the name is no coincidence, Walter," she added in a tone of voice so uncanny and eerie it made Walter's skin crawl.

"I have been given many names and called many things; but I am Lithilia.," she hissed. "And you, Walter, have a special role in my plan."

Walter's body quaked between mind-numbing ecstasy and paralyzing fear at the full realization that his jackpot winnings were about to pave a path of no return to a destination that could only be Hell itself. Right before he climaxed, Lithilia leaned closer to his face and opened her mouth. A glowing orange mist rushed from her mouth into his as he moaned with literal soul-wrenching ecstasy. In his moment of climax, Walter was most vulnerable and the glowing, orange mist burned his essence to nothingness. Everything he knew, and everything he was, evaporated in an esoteric blast as the human life he had burned away; and, instead of giving seed, Walter's soul was scorched.

That morning, Walter Peabody woke up a human. But now, he was reborn as a new creature; one that was neither demon nor human, luper nor chuper. Walter Peabody opened his eyes, and they glowed with a bright orange hue, the shade of a sinister. He became flaccid with his rebirth and Lithilia ceased her gyration. She removed herself from him and stood beside his bed. She gazed down on the vermin that Walter had become with the utmost disdain.

"Welcome to the new life, Walter," Lithilia said coldly. "Are you ready?"

Walter stripped himself from the bed and prostrated before Lithilia.

"I am at your service… my queen," Walter replied.

"Hope you enjoy your lottery jackpot," Lithilia scoffed and summoned clean garments over her body before she teleported back to Hell Realm.

CHAPTER ELEVEN

WINGLESS

DIRECTIONAL UPS AND downs are relative to one's physical location or current vibrational frequency within Creation. An ascension is a move to a dimension of higher vibrational frequency and a fall is a move to one with a lower vibrational frequency. No angel or archangel had ever ascended but many had fallen before. Some had returned and while others had not for various reasons.

Michael, Uriel and The Edge gradually receded into the distance. Eliel was aware that the feeling a weightlessness as he fell was just an illusion. Everything that happened recently up to his fall still felt surreal to him. One moment, he was watching over Baby JEM and, before he knew it, he appeared in Michael's domain, dueling for his life. Then Uriel had provided him with enough evidence to convince him that he was an angel of promise and now, he was falling.

Oh yes. This is happening. I'm actually falling, Eliel heaved his shoulders. *Where to? I have no idea. I'll find out soon enough, anyway.*

Eliel continued falling. Celestia was no longer in sight, but his essence still resonated with the vibrational frequency of the dimension: Lemuria.

Home... it's... gone....

He left home to embark on a journey into the unknown; and in that unknown, he would have to find himself again.

I will find myself again. My brothers and sisters depend on my success. I must return and for that to happen, I must remember.

This begged the question: how could he remember in amnesia? Uriel's words came to memory.

"But even though they say there is total amnesia, there's a part of us that never forgets. It just gets buried in the far recesses of one's mind..."

Thus, instead of wasting energy and precious moments analyzing the situation, he decided to focus on something that could act as triggers during his journey to remembrance later. He thought of Baby JEM and his heart warmed the sweet memories of her cuteness. He smiled.

I miss her a lot already, he chuckled. *I wonder if I'll get to meet her after my fall? Assuming I'm falling to Earth Realm, that is.*

However, as quickly as sweet thoughts of the infant came to mind, Eliel quickly brushed them aside.

"Thoughts of the baby will not help me remember," he said out loud.

Eliel continued to fall and, as he fell, he came up with a mantra.

Celestia is my home. I am on a mission. I am The One.
Celestia is my home. I am on a mission. I am The One.
Celestia is my home. I am on a mission. I am The One.
Celestia is my home. I am on a mission. I am The One.

Suddenly, pangs of searing pain pounced on his form as the edges of his wings burst aflame. He screamed as the flames burned their way at a steady speed from his wingtips towards his scapulae. He did not even recall summoning his wings. His wings had popped out of their own volition. He also realized that his essence no longer resonated with his home dimension and everywhere looked strange to him. Panic set in. He flailed wildly as he tried to douse the flames on his wings with his hands. Unfortunately, his level of flexibility did not allow him to reach what was left of his wings and scapulae.

I must have entered a lower dimension, he thought.

His essence also initiated a resonance with this lower dimension, a process which resulted in excruciatingly painful spasming of his body, which also looked and felt denser than his Celestial form. Moments later, the spasming of his form subsided once his form attained resonance with the vibrational frequency of the new dimension

Celestia is really gone, he thought.

His chest area heaved with the sadness that came with this realization. He stole a moment to survey a nearby realm. Creatures with spherical bodies of various sizes with five pairs of legs traversed the realm. Many of them pointed a pair of legs in his direction and waved them in the air in what Eliel thought was excitement. Some stretched their top two pairs of legs forward and lower their bodies to the ground, as if in prostration. Eliel resumed his mantra.

Celestia is my home. I am on a mission. I am The One.
Celestia is my home. I am on a mission. I am The One.
Celestia is my home. I am on a mission. I am The One.
Celestia is my home. I am on a mission. I am The One.

The first wave of a sense of loss hit Eliel as the flames burned the last portion of his wings away.

This is what Uriel meant when she talked about a loss of identity during a fall. Anyway, I must focus. I can't allow any changes within me affect my mission now.

Celestia is my home. I am on a mission. I am The One.

Celestia is my home. I am on a mission. I am The One.

Celestia is my home. I am on a mission. I am The One.

Celestia is my home. I am on a mission. I am The One.

Eliel screamed again, louder this time, as more excruciating pain ravaged every iota of his constitution. He clawed at his face and body as if to rid himself of a million pins stabbing his flesh from the inside at the same time. Pointless. His garments burst into flames and his vibrational frequency dropped to resonate with that of the lower dimension he just entered, thereby resulting in his body becoming denser than before. Moments of suffering later, the pain subsided with the completion of the resonation of his body with that of the new dimension.

He fell past a realm. A countless number of dead bodies littered its surface.

"This carnage is not from a natural disaster," he said. "That enormous pit does not look natural to me. They brought this upon themselves. Pity."

Eliel could have been wrong, but it did not matter.

Celestia is my home. I am on a mission. I am The One.

Celestia is my home. I am on a mission. I am The One.

Celestia is my home. I am on a mission. I am The One.

Celestia is my-

Eliel grabbed his temples, squeezed his eyes shut and gritted his teeth as his head threatened to implode from the pain that pounded within. Flashes of light blazed in his vision repeatedly and rhythmically. If he could open his mouth, he would have screamed louder than he had ever screamed because the pain in his head dwarfed all the pain and suffering he had ever experienced in his entire existence. Alas, his efforts to drown out the pain proved worthless and his head pulsed with every pounding within.

Wait, I just swallowed, he exclaimed mentally.

The pain subsided and he smacked his lips.

My mouth is watery, like those of creatures of lower realms, he realized. *But how? Why? What's happening to me?*

He swallowed again and coughed.

What's happening? he panicked. *Angels don't have watery mouths. Angels don't swallow. Angels... Ang... What? I'm losing my mind. Oh no. I'm losing my memory. I must fight it. I must fight it.*

Fear and panic took his spine in a murderous grip. He attempted to recite his mantra with renewed vigor.

Ce… Ce… I am… Where? Ce…

Eliel could not remember the words. His home was… A tear of sadness and hopelessness rolled down the sides of his eyes.

Liquid from my eyes, he swiped at his eyes and rubbed the tears between his fingers. *How can this be?*

He sighed.

At least I remember my name and what I am.

As such, he came up with a new mantra.

My name is Eliel, and I am a fallen angel
My name is Eliel, and I am a fallen angel
My name is Eliel, and I am a fallen angel
My name is Eliel and I am a fallen angel

"There," he exclaimed. "I may not remember where I'm from, but I know what I am and I know my name. I shall keep this mantra."

Pain flared through his body suddenly, but not as much as any of the earlier attacks. His body did feel denser though. He ignored the realms he fell close to. He had to save his mental strength to combat the amnesia that loomed ahead.

My name is Eliel, and I am a fallen angel
My name is Eliel, and I am a fallen angel
My name is Eliel, and I am a fallen angel
My name is Eliel, and I am a fallen angel

Why am I even saying, 'I am a fallen angel' instead of 'I am a falling angel?' He wondered.

Was it his surrender? Had his psyche and will already accepted his current situation? He was wingless, his body was denser, his memory was fading, and he had lost much of his identity.

Yes, was his answer.

He was an angel only in his fading memory. He did not feel like an angel. He could not even feel the new vibrational frequency of this lower dimension and he could not feel his… essence. Still, many questions lingered.

Where was he falling from? Where was home? Where was he? And what are angels?

Strange term, 'angel', he thought. *I know this word somehow. Yet, I don't even know what it means. And why do I keep repeating these lines? What is the purpose?*

So many questions and no answers. The feeling of loss and sorrow grew even deeper with every passing moment.

My name is Eliel, and I am a fallen angel
My name is Eliel, and I am a fallen angel
My name is Eliel, and I am a fallen angel
My name is Eliel, and I am a fallen angel

Suddenly, millions of memories of faces and names flashed through his mind at once and disappeared immediately: Gahel, Michael, JEM, Jemma or something like that.

Who are these creatures?

An image of a creature with a flaming sword and flames spewing out of his eyes and mouth flashed in his mind and disappeared.

Who are these people?

"*Hang in there, Eliel,*" a sweet, feminine voice said. "*Remember to hold on to something and trust your instincts. They will never lead you wrong, Eliel. Remember…*"

What was this voice trying to say? Hold on to something? What was going on? Why was he losing his mind? And why did it seem like he was falling?

What's happening? Why was that voice talking to me from inside my head?

The panic, confusion and fear took a life of their own.

"*Listen, Eliel,*" a masculine voice said, more like commanded, though his voice carried no sense of urgency.

"*You are entering the final stages of your fall. Perhaps right now, you do not even know that you're falling; let alone, know why you are falling. Rest assured, it is alright; I have been there before, and I know exactly what you are going through. But like Uriel just told you, all you have to do right now is hold on to something and trust your instincts. Remember, you are Eliel, and you are The One.*"

Somehow, in the insanity of the situation, Eliel found some peace and serenity. He did not know why nor did he care to know why anymore. His body relax with the letting go of the tension within. He closed his eyes and took a deep breath.

Breathing. This is new.

He sucked in a lungful of air and held it. He listened to his heart beating rhythmically.

Heartbeat… another new sensation.

He let out the air he was holding in his lungs.

My heartbeat, he sucked in another lungful of air and held it. *Sounds like music to my soul. Wait.*

He let out the air.

Soul? Where did that come from? What is a soul?

Eliel shrugged and examined his hands.

I have much to learn.

He felt his forearms, biceps, triceps, and shoulders becoming even denser. He rubbed his hands along his core; strength, and definition. He wiggled his toes, cracked his fingers and smiled weakly.

My name is Eliel, and I am a fallen angel

My name is Eliel, and I am a fallen angel

My name is Eliel, and I am a fallen angel
My name is Eliel, and I am a fallen angel
And then, following his instinct, he added one more line.
This is not my home. And I am the one.

He broke through the dimension in which lay his destination. No pain this time,; only total peace and total amnesia. He continued his fall as his body became even denser. He fell towards a new realm, a blue one. Another smaller, gray realm floated near the blue one. A much bigger and brighter yellow realm was visible and very far away from the blue realm. It gave light to one side of the blue realm, causing the other side of the blue realm to be in the dark. Eliel fell past the gray realm and headed towards the dark side of the blue realm. And then, Eliel closed his eyes and lost consciousness.

***

Newman Weinberg was a lowly farmer in a small farm town, about forty miles from Oklahoma City. It had been two years since the fifty-nine-year-old became a widower, no thanks to ovarian cancer. His children, Paul and Paula, were grown up and had moved out of the State of Oklahoma. Paul had a job in Michigan as an engineer. Paula worked as a registered nurse in Maryland and was currently on maternity leave. She and her husband had just had their first children; twin girls, whom they named Donnie and Maria, after Paula's mother, Donnie, and her husband's grandmother, Maria. Paul was engaged to his fiancée.

The time was 2:17 a.m. when Armstrong, Newman's bulldog, started barking wildly at the back door. Newman roused from slumber. He slid out of his bed, retrieved his shotgun from under the bed and quietly made his way, barefoot, towards the kitchen. He peeked into the kitchen. The full moon provided sufficient illumination. With the certainty that no one else was in the kitchen, he called out to his dog in a whisper.

"Here boy. What's wrong, big guy?"

Armstrong continued barking and clawing at the door. Newman relaxed, thinking his friend wanted to go take care of business outside. He lowered his gun, walked towards the back door and opened it. Armstrong dashed through the first available crack in the open door and ran into the backyard. It turned, looked at its owner and barked. Newman stepped into his backyard. He crouched near his friend and scratched it behind its ears..

"What's da matter, boy?" he asked. "What ya tryna show me?"

Armstrong turned its head towards the sky and barked. Newman followed his friend's gaze. He recoiled with shock.

"Dear God," he exclaimed.

Something like a shooting star, though much bigger and brighter, blazed through the night sky. However, it did not just travel across the sky and disappear like shooting stars did. Instead, it headed straight towards Newman's farm at an incredible speed. Armstrong barked even louder and more ferociously. Newman rose to his feet as he gaped at the accelerating ball of fire from the sky. Finally, his adrenaline kicked in and snapped him out of his daze. He scooped Armstrong from the ground and ran for the house.

If I don't make it, then I'd be glad to join my darling wife, he thought.

The night turned brighter than a cloudless midday with the impact of the blazing object. Yet, neither sound nor shock followed the impact of the blazing object. The brightness lasted no more than three seconds before the darkness of the moonlit night resumed command. Newman froze mid-stride, surprised and confused he was still alive. He felt his body to ensure he was still in one piece. Armstrong's barking was the final confirmation that indeed he was alive. Newman set him down on the ground, thinking the dog would dash for the kitchen. Instead, it dashed towards the impact zone.

"No boy," Newman cried out but Armstrong ignored him.

Newman chased after his dog. Armstrong stood at the edge of the impact zone and barked into the small crater in the ground. Newman stopped at the edge of the small crater; 10 feet in diameter and six feet deep.

"That's a small crater for such an impact," Newman wondered. "But how?"

He peered into the cloud of dust that gradually settled. Finally, he could see the bottom of the crater.

"Oh my God," Newman exclaimed.

The body of an adult male lay motionless at the bottom of the crater in fetal position. Newman swallowed nervously.

"What in the world is that?" he wondered and took a cautious step towards the edge of the crater.

A million thoughts raced through his mind. He was certain that UFO's and aliens were real and believed he had even seen a few when he was a child. But when he had told his grandfather, his grandfather had brushed away his story as a figment of his imagination. Newman was not entirely sure if this person in the crater was an alien or not.

"No spaceship, unless he's some special kind of alien that doesn't travel with a spaceship or clothing for that matter," Newman surmised and wrinkled his nose. "Jesus Christ."

The man in the crater roused and groaned. Newman tripped and fell backwards as he staggered away from the crater. The man slowly rose to his feet, as if he was in a drunken stupor. He shook his head as if to clear it and looked up. Newman crouched on one knee and stared back at the human in the crater while Armstrong barked incessantly. He tightened his grip around in gun.

"Don't come any closer, alien," Newman ordered, trembling as he spoke. "I promise you; I will shoot. So, stay where ya are."

The man in the crater regarded Newman quizzically. He rubbed his temples and shook his head again. Suddenly, the air seemed to pulse with a surge of energy as the last wave of his erased identity was about to leave him.

"My name is Eliel," he said. "I am a fallen angel. This is not my home. I am The One."

With those words, Eliel opened his arms. Bright, golden light coalesced from his shoulder blades to form wings. Then the wings of light dissipated into tens of thousands of tiny specks of light, which floated away into the darkness of the night. The amnesia was complete and Eliel collapsed back into the crater.

"Oh... my... God...," Newman cried

And without thinking, Newman rushed into the crater, towards the man who just identified himself as a fallen angel.

CHAPTER TWELVE

WHO AM I

NEWMAN STUDIED THE stranger lying on his son's former bed in his son's former bedroom. Thirty hours later, the man from the crater, who claimed to be a fallen angel, was still asleep. Newman did not want to miss the moment when this 'wannabe fallen angel' woke up from his sleep. However, caffeine binging could only pump his system with enough adrenaline to keep him awake for so long. He slumped in his chair from weariness as the excitement of all that happened wore off. Even his hair seemed exhausted. In a baffling turn of events, neither Newman nor his neighbors called the cops.

How could anyone have missed such a spectacle? He wondered.

Still, Newman wrestled with the thought of alerting the authorities.

But what if this man, who was unscathed by the fires of his vessel, was a fallen angel? I know what I saw. Those were wings of light. WINGS, for God's sake. Perhaps the Almighty God has chosen me for something very important? Newman scratched his chin. *God does work in mysterious ways.*

Nothing made sense. While his logical mind insisted he called the cops, his gut dictated he do the right thing; and the right thing was not to hand over this stranger to the authorities. As such, Newman found the strength to pull the man out of the hole, drag him into the house and up the stairs into his son's room. It only took him twenty-seven arduous minutes.

"This is too much work for an old man," he said to Armstrong.

The dog barked once.

"But hey, not bad huh," he slurped his dark brew. "I may be old, but I'm far from done."

Armstrong whimpered and buried its face in its paws. Newman chuckled.

"Thought you had my back, buddy."

Newman's head bobbed constantly and each eyelid weighed a ton from lack of sleep. He stood up and paced around his son's room for the millionth time and for the millionth time, he asked himself the same set of questions.

First question: is this human-looking creature really an angel?

The grand entrance, the wings of light, the final words before passing out, and the seeming disregard for being naked.

Why did that last part even cross my mind? he wondered.

"Oh well," he shrugged. "I'll just have to take his word for it."

His Christian upbringing validated his belief in the existence of angels and their role as messengers of God. Artworks depicted them as creatures with wings and various visions from many folks confirmed this assertion.

Faith… it's all about faith.

However, something was odd about this alleged 'fallen angel'. Every picture of angels he had seen depicted angels as Caucasian. Not that Newman was racist, but when the man in the crater said he was an angel, Newman's initial sentiment was one of doubt because the man from the crater was clearly African American. However, Newman chose not to let subtle brainwashing cloud his judgment.

Second question: what do I do when this 'angel' wakes up?

Calling the authorities was out of the question. What would he say?

"Hello. I found a naked man in my backyard who claims to be an angel. Please, send help."

"Yeah. Help's gonna come alright; straight jacket and all, Newman scoffed. And not that I'm a fan of conspiracy theories and all that. But what if it turns out that he is an angel for real? I'm gonna have some secret government organization storm out here and next thing you know, ma kids won't even know what happened to me. They'd erase me down to my social security number," Newman shook his head vehemently. "Ain't calling no cops or nobody."

This led to the next question.

When the angel eventually starts blending with society, hopefully in his 'human' form, what would his back story be?

Newman came up with a quick back story. Eliel, that was what the angel called himself, was the son of a long-lost friend of his. They fought together in 'Nam. Eliel wanted to learn about the farm life first-hand before going to study agriculture in college. So, his friend sent Eliel over to live with him in the meantime until Eliel was ready to return to Texas.

Weak, I know, Newman thought. *But folks should mind their damn business.*

Fourth question: why did Eliel fall?

According to Christian doctrine, Newman remembered reading about angels coming down to earth and sleeping with women. This happened before the deluge in the story of Noah and his ark. The women got pregnant and gave birth to giants called Nephilim. Similar stories permeated various ancient mythologies. The Nephilim were 'full of wickedness and they ravaged the Earth with their wickedness' or something along those lines according to the Christian bible.

"So, if Eliel's claim was true," Newman supported himself against the chair.

His legs protested against the constant back-and-forth pacing.

"Does that mean his mission is to spawn a race of giants, like a new Nephilim race, who are gonna wipe out the Earth?"

Newman shook his head at the absurdity of his train of thought.

"Only Hitler and his sympathizers will love the ideal of cleansing mankind," he added. "And last I checked, Hitler did not take too kindly to folks of this fallen angel's color. Wait a minute. How do giants and racial cleaning even relate? I'm starting to lose my mind."

Newman massaged his forehead and shook his head. Armstrong lay still on the floor.

"Besides, my gut tells me this angel ain't the type to go around killing people," Newman straightened himself and yawned loudly, startling Armstrong.

"Look at me," Newman shook his head slowly and chuckled. "A damn angel is in my house. I've got so many questions for you, mister, that is, if I don't die from lack of sleep."

He stretched, turned and twisted his body. He smacked himself across the face, but even that did nothing to help keep him awake. The nerve endings on his face seemed to be losing the battle against sleep.

"Gotta give him a name too," Newman added. "For God's sake, what kinda name is 'Eliel'?"

Eliel finally roused from his sleep and opened his eyes. He squinted and shut his eyes. Newman bolted with a new surge in adrenaline and moved closer to Eliel. He reopened his eyes before he slowly sat on the bed. He examined the clothes he was wearing. The plain white tee shirt and checkered pair of shorts were a size too small. His eyes surveyed the room.

"Sorry 'bout the clothes, young man," Newman said. "My son didn't have your body type."

Newman studied Eliel carefully as Eliel leveled a blank gaze at him.

"Do you understand what I'm saying, son?" Newman asked, noticing the quizzical look on Eliel's face.

"Wh-" Eliel cleared his throat, swallowed and tried again.

"Where am I?" he asked in a husky voice.

"Good, you speak English," Newman sighed with relief and puffed his chest. "Don't know how you can, but that's alright. You're in my house."

"Where is your house?" Eliel asked.

"I'll ask the questions here" Newman replied with false bravado. "Hope ya don't mind."

Eliel nodded, not that Newman needed his approval, anyway.

"Good," Newman said. "First question: where ya from?"

"I don't know," Eliel replied and stared blankly at the floor.

"What do ya mean you don't know?" Newman asked.

"I mean I don't know where I'm from," Eliel replied.

Newman sighed heavily.

"Okay then. What's ya name?"

"My name…," Eliel began and then stopped. "My name is…."

Eliel furrowed his eyebrows and massaged his forehead with his fingers. Then, he looked up Newman with sad, confused eyes.

"I don't know my name," Eliel said.

Newman leaned back in his chair and studied Eliel. Unable to arrive at any conclusion, he continued with his line of questions.

"Okay. This is getting interesting," Newman said with exasperation and leaned forward. "Do you remember how you got here?"

"I remember blackness and then I woke up here," Eliel replied, barely above a whisper, and gestured around the room. "I don't know how I got here."

"Let me get this straight," Newman inched to the edge of his seat. "You don't know where you're from, your name, and how you got here. You tryna tell me ya don't know who you are?"

"I'm afraid so," Eliel sighed. "I don't remember anything."

Eliel buried his face in his hands, rubbed his eyes and sniveled.

"I don't know what's happening to me. I don't remember anything."

Newman studied Eliel very closely.

He's either a very good actor or he's got a terrible case of amnesia, Newman thought. *If he can't remember anything, what next?*

Eliel sniveled and wiped his eyes and nose.

Guess I could teach him about the ways of the people of Earth, Newman concluded. *Wait a minute. Why am I even thinking about teaching him about the ways of earthlings?*

Newman sighed.

Because I already made up ma damn mind to help him, until he regains his memory. God help me. Wish Donnie was here. She would've been of much greater help than I'm gonna be. And if his mission was to spawn a bunch of Nephilim on Earth, then this amnesia is a blessing in disguise because I can change his heart or something before he remembers. God does work in mysterious ways.

Shut up, you old fool, Newman scolded himself. *Do you hear yourself?*

"Thank you for everything, sir," Eliel said softly.

Eliel never took his eyes off the floor.

"You're welcome, son," Newman replied.

Eliel's words of gratitude erased the last traces of reservation Newman had about helping him.

"Tell you what's gonna happen now," Newman leveled a hard gaze at Eliel. "First of all, this is very odd for me, and I think it'd be odd for anyone else as well to just help a random stranger like that. For all I know, you could be out to kill me, you know?"

"And why would I want to end the man who has been good to me?" Eliel met Newman's gaze.

"I don't know," Newman replied weakly. "Just because?"

"Sir," Eliel spoke firmly. "It is wrong to end another 'just because.' All life is sacred and must be respected and protected."

Newman smiled with pleasant surprise.

"The strong should protect the weak and power must be used for service," Eliel continued as if he were reciting a pledge or an oath. "So again, I ask you, sir, why would I want to end the existence of one who has been good to me?"

Newman thought it wise to calm Eliel down.

"Whoa, whoa, whoa. Easy now, son." Newman said. "Just testing the waters."

Newman wiped an invisible bead of sweat from his forehead with the back of his hand.

"Okay, here's what we'll do," Newman said. "Until your memory returns, I'm gon' give you a name and a cover story and you're gonna play along. You with me so far?"

"Yes, sir," Eliel replied hesitantly.

"Good, I like your manners, by the way," Newman said. "So, your name is Donald and you're a friend of mine's son from Texas."

"What is Texas?" Eliel asked.

"Just a place a little far from here," Newman replied dismissively. "Details will come later. For now, we'll work with these basics. Okay?"

"Okay," Eliel replied.

"Good, I'll start over," Newman adjusted himself on his chair. "Your name is Donald Smith. Your father's name is Tyrone Smith. Your father and I are friends from way back in 'Nam. Your mother is Anna Smith. She passed away a decade ago. You're from Texas, and you're here to learn about farming first hand."

"So, my name is Donald... Sims?" Eliel asked.

"No, Smith. Donald Smith."

"Donald Smith," Eliel repeated. "My father's name is Tyrone Smith, and my mother's name is Anna Smith. I am from Tex... Tex...?" he tapped his head as he tried to remember.

"Texas," Newman offered.

"Texas," Eliel repeated. "And I am here to learn how to farm."

"You sure you an amnesiac?" Newman asked with a smile.

"Thank you, sir," Eliel said, smiling weakly for the first time since his fall.

"You're welcome," Newman replied.

The tension in his body gave way to ease as he began to feel more comfortable with Donald, formerly known as Eliel.

"Are you tired, sir?" Eliel asked.

"You have no idea, son," Newman replied with a long stretch and yawn.

"You're right. I don't, sir," Eliel added honestly.

"I didn't mean it like that," Newman apologized and sighed. "You gonna get used to certain expressions with time. But for now, just go easy on yaself and don't worry too much about certain things. Okay?"

"Okay, sir," Eliel replied.

"One more thing," Newman said. "During this period of learning, I think it's best you don't make any contact with the public."

"Learning?" Eliel asked.

"Yes, learning," Newman replied. "Gotta get you familiarized with our culture and mannerisms, yadi yadi yada... You know, the whole nine yards."

"Nine yards?" Eliel asked innocently once again.

Newman chuckled and shook his head.

"Like I said, Donald," Newman continued. "No contact with the public until I bring you up to speed. Last thing I need is any unnecessary attention to you and me right now. Do you understand me?"

"Yes sir, I do," Eliel affirmed.

"Good," Newman stood up and headed for the door. "I trust you won't leave the house while I go catch me some shut eye, would ya?"

"No sir," Eliel replied. "I'll stay right here."

"Fast learner," Newman said and winked.

"Sir?" Eliel called.

"Yes?" Newman stopped at the door.

"What's your name, please?" Donald asked.

"Oh my, where are my manners?" Newman slapped himself on the head and walked over to Donald.

"Weinberg. Newman Weinberg," he extended his hand.

Donald stared quizzically at Newman's extended right hand.

"Put your right hand out, son," Newman said.

Eliel did. Newman took it and shook it.

"There," Newman said. "That's how folks out here greet. And this," Newman pointed to the dog, "is Armstrong. Here boy."

Newman headed for the door and Armstrong trotted behind him.

Newman closed the door behind him. He had decided at the last minute not to tell Donald his real name. He was unsure how Eliel would handle a sudden recouping of his memory, especially after falling.

Eventually, I'll tell him the truth, Newman promised himself as he glided dizzily into his bedroom.

He fell on his bed, closed his eyes and plunged into the blackness of near-death sleep in less than a second.

Donald lay back on the bed and stared at the ceiling. Within seconds, he drifted back to sleep. His body was still trying to recoup and resonate completely with the vibrational frequency of Earth Realm since he completed his fall; hence, the two-day sleep.

"Do you think he'll adjust quickly," Michael asked.

"I'm sure he'll be fine, Michael," Uriel replied. *"He's very strong."*

"The next cycle is nigh," Michael said flatly.

"And Michael thinks I do not know that," Uriel replied sarcastically.

"I've never seen any fallen angel or archangel display wings of light after their fall like Eliel did," Michael admitted. *"He really is special, is he not?"*

"I thought that was a given," Uriel took his elbow. *"Come. Let's leave him be."*

"Do we have anyone assigned to him?" Michael asked.

Uriel bent over and kissed Eliel on the head before replying.

"You know the rules, Michael," Uriel said. *"No angel or archangel is to watch over The One. He is on his own, and he must find his way on his own."*

Michael nodded.

When Michael and Uriel teleported away, Eliel roused in his sleep. He was having a dream about two creatures, a male, and a female, standing over him and having a conversation.

CHAPTER THIRTEEN

A BALL OF FIRE

SHI'MON RELISHED THE fact that his psyche was free from the burden of his guilt for betraying his mentor, as well as the fact that Yehuda was no longer his mortal enemy. Plus, he had undergone an esoteric upgrade after his rebirth from surviving the Shadow of the Soul. Despite getting rid of the Bright Eyes, a major achievement, other threats to the realm beckoned still; like Maduk and Beelzebub. His coffee steamed on his night stand. He only ate and drank in front of others as a cover. Why settle for the process of feeding and digestion when one could spark the ethers into directly nourishing the body? Well, he had to maintain his cover and let the world know he was 'human' just like the rest of them. This was a rare morning for him because peace and relaxation filled the air, something he had not experienced in too many centuries to remember. His cell phone rang. He sighed, picked it up and when he saw the caller ID, he sighed again, heavier this time, before accepting the call.

"Yes, Antonio," Shi'mon said flatly.

"There was a massive spike in the realm's auric frequency, sir," Fr. Antonio spoke with urgency.

"How massive?" Shi'mon asked.

And how did I not feel that? he thought.

"Category 5, sir," Fr. Antonio replied.

"The most we have ever registered was a 2," Shi'mon said almost to himself.

"Affirmative, sir."

A moment of silence lingered.

"I am on my way," Shi'mon said and ended the call.

Shi'mon reached for the phone on his nightstand and pressed a button. A click followed a dial tone.

"Yes, your supremacy," said a husky voice on the other end of the line.

"I'll have breakfast in the car, Vincenzo," Shi'mon said. "Do you think you could quickly work some of your culinary magic for me?"

"Of course, your supremacy," Vincenzo replied. "Any special request?"

"I defer to your infallible judgment," Shi'mon replied.

"Only God and the goodly pope are infallible, your supremacy," Vincenzo countered with a chuckle of appreciation.

"Then you are the third person on my list," Shi'mon asserted.

"His supremacy has made my day," Vincenzo spoke with gratitude.

"Thanks, Vincenzo," Shi'mon ended the call.

Vincenzo, the chef, was one of the few people Shi'mon conversed with in an almost friendly manner. Why? Shi'mon was unsure and did not care.

Despite the serious nature of Fr. Antonio's call, Shi'mon took his sweet time getting ready for his ride to work. After his call with Fr. Antonio, he tapped into Earth Realm's esoteric signature and scanned the realm. He detected nothing majorly variant of the level of the vibration of darkness the realm normally emanated. Therefore, whatever caused the Category 5 disturbance in Earth Realm's auric frequency was not aligned with the vibrations of darkness. On his way to the car, he made a pit stop in the kitchen and snatched his packaged breakfast himself. He wolfed it down in the car as they headed to the Vatican.

Given the contents of this breakfast, it is a good thing I am only Jewish by birth, he thought.

The drive to the headquarters was surprisingly smooth for a Tuesday. During the drive, Shi'mon reminisced on the era of the space war. Humanity's childishness never ceased to amaze him. He had lived for over two millennia and the hearts of men had not seen much evolution in inclusiveness during that span of time. In fact, humanity had ensured individualism was the modus operandi. During the space war, he took the initiative to attach special devices on the satellites and space stations orbiting the realm, without the permission or knowledge of the countries that owned these structures in space. The greatest minds the realm had to offer could not device means to detect teleportation even if they tried. The rest of the O.R. assumed they had received permission from the owners of these satellites and space stations. Only he knew the real story.

The O. R called these attachments auric sensors. Auric sensors were designed to monitor and track changes in Earth Realm's auric frequency.

"An auric frequency is the frequency of the collective consciousness of a realm, dimension and even cosmic cluster," Yeshua told him during training once.

The O.R. labelled Earth Realm's auric frequency 'Category 0', or reference point. Earth Realm also shared the same auric frequency with other realms within Solaris, the dimension in which Earth Realm was located. Shi'mon always thought this was odd. Yet, he saw the advantage this shared auric frequency represented.

As such, if anything or any creature entered Earth Realm's atmosphere from another realm within Solaris, then it would cause no change in Earth Realm's auric frequency and will, therefore, register as a Category 0 disturbance. If the intrusion, however, was from a dimension higher than the Dimension of Solaris, the higher vibration frequency of the intrusion would cause a disturbance in Earth Realm's auric frequency and the auric sensors would register and categorize the level of disturbance. Nothing ever entered a higher dimension from a lower one by default, unless their vibrational frequency increased enough to resonate with that of a dimension higher than theirs was. An increase in vibrational frequency of a dimension indicated transcendence and resonating with the vibrational frequency of a dimension of higher vibrational frequency indicated an ascension.

Sinisters came to Earth Realm from Nimbu Realm, another realm within Solaris, via portals. Therefore, Sinisters did not cause any disturbance in the auric frequency of Earth Realm. As such, the O.R. had to devise other ways of detecting and tracking them when they entered Earth Realm.

"Category 5," Shi'mon said to himself. "Whatever caused this disturbance, subtlety is not its forte."

The car pulled up at the Vatican. Shi'mon quickly let himself out. He returned the greetings of his agents with quick nods and curt waves as he marched down the hallways to take the elevator underground to the control room. He pushed the door and walked into the control room and walked straight towards Fr. Antonio, who was hunched over another priest. Both of them stared intensely at a 120-inch screen.

"Any updates?" Shi'mon asked.

"No, your supremacy," Antonio squinted at the monitor. "No word from the locals, government or the internet."

"Images?" Shi'mon asked.

"This is what the auric sensors picked up," Antonio replied.

He turned his attention towards the young priest over whom he loomed.

"Send the feed to the big screen."

The young priest obliged. On the screen, something that looked like a comet suddenly appeared in space and raced towards Earth Realm at an astonishing speed until it crashed. Shi'mon rubbed his chin in thought.

"What do you think it is, sir?" Antonio asked.

"It's not a cosmic body," Shi'mon replied. "Did you notice how it suddenly appeared from nowhere? That means, it was already in the process of travelling but was still at a vibrational frequency that was higher than that of our dimension. So, it was invisible until its vibrational frequency dropped to ours, to what we could detect."

"And why could the other satellites not pick up any images of this outer-dimensional object or being?" Antonio asked.

"Remember, auric sensors are set to register changes in auric frequencies," Shi'mon explained. "The sensors locate the cause of the auric shift and create an image of whatever is causing the shift. Satellites, however, can only register images visible to the naked eye."

Antonio rubbed his chin in comprehension. It now made sense why there were no stories about any meteorites, UFO's or something in that light. He did have one question that bothered him, though.

"If that is the case, how come there was 'impact' without any major physical disturbances?" he asked. "I mean if a ball of fire crashed somewhere in the middle of the night in a populated area, wouldn't that cause a stir at least to the locals? And wouldn't the authorities have been alerted already?"

"And we would have been on it," Shi'mon interjected. "But we got nothing."

"Agreed, sir," Antonio narrowed his eyes in thought.

"There was a crash but no explosion," Shi'mon said. "Why?"

"I was wondering myself, sir," Antonio agreed.

"Because of the absence of any buzz about a crash in that area," Shi'mon said. "I think our ball of fire contained a living creature."

"That's quite possible, sir," Antonio agreed.

Antonio pulled up a chair and sat next to the young priest. He took the mouse from the younger priest and clicked a few times on a still shot of the video. Then he right-clicked and tapped two keys simultaneously on the keyboard. The image magnified to twice its size. He continued tapping on the same keys until the image was enlarged to his satisfaction. He then returned the mouse to the young priest.

"Filter and enhance the image layer-by-layer," Antonio said.

"Yes, sir," the young priest replied and proceeded to do so.

As he did, a silhouette began to form within the ball of fire. He stopped.

"Keep filtering," Antonio ordered, and the young priest obliged.

After filtering through twelve layers, a faint, but distinct outline of a human form curled up in a fetal position became visible. The young priest gasped, uttered a few expletives and then quickly apologized after realizing that he was in the presence of his two most senior supervisors.

"You were absolutely right, sir," Antonio beamed with excitement.

"And to explain why there was no explosion on impact," Shi'mon added, ignoring Antonio's comment, "this being was still at a vibrational pattern that was just above ours. His materialization reached 100% only on impact. This is a highly evolved being to be able to demonstrate such control during its fall and – "

Shi'mon suddenly stopped and his face went pale from shock. He swallowed and took an involuntary step backward. Usually, he could maintain his composure even in the face of adversity. But not after the realization of what the image on the screen represented.

"What is it, your supremacy?" Antonio asked shakily.

"Where was the crash?" Shi'mon asked.

"Here, sir," Antonio replied, pointing at a spot on a tablet he held. "It's a rural, not-so populated area in Oklahoma City in the US."

"How many agents did you dispatch out there?" Shi'mon asked.

"One, sir," Antonio replied, suppressing a smile of pleasure for adequately preparing himself for his boss' questions.

"Send two more immediately," Shi'mon ordered.

He turned to face Antonio.

"They're to locate but not, and I repeat NOT, to liquidate the target. Clear?"

"Yes, sir," Antonio affirmed.

"Once they locate the target, they are to report to you directly and immediately and you are to report to me immediately. On absolutely no occasion are they to let the target out of their sight. They will become this creature's guardian angels. This is a high priority mission from now on. I want instant updates on the target."

"Aye aye, sir."

"One more thing," Shi'mon added. "Should the target prove to be dangerous then our boys are to do what they do best, but only with my blessing."

"Yes, sir."

Something about Shi'mon made Antonio turn white with fright and it was not the sternness in his boss' voice. When Shi'mon turned to leave, Antonio called out to him.

"Sir," he swallowed.

"What is it?" Shi'mon asked without turning around.

"What or who is their target?" Antonio asked.

"A new guy in town," Shi'mon replied flatly and exited the control room.

Antonio whipped out his phone and dispatched two more agents to the site of the crash. His mind kept returning to that moment when he had been paralyzed by fear; fear at the realization of what his boss was. His world was about to crumble around him, but he would have to err on the side of caution from now on. It might turn out to be an impossible feat, but he will do his damnedest best.

After all, he thought, *it's not every day you get to learn that your boss is a Bright Eye.*

For the briefest moment, Shi'mon's eyes flashed. But Antonio had seen it.

So many things now make sense, Antonio rationalized. *His supreme fighting skills, his special missions, meeting Yehuda by himself and so many other things. Who is he really? What's his endgame? Is the O.R. a sham? Nevertheless, he is an enemy of humanity and I took an oath to protect Earth Realm and humanity from all enemies, within and outside of the realm.*

While Antonio's thoughts churned in his mind, he never paid much attention to a priest telling his coworker he was going to use the restroom. While in the restroom, the priest ensured he was alone. He stepped into a stall, locked the door and whipped out his cellphone. He speed-dialed a number and waited as the phone rang on the other end. After three rings, someone picked up.

"Ball of fire crashed just outside Oklahoma City. Big boss very concerned and issued rapid orders. Must be something big. Out now."

The priest quickly ended the call. He flushed the toilet, walked out of the stall and washed his hands in one of the sinks. He complimented himself for his sense of hygiene, though he could not say the same about his allegiance to the O.R.

Meanwhile, in a studio apartment in a town on the outskirts of Liverpool, Walter Peabody set his phone down and smiled. The queen would be very thrilled with this update.

Time to get busy.

Shi'mon resisted every urge to teleport into his office. He took quick strides along the hallway and the elevator could not go up fast enough. He issued orders to his administrative assistant not to let anyone disturb him for any reason. He locked the door and sealed the office completely. He sat in his chair and breathed in deeply and let out the air slowly a few times. His mind kept going back to the image on the monitor. The creature in the ball of fire was wrapped around something that looked like fire. But it was not fire. The creature was extra-dimensional. If the others had seen it, they must have thought it was just a pattern of the flames. But to Shi'mon, the pattern around the creature's body was as clear as the fact that Antonio had seen his eyes flash, which was a deliberate but harsh introduction to a truth Antonio was going to be privy to eventually at the right time, anyway.

Some people throw parties, others don't, he thought. *Me, when I'm about to retire, I flash my eyes to my next-in-command.*

"Something big is coming, brother," Shi'mon said telepathically.

"What do you mean?" Yehuda asked.

"We have a fallen angel among us," Shi'mon replied.

Brief silence.

"I know it's their fight," Yehuda said, *"But I think we must speed things up on our end. If it gets nasty up there, and they want to bring it down here, we can't go down without a fight."*

"You don't say," Shi'mon replied. *"Assemble everyone, including Miriam and Marissa. I want Maduk and Beelzebub located and liquidated immediately."*

"ROGER," Yehuda replied and disconnected the telepathic link.

CHAPTER FOURTEEN

ONE YEAR LATER

"COME ON, SARA, one more shot," Johnson slurred at the bar.

"I'm gonna call your wife," Sara admonished. "You're more drunk than a skunk. You best be on your way now."

Sara reached over and seized the shot glass from Johnson's hand.

"Will you please take him home, Jimmy?" Sara said.

"Sure thang, Sara," replied Johnson's friend, Jimmy. "Come on, buddy."

Jimmy tapped Johnson on the shoulder and helped him off the stool. Johnson took two wobbly steps and face-planted on the floor. The bar erupted with laughter. Jimmy sighed and shook his head.

"Gimme a hand, Bob, will ya?" Jimmy urged.

Bob reluctantly stepped away from the two girls he was conversing with.

"Don't you ladies go nowhere now," Bob said and winked at the girls.

"You keep dem dranks comin' and we ain't goin' nowhere, mister," one of the girls replied.

"Ya gonna gimme a hand or what?" Jimmy called out to Bob.

Bob obliged, knowing his 'gesture of goodness' was going to eventually earn him a free drink or two later.

"Another day in paradise, ma'am?" said a stranger to Sara.

"Sometimes, I just wanna bend them over and do what they mommas shoulda done a long, long time ago," Sara replied.

"You can do that to me anytime you want, honey," offered a customer.

A regular, probably in his mid-sixties and he looked like he had been baked in the sun all his life. He sounded like Conway Twitty on helium and his sheepish grin exposed teeth nearly blackened from a lifetime of chewing tobacco.

"And Hell freezes over," Sara replied with exasperation.

The older gentleman smiled mischievously and inched closer towards Sara, rudely pushing past the stranger. He reeked of alcohol, tobacco and liver cirrhosis.

"You gotta tell me, Sara," he said, looking around as if he was trying to share nuclear launch codes with Sara. "What's ya secret, huh? I mean, I been comin' to this bar since you opened it twenty-five, thirty, years ago and you still the same young gal you was back then."

"And Imma tell ya what I done told ya many times already," Sara replied without missing a beat. "I keep my tail away from the sun and I don't get drunk on my own stash."

"That's a pile of horse crap, Sara," the older gentleman slurred, spraying spittle from his foul-smelling mouth.

"Excuse me, sir," the stranger said, "I was tryna have a conversation with the lady before you rudely interrupted."

"And who da hell are you?" the older gentlemen spat.

He tried to stand up straight but staggered backward.

"Who I am, ain't important," the stranger replied. "But you best pay your tab and head on home now before you hurt yourself."

"You-, you not my daddy-" the older gentleman slurred his words before he dropped his empty bottle to the ground. "Don't talk to me like... like... that."

The bottle rolled away from him. Two cops walked in and scanned the bar. Sara waved at them and then gestured at the drunkard. The cops took him away.

"'Preciate you tryna stand up for me, sir," Sara said. "But I can handle myself."

"Meant no offense, Ms. Sara," the stranger said. "Hope you don't mind me calling you Ms. Sara. Heard everyone calling you by that name."

"I know you meant no offense and you certainly can call me Ms. Sara," she replied. "It's rare to find such manners these days in these parts. Your next drink is on me."

"That's mighty kind of you, ma'am," the stranger replied. "But I must insist on paying-"

"I won't take 'no' for an answer," Sara countered, smiling.

"Much obliged, ma'am," the stranger conceded, smiled lightly and tipped his black fedora at Sara.

"And it's Sara," she said and started wiping the space on the bar next to the stranger as another customer eased onto the seat next to the stranger.

"Hey, Don," Sara flashed a smile while opening a bottle of beer and snatching a $20 bill another customer had left of the bar with the kind of coordination that only a bartender and owner like herself could exhibit.

"Hey Sara," Donald smiled and waved at her. "Great night so far?"

"Don't even get me started, hun," Sara replied as she served a couple a shot of whiskey each.

"Let me guess," Donald said. "Johnson, Paulson, and Mrs. Stadbury?"

"First two are correct," Sara said. "But Mrs. Stadbury's a no-show."

"Awww shucks," Donald chuckled. "I missed one this time."

The stranger's keen eyes raked through the approximately 500sqft of space that passed for a bar. The dark, grey walls could use a fresh layer of paint but the dim lighting of the bar did a great job at negating this need. A non-functioning juke box and a pool table occupied the right-hand corner of the bar, while the pictures of a few country music and rock stars adorned the walls. Thirty to thirty-four folks, most of them blue-collar workers, added more life to the bar besides the country music blaring from speakers that hung from four, top corners of the bar. A symbiotic relationship brought horny men and ladies who preyed on the men's horniness: drinks and maybe bar food in exchange for flirtations and maybe fleeting moments of intimacy between the sheets later.

Sara's bar was one of three in this small, suburban town with a population of just over 3,000, and her bar was the busiest of the three. Maybe the cleanliness and size of it contributed to its repertoire of being the busiest. Maybe it was Sara's magnetic personality radiating from her five-foot-eleven, heavily-toned, bosomy body with baby-smooth skin and blindingly white teeth that shone every time her naturally luscious lips peeled back. Whenever she turned around to reach for a drink, or whatever, her big, firm-looking buttocks gently curved into her thick, strong thighs, which flowed into beautifully formed calves: not too large, not too small. Short black hair never looked better on any woman the stranger had ever seen. Three other employees assisted her and they all wore black tops and a blue pair of jeans. Sara, however, wore a black tank top, a blue pair of daisy dukes jeans shorts and a pair of black, low sneakers.

You're definitely the reason why they all flock here, the stranger said to himself.

He turned on his clairvoyance, clairsentience and clairaudience. Everyone's aura indicated they were human, except for Donald's, the gentleman who just sat next to him. The stranger knew that already. However, Sara's aura was different from everyone else's, including Donald's. Clairaudience did not help much. Her thoughts were all geared towards taking care of her business and employees.

Remarkable focus, he thought. *All business. That's good so far.*

Clairsentience indicated she was not aligned with the dark side.

Be that as it may, the stranger thought. *That glow on your throat is the first I've ever seen and I must get to the bottom of this.*

He took a swig from his glass and savored the burn of the alcohol as it made its way down his gullet.

Who or what are you? the stranger's curiosity quaked with deep interest and an unexpected desire for Sara.

He swirled his drink and nodded slowly.

Seems like I just gave myself a new assignment,

"You must be from outta town, stranger," Donald said.

"Is it that obvious?" the stranger asked with a smile.

"Well, aside from the fact that everybody knows everybody and they momma in this town," Sara chimed in, "a fine black man like yourself kinda sticks out."

She winked at him.

Flirty bartender, the stranger thought. *Keeps the business entertaining.*

"Never took you for a poet, ma'am- I mean, Sara," the stranger said.

"You'd be pleasantly surprised," Sara replied.

"Surprise me then," the stranger flashed the sexiest smile he could summon.

You're not the only one who can be a tease, creature, the stranger thought.

"He giving you any trouble, hon?" Donald asked playfully.

"Not at all, sweetie," Sara replied. "He's taking real good care o' me. Defended my honor against Paulson. I feel safer with him here already."

"Don't listen to her, partner," Donald nudged the stranger in the arm. "Said the same thing to me when I just started coming here."

"Hey, stop ruining my game," Sara wagged a finger playfully at Donald.

"'Preciate the tip, partner," the stranger raised his glass at Donald.

He realized his glass was empty and signaled to Sara.

"May I have a bottle o' beer this time, please? And a bottle for ma friend over here as well. Owe the man ma life."

Sara, Donald and the stranger burst out laughing as Sara opened two bottles of beer for the men. Donald and the stranger cheered.

"Much obliged, sir," Donald said and took a swig from his bottle.

"Not at all, partner," the stranger replied and took a swig from his bottle as well. "So, ready for the game on Sunday?"

"Hell yeah," Donald replied. "Who you with?"

"Ravens baby," the stranger said.

"You gotta be kidding me," Donald' eyes bulged like a kid who had just received the best toy ever for Christmas. "I'm a Ravens fan too."

"I'll be damned," the stranger replied, incredulous himself. "What are the odds. You must be the only Ravens fan in these parts."

"And Imma leave you two chocolate wonders be," Sara chimed in. "Y'all just lemme know when y'all need something else."

"Thanks, Sara," the stranger said.

Sara smiled and walked to the other end of the bar.

"So, where you from?" the stranger asked.

"Texas," Donald replied. "I live with Mr. Weinberg at his farm. My dad and him is friends since 'Nam. Here to learn how to farm first-hand before I head on up to college. What about you, sir?"

"Born in Cameroon, but I was raised in Alabama," the stranger said. "My dad had a scholarship up there. Took me and ma momma with him when he came to this country. I was about nine years old then."

"Cameroon…" Donald repeated. "That's in Africa, right?"

"Central Africa, yes," the stranger replied.

"Oh, that's neat," Donald remarked. "What happened to your accent?"

"What happened to yours?" the stranger retorted.

The two men burst out laughing.

"I'm Donald, by the way," Donald extended his hand.

"Pleased to meet you, Donald," the stranger shook Donald's hand. "I'm Patrick."

The two men chatted the night away. Six-bottles-of-beer-each later, Donald slid off his stool.

"Gotta run now, man," he said. "Early day tomorrow. We should hang out some more before you return to the East Coast."

"Sure thing," Patrick replied and shook hands with Donald. "Sure you don't need a ride home?"

"I'll be fine," Donald replied. "It's just beer. I'm concerned about you though, big guy. You violated the #1 rule of drinking."

"Never mix your booze?" Patrick cocked an eyebrow. "I'm fine. Drive safe."

Donald gave a partial military salute, turned around and left the bar.

Patrick glanced at his $6,000-watch. 11:27 pm.

"Hey, Sara," he waved at her. "One more bottle please."

Sara obliged. The bar slowly emptied as the minutes ticked by.

Donald is completely oblivious of his true identity, Patrick sipped his beer. *Anyway, we're here to keep him safe.*

He pressed into his left ear.

"Yes, sir," a male voice crackled over the earpiece.

"How's his driving?" Patrick asked.

"Steady, sir," was the reply.

"Good," Patrick said. "Is Li with you?"

"Li here, sir," another voice replied.

"Keep me posted," Patrick ordered.

"Aye, sir," the two agents chorused their reply.

When the first three agents dispatched to this location started reporting sightings of Sinisters within forty-eight hours of their arrival, the O.R. realized they had a mole within the organization and it had to be someone who was in the control room when Father Supreme gave the set of orders. A surgical process of elimination ensued, which identified the mole. He was subtly fed much false information that led to the systematic elimination of so many Sinisters that a few months later the mole stopped coming to work. His lifeless, rotting corpse was found in one of Rome's filthiest slumps. Someone in Sinister Camp was not a happy camper. No one at the O.R. missed the mole.

The first three agents did a phenomenal job at locating the target of interest. They narrowed down the coordinates of the crash site to within a two-mile radius and had begun investigating immediately. Eighteen hours of nonstop searching later on foot, their search brought them to Newman's house, which gave off-the-chart readings on their portable auric sensors. Under the cover of darkness, they found a large piece of plywood in the backyard of Newman's house and when they lifted the plywood, they found a hole in the ground. An agent reached into the hole and felt it. It felt smooth to the touch like glass.

"We found it," declared an agent. "We must inform Fr. Antonio at once."

His comrades nodded.

Then, the Sinisters started pouring in. On the first day of attack, one agent died but the other two held on. Week after week, they watched and protected their target as they fended off Sinister after Sinister. Thankfully, their target never left the house for some reason. Eventually, the Sinisters eased off and the agents had one less thing to worry about in the meantime. Then, word reached the O. R of a Sinister secret weapon, who was undetectable to the O.R. sensors designed to sense and locate Sinister portals. That was when Shi'mon tasked Patrick to pay the small town a special visit. The agents in the field were to answer directly to Patrick from then on.

"You're still here," Sara's words snapped Patrick out of his reverie.

"Fixin' to finish this last man standing," he replied brandishing his bottle.

"What a chore," Sara rolled her eyes.

She snatched the bottle from Patrick's hand, took a swig from it and returned it to him. Patrick smiled and took a swig as well.

"When do you close down for the night?" Patrick asked.

"Why ya wanna know?" Sara asked in return.

"Damn curiosity," Patrick replied with a weak smile.

"You could've at least tried to come up with a lie or something, ya know," she flirted. "Like, 'Was just tryna make sure you got home safe.' Or whatever your male instincts ask you to say."

They both laughed.

"I could," Patrick agreed. "But would you rather I lied or told you the truth?"

"I'd rather you told me the truth, stranger," Sara replied in earnest.

"Here's the truth," he said.

He leaned forward and stared deeply into her eyes. Sara did the same. He reached even further and placed his lips very close to her right ear.

"Just asking," he whispered.

"You snake charmer," Sara exclaimed and threw a playful punch at Patrick's shoulder.

Patrick effortlessly redirected her punch back towards her and something about the gesture made Sara weak in the knees. His clairvoyance revealed her colors changing and clairsentience revealed she burned with desire for him.

Bingo, he said to himself.

"1:45," Sara said and straightened.

Her chest heaved up and down slowly and her massive bosom threatened to jump out of her tank tap.

"You know where to find me," Patrick said, sliding a $100 bill towards her. "Keep the change." he added and walked out of the bar.

Patrick sensed her passion burn hotter than that of any other person he had used clairsentience on before.

She is extra-dimensional, alright, he concluded. *But from where? Anyway, I'll find out soon enough.*

He glanced at his $6,000-watch. 11:42.

See you soon, Sara, he said to himself as he rounded the corner past the door.

Partaking in local distractions was never his intention. Yet, stuff just seemed to happen all the time; unwarranted, but very much appreciated. Resistance was pointless. He adjusted his leather jacket and walked towards his rental.

Wish I could just teleport, he sighed as he fished for his keys. *Driving is so boring.*

He unlocked the car remotely and right before he slid behind the wheel, he heard someone call out to him.

"Care to give a girl a ride, mister?" said a farm girl in too short a skirt and low-cut blouse that also showed her flat tummy as she walked towards him.

Normally, he would have declined. He had a prior engagement already.

Well, can't say 'no' to a girl in a pair of boots and red lipstick, can I now? he thought.

"As long as you don't try to hurt me, miss," Patrick flirted.

"Well, I just might," she slid in the front passenger seat. "But I got a feeling you gonna like it."

She batted a pair of big, seductive, green eyes at Patrick

"Careful what you wish for," Patrick said with a flirtatious smile.

Patrick revved the engine and headed towards the only motel in town. Two hours later, he drove the girl to her home.

"I'm sore as hell," she beamed. "Might even walk funny for a few days, but you know what?"

"What?" Patrick asked.

"It's all for a freaking great cause, literally," she exploded with laughter at her own words.

"Glad you feel that way," Patrick said in a monotone.

She took him by the lapels of his leather jacket.

"Promise me we're gonna hang out again before you leave town," she begged.

"I promise," he lied.

She grinned, smooched him and exited his car. Patrick made sure she was safely inside her home before he sped off towards the motel. He thought of Sara on the way back to the motel.

"What the hell am I doing?" he smacked himself in the forehead. "Anyway, it's all part of the mission. Yes, my mission."

He pulled into a parking spot at the motel five minutes later.

Can't believe I had a drink with an angel, Patrick smiled as he took the stairs to his room, two at a time. *How cool's that? I wanted to ask for his autograph but Father wouldn't have taken too kindly to that.*

He entered his room, left the door slightly open, undressed and kept only the bathroom lights on to dimly illuminate the room. Four minutes later, there was a gentle knock on the door. He placed a pillow over his pelvis.

Cut it too close, he thought.

The door creaked opened slowly. A freshly showered, long-wet-haired, sweet-smelling, high-heeled-boots-wearing and red-lipsticked version of Sara walked in. The sound of her boots, gentle on the hardwood floor, echoed into the quiet of the night. She locked the door behind her, without taking her eyes off Patrick.

Glad I had some earlier sessions, Patrick thought. *Could've burst a nut just staring at all that hotness. And didn't she have short hair at the bar? She knows what she's doing.*

He sat up slightly.

You like your hair pulled, don't you? Patrick mischievously smiled in the darkness. *You got it, creature.*

"Nice coat," Patrick said out loud.

"Nice pillow," Sara replied. "Whatcha hidin' under there?"

"I'd show you, but I don't wanna give you a heart attack," he replied without missing a beat.

Sara could not contain her laughter and Patrick smiled.

"Oh my God, Patrick," Sara said between fits of laughter.

"You finally said my name," Patrick remarked.

"I pay attention, ya know," Sara replied.

She bent over to take her boots off.

"No," Patrick said.

Sara froze.

"Leave 'em on."

"Had a feeling you'd say that," Sara said.

She straightened and leaned against a small table by the door.

"How about you show me yours and I show you mine," she added in the most flirtatious voice Patrick had ever heard.

"Sure you want me to do that?" he asked.

Patrick stood up and let the pillow fall to the floor, revealing his nudity.

"Y- yes…" Sara stammered and swallowed.

Sara breathed more heavily, but steadily, as the promise and anticipation of what was to come grew with every second. She stood transfixed by his nether region, as if it was a world wonder. Patrick approached her and reached for the belt of her trench coat. One tug later, the belt came untied and the lapels of Sara's trench coat came apart, revealing Sara's resplendent and exquisite nude physique. Patrick swallowed involuntarily and cautiously reached for her skin, as if he was hypnotized by the surreal nature of the situation. He turned on his clairvoyance, clairsentience and clairaudience. Whatever she was, wherever she was from, Sara was definitely a creature that evoked every iota of his caution, curiosity and carnality in one logic-defying conundrum.

Sara's skin looked and felt surreal as Patrick slowly ran his fingers over her belly. Normally, when he came close to or was intimate with other humans, his aura and theirs behaved like two immiscible liquids. With Sara, however, their auras merged.

How? he wondered. *She's from another dimension. How is this possible?*

Her energy danced between his fingertips like jagged sparks of electricity. It flowed through his fingertips and coursed through his being. Patrick pulled his fingers about an inch away from her body. Her energies danced between his fingertips and her skin like violet sparks of electricity. She closed her eyes and moaned. His lips parted with surprise and curiosity. He raised his gaze to look at her face.

Who is this woman? He asked himself. *Better yet, WHAT is she?*

He slid his fingers up her sternum. The inner parts of her bosom smothered his hand.

So smooth and firm, just the way I like it.

He gently wrapped his hands around her neck and she arched her head backwards, as if begging him to grab her neck and squeeze. Her breathing became more erratic as more sparks ignited on his fingertips around her neck.

I should end her right now, he thought. *She's extradimensional and could be dangerous.*

Sara moaned some more and more sparks danced between his fingers and her neck. Patrick gritted his teeth and increased his grip around her neck.

But who am I to be judge, jury and executioner? he unclenched his jaw and loosened his grip around her neck. *She may be extradimensional, but she's far from evil.*

Patrick gently tugged at her neck, forcing Sara to straighten her neck and face him. She gently placed her hand around his hand on her neck.

Besides, our auras are merging. Something in her beckons to me and I must find out what that is.

And thus, instead of ending her, Patrick angled his head and planted a long, soft kiss on her neck. She gasped and almost lost her balance at the edge of the table. He kissed her neck, passionately, feeling and hearing the crackling of energy bouncing back and forth between their close, exposed flesh.

"Wh, whatever you're doing," Sara stuttered. "Plea, please… don't … stop."

Her passion was unlike any Patrick had ever experienced and he had had his fair share of women during his short existence. He cupped her left breast, squeezed gently and played with her nipple.

Sara moaned some more and her body glowed with a violet hue. Again, Patrick considered ending her. But then, she parted her limbs slightly, granting him total access to her innermost sanctum and the thought of ending her evaporated from his mind faster than a drop of water on the sands of the Sahara. Patrick reached in between her legs with his free, right hand. Sara gasped and shuddered as ecstasy supercharged with extradimensional, resonating energy swept through her body. She frothed some more before she seized his face and locked lips with him.

Patrick played with the drenched and still drenching protuberance in between her lower lips. Sara gasped louder as more violet sparks of energy danced between his fingertips and her drenching nether region. She clutched the back of Patrick's neck and buried her chin in the crease between his right shoulder and neck as Patrick worked his magic. She convulsed and spasmed before her body tensed up so much that Patrick thought she was about the shatter into in billion China pieces. But then, Sara let out a scream of exhilaration and release before she collapsed onto his body. While she panted and savored the first round of climax, Patrick summoned supercharged chi and healed his shattered eardrum. Then, Sara took over.

Sara groped for Patrick's hardness after he slid her coat off her body. Her coat fell in a lazy pile on the small table she was leaning against. As violet sparks of energy danced between her and his hardness, Sara was the closest thing to perfection he had ever seen, the closest thing to perfection he had ever touched and, as Sara stooped and took him in her buccal cavity, she was the closest thing to perfection he had ever experience. Sparks of energy played in her mouth as she worked her magic.

Her life force encase him and she savored in his as they glowed together in a most beautiful violet hue. Every ether of his being flared alive with the supercharged energy of the extradimensional creature that was pleasuring him in ways that he was sure he would never experience with anyone else. Their beings tingled to a resonance that Patrick could not explain. All he knew was that Sara's esoteric makeup far superseded his and, for a moment, in the moment of resonance, his esoteric signature underwent an upgrade. Even though his basic instinct to remain cautious waxed strong, he could not help but relish the new sensation he was experiencing. Whatever this... creature... was, he would let her have him, all of him, however she wanted.

As such, he cast caution out the window. He let go of his fear, the final frontier to this far-reaching feeling of exuberance and exhilaration he could neither conceive nor put to words. When he surrendered, he sensed Sara had also done the same. In an unspoken symphony, the pair relinquished all they had, and all they were, to that present moment. She stood up, eyes closed, and pushed him on the bed. She slid atop his body like a serpent of seduction and straddled him. When she opened her eyes, they glowed with a violet brightness. Sara took his metallic protrusion and guided him in. Violet sparks of energy danced around her body and his in jagged patterns.

Patrick's energies went esoterically nuclear, infused and resonating with the much higher energies pulsating from an extradimensional perfection in the flesh. The feeling was beyond sexual, beyond giving and receiving. It was a feeling of arriving, of an awakening to something that could only come from letting go and accepting; a feeling beyond words that only the experience of the moment could tell. He entered her warm, drenched tightness and, in that moment, as the violet sparks of energy went berserk all over their bodies sizzling with otherworldly passion, illuminating the dimly lit motel room with its bright violet flashes, Sara became the perfection Patrick had never imagined.

The pair lost control and gave in completely and unreservedly to every carnal inclination they could muster. Hours burned away, but not nearly as quickly as the couple burned their interchange of energies. During the final stretch, Sara slid her legs from Patrick's shoulders and wrapped them around his waist. With the fluidity of a violet, humanoid amoeba, she flipped Patrick over and straddled him. Her hips ground, pushed and pounded against his in a rhythm so perfect that could only come from countless sessions of erotic escapades. Their sweaty bodies and the secretions from her southern sanctums provided sufficient lubrication to minimized bruising; not that either of them cared about that, anyway. Suddenly, violet sparks began crackling from their joint waistlines in more erratic patterns and Sara went to town.

Sara built towards something that transcended an orgasmic climax. For a fleeting moment, fear gripped Patrick's spine as a new level of energy seized his being and invoked another level of energy within his being that he was ignorant of its existence. Sara's face contorted and her body stiffened as she increased her frequency of her pelvic pounding. Her breathing became more erratic, her eyes sealed shut and her lips parted as if she was about to scream.

Sara leaned forward and dug her fingers into Patrick's chiseled chest. As she sailed towards her grand finale with every gyration, Patrick inched closer towards his. He squeezed his eyes shut and pursed his lips as his body stiffened. Their energies synced, their energy frequencies attained resonance and, in that moment, Patrick and Sara, two creatures from different dimensions, shared a bond that made them one and inseparable. They felt every ether and energy from each other's existential experience. The bond transcended body and mind. The bond was something birthed in being. A violet, non-consuming flame slowly formed all over Sara's silhouette as she raised her head to the ceiling and her body tensed in a prelude to-

A scream of ecstasy and release resonated through multiple sonic frequencies at the same time. Creatures far and near, across various realms and dimensions heard Sara loud and clear. But that was nothing compared to what Patrick's eyes did not see as he himself shared in Sara's scream of indescribable release. But Patrick did not need his eyes to behold what he was already experiencing in their momentarily unified and inseparable being. He had clairvoyance, clairsentience and clairaudience as his tools for much higher levels of perception. Besides, his eyes would have tainted the knee-bending, awe-inspiring, worship-worthy sight of the violet, non-consuming flames on Sara's silhouette exploding with the beautiful brightness of a supernova, as the couple achieved a simultaneous climax worthy of an applause from Creation itself.

Their individualisms kicked in, separating their beings as an aftereffect which followed the brilliance of their culmination. Sara collapsed into Patrick's arms. She remained in that position, on top of him, for a few minutes. Neither of them uttered a single word, for more was communicated in ways beyond the tongue. Experience, esoteric and surreal, sufficed. For Sara and Patrick, they truly each were the perfection that each of them had never, ever imagined.

Patrick adjusted a passed-out Sara on the bed. He held her sleeping form close to his body. Six hours of non-stop erotic ecstasy and worldly wildness had gone by and while Sara slept peacefully in his arms, Patrick stayed awake, wondering who or what Sara was. She was neither luper nor chuper, nor was she Sinister, angel nor demon. Sara was unlike anything he had ever encountered in his line of work. Besides her extradimensional nature, she was unique; remarkably beautiful and unique.

***

At the concierge of the motel, a stranger walked in and rang the bell. A young lad emerged from the back room and approached the counter.

"Top of the mornin' to you, sir," he said with unnecessary glee.

Marijuana had that effect on people sometimes.

"Good morning to you, sir," the stranger replied. "I'd like a room, please?"

"How long, sir," asked the lad.

"Just a day," the stranger replied.

"Alrighty. Please fill out your name and sign here," the lad marked an X on two spots before handing the stranger a clipboard with a form and a pen. "And I'm gonna need some ID, as well."

The stranger obliged and handed the lad his passport. The lad made a copy of it and returned it to the stranger.

"And that'll be $30 please," the lad sniveled.

The stranger handed the lad two $20 bills.

"Keep the change," the stranger said.

The lad's eyes lit up as he envisioned replenishing his stash of weed with the extra $10.

"Wow, thank you-" he turned the form around – "Mr. Peabody. Here's your key. Room 221. Up the stairs and to your right. Third door down. Hope you enjoy your time with us."

"You're welcome and thank you," Walter picked up his suitcase and headed for his room.

CHAPTER FIFTEEN

PUZZLE PIECES

"DID SHE SHOW up?" Lithilia asked as Kazuk entered their domain.

"No, she did not," he replied and sat on a chair he summoned.

"She must've had her reasons, my love," she said, walking up to him.

"Maybe," Kazuk replied grumpily. "Just reminding me who's boss. Uncalled for, I'd say,"

"Sorry about your ego," Lithilia smirked. "Everything doesn't have to happen the way you want it to. Everything doesn't have to be perfect."

His pettiness is becoming insufferable, she thought.

"This has to be perfect, Lithilia," Kazuk glared at her. "*EVERYTHING* has to be perfect for this to work. Don't you get it?"

"I do understand that everything must be perfect," Lithilia said. "Despite what you may think."

Kazuk closed his eyes, summoned his wings, flapped them twice and dismissed them before he opened his eyes and glared at her again.

"By 'everything' I meant everything concerning this plan," Kazuk said.

"Because you can't tolerate another fiasco like last time," Lithilia finished his statement for him. "Yes, my love, I know. I'm only trying to offer some support."

"If by 'support' you mean reminding me about how the plan is falling apart, then you and I clearly have different definitions for 'support'," Kazuk said rudely.

"I agree with you, my love," she replied with deliberate calm, which made him squirm with frustration. "To me, 'support' includes, among other things, letting you transfer your aggression on me in hopes that you will feel a little better."

Lithilia paused to let her words take effect on him. His features softened, his glare vanished and he heaved his shoulders before he settled further into his seat. Then, he leveled a gaze at her, which she had come to understand was one of his ways of apologizing.

Maybe I should go easy on this childish buffoon, she considered.

"Are we really arguing because of Akasha?" she asked.

"No," Kazuk replied. "We are arguing because I let my emotions get the better of me."

"But you do this whenever something doesn't go your way, my love," she averted her gaze of feigned frustration. "Every single opportunity. Is that all I am to you; a punching bag for your emotions?"

"You know that's not true, my love," Kazuk shook his head. "I'm sorry. I didn't mean anything I said."

What a sissy, Lithilia thought. *He will certainly not last half a moment when all Hell breaks loose, literally.*

"Let's ditch Akasha altogether and work on a plan of our own," she proposed. "There must be some way to deal with The Scribe that does not involve her."

"The Scribe is too powerful," Kazuk yelled in frustration.

"True," Lithilia agreed. "But he's not unstoppable. There has to be a way."

"Finding another way to deal with The Scribe without seeking Akasha's help would be adding more to our already full plate," Kazuk replied, trying to let her know her reasoning was valid, but it may not be feasible.

"Too much on our plate?" Lithilia narrowed her eyes in confusion.

"Right now, we want to obtain the Zarark, capture Michael, take out The One, and we still have not yet even thought about what happens when she returns," Kazuk explained.

"Obtaining the Zarark sounds like the easiest item on our agenda," she sighed.

"Which will help us capture Michael," Kazuk affirmed.

Passion burned in his eyes and strengthened his tone of voice.

Good, Lithilia thought. *Can't have you moping around when there are more important matters at hand.*

"Metatron is now under control, and he will oblige," he added

"Wait," Lithilia snapped her head towards Kazuk. "What do you mean by Metatron is 'now under control'?"

She asked with peaked interest.

"Let's just say I had a small conversation with him earlier," a mischievous grin crept across his face.

Lithilia could not help but smile.

"I'll be damned," Lithilia grinned like a hooker who just saw more bills from a client than she had expected.

Kazuk summoned a seat in front of him. She settled into it and waited for him to continue. Instead, he just stared blankly at her.

"Well, don't leave me hanging now," Lithilia almost begged.

They both burst into laughter.

"Alright," Kazuk grinned. "We had a small conversation and he now knows who the boss is in this realm. We have his unwavering loyalty."

"Ooohhhh honey. You're making me all warm and fuzzy," Lithilia said.

She leaned forward and kissed him on the lips.

"Only because I have a strong woman by my side," Kazuk complimented her.

She smiled her appreciation at him.

"So, we obtain the Zarark and then capture Michael," she returned her focus to the plan. "What about The One?"

"I still think we should just send a bunch of demons down there-" Kazuk started saying.

"And hand victory over to Celestia on golden wings?" Lithilia asked. "You know damn well that is not an option, Kazuk."

"I don't care what *The Book for the Fallen* says," Kazuk retorted.

"Oh, I'd strongly recommend you care," Lithilia rebutted. "Those words were transcribed for a reason."

"I know, I know," Kazuk conceded and heaved his shoulders. "I just don't know how to get around that. The One could ruin everything for us if he returns to Celestia."

"And this is where I come in," Lithilia interjected.

She adjusted herself in her chair before continuing.

"Remember how you have been accusing me of being 'busy'-"

"And keeping me in the dark? Yes, I do," Kazuk replied.

"Yes, I've been busy," Lithilia continued. "With good reason. I was waiting for the right moment to bring you in."

"Like now?" he asked rhetorically.

Lithilia glared at him before replying.

"The prophecy says creatures from dimensions outside of that into which The One falls should not influence The One in any way while in amnesia and all that gibberish, right?" she said. "So, no influences from archangels, angels, cherubim, seraphim, demons and all that, are welcome. The One, Eliel, fell to Earth Realm and the timing could not be more perfect. The Logos, in their infinite wisdom," Lithilia rolled her eyes, "probably did not think the creatures from Earth Realm could have any influence over an angel. Anyway, guess who's from Earth Realm."

"You," Kazuk's eyes popped with understanding

"Indeed," Lithilia winked. "Even though I can live in different dimensions, I am still of the Dimension of Solara. And so are my sinisters…"

"Woman," Kazuk exclaimed. "The things I want to do to you right now."

"Shortly, honey," she flirted. "So, I've been working with Maduk, and on my own sometimes, to get the sinisters to eliminate Eliel. But that damn organization has found a way to detect my creatures."

Lithilia let out and expletive and clenched her fists. Kazuk reached out and touched her hand.

"See," Lithilia snapped. "This is what happens when creatures do not follow orders. I specifically told Maduk not to enter Earth Realm yet, but he wouldn't listen. Now I have to shield him from the O. R. until the perfect moment."

Lithilia screamed, pulled her hair in frustration and bared her teeth.

Kazuk did everything to suppress a smile.

Feel what I feel when a perfect plan is no longer perfect, he thought. *Look at you, thinking you are the queen of serenity and calm or something. For Hell's sake, you live in Hell and you're married to the King of Hell. There's absolutely nothing serene in that, you bitch.*

"Would you prefer to talk about it later?" Kazuk offered.

"No, my love," Lithilia sighed. "I'm fine now. Sorry for the outburst."

"It's okay, honey," Kazuk assured her. "You sure you want to continue?"

"Yes, I am," she replied more firmly.

"Okay then, let's hear it," he said.

"Where was I again?" she asked.

"Something about children not listening to their mothers?" Kazuk smiled.

Lithilia smiled back and shook her head in amusement.

"Try harder. Not working on me," Lithilia stuck out her tongue.

"Can't blame a fallen-archangel-turned-demon for trying," he replied. "It's amazing how much of your human tendencies you still retain."

"I am human essentially, am I not?" Lithilia said.

"For the most part, I think you are," Kazuk spoke honestly. "Or maybe I should say, you're a very special kind of human."

"I still have a soul at least," she agreed.

A cloud of sadness hovered over her and her eyes watered.

"To them, you having a soul is only in the metaphorical sense," Kazuk said. "You're not exactly held in high esteem among your kind."

"They don't understand me," Lithilia spoke softly.

"They don't know you well enough," Kazuk offered.

"They think I'm some demon," she spat and immediately regretted her words. "I'm very, very sorry. I didn't mean it like that at all."

"I'm neither angry nor offended," Kazuk spoke in earnest. "I've accepted my fall from an archangel and my new identity as a demon. Perhaps someone could use a little self-acceptance as well," he winked playfully at her.

Lithilia smiled weakly back at him.

"Perhaps someone needs to finish her story," Lithilia countered.

"Indeed," Kazuk agreed.

"Children. No, they never listen," she said. "So, I had to revise the plan. But that's okay. Anyway, sinisters have been trying to pay The One a visit, but they've always encountered stiff opposition. Those agents are quite good, I must admit."

"They can't be that good, can they?" Kazuk asked.

"They are, and the best of them is that one called Patrick," Lithilia sneered at the name. "In due time, I'll deal with him personally."

"So, does the O.R. have a way to detect Sinisters?" Kazuk asked.

This moron never pays any attention, Lithilia exclaimed in her mind.

"They do," Lithilia replied. "And they're becoming more adept with their systems. The odds were not looking in our favor, and so I had to adapt. I did not even bother to let Maduk know."

"And this is why you have been so busy lately," Kazuk said.

Yep. Super, inattentive moron. How did he even manage to be king of Hell Realm again? Lithilia managed a weak, sympathetic smile.

"Yes," Lithilia replied patiently. "Had to create a sinister hybrid; one who was more human than he was sinister. It was a random selection process, but I picked one human. His name is Walter Peabody."

"Had a feeling you would pick a man," Kazuk joked.

"Sniff, sniff, do I smell jealousy in the air?" Lithilia joked along.

"Only if he's bigger than me," Kazuk replied and Lithilia play-punched him in the arm as they both burst into fits of laughter.

"No, he's not," Lithilia said. "Feel better now?"

"Yes, love," Kazuk replied with exaggerated relief. "I do, thank you."

"They don't call me succubus for nothing, do they?" she asked rhetorically.

"They should call you by your real name," Kazuk replied. "'Lilith' irks me."

"If *you* feel like that, then imagine how I feel…" Lithilia smiled.

"We just can't help but digress, can we?" Kazuk said.

"Nope, we just can't help it," she agreed. "But back to Walter Peabody. So, I turned him into this hybrid a few moments prior to The One falling. In earth terms, that would be about three years before the fall. My thinking was that, if the sinisters fail to get to him, and knowing that Michael and Uriel would not allow any angel or archangel near him, and also that Hell's citizens would be foolish to interfere, I had to come up with a backup plan."

"And this Walter P. was your backup plan," Kazuk interjected.

"Indeed," Lithilia replied.

"And where is he this moment?" Kazuk asked.

"He just arrived in the town where the angel fell," Lithilia replied.

"Expecting any trouble?" Kazuk probed.

"Not from the agents," Lithilia replied as a look of worry strolled across her face. "I'm positive that with all the training he has received so far, those agents must be easy for him to eliminate."

"So, what is the possible problem then?" Kazuk asked.

"Patrick," Lithilia replied with a sneer. "He's really that good. They say he was specially trained by Shi'mon himself. Like some protégé."

"I'm not versed in the affairs of the humans of Earth Realm," Kazuk said. "But if what you say is true, then I'm also confident that this Walter will prevail. I assume you trained him yourself, right?"

"Yes," Lithilia agreed.

"Then there's nothing to worry about," Kazuk assured her. "I've seen you in action and woman; you're phenomenal. Walter has been in good hands. Literally."

The couple erupted in laughter.

"You're right," Lithilia agreed and smiled. "I think I'm just overreacting."

"You are overreacting for nothing," he affirmed. "And I'm curious, why don't you… distract… this Patrick yourself?"

Lithilia understood what he meant.

"Because he would detect that I am not 'normal'," Lithilia replied.

"So?" Kazuk prompted.

"My cover could be blown," she replied. "The last thing I want is to have any of the apprentices showing up. Especially Miryam."

"What's so special about this Miryam?" Kazuk asked.

"Oh, honey," Lithilia said, shaking her head. "Miryam and I go a long way back. Another story for another day."

"I'm really curious why this Miryam scares you so much; but you're not the least afraid of the incarcerated one," Kazuk tried to probe some more.

"And I promise you, I'll tell you eventually," she tried to mask her discomfort with a little firmness in her tone of voice.

"You've been saying that for a very long while now," Kazuk retorted.

"I know and I'm sorry," she replied. "I will fill you in later, please. Okay?"

"As you wish," Kazuk shrugged. "But I still think you should give it a try."

"Give what a try?" Lithilia asked.

"Distracting Patrick, if not eliminating him yourself," Kazuk replied.

Lithilia bit her lower lip as she considered her husband's proposal. The more she did, the more she agreed that it was a risk worth taking.

"The main goal is to eliminate The One, right?" Kazuk asked.

"Yes," Lithilia agreed.

"So, what if you just caused enough distraction, even if it's just to allow Walter to see the mission to completion? Would that still not count as success?"

"It would," she agreed.

"And wouldn't you say it's worth the risk?"

"It certainly is," Lithilia concurred. "Patrick would detect me though-"

"Let him detect you," Kazuk interjected. "That is the whole point of you being a distraction to him. He will not be able to focus on you and Walter at the same time, thereby clearing a path for Walter to take out The One."

"I see your point," Lithilia nodded. "It is certainly worth the risk, and I will do it. I think I may already have a plan in mind."

"And why am I not surprised?" Kazuk smiled broadly.

"Because you know me too well, my love," she replied.

Lithilia stood up from the chair and walked towards the bed. As the chair dematerialized into the floor, her clothes also dematerialized from her body with each step she took. Her naked form slid onto the bed with the grace of a serpent. She turned around and faced her husband with eyes burning with invitation. Kazuk stood up from his chair, which dematerialized into the floor. He summoned his wings as his garments also disappeared. He rose upwards in the air. His naked form stayed in the air for a moment as he gazed down at Lithilia's naked form on the bed with ravenous eyes. Then he glided towards her. She parted her legs to welcome him as his wings wrapped around their bodies.

As Kazuk filled her up, Lithilia remembered the day Father introduced her and her first love to the garden for the first time. She remembered how they played in the stream, how they bonded that day and how it was the most beautiful day in her life. With these thoughts, she could survive the utterly disgusting ordeal of faking love and pleasure to someone she considered a mere pawn in her grand plan. It still truly amazed her how Kazuk, after all this time, could not tell she was so not into him at all. But then, Lithilia had concluded many millennia ago that, no matter the realm or dimension, men were all the same.

They are only as smart as their genitals allow them to be.

***

The Scribe was not going to stick around and watch Lithilia and Kazuk engage in such primitive acts of copulation. He teleported to another realm in another dimension in another manuscript that was too far from *The Soulless Ones* for any creature within Lemuria to even conceive. He had business to attend to and many more catalysts to prepare for his grand plan. Without Kazuk knowing, of course, he had planted the thought of Kazuk meeting with Akasha to end him in Kazuk's mind, The Scribe. During the meeting, he posed as Akasha.

I thought it was going to be a funny joke, The Scribe said. *Despite my extensive sense of humor, laughter is one of the luxuries I never really awarded myself.*

The Scribe rubbed his chin.

Well, first time for everything.

And then, The Scribe did something he had never done while existing as The Scribe. He erupted in wild, derisive laughter, causing over a trillion uninhabited realms to become obliterated and erased from existence.

CHAPTER SIXTEEN

BASIC INTRODUCTIONS

THE SUBCONSCIOUS REALIZATION that the time was way past noon yanked Patrick from deep sleep to sudden alertness. Heat and humidity filled the motel room, thanks to poor air conditioning, lending a new definition to the stale smell of sweat and sex to the room. He could easily charge his chi to render his body and room to optimal temperatures but preferred the aphrodisiac purveyed in the after-smell of baked-up genital juices and sweat. His body glistened with a sheen of sweat and so did Sara's. He could have sworn he had just blinked, but the blink had lasted more than six hours. Sara still lay fast asleep in his arms. He reached for his phone on the nightstand; no missed calls, no messages. When he reached out to return the phone, Sara tightened her grip on his free arm.

Patrick froze in mid-reach, not wanting to wake her up. Instead, he returned the phone on the nightstand using telekinesis.

But why don't I wanna wake her up? he wondered. *Why am I being so nice to her?*

She looked so peaceful, snuggled against his body. He settled back in the bed and gathered her closer to his body. Sara moaned slightly.

Can't believe I'm doing this, he thought.

This violet, bright-eyed, extradimensional stranger posed no threat, yet, but she remained a total mystery.

About last night.

Last night, he sensed and experienced pent-up passion like he had never sensed or experienced from anyone else before, which had nothing to do with the violet sparks that danced between their bodies.

Should I include this in my report? he smiled, knowing the answer to the question.

And now, she's happy? Relieved? At peace? Not sure. Maybe a combo of all that and more.

His nose and lips rested on her occiput. Yet, he ignored the scent of her hair. His mind had more important things to busy itself with.

She's passed out, as if she hasn't had much sleep in a long time.

Patrick caressed her hair and kissed her head softly.

Let her get all the rest she needs. The interrogation will come later, unless she turns all violet evil on me or something.

Sara moaned, turned around to face him and snuggled closer to his body. She wrapped a leg around his and pulled it in between her legs. Her eyes were still closed when she smiled sleepily. She adjusted her head to a more comfortable spot on Patrick's arm. Her smile slowly disappeared as she fell asleep once more. Patrick admitted that her gesture was cute and before he knew it, he was stroking her hair. Still, he remained cautious, but not concerned. In just a few hours, he had developed a deep caring for this beautiful, human-looking stranger.

Before last night, I'd have treated her very differently. Shoot first ask questions later. But I must follow my gut, just as Father taught me. Although if Father finds out, he'll probably have my guts for breakfast.

Patrick smiled a little.

Regardless of what I may think, I can't ignore what I saw, felt and experienced with her last night. Anyway, I'll have answers soon, hopefully.

An hour went by and Sara was still asleep. Patrick wanted to use the restroom. He started slowly sliding his arm from underneath her neck.

"You're not afraid of me," Sara said, her eyes still closed.

"You've been awake?" Patrick asked.

"Just woke up," she replied and snuggled closer to him.

"Okay," he said. "Must use the restroom. Be right back."

Eyes still closed, she kissed him on the lips. He used the opportunity to pull his arm away from underneath her neck. He took care of business and returned a few minutes later. He cracked open the bathroom window, not because he did a Number Two, but because he wanted to allow some fresh air into the room. He slid back into the bed. She snuggled against him again.

"You're not afraid of me, Patrick," she repeated.

Sara still did not open her eyes.

"No, I'm not," Patrick replied.

"Why?" Sara asked. "After everything you saw and everything you felt last night, why aren't you afraid of me?"

"More importantly, who are you, Sara?" Patrick countered.

Sara remained silent for a few seconds.

"I'll answer all your questions," Sara replied. "I promise. But first, if you don't mind, I'd like to ask you some questions. After you answer them, I'll tell you everything you wanna know. Deal?"

"Depends," Patrick replied.

"On?" Sara asked.

"On whether I think you'll tell the truth or not," Patrick replied.

"I'll tell you nothing but the truth, I assure you," Sara promised. "I feel like I can trust you."

Not a good sign, he thought.

"And what makes you think that?" Patrick asked.

"Because, if you're not afraid of me after last night, then you won't be afraid of what I tell you about me," Sara replied calmly.

Logical, he thought.

"Very well, you may ask away," Patrick said.

Sara opened her eyes and sat cross-legged on the bed. Patrick stole a quick moment to appreciate her physique. She pulled her hair back with both hands and her bosom danced with her arm movements. Patrick started hardening again. He quickly switched his mind to naked senior citizens doing mud wrestling, but the hardening continued. He focused his thoughts to his hatred for watermelons. However, the subliminal idea of 'melons' got the better of him. He mustered the strength to peel his gaze from her bosom. Finally, he focused on the mission and that caused an instant deflation.

"Is your real name Patrick?" she asked.

"Yes."

"Are you human?"

"Yes."

"From this world?"

"Yes."

"Are you sure?"

"Yes. I'm just something like an 'upgrade' and by that I mean I've developed a few of my latent abilities," Patrick explained.

Sara nodded.

"Thank you," Sara said. "I believe you. I've never met an 'upgrade' before. First time for everything. Okay, your turn. Ask away."

That was easy, Patrick thought.

"What are you?" Patrick asked.

"I don't know," Sara replied.

"Is Sara your real name?"

"That is the only name I go by; the only name I remember."

"Where are you from?"

"I don't know."

"How old are you?"

"25,798 years."

"JESUS CHRIST," Patrick exclaimed and leaped from the bed, not out of fright, but out of pure shock.

He expected her to say something like 200, 500 or even 2,000. He regained his composure and returned to bed. Sara remained calm and expressionless, despite his reaction.

"I'm sorry," Patrick apologized. "I just didn't expect that number."

"It's okay," Sara replied. "I'm honestly surprised you're still here."

Me too, Patrick wanted to say, but he changed his mind.

Sara managed a sad smile.

"How come?" Patrick asked.

He realized the question was too vague and too broad.

"I mean…" Patrick hesitated. "You know what, why don't you just tell me everything you can?"

"I actually prefer that," Sara replied.

Sara's eyes darkened with sadness. She stared blankly at the sheets.

"Sure you wanna hear it all?" Sara asked.

"Absolutely," Patrick replied.

"As you wish," Sara adjusted her posture. "Just gonna be the basics though. Too many unimportant details stashed in 26,000 years."

"Agreed," said Patrick.

"Oh, hold on a sec, will ya," Sara sprang from the bed.

Sara let out a few expletives as she reached into her bag. Patrick tensed in preparation for any possible attack from her. He relaxed when she whipped out her cell phone and hurriedly tap on the screen a few times. She set the phone on the counter and Patrick could hear a dial tone.

"Come on, come on," Sara said.

After four rings there was a crack, and a male voice that sounded like Conway Twitty on helium burst through the speakers.

"Hello?"

"Hey Joe, it's Sara," she said. "I'm sorry, but I'm gonna be late today. Could you guys go on and take care of stuff before I show up?"

"Sure thang, Sara. You okay though? You sound like you could be comin' down with somethin'," said a slightly concerned Joe.

"I'm fine, thanks," Sara replied. "Just hungry, I think?"

"Come on now, Sara," Joe urged. "I've known you since I was a kid and I can tell when you're lying to me."

"Okay, maybe it's just these damn allergies," Sara lied. "But I promise you,

I'm fine. I'll just be in a little late."

"You know you're entitled to a day off, right?" he pushed on.

Sara turned towards Patrick and rolled her eyes. Patrick chuckled.

"I do, but I'll be there Joe," Sara replied and thought she may have come off as a little rude.

"Okay now, see ya later then," Joe finally said.

"Thanks, Joe. See ya later."

She ended the call and rubbed her temples.

"Looks like someone's got the hots for ya," Patrick said.

Sara smiled at Patrick as she walked back towards the bed.

"Nothing compared what I have – had – for you, Patrick," Sara's cheeks reddened just a tiny bit. "Thanks for last night, by the way. Haven't felt this way in a very, *VERY* long time."

"My pleasure, literally," he replied with a kind smile. "And just out of curiosity, how long are we talking about?"

"25,798 years," Sara replied and grinned.

"Jesus H. Christ," Patrick exclaimed. "You mean you haven't bumped pelvises in twenty-six millennia?"

"Oh God no. That's not what I meant," Sara replied, unable to control her laughter. "If that was the case, then I sure dunno what woulda happened to ma lady parts by now. Probably sealed shut or somethin'."

Sara laughed so hard that tears streamed down her eyes.

"Sorry hon, haven't laughed this hard in a while," she said.

"I'm not gonna ask how long," Patrick chuckled and Sara guffawed.

"Okay, okay," Patrick raised his hands in the air. "I give up."

"Okay, I just meant even though I've had sex, obviously," she sniveled, "I ain't felt this way for as long as I can remember."

Her laughter eased up a little. Patrick nodded his understanding.

"Sorry about earlier. Had to take care of business real quick," Sara added. "After all, I do have a business to run, don't I?"

"Can't even imagine how much money you have right now," Patrick said.

"Nah. You can't," Sara agreed. "So, where was I?"

"The beginning," he replied.

"Yes. The beginning," Sara cracked her knuckles and flexed her shoulders. "I can only remember my life leading up to twenty-six millennia ago. Before that, I have no recollection of who I am or where I'm from."

"No memories at all?" Patrick pressed.

"Absolutely none," Sara confirmed. "Woke up naked, confused and shocked in the middle of a desert, the sun burning my skin and the desert sands showing even lesser mercy. As days turned to weeks and weeks turned to months,, I learned how to survive and adapt. Long story short, I moved around a lot. I started noticing that I was different when after a few decades, I hadn't aged one bit and everyone else around me was aging and dying.

"I've also never been sick," Sara continued. "Not even a cold. Plagues and diseases would wipe out entire communities and I'd be the lone survivor. I've had it all, I've seen it all, and I've lost it all. I've been married several times, but I could never have kids for some reason. Sometimes, the violet light would flash from my eyes or hands. Last night was the first time it ever flashed from my heart. That was when I knew there was something extraordinary about you, Patrick. I don't know what it is and maybe you don't know either but eventually, you will."

"The very first time?" Patrick asked, a little surprised.

He ignored the part about her telling him he was special.

"Yeah, the very first time," Sara confirmed. "I did mean what I said before about last night. So once again, thank you so much, Patrick."

"I'm sorry, it's a little hard for me to understand that with all the options you've had over such a long span of time, that last night wasn't just another sexual experience for you," Patrick explained.

Sara stared at Patrick with the prettiest, most violet-colored eyes Patrick had ever seen. It was the first time he noticed the shade of her eye color and how unique that shade was.

"Last night…" Sara said, and her voice trailed off.

Her violet eyes flickered with sadness, as if a sudden realization of the unhopeful genre dawned on her. However, the flicker of sadness vanished almost as quickly as it came in the manner of an expert reaction borne out of multiple millennia of unwanted and unavoidable practice.

"I mean, you saw it all and felt it all last night," Sara continued. "That was me, unhinged, unapologetic and holding nothing back. That was me letting go and offering you all that I am, the me I know and the me I don't remember, without reservation or fear. And you honored me by accepting my offering to you without fear or reservation."

Her country accent is gone, Patrick noticed.

Patrick opened his mouth to say something, but it closed of its own will. For the first time in his life, he was speechless. His shoulders slumped and in the silence of the situation, he said more than he ever could have said with words. Sara nodded her understanding and her eyes welled up with tears.

"It's okay, and it's also okay that you don't understand," Sara assured him, and a resplendent, sad smile graced her perfect face. "Believe me, I've lived a life with men and women either fearing me eventually or just wanting to bed me. But you were the only one who talked to me like a normal person and you still do not fear me. Even at the bar, you didn't try to make a move on me. I made a move on you. I seduced you instead. You just don't know how wonderful it felt being with you last night, Patrick. I mean it. It wasn't just the sex. I can have sex, great or not-so great, anytime I want. Last night, you brought out a feeling of aliveness and being in me. I was 100% myself."

As Sara spoke, tears of happiness and sadness ran down her cheeks, and a violet glow beamed in her chest, between perky, bigger-than-one-palm breasts. She smiled and touched her chest lightly, as if it were the most fragile thing she had ever touched.

Maybe she literally has a fragile heart? Patrick wondered.

Sara leveled a tear-filled gaze at him and laughed weakly as she sniveled. His clairsentience indicated she was truly happy. A huge burden had come off her shoulders. Just talking to him had made her feel so much lighter and happier. The tears kept rolling down her cheeks as the light in her chest grew even brighter.

Must admit, this is so… beautiful, Patrick thought. *She is so beautiful.*

It was a wonderful feeling to be in the presence of a stranger without a single ounce of aggression or evil in her bones.

These are tears of joy and appreciation for the gift of being that you bestowed upon me in a single night of intimacy with you, he heard Sara's thoughts via clairaudience. *Even if our paths never cross again after this, I'll forever cherish our fleeting encounter for the rest of my days. I wish I could say these words to you, but I fear my words may chase you away.*

Patrick still did not know exactly what he had done. Maybe it was the fact that he chose not to treat her as an impromptu mission or adversary. Maybe it was because he chose to let his humanity dictate his course of action as opposed to his training, for which he was glad he did. It had been a long time since he had seen so much joy and appreciation in one place and it gave him a great sense of accomplishment, even if it was from a single person.

My mind is made up, he steeled his resolve. *I must not reveal what I know about her to Father. Who knows how Father will handle the situation. Sara must be protected.*

Patrick was so lost in his thoughts that he did not realize that she had leaned forward and hugged him around his neck. He adjusted his body and held her waist. She wrapped her legs around him, her naked body pressing against his even more. She sobbed silently against his shoulder. Patrick rubbed her back and stroked her hair softly. He kissed her on the temple.

"It's okay, Sara," Patrick whispered in her ear.

"You're right," Sara agreed amid sobs. "It *IS* okay. Thank you so much."

"You're very welcome, dear," Patrick replied softly.

Patrick held Sara like that for a little while until her sobbing subsided. He did not know what to think anymore and neither did he care. He just held her and let her relish her moment.

"Make love to me, Patrick," Sara pleaded softly.

Patrick obliged. This time the bonding was more passionate than before. This time, more violet streaks of energy fired from every touch and taste. This time, every gyration and thrust flared with sensations deeper and more sensual. This time, her eyes and heart beamed brighter with violet luminescence. Two hours later, they lay in each other's arms, satiated and spent, but none would take a nap. Dusk beckoned and Patrick was still on a mission.

"You here for Donald, ain't ya?" Sara asked, reverting to her country accent.

Patrick said nothing.

"You don't gotta say nothin'," she peeled herself away from him. "Knew there was somethin' 'bout him. I'm guessing he's been around for a year or so 'cause that's right around the same time strange stuff started happening 'round here."

"What do you mean?" Patrick asked.

"Well, it's more like the energy levels around here changed," she explained. "I could tell because… Well, you know."

She's clairsentient, Patrick remarked. *Does she know?*

"I understand," Patrick replied and sat upright on the bed. "Yes, I'm here for him, but not to harm him."

"I know," Sara said. "He tells everyone he's from Texas and all that, but I don't buy it. Everyone else does though, but not me. His color is also different. Unlike anything I've ever seen."

Clairvoyant, Patrick furrowed his eyebrows. *What else is she? Clairaudient?*

"He may be in danger and that's why I'm here," he said. "To protect him."

"He has the same countenance I had when I found myself in the middle of nowhere," Sara continued. "He has also lost his memory and his Texas story is just a cover story to keep the nosy folks at bay. That's my best guess and my gut tells me I'm right."

"I see," Patrick said. "Thanks for the heads up."

"You're welcome," Sara smiled. "Well, guess we better get on with business."

Patrick got up from the bed and walked towards the bathroom. He relieved his bladder of its contents, flushed the toilet, washed his hands and then stood by the door. He regarded Sara for a moment as she lay naked across the bed. She returned his calm stare.

"Please don't let anything happen to him," Sara pleaded. "He's a good man, whatever he is. May be one of the very few good men this town has left. Plus, I could use a friend in these parts."

"I'll do my best," Patrick replied. "Just stay at home tonight when you close the bar. Do not come outside for any reason. It may get a little nasty later. Okay?"

"Aye aye, sir," Sara exclaimed.

Patrick smiled at her cuteness. Sara stood up from the bed and clapped her heels. Her breasts bounced in unison as she did, and she added a salute.

"Sir, permission to join you in the shower, sir," she said.

"Permission granted," Patrick played along.

Sara beamed like a child and joined him in the shower. They emerged from the shower an hour later all fresh, clean and ready to take on the rest of the day.

A few hours later, Patrick peeled himself from the motel bed. He had taken a nap after his shower. Sara had insisted on making the bed as he got dressed and talked to the other agents. Their numbers had been increased from 6 to 14, and they kept a constant eye on Mr. Weinberg's house. Solara had already disappeared over the horizon when Sara returned to the bar after making a pit stop at her house to put some clothes and makeup on. Patrick glanced at his phone one more time and, satisfied that the battery was 97% charged, he unplugged it from the charger and slid it into his right jean pocket. He scooped up his watch and snapped the clasps shut after it made its way past his left wrist.

"No fedora tonight," he said. "Don't want to mess it up with Sinister goo and guts. Those orange critters won't go down without a fight, especially that so-called 'secret weapon'."

Patrick scoffed.

"Secret weapon. We'll see if you live up to your reputation."

He scooped up his keys from the dresser in one hand and, in the same fluid motion, he swung his black leather jacket that was placed on the only chair in the room over his shoulders.

"I don't like this design," he said and sparked the ethers of his leather jacket into a different design.

"There."

He adjusted the jacket over his shoulders as he walked out of the door, down the stairs and towards his car. As Patrick drove off into the night, he was oblivious to the fact that he had just walked past a room that harbored a human-sinister hybrid and deadly enemy by the name of Walter Peabody.

CHAPTER SEVENTEEN

STANDOFF

WALTER STARED BLANKLY out his window. He had some time to kill before he embarked on his mission. He considered commingling with the townsfolk but decided it was best to keep the lowest profile possible, especially if things got nasty out there. He twirled his favorite whiskey in his glass. The rest of the bottle, which he brought with him, sat atop the night stand. His research suggested a total lack of quality liquor in this dump of a town. Ever since the queen gave him a new life and purpose, his world had changed. He was stronger, more confident and most importantly his bank account was fatter than he could ever have imagined. The girls came easily, life was good, and all he had to do was be the queen's bitch. A remnant of his humanity still writhed and rebelled occasionally. But thank the skies, and the queen, for liquor and ladies. No drugs, though. Never. None needed. Life was a high by itself. He took another sip and continued staring out into the night.

An average-looking guy with an above average persona, as per Walter, walked past his window. Nothing stuck out more prominently than a strong, black guy in a tiny town dominated by white folks, sporting expensive clothing, an even more expensive watch and driving a rental with out-of-state license plates.

"You must be the famous Patrick the queen warned me about," he chuckled derisively. "Not sure if your being flashier than a neon sign in Vegas was just you being careless or over-confident."

He sipped some more whiskey.

"Doesn't matter, anyway," he added. "Tonight, you'll die with the rest of your boys. I'll save you for last, just because."

Walter had his doubts when the queen told him that he could not be detected by the organization. Patrick walking past him just now without any hint of recognition or awareness of his presence confirmed what the queen told him.

"I'm going to enjoy myself tonight," Walter finished his drink, which caressed his gullet like life-giving water.

He shivered involuntarily and not because he was cold. Far from it. His body tingled with excitement and anticipation for an assignment worthy of his status: agents of the organization, a fallen angel and Patrick. Walter closed his eyes. His raging thoughts eased up and his mind drifted into the past.

The night he was transformed; the night he experienced the ultimate pleasure, death and rebirth all at once, was baptism of the esoteric kind. In his ultimate pleasure was his death and out of his death, he had been reborn. His new self awoke and stared into the eyes of the queen as they burned with a bright orange hue. Something within him that he could feel, but was not a part of his physical body, seared and pained like he had never imagined. Innately, he recognized the searing was of his soul and his very soul was being scorched to submission as the flames of the sinister life flooded his being from the queen's mouth into his.

A kiss of death and life all at once.

His old self plunged into a dark nothingness and a new self waking up to a burst of orange brightness. He died a human and was reborn a Sinister.

He called her 'mother,' but she gave him a stern, one-time warning never to desecrate her status thusly again. Only one could call her that. Every other sinister was to address her as 'queen.' Over the next year, she personally furthered the transmutation of his new being to render him imperceptible to the organization's sinister sensors. She could scorch his soul, which she did too many times for him to remember, but she could not render him soulless. Thus, she bruised his soul repeatedly to near-soullessness. He experienced different levels of pain that he could only wish on his worst enemies. Yet, he endured everything with honor, pride and loyalty to the sinister cause.

"And here I am, tasked with this special mission," he said. "This is my time to shine and rise above my peers. My promotion beckons. Who knows, maybe I can even be consort to the queen."

A mischievous grin spread across Walter's face before he peeled his gaze away from the window and headed for the nightstand. He poured himself some more divine liquid.

"Tonight, the angel and Patrick die," he swallowed the contents of his glass in one swig. "Tonight, I will not fail my queen."

Patrick sat at the bar and sipped on a beer. Sara and her staff were busy tending to the tipsy, the drunk and the horny as usual. Two O.R. agents comingled with two girls who were looking for an interested party to pay for their drinks and flirt with them. If Donald showed up, they would tail him all the way home, and Patrick would provide any form of backup if needed. He entertained the approaches of some girls, but only long enough to indicate to them that he was not interested in buying them drinks or sleeping with them. Out of the corner of his eye, he caught Sara eyeing him with intense amusement and clairsentience revealed no jealousy or sinisters for that matter.

Good, he thought. *So far.*

Two girls flanked him at the bar.

"Say, mister," one of them cooed and batted her eyes at him. "Why you sitting here all by yaself?"

"Girlfriend ditched ya?" the other teased.

"No reason, ladies," Patrick replied and sipped on his beer.

"Is that right?" asked the first one rhetorically.

"I think he could use some company, Cindy," said the second girl.

"I think so too, Mandy."

Porn star names, Patrick thought and flashed a fake smile. *How cliché.*

"What da hell," he shrugged with resignation. "Can't say no to two fine gals like you now, can I? Barkeep."

He signaled at Sara. Sara approached them.

"Whatever the ladies want," he gestured at Cindy and Mandy.

Fifteen minutes later, Cindy and Mandy were still talking his ear off. Normally, their behavior would stir his loins. He could think of a few pleasurable ways to shut them up; but not tonight.

No interest, he said to himself. *None at all and Sara has nothing to do with it. Tonight is all business.*

"And this one time, Cindy and I was…"

Patrick tuned them out. When they laughed, he faked a laugh as well and when they regarded him as if they expected him to agree with whatever they said, he nodded and chuckled a little. Sometimes, he used words like 'absolutely', 'no way', 'really' and so on.

Although, she's the kind of girl I'd want as a girlfriend, Patrick thought. *If I were to have a girlfriend. That age, though. Anyway, at this point, she's too old for anyone, though she could easily pass for someone in her early 30's.*

Patrick let out an expletive and his phone vibrated in his pocket.

"What's the matter, big guy," Mandy slurred slightly.

Four bottles of beer and a shot will do that to a light weight alcohol consumer.

Patrick reached into his left jacket pocket.

I just sent a personal record, Patrick exclaimed in his head. *I banged a 26,000-year-*

old chick.

"'Scuse me, ladies," Patrick said and reached for his phone.

"What's up boss…? Nah, just having a little bit of fun with two lovely ladies over here…" he spoke on the phone.

"Hi, boss," screamed Mandy into the mouthpiece.

Patrick pulled away from them smiling as they giggled away.

"Yeah… Okay… Maybe in two days… What was that? Okay, that sounds great… Later then, and good night," he said.

Patrick ended the call and returned to his seat.

The first agent understood the message and left to use the restroom. He never re-emerged from it. The second agent finished his drink and asked his companion to walk with him to his car. She obliged with a mischievous grin. Patrick focused his clairaudience on them.

"How about I drop you off at your place, since you don't wanna join me at my motel room?" said the agent.

"Fine by me," she said. "Sorry, don't go with no strangers to no motel. You comin' to ma place tonight."

"Yes, ma'am."

They left the bar.

"Sorry, ladies," Patrick said. "Got some business to take care of."

Cindy and Mandy whined in perfect harmony.

"But the night's still young," Mandy made a face.

"Tell y'all what," Patrick whipped out his wallet and fished out a $50 bill. "Go to the motel and get us a room. I'll join you ladies in about an hour."

"Promise?" they chorused together.

"Cross ma heart and hope to die," Patrick lied.

"Alright, see ya soon big guy," they blew him a kiss and headed for the door.

Patrick waited four minutes before he slid two $100 bills across the bar, which was a lot more than what he owed. Sara swiped the bills and stashed them in the register. A look of worry creased her face.

"I'm worried about Donald," she said via telepathy.

Great, she's also a telepath, Patrick sighed.

"Donald will be fine," he replied telepathically. *"I'll keep him safe, don't worry."*

"I know," she said. *"I'm also afraid of what you may have to do to ensure he's safe."*

"That's very sweet, Sara," Patrick said as he headed for the door. *"See you later."*

Patrick slid into his rental and started the engine. Two girls approached the car and stopped in front of it.

"Thought you could get rid of us that easily?" Mandy cocked an eyebrow.

Cindy wagged a finger at him.

Patrick let out an expletive before he rolled down the window.

"So, y'all just gonna stand there all night?" Patrick asked.

Mandy and Cindy giggled with drunken glee and slid into the car, Cindy in the front and Mandy in the back. Cindy immediately reached for his zipper.

Not going to fight this, Patrick sighed.

They arrived at the motel and Patrick booked another room on the ground floor. He guided the drunken duo into the room. They immediately pounced on him. As the three engaged in foreplay, Patrick suddenly applied pressure on a specific nerve on the back of their necks. Both girls instantly passed out in his arms. He tucked them in bed, walked out of the room, closed the door, got into the car and hit the road. Mr. Weinberg's house was eight miles away from the motel according to the navigation. Four miles later, a pretty lady stood idly in the middle of the road. She wore a pair of black, tight-fitting pants, a black blouse, and a black leather jacket. She also had on a pair of black boots and her thick black hair was pulled back in a tight bun. She was as beautiful as she was evil and Patrick knew exactly who she was even before her eyes glowed orange.

"Lithilia," he grinned evilly. "Finally, we meet."

Patrick gunned the engine, but the woman did not move. He drove the car right through her as if she were made of air. He hit the brakes and quickly parked the car on the side of the road. He zipped out of the car and charged towards her. She charged at him as well. His punched whizzed over her head as she ducked and her uppercut whooshed towards his solar plexus in a counterattack. He angled his hips to the right, just enough for her punch to brush his jacket and miss its mark. He followed his swing with a left knee towards her kidney, but she sank her hips lower and connected her elbow into his left, floating ribs.

She added a knuckle punch straight into the bridge of his nose, faster than the sound of his broken lower ribs reaching his ear and completed her turn with a straight sucker-punch into his left jaw. Patrick's jaw came apart with a loud pop and he crashed into the ground a few feet away. He executed a backward roll to absorb his fall, while he instantly healed his ribs, nose and jaw with supercharged chi. An orange streak accelerated towards him and he shot his left foot upwards as he did a second backward roll. His left foot connected with her chin and sent her sailing seven feet into the air. She landed into the ground, rolled and crouched immediately, waiting for another attack.

"Pleased to finally meet your acquaintance, Lilith," Patrick stood up.

"The feeling is not mutual, Patrick," Lithilia glowered.

"You really don't like that name, do you?" Patrick grinned and leaned forward. "Lilith."

Lithilia let out a scream of fury, rolled forward and blazed towards him. Patrick side-stepped and drove his right knee into her temple. Her head snapped sideways, her cervical vertebrae came apart, breaking her neck without severing her spine. Lithilia healed herself before she rolled several times on the asphalt under the force of Patrick's blow. Patrick was on top of her before she assumed battle stance. He grabbed her by the hair and slammed her face into the tarmac with extreme prejudice over a hundred times within a few seconds. Then, his phone vibrated in his pocket.

Something's not right, his gut tightened to the feeling of unwelcome tidings.

He let go of Lithilia's hair and stood up.

"Kill you later, Lilith," Patrick straightened his jacket.

He turned his back to her and made to teleport. However, out of the corner of his eye, an orange form glared in the darkness of the night. Within less than a thousandth of a microsecond, Patrick realized his mistake and prepared himself for a brutal, if not fatal, attack. However, nothing happened. Instead, a brighter violet brilliance smothered Lithilia's orange glow. He slowly turned around and a smile of gratitude spread across his face.

Sara stood tall as an embodiment of purple light, with an outstretched right hand. She neither glowed nor flamed up. Her entire form was luminescent and glorious. A sphere of purple light hovered in the air and within that sphere, the orange-glowing body of Lithilia writhed and raged, and in her hand, a smoldering dagger. Patrick swallowed.

That's no normal dagger, he thought.

He returned his attention towards Sara.

"I owe you, Sara," said Patrick telepathically.

"Thank me later, my friend," she replied in like manner. *"Go check on your friends. I'll deal with this creature myself."*

"No, you will not," Lilith screamed and engulfed herself in an orange ball of light, which disappeared as quickly as it had appeared.

Lithilia was nowhere to be found.

Sara and Patrick stared at each other for a moment. She lowered her hand.

"Hurry now," Sara yelled to him telepathically. *"Your friends need you."*

Patrick teleported towards Newman's house.

Walter blended with the darkness. He had already eliminated two O.R. agents half a mile south of Newman's house. He half-jogged towards the house. He hid behind a house and scanned the area some more. He noticed two other agents on the west corner of Newman's house. Each faced a different direction.

Poor formation, he thought. *Makes my job easier.*

He moved in closer towards them.

Pathetic, he smiled with conceit. *Expected a real challenge. Nothing so far.*

Walter Peabody shook his head in disappointment and approached his targets. One of the agents raised a walkie-talkie to his mouth and spoke into it.

The agent waited for a second and then raised the device to his mouth again. Then, the agent raised it one more time to his mouth, talked some more into the device before he returned it to his pocket and pulled out a cell phone.

Walter let out an expletive when he realized his mistake.

According to what another mole had told them, the O.R. had set up a monitoring system around Mr. Weinberg's house to detect any 'outer-worldly' presence. Walter could hide behind the camouflage of his vestigial humanity. To teleport or zip, he would have to shift to his more Sinister form, which would trigger an alarm.

Can't let that happen, he said to himself. *Can't even open up portals.*

Basically, anything that changed the energy field anywhere near any of the detectors would set off an alarm. That was why sinisters were easily picked off one by one when they created and emerged from portals.

The agents of the organization were good, but their mistake was their reliance on the monitoring systems instead of relying on their training. Walter made them pay dearly for this mistake by taking them out one by one as he made his way towards Newman's residence with the kind of stealth that would make a ninja master puff with pride. However, he too became sloppy with overconfidence. He had taken too much time and his stupid pride cost him the element of surprise, which was his biggest advantage yet.

"Time to speed things up," Walter muttered.

The agent with the cell phone raised an alert when two of his comrades did not respond. The agent then tried to call Patrick, but even Patrick did not respond. Walter moved with the speed of a cheetah doing a 50m dash. Within half a minute, four more agents had been decapitated and a fifth had almost lost an arm, thanks to Walter tripping over a rock when he was going for the agent's neck. Yet, as quickly as Walter hit the ground, he was back on his feet and charged at the agent and the agent's comrade. They fired shots in rapid successions from their silenced handguns, but the bullets neither stopped nor slowed Walter. The wounded agent pulled his knife and stood his ground, ignoring his friend's call for him to move to safety.

"We stand our ground against evil," the wounded agent gritted his teeth.

He staggered from the pain but his resolve was titanium-strong.

"To the death," his comrade chimed in and pulled out a dagger as well.

"How noble," Walter smirked. "For your courage, I'll make it quick."

"Hey," a voice called from behind him.

Walter stopped and turned around slowly to see a figure standing in the full glow of the moonlight.

"Yeah, freak show," Patrick said. "I'm talking to you."

"Ah, you must be the famous Patrick," Walter mocked. "Finally, maybe I'll have some real competition. A real fight…"

"Get him out of here," Patrick ordered the unharmed agent.

The unharmed agent obliged and escorted his wounded comrade away.

"The queen told me about you," Walter sneered as he circled Patrick.

"You mean the bitch I just iced down the street?" Patrick asked. "Lilith, right? That was your queen? Oops. Sorry, but not sorry."

"You wish you did. You won't even last a second in her presence, let alone her might," Walter scoffed.

"Was that how long you lasted when she was riding that tiny English dick of yours?" Patrick taunted in a perfectly mastered British accent. "After all, isn't that all she's good for? Sucking and riding dicks?"

"If only you knew," Walter replied, still circling Patrick who did not move from his position. "And to think of such blasphemy, claiming you 'iced' her."

"Think what you want, but what happened, happened," Patrick rebutted.

"I'd love to keep chatting," Walter lied. "But I have a fallen angel to kill."

Walter zipped towards Newman's house, tossing discretion to the wind. But Patrick teleported and appeared in front of him. He delivered a right, downward punch into Walter's left jaw as he appeared. Walter crashed face-first into the ground and Patrick added a harsh kick into his floating ribs for good measure. Walter slid about ten feet away from the door, crouched and zipped again. Patrick read Walter's zip trajectory and zipped as well. When he was close enough to Walter, he teleported both Walter and himself eight miles away from Newman's house. The activities around the house triggered multiple alarms, and though the agents knew Patrick would take care of Walter, they zeroed in on the house regardless, just in case.

Walter's raged with mounting frustration. He had grossly underestimated Patrick. The many briefings he had received about Patrick did not mention that Patrick could teleport; but maybe no one actually knew that he could.

"You know, we could do this all night," Patrick mocked. "I've got nothing but time. Can't say the same for you though."

"Is your ego as big as your mouth?" Walter scoffed.

"Look who's talking about ego," Patrick took a step forward.

Walter backed away.

"You know it's rude to walk away from a conversation," Patrick smirked. "I thought you British cats were all about politeness. Or did the bitch also ride your manners away?"

Walter's skin color started turning into orange, the color of a Sinister.

"Does 'ball of orange light' for a hot bitch mean anything to you?" Patrick taunted further.

Walter winced a little and Patrick grinned with evil delight.

"Yep, that's right," Patrick said. "That slut-bitch exploded in an orange ball of light right before I drove this-" he sparked a katana from the ethers and it manifested in his right hand- "into what passes for her heart."

If Walter was furious before, he never showed it. But even in the darkness, Patrick's clairsentience indicated that he had struck a raw nerve with Walter and clairvoyance showed the color of Walter's aura changing from dark orange to blood red.

"And now, you pay," Walter attacked.

Walter gave all he had and more. Patrick toyed with him briefly. His next move saw to the cleaving of Walter's sword-bearing hand. He watched with sadistic delight as Walter squealed like a pig. Next came interrogations. Whenever Walter proved to be headstrong, Walter lost a part of a limb.

"Your friends died begging for mercy," a nearly toothless Walter said with unapologetic scorn.

Patrick took a deep breath to calm his raging emotions.

"I'll keep you alive until I decide you're of no further use to me," Patrick spat and resumed his interrogations.

An hour later, a squirming, bleeding, limbless, toothless, eyeless, no-genital Walter mumbled his plea for mercy as Patrick set what remained of Walter's body ablaze with fires he sparked from the ethers. He cut Walter's throat and Walter's screams turned into incoherent gurgling as he slowly drowned in his own blood, while he burned slowly from inside out. Seven minutes of unimaginable pain later, Patrick sparked the ethers into a katana and severed Walter's head.

"Sinister threat neutralized, boss," he reported via telepathy. *"Sinister knew nothing of value."*

"Excellent work, son," Shi'mon replied in kind.

"Father, I think this fallen angel is costing us too many of our brothers," Patrick tried to contain the anger that bubbled within his soul for the loss of his friends.

"I agree, we can't afford any more losses," Shi'mon said.

"I can have a little chat with Mr. Weinberg first thing tomorrow when he's alone," Patrick suggested. *"He must know something about Donald that we don't."*

Silence lingered between mentor and mentee as Patrick waited for his boss' response.

"Show no restraint," Shi'mon ordered. *"Do what you must. Those are your new orders. This fallen angel must return whence he came."*

THE END OF PART TWO

PART THREE

THE BOOK FOR THE FALLEN

CREATURES OF CELESTIA! Heed to the dictum of The Logos!

And it shall come to pass that all angels and archangels in the Realm of Celestia shall be free to fall to a realm in a dimension of lower vibrational frequency than that of yours. It shall come to pass that in your fall, you shall address the situation that is your polarization. In your fall, you will forget who you are and whence you came. Your identity as a creature from the Realm of Celestia will elude you, and it will be your responsibility to remember. This will be an esoteric amnesia.

And it shall come to pass that none other from the Dimension of Lemuria shall interfere with the sojourn of another who has fallen. Heed to this warning, you creatures of Lemuria! For your sake, do not undermine this warning! Not only will you instantly cause the fallen one to rise again and align to the light by default, but you will incur the very wrath of The Logos upon yourself! You have been warned!

When Malichiel finished transcribing the message, he rushed at once to his good friend, Michael, and showed him. This was the fourth message from The Logos. Michael read the message over and over and summoned his inner circle. He shared the transcription with them. Uriel was late, which was unusual for her, but she quickly caught up with everyone.

"At least," Uriel said when she finished reading the transcription, "we now know that The One and the rest of our brethren who choose to fall, will definitely not be interfered with."

The inner council nodded their agreement, while Michael eyed Uriel in a way he had never done before; with suspicion.

CHAPTER EIGHTEEN

START TALKING

LITHILIA SCREAMED WITH maniacal rage in her domain in Hell. She repeatedly summoned and smashed furniture and breakable items to smithereens and splinters against the walls of her domain using telekinesis, the sounds of which neither soothed nor abated her fury. Staccatos of expletives fired from her lips. Her face and body shapeshifted into those of a variety of creatures she had encountered and even been intimate with on many of the realms and dimensions she had visited. How could any creature make her feel so useless and powerless? Worst of all, that arrogant buffoon called Patrick matched her in hand-to-hand combat! Damn it! But even as she directed her frustration and humiliation towards everything else but herself, she realized that her impromptu plan to be a distraction to Patrick was just that; an impromptu plan. As such, in her arrogance, she had underestimated her opponent. More expletives, curses and screams fired from her lips and many more pieces and breakable items appeared and shattered under the force of her will.

"Patrick," she screamed and bared her fangs. "Damn you. Damn you, Damn you, you-"

Another round of expletives followed her outburst. She raged for many more minutes until finally, she summoned a chair and sank into it.

"That arrogant piece of-"

More expletives followed. Her anger began to ease, followed by a moment of reflection and analysis.

What the name of Hell Realm went wrong? she asked herself.

She closed her eyes for a second.

I underestimated him, despite his reputation.

Her face shapeshifted into that of a black-and-green reptilian creature with three horns and no earlobes, which she encountered in a realm in a dimension one level above Solara, Earth Realm's dimension. Her hatred for these creatures burned with searing passion, mainly because her powers of seduction proved most ineffective on them. No copulation meant she could not steal their essence and add to her collection of essences. She shapeshifted her face back to normal after a few seconds.

In my defense, I didn't expect that brat to have help and, speaking of help, who is she?

Lithilia sat up and rested her elbows on her thighs.

It is definitely a 'she' and her esoteric signature is unlike anything I've ever heard of or encountered. I couldn't do anything against her. Had to use that one-time spell Anuck of Muebong Realm gave me. Damn it.

Lithilia clenched and unclenched her fist and gritted her teeth.

And I can't get that spell back. Anuck will definitely not welcome me back with open arms after the way I scissored her and scrammed.

Lithilia sighed, though she did not need to. Her Earth Realm tendencies still followed her wherever she went.

Who and what is she? How did Patrick have her on his side? Is she with the organization?

Lithilia tapped and index finger on her chin.

I'll get to the bottom of this.

"I take it your mission did not go so well?" Kazuk asked from the doorway.

Lithilia was too engrossed in her thoughts to notice her husband's presence.

"How long have you been standing there?" Lithilia asked.

"Long enough," he replied calmly and walked into the domain.

"Have you come to gloat?" Lithilia smirked.

"What do you think?" was his reply.

"What are you waiting for then?" she snapped at him. "Let's hear it."

"You do realize that transferring your aggression on me will not change the fact that what happened, happened, right?" Kazuk said calmly.

"Oh, I see what you're doing," Lithilia wagged a finger at him. "You're just getting back at me for what I did to you earlier, aren't you?"

"So, you're saying you weren't being genuine earlier about being supportive," Kazuk stated.

Lithilia realized her mistake and regretted it.

"I'm sorry, I-" she started apologizing, but Kazuk cut her off.

"I'm not going to lose any energy on that," he dismissed her apology with the wave of a hand. "But if you'd prefer I leave you alone, I can do that."

Lithilia paused for a moment and took a few breaths. She raised her gaze to meet his.

"I'm truly sorry, my love," she spoke genuinely. "My behavior was childish.

Please forgive me. And I'd like you to stay… Please."

"I accept your apology," Kazuk replied.

He summoned a chair, sat down and crossed his legs. Lithilia stood up, folded her arms and bowed her head in thought. Kazuk opened his arms in a gesture of invitation. Lithilia smiled weakly and walked into his open arms. She cuddled against him and he gently caressed her hair. Lithilia closed her eyes, relaxed and her fiery emotions quieted.

"Would you like to tell me what happened?" Kazuk asked.

"Too humiliating," Lithilia replied.

"I understand," Kazuk said. 'Still, I would like to know."

"First, it was Patrick," Lithilia exclaimed.

Her voice rose with the return of her anger.

"What about him?" Kazuk asked calmly.

"His insolence. He thinks he's Creation's gift to humanity," she hissed. "I know he's really good, but the ego on that man."

"Did he beat you in hand-to-hand combat?" her husband asked.

"We were almost evenly matched," Lithilia lied.

"Did you use any spells on him?" Kazuk asked.

"Would've been too easy," Lithilia sat upright on his lap. "I wanted to beat him at his own game, in his own territory, on his own terms. But he had help."

"Help?" Kazuk narrowed his eyes with curiosity.

"Yes," she affirmed, "from some creature bathed in violet flames. The thing is, I never saw or sensed her coming. Worse, I was powerless against her. Only when she showed up was I forced to use a spell to protect and save myself."

Kazuk rubbed his chin pensively. Then he lowered his hand to the armrest.

"I wonder what kind of creature this could have been…" he said more to himself than to Lithilia. "Violet flames…"

"And I was powerless against her," Lithilia added.

Kazuk's pensive look lingered.

"My guess is that given what you can do," Kazuk said, "she must be from a much higher dimension than ours to be able to render you powerless."

"But what *IS* she?" Lithilia insisted. "That's what I really want to know; what she is and where she's from."

"We could do some digging," Kazuk offered. "Maybe we could contact The Scribe or Akasha."

"I think we could, but I'd prefer we do this ourselves," she suggested.

Kazuk agreed.

"And your secret weapon?" Kazuk asked, referring to Walter.

"He was expendable, anyway," Lithilia replied dismissively. "It would've been nice if he had succeeded before he got iced though."

"True," Kazuk agreed. "So, what next? Dispatch more sinisters? Carry out an all-out overt attack?"

"That violet, flaming creature is there," she snapped with frustration at his seeming lack of appreciation for the situation. "And if I couldn't do anything to her, do you think the Sinisters stand any chance against her? Numbers or not?"

"I see," Kazuk conceded. "So, what's the plan now?"

"We wait," Lithilia answered. "And hope The One joins our cause whenever he awakens. We can't afford to make things easier for the other side."

"Alright then," Kazuk said.

"And if he does, are you ready to give up your position as King of Hell?"

"From what I understand, if The One does come over to our side, I won't have a choice, would I?" Kazuk replied.

Lithilia shook her head, lay back in his arms and closed her eyes.

***

Patrick sat in his rental a quarter of a mile from Newman's house. He glanced at his watch and back at Newman's house for the millionth time. Close to midday and neither Donald nor Newman had left the house. If Newman left the house, he would tail Newman and catch up with him. If Donald left the house, even better. He ached for that face-to-face conversation with Newman. His blood still boiled from the loss of his fellow brothers.

"All because of that damned angel," Patrick fumed. "Their deaths better be for an actual greater good or so help me God, someone will have to pay."

Patrick breathed in and out slowly to calm his nerves; not much success.

The front door to Newman's house finally opened and Donald strode out, dressed in a tucked-in red and black flannel shirt and a pair of nut-hugging, sperm-killing jeans. His brown boots glistened in the sun. His keys dangled from his left hand as he headed towards one of Newman's pickup trucks. He was about to back out of the compound when Newman came running out of the house, waving at him and saying something Patrick could neither hear nor interpret. The truck stopped and Newman approached the driver window. Patrick enhanced his hearing to the point that he could hear an ant crawling on Newman's rooftop.

"Nothing important," Patrick said. "Just an overprotective, fatherly man."

Newman returned to his front porch, turned around and watched Donald back out of the driveway and hit the road. When Newman entered his house and closed the door, Patrick exited his rental and headed for Newman's house. He pressed the doorbell and waited.

"Keep calm now," he muttered to himself.

The door opened and the surprised face of Newman peered through the glass partition.

"Can I help you, son?" Newman asked.

"Yes, you can, Mr. Weinberg and I'll make this simple," Patrick replied.

Newman narrowed his eyes and his features tightened

"Okay…," Newman said.

"I wanna talk about the fallen angel who lives with you," Patrick said a matter-of-factly.

Newman turned as pale as a ghost, much to Patrick's satisfaction.

"I don't know what you're talking about," Newman lied and made to shut the door. "You best be on your way now, son, before I call the cops."

Newman closed the door and locked all the latches and locks on the door. He turned around to head upstairs but instead, he almost collided with Patrick standing behind him.

"This conversation ain't over, old man," Patrick loomed menacingly over the senior citizen.

Patrick was pleased to see that Newman was petrified with fear.

"H- how…" Newman stammered and swallowed, petrified with confusion and morbid dread.

"You're housing a fallen angel and a little teleportation scares you?" Patrick asked. "Come on now, old man. Just wanna talk."

Newman wanted to make a quick dash up the stairs to retrieve his rifle.

"Look here, old man, really think you can run faster than me?" Patrick asked. "For God's sake, I just popped up in your living room. Shouldn't that ring some kind of bell in that old head of yours?"

Newman froze mid-stride as Patrick turned around to face him.

"Please, sit," Patrick ordered. "One more stupid move and you won't like what Imma do to you. And yes, I will hurt you; pretty badly, if I have to. Up to you how you wanna do this."

Patrick waited for Newman to comply, but Newman remained frozen in place.

"I said SIT," Patrick yelled.

Newman readily complied.

Patrick pulled up a chair and placed it a few feet in front of Newman. He whipped out his phone from his pocket, scrolled through some apps and tapped on what he was looking for. He handed the phone to Newman, who took it with trembling hands.

"Press 'PLAY'," he ordered.

Newman swallowed nervously and did as he was told.

"Dear God," he exclaimed in horror and more color drained from his face.

In the video, two men lurked in the shadows, watching over a house that looked like his. Suddenly, a circular burst of light, like a portal in one of those fantasy movies, appeared and three creatures that looked like humans with orange skin jumped out of the portal. The two men attacked the creatures and killed all three of them with the expertise of well-trained assassins. But in the process, one of the creatures had dealt a fatal blow to one of the humans, and he eventually died. The video stopped and Newman returned the phone to Patrick. His skin looked more wrinkly and his body trembled visibly.

"We call those creatures 'Sinisters' and those two men, Kim and Juan, are my good friends," Patrick said, returning his cell phone to his pocket. "Well, Kim is dead now. And yes, the house in the video is your house."

"But...," Newman tried to speak, but no other words came out.

"What you saw in the video has been going on for a while now. Ever since the angel showed up in your backyard. The sinisters came to kill him, and many of my brothers have died trying to protect him and consequently you." Patrick spoke with ice and anger in his voice. "Do you understand what I'm saying so far, old man?"

"Yes," Newman replied weakly and swallowed.

"Good, and now, before I lose my cool, you will tell me every single thing you know about this angel or so help me God I'll send you to join my fallen brothers," Patrick assured Newman.

Patrick spoke with unremorseful, unapologetic promise and assurance for the consequences that would follow an unsatisfactory compliance on Newman's part.

"I don't know anything..." Newman lied.

Before he finished his lie, Patrick sparked the ethers into a small knife in his right hand and threw it between Newman's legs. The knife stuck dangerously close to Newman's testicles, eliciting a yelp and recoil from Newman.

"Listen, old man," Patrick continued and made the knife disappear. "It doesn't have to come to this. I know you're lying. I can read your mind and hear your thoughts, literally. You don't want to test me again. At least, for the sake of those who have given their lives to protect you and that freaking guest of yours, tell me everything you know about the fallen angel."

Newman swallowed and stifled a whimper.

"Today, old man," Patrick yelled.

Newman leaped in his seat.

"I haven't told him yet," Newman replied, his body still trembling visibly.

"And you think I don't know that?" Patrick asked rhetorically. "I know he doesn't remember anything before his fall and you haven't told him anything either. What I'm asking is for you to tell me what you haven't told him yet. Can you do that without me making you?"

Patrick sparked the ethers into a double-edged, serrated dagger.

Newman's body stiffened with fright. Patrick leaned forward and glowered.

How did he do that? Newman wondered. *He just made that thing appear out of thin air like magic. Is he even human? He's not human. No, he's not.*

"My patience runs thin, old man," he warned.

Newman jumped on his seat and recoiled.

"Please, sir," Newman swallowed. "Just… put that thing away and I'll tell you everything you wanna know."

Patrick held the dagger a moment longer before he dismissed it.

"Start talking," Patrick ordered.

"There may not be enough time-" Newman started saying

"Then quit stalling," Patrick barked.

Newman heaved a sigh and started narrating the events of the night of the fall. Patrick asked many questions and Newman answered as many as he could. Forty-five minutes later, Patrick rose from his seat to leave. Much remained for him to assess. He may not want to overwhelm the angel suddenly because, after all, the old man could be right. What if this fallen angel's agenda was not one that would benefit mankind? Regardless, this fallen angel's memory has to be restored.

And how do I do that? he wondered. *What happens after he regains his lost memory?*

. The O.R. had no experience or standard operating procedures on dealing with fallen angels, but there is a first time for everything.

We'll just have to pray for the best and prepare for the worst, Patrick teleported to his car, started it and drove into town to stalk Donald.

***

Donald made a stop at the gas station on his way home. As he was pumping gas, a car pulled up on the other side of the gas pumps. A few seconds later, a gleeful, smiling little girl, jumped out of the car and ran towards Donald. Donald smiled back. He picked up the six-year-old, threw her in the air and caught her on her way down. He repeated the gesture four more times and each time the little girl screamed with pure joy. Her parents smiled at the playful pair. Donald cradled her on his hip, and she wrapped her arms around his shoulders as he walked back towards her parents.

"How is my little angel doing?" he asked her.

"No, *YOU'RE* the angel, Mr. Donald," she replied and turned to face her parents. "Mommy, daddy, don't you guys see his wings?" she stabbed at the air above Donald's shoulders. "They go all the way from there to there."

Donald shook hands and exchanged brief pleasantries with her parents.

"And you, my little angel, are a muse in the making," Donald kissed her on the forehead. "Who did you get that from? Mommy or daddy?"

"I'm serious, you guys" she insisted. "Look. He has wings, and they're here."

The little girl pointed at the space behind Donald's back and traced what were supposed to be Donald's wings.

"Told you not to call her your little angel no more," her mother joked.

Donald set her back to the ground.

The little girl reached up as if to touch something on Donald's back; but her hands brushed through air.

"She is an angel, ma'am," Donald said. "I can't help it."

"Well, that she is," said her father. "Say, you should stop by the house for dinner sometime, Donald. Been a while."

"I sure will Mr. McCoy," Donald replied. "Thank you kindly."

Donald then turned his attention to the little girl and waved at her. She waved and pointed at his shoulders with her little index finger. She then spread out her arms and flapped them like wings. Donald smiled and did the same. Her grin broadened as Donald made to enter his truck because she saw Eliel spread his wings outwards and flapped them twice. But Donald had no idea what was going on with him.

CHAPTER NINETEEN

A TINGLING

A SMILE REMAINED on Donald's face, thanks to his little friend, whom he called his little angel. She always had that effect on him, no matter the mood he was in. Such infectious cuteness. The world could use more of her spirit. The McCoys were a great family, and he had had dinner with them twice over the past year. The McCoys were friends with Newman and had taken an instant liking to Donald the moment Newman had introduced Donald to them. Meredith, their daughter and Donald's little angel, was the icing on the cake when she swore Donald was an angel, despite her parents' attempt to explain why they thought she was wrong. That was also the first time in Donald's life, or the life he could remember, that anyone had called him an angel. Her purity of heart and mind, coupled with her unrivaled cuteness were a perfect panacea to his ego.

The dreams were recurrent and sometimes with two recurrent characters, a male and a female angel. At times, he dreamed of being an angel or lived with other angels in a place that looked like what Newman and his Christian friends could easily describe as heaven. However, these dreams felt too real, almost like a memory. The female had the kindest eyes and loving heart. The male exuded authority, strength and leadership, but his eyes pointed towards a psyche wrought with deep pain and sorrow. The female wore a gold bracelet on her left wrist and the male wore a gold bracelet on both wrists. Donald wrestled with the idea of sharing his dreams with Newman. However, he decided not to.

They're just dreams, he surmised, though his gut riled against this conclusion.

Donald slowed to a stop as a traffic light turned from yellow to red. He tapped on the steering wheel with his left index finger and hummed a tune.

Dreams. Memories. Who knows? he thought. *But why am I even entertaining the thought of these dreams being memories in the first place?*

He scoffed.

But, for the sake of argument, if these dreams are memories, then the implications are as dire as they are irrational.

"Come on now," he said out loud. "Angels and heaven aren't real anyway."

He chuckled a little.

But how did I even get to Newman's house? he thought. *Where am I from? Why does Newman keep telling me to give myself time to let my memories return? He knows more than he's willing to admit. And I must-*

Someone honked their horn and snatched Donald out of his mental dialogue. The light had turned green. He released his foot from the brake paddle and waved a hand outside his window to apologize to whoever was honking. Donald continued his drive home, but was it really home? Granted, Newman's house was the only place he could call, or remember as, 'home'.

I must have come from somewhere.

Newman had come up with his cover story. Given what he understood of the society, Newman could easily have called the police and they would have most likely helped him find his home and even help with his identity.

But he chose not to go to the police. Why? Donald made a right turn. *Why didn't he call the police? Either he's insanely foolish for harboring a complete stranger, or something much bigger than himself and possibly the police is going on.*

Donald sighed and made a left turn after a stop sign.

I've known Newman long enough to know that he's not a bad person and will never condone anything that was on the other side of the law, Donald thought. *This means he's not hiding me from bad people. He's trying to protect me. But from who? Or better yet, from what?*

Home was now three miles away. Donald pulled over to the side of the road, killed the engine and sat quietly. He weighed his options for a few minutes before he made up his mind.

I'll have a chat with Newman, whenever the timing feels right, he concluded.

He restarted the car and drove home. He focused more on the road this time. Safety first. Seven minutes later, he stepped out of the truck and retrieved the groceries from the back seat. Using his legs, he closed the back door of the truck and walked up the porch. He used his nose to press the doorbell and was thankful Newman would never know what he had just done with his nose. A weary, much-older-looking version of Newman opened the door and let him in. He placed the groceries on the kitchen counter and leveled a gaze of concern at Newman.

"Is everything alright, Mr. Weinberg?" Donald asked.

"Yes, everything is fine. Thanks," Newman half-lied.

"You look a little ill, that's all," Donald prompted.

"Not enough sleep last night," Newman lied with a forced smile. "And these old bones need their beauty sleep,"

"When I grow up, I wanna be as strong as you are now, sir," Donald joked and smiled. "Told you before, you don't look your age at all."

"Well, thank you kindly for the compliment, young man," Newman said and walked over to Donald. "A compliment always brightens one's day."

"You don't say," Donald beamed. "Speaking of compliments, guess who I ran into at the gas station today."

"Shamus?" Newman asked.

"Nope. Guess again," Donald said.

"Billy Swanson?"

"Nope. Last try."

"I give up," Newman said, after giving it some thought.

"The McCoys," Donald said. "And guess who was with them?"

"Meredith," Newman rolled his eyes.

"See? You got one right," Donald spoke with an equal pinch of sarcasm.

Both men laughed a little.

"They invited us for dinner, by the way," Donald added.

"Did they invite you or us?" Newman asked.

"Well, they said 'you should stop by for dinner sometime.' So, I'm not sure if the 'you' was used in the singular or plural," Donald explained. "But I'd prefer to think they meant us."

"They weren't specific, Donald," Newman almost whined.

"Now I'm absolutely convinced something other than lack of sleep is wrong with you today, Mr. Weinberg," Donald rebutted.

"And what makes you think that?" Newman asked.

"You're whining about accepting your friends' invitation to dinner at their home. That's why," Donald replied as he put the last of the groceries away.

"Am I that whiny?" Newman asked, managing a weak smile.

"Yep," Donald replied.

"Okay then, I'll get my happy pills," Newman joked.

But Donald did not laugh.

"You don't gotta go if you don't wanna," Donald offered.

"No. I'll go. Sorry, it's just been a tiresome day so far," Newman was almost sincere. "But I'll be fine. The feeling will pass."

Donald assumed that Newman was talking about the loss of his wife. So, he let the situation be. He understood that sometimes Newman relived the pain of his loss.

Poor guy, Donald thought. *Wish I could do something to help.*

"So where were we again?" Newman asked.

"Huh?" Donald seemed a little confused.

"Something about compliments and brightening of days, I think," Newman replied.

"Oh yes," Donald remembered. "We were talking about that, and that's how the McCoys came up. Funny, Meredith kept insisting on calling me an angel."

He chuckled and missed Newman wince when he turned around to place away some canned food in the pantry.

"She's so cute," Donald continued as he returned to the kitchen island with a can opener. "She sounded so convinced. She even asked her parents if they could 'see my wings' and all that."

Donald chuckled some more and shook his head as he opened a can of tuna.

"She sure is a cute one," Newman managed to say.

He bent over to pick up something from the floor.

"Needless to say, *that* made my day," Donald added. "I'm looking forward to seeing her more than to having dinner with her parents."

Donald winked at Newman and Newman managed a weak laugh.

"Don't worry," he added. "I know the McCoys can be a handful at times."

"And you'll be playing with Meredith while I'll be stuck with them," Newman spoke smugly.

"I call that a fair trade," Donald emptied the contents of the can of tuna into a frying pan.

Donald stirred the contents of the frying pan as he added some vegetables, adobo seasoning and black pepper. He cracked two eggs into the mix and let the frying pan sizzle its magic, as he liked to describe whatever he was cooking. He placed some slices of bread in the toaster, and a few minutes later, his meal was ready. He poured himself a glass of orange juice. He chatted with Newman the whole time and, somehow, he forgot to ask Newman about the thing that bothered him during his drive home from the store.

"I'm gonna take a nap," Newman said and headed towards the stairs.

"Oki doki," replied Donald.

Donald followed behind, munching on the calorie bomb he called an omelet sandwich as if it was the best thing ever made by man. Newman sighed and shook his head. When Newman entered his room and shut the door, he lay on the bed and stared at the ceiling. Sleep was not going to come easily, but he was aware of that already. especially with his thoughts going Formula One in his head.

"I came this close to telling him everything," he muttered to himself.

After that fateful night when Eliel crashed in his backyard, he resolved never to reveal Eliel's identity to anyone, including Eliel. However, as the days turned into weeks and weeks to months, he realized his hesitation stemmed from something else.

Fear.

The fear was not from the possibility of Eliel being a dark angel with evil intent. The fear came from the thought of loneliness once again when Eliel returned to wherever he came from after Eliel regained his memory. Over time, Newman had grown quite fond of and attached to this fallen angel. Eliel had become like a son to him and Eliel respected and treated him like a father, forging a wonderful father-son relationship between the two of them. Newman was not ready to let go, at least not yet. As he let the thoughts run through his head, Newman's paternal instincts took over. He realized that though his motives seemed harmlessly selfish, a good parent knew when it was time to let the children leave the nest. And so, Newman Weinberg made up his mind.

"I will have that conversation with him... tonight."

The rest of Donald's sandwich disappeared quickly. He drank the last sip of his juice and set the mug on the night stand.

"I'll take y'all downstairs later," he burped.

The soft, soothing hands of food coma caressed his soul and his eyelids felt as if a 50lb kettle bell was attached to each of them. He stretched lengthily as he yawned and made himself comfortable on his bed. He remembered his first day on this bed when he awoke as a blank slate. He recalled his confusion and apprehension for the stranger who sat across from him. He remembered going back to sleep almost instantly after the stranger had left, the stranger who had been so kind and generous to him; the stranger who had acted like a father to him. Donald also remembered his dream; the two angels, a male, and a female, standing over him in this same room, and having a conversation. These same angels featured in most of his recurrent dreams over the past year. Donald sighed and narrowed his eyes.

"As crazy as it may sound, these are not dreams at all," he said to himself.

Donald lay on his back and faced the ceiling.

"Something is definitely different between what I felt that day and what I feel when I dream," he said to himself. "On Day one, it was more like a presence from them two angels, though I was dreamin'. But they were here, at least they felt as if they were here, looking down at me. No, watching me... checking up on me or something."

Donald furrowed his eyebrows.

The other dreams felt more like memories, he thought. *They say dreams are just the subconscious replaying things sometimes. Could my dreams then be memories of me where I was? Where I'm from?*

Someone once told me to trust my instincts. But who was it? And why did they tell me? I

177

can't remember and it's driving me nuts. Nothing makes sense, and yet my gut tells me otherwise. I must follow this gnawing in the pit of my stomach. I must trust my instincts, regardless of how irrational the conclusions they present.

Indeed, the logical conclusion was clear. But he feared this line of logic.

Why am I afraid? What am I afraid of? I'm either a very special human being or I'm not human at all. And if I'm not human, then what am I? An angel from heaven?

Donald tried to laugh off the situation but fared poorly.

But aren't angels supposed to be creatures of purity, serving in the presence of God for all eternity? I can count at least five girls who will attest to my 'impurity'.

He turned and lay on his left side.

Maybe I'm a special kind of human being with ties to angels? Anyway, I can run scenarios in my head all day or I make things simple.

Donald sighed and closed his eyes.

I'll have that conversation with Newman this evening after his nap.

With those final thoughts, Donald drifted off to sleep immediately.

***

Michael watched from his domain. He nodded with satisfaction, pleased to see Eliel was starting to go through an awakening. He took a moment to relive his own period of awakening after his fall. The first wave of confusion was not kind to his psyche. That confusion gradually morphed into curiosity and curiosity birthed comprehension. When Michael's memory returned with the completion of his awakening, he innately knew he had been reborn into a new kind of archangel, one who had had a taste of the dark side and triumphed. Perhaps being the first in Celestia to fall helped to solidify his status as archangel supreme.

"At least, I have something good to turn to while I remained steeped in the gloomy side of my past," he said to himself. "Never again, Celestia. Never again."

"Still thinking of your glory days as a fallen archangel?"

Uriel's words yanked his attention back to the present moment.

"Your stealth improves constantly, my friend," Michael said, without turning around to face her. "Soon, you just might be able to avoid my detection entirely."

Uriel summoned a chair next to him.

"You're also getting better at reading my mind," Michael added.

"What's on your mind?" Uriel asked jokingly.

"You don't want to know," Michael smiled dryly.

Uriel sat down and took his hand in hers. They interlaced their fingers and she had known him long enough to tell he was grateful for her timely company.

"He'll be fine, you know," Uriel tried to reassure him.

"I'm more confident in him now than I was before," Michael said..

"But not confident enough," Uriel interjected.

"For now, his inclination is still towards our side. That is good news," Michael replied and sighed. "But he still has to go through his tests."

"If I know Eliel well enough, and I think I do, he will make it," Uriel's tone of voice indicated her unwavering confidence in Eliel.

"I'm not saying he's weak, Uriel. His strength and resolve are unquestionably remarkable. I am merely concerned about what happens when he has a taste of the other side,". Michael explained.

Uriel nodded. She relaxed her grip on his hand. Michael did the same, though unwillingly.

"I don't mean this in a bad way, Uriel. But you have not tasted the other side either," Michael said. "Honestly, I'm glad you have not. I'm sure you would handle it wonderfully. But that does not take away the seduction and addiction that could come with the other side. Eliel is humble and loyal to Celestia. But who knows what will happen when he goes through the tests?"

"No offense taken, Michael," Uriel said and gently took his hand in hers again. "And thanks for your confidence in me. Now, you and I must focus on believing more in Eliel. He may need it after all."

Michael nodded almost imperceptibly. Uriel smiled weakly, reached across and kissed him on the cheek. He felt her reassurance and encouragement, and he deeply appreciated it. Uriel's hand rested on his cheek as she turned his face towards hers. Uriel gazed at Michael deep in the eyes and the most beautiful smile Michael had ever seen appeared on her face. She had stood by his side from the very beginning, through the Great Rebellion, through the rebuilding process and even in his darkest hour. Ironically, maybe Eliel falling was Michael's darkest hour. After all, the prophecy spoke of The One rising to the highest rank of angels, did it not? Who knew? Maybe Uriel was with him right now to keep him in check; to make sure that he, Michael, did not do something stupid upon Eliel's return. As likely as that was a possibility, Michael's chest became heavy with guilt.

I should not harbor such vile thoughts against a most loyal and trusted friend like Uriel, he thought. *Whatever her reason for being with me right here and now, I remain grateful. She means me no harm and will never mean me any harm.*

"I'm sorry," Michael murmured.

"What for?" Uriel asked.

"For not reciprocating your faith in me," Michael admitted.

"I know that already," Uriel said. "You wouldn't be you if you didn't entertain all the possibilities. That's part of what makes you archangel supreme and a leader I'll follow to my very end. Besides, I also know that you've had a change of heart."

"You know me too well," Michael said.

Michael leveled his gaze at Uriel. Uriel's lips parted slightly with her smile.

"If that is what you think, then you must also know that my answer is no," she said.

"No? But I did not even ask you anything," Michael recoiled slightly from her statement.

"No, you didn't. But you were about to," Uriel said.

"I do not understand," Michael admitted.

"I've seen that look too many times to know what it means, Michael," Uriel explained, smiling softly. "It was the same look you gave her every other time you were not talking about Celestial affairs. Does that help?"

"By Celestia," Michael exclaimed.

Without even realizing it, he was actually falling for Uriel. The feeling was subconscious and but there all along. But now that Uriel mentioned it, he realized how true her words were. He had gone weak in the knees when she had taken him by the elbow and led him away from Eliel's room after the fall. He had wrapped his fingers around hers involuntarily. A warm sensation had filled his chest when she kissed him on the cheek and placed a hand on his chest. The list went on and on.

If she knew all along, then either she has been taking advantage of me for personal gain or she is actually working for the good of Celestia, Michael thought. *By Celestia. Should I be concerned about my most trusted friend and ally? The last time someone had this kind of effect on me, a rebellion had ensued.*

"You may have trust issues right now," Uriel spoke calmly and soothingly. "But I assure you, I'm not like her. There are many other female archangels and angels here who are also not like her. You just have to learn to trust again."

"But none of them is you, Uriel," Michael blurted. "None of them is you. Despite my history and everything else, I can trust you, and I do trust you."

Michael had made his decision and he wanted Uriel to reciprocate.

Uriel's features softened and she closed her eyes. His words bore sincerity and surrender in them, the latter which she had not seen in Michael since the Great Rebellion. She slid off her chair, knelt in front of Michael and took his face in her hands. She looked at him in the eyes and, for a moment, their beings merged into one. She closed her eyes, inclined her head and kissed him deeply and passionately in the mouth. Michael reciprocated. In that moment, the two archangels glowed in unison as their beings became intertwined. In that moment, flames spewed from the corners of their closed eyes and locked lips and their passion burned even more. And in that same moment, a sad truth was birthed to both parties.

Michael and Uriel slowly peeled away from each other.

"As much as I would love to be yours and to have you as mine, I'm afraid I just can't, Michael," Uriel said and bowed her head. "My heart belongs to another and I can only hope he will feel the same."

Uriel stood up as her archangel flames slowly died out.

"I'm very sorry, Michael," Uriel said and teleported back to her domain, leaving a very disappointed Michael alone in his domain.

CHAPTER TWENTY

I MUST BE DREAMING

DONALD AWOKE TO an unfamiliar feeling of the sun's heat burning his skin and a breeze cooling him off at the same time. He lifted his hand to shield his eyes from the glare of the sun. He squeezed his eyes shut, opened them again and propped himself on his elbows after his eyes adjusted to the brightness of the afternoon sun. The ground beneath him felt soft. He scooped a handful. Sand. He examined his surroundings.

This is definitely not my bedroom, he thought.

A forest lay to his left. An endless beach with white sands and smooth pebbles stretched for miles in front and behind him. To his right, a large body of greenish-blue water spanned into the horizon.

I'm on a beach, he cried out in his mind. *A freaking beach. Wait. Am I on an island?*

Uncertainty was his reply.

First trip to the beach and it feels... different from what I expected.

Donald stood up and wiped off the sand that clung to his shirtless torso and the front part of his legs his pair of flowery shorts did not cover. He took a few careful steps on the sand, expecting the heat from the hot sands to singe through the soles of his feet. Nothing happened. He rubbed his chin as his mind pored over the irrationality of the situation. Finally, he shrugged and let it go. He was alone in an unfamiliar but friendly-feeling territory. He scanned for signs of any form of life other than the trees in the forest. Nothing. All was quiet except for the rhythmic caress of the waves along the shoreline and the winds whistling through the trees.

This is quite serene, Donald admitted. *Creepy but serene nonetheless. Peaceful and perfect too, if I may add.*

He closed his eyes and relished the moment. He filled his lungs with as much clean and fresh, salty air as possible, held it in his lungs and then slowly exhaled. He moaned with the sweet sensation that came with the deep-breathing and opened his eyes.

A round of waves washed up the shore but not up to where he stood. Donald smiled and watched as the waves retreated and a second round surged forward. This time, the waves washed over his toes and ankles. The coldness of the water sent shock waves up his legs. He flinched slightly. He walked closer towards the water until the next round of waves rose midway up his sheen. When the waves retreated, a broken seashell, no larger than his big toenail, rested between his feet.

Donald bent down and picked up the broken shell before the next round of waves, which almost reached his knees, washed it away. He tried to wipe the sand off the shell, but not all of the sand came off. So, he took a knee and quickly rinsed off the shell with the next round of waves. When the waves retreated, a small hermit crab sat in the shell.

"How did you get in here, big guy?" Donald smiled at the tiny creature. "Did you come with the waves just now?"

"You should keep it," a voice called from behind.

Startled, Donald whipped around to face his unexpected companion. A lad, barefoot and shirtless with a pair of shorts that were a size too big for him, stood about twenty feet away. His dreadlocks rested on his chest and he held a soccer ball against his right hip with his right arm. He was probably no more than nine years of age.

"You should keep it," the little boy repeated.

"Why should I?" Donald asked.

"Because you found it, silly," the little boy grinned. "So it's yours. Keep it."

"Well, young fella, just 'cause you find somethin'; don't mean you gotta keep it," Donald explained. "Besides, it belongs in the sea. So, I'll put it back there."

"If it was me, I'd keep it," the little boy shrugged.

"And what would you have done with it?" Donald asked, still cradling the hermit crab in the palm of his right hand.

"I don't know; maybe raise it, feed it and take care of it?" the little boy replied, shrugged and transferred his ball to his left arm.

"Very thoughtful of you," Donald replied as he turned around and walked further into the water. "I'd do the same, but I prefer to let the water take care of its own."

He waited for the little boy to respond. But the little boy said nothing.

"Sometimes, no matter how good our intentions, we just gotta learn to let go, my little friend," Donald added.

The waves now reached Donald's knees. He gently lowered the hermit crab in the water, and it disappeared therein.

"Have a great life," Donald said softly.

Donald turned around and headed towards dry land. The boy watched him emotionlessly. When Donald was ten feet away from him, the little boy started tossing his ball in the air and catching it repeatedly with both hands.

"Would you like to play?" he asked Donald.

"I'd love to, but I don't know how to play," Donald replied.

"I can teach you," the little boy flashed a broad grin, revealing two missing upper incisors. "It's really easy."

He let the ball drop on the sand in front of him and placed his right foot on the ball.

"Thank you, my friend," Donald stretched. "Would you like to tell me your name before you teach me how to play?"

"I go by many names, Donald," the little boy replied.

Donald froze in shock from the little boy's response.

"How do you know my name?" Donald asked.

"How I know your name is not important," the little boy juggled the ball with his right foot. "But to answer your initial question, you can call me AK."

AK then kicked the ball a short distance away and chased it. When he caught up with it, he raised it in the air with his right foot, juggled it three times in the air with his head, and brought it to his chest before letting it rest on the sand. Donald nodded and smiled at AK's adept maneuvering of the ball.

"Okay, AK," he said with resignation. "I definitely can't do what you just did. Perhaps we could start off with something less complicated?"

"Sure, Donald," AK replied. "Would you like to start with remembering your name, maybe?" AK resumed expertly juggling the ball

"My name is Donald."

"Just as mine is AK," AK replied and kicked the ball towards Donald.

Donald caught the soccer ball with his hands. It burned his hands and he dropped it on the sands.

"No hands," AK wagged a finger at him. "Any other part of your body is acceptable; just no hands. Okay?"

AK raised a thumb in the air.

"Got it," Donald replied, shaking his hands. "No hands."

"Good, now kick the ball towards me," AK commanded.

Donald took a step backward and moved to kick the ball. However, he had a change of heart. He raised the ball in the air with his right foot and let it bounce on his chest. Instead of letting it hit the sand, he juggled it with his right knee and then his left knee. He repeated the sequence three more times, and on the fourth try, he kneed the ball with a little more force so that it went higher into the air.

Then Donald juggled the ball three times with his head and let it fall towards the ground. Just when it was about to hit the ground, he used his inner right foot and tapped the ball back into the air. He did this twice and switched to the outer part of his left foot. He juggled the ball three times and, on the fourth time, he kicked the ball towards AK. AK absorbed the momentum and speed of the ball on his chest, juggled it once with each knee before catching it in his right foot in midair. He brought down the ball gently to the ground and smiled at Donald.

"And who says you cannot do what I just did?" AK asked.

"How did I do that?" Donald asked, full of surprise.

"Again, you ask the wrong question," AK replied flatly.

"Where are we?" Donald asked, looking around.

"We are wherever you want us to be," AK replied.

"I don't understand," frustration brewed within Donald.

"'Cause you're trying too hard," he replied. "And asking the wrong question."

"So, what is the right question, AK, if that is even your name?" Donald rubbed his temples.

Black, thunderstorm clouds suddenly gathered in the sky, heralding a storm a coming by casting the beach in a dark shade of grey.

"Ah. We're making progress," AK replied ignoring Donald's questions.

Donald's brewing frustration quickly turned into a broth of fury.

"Just tell me your name," Donald ordered.

The skies grew darker and the winds howled with enough ferocity to uproot a small tree.

"Wrong question," AK replied with all the calm in the world.

Donald gripped his temples. A deafening throbbing in his head threatened to blow his skull apart and the dark skies lit up with multiple flashes of lightning chased by booming applauses of thunder. The waves rose to more than thirty feet high, and with each passing second, the pain in Donald's head promised to render him insane shortly. He fell to the ground and screamed into the raging storm. AK slowly approached and loomed over him. He dropped to one knee, leaned forward and whispered softly in Donald's ear.

"What do you want, Donald?" he asked.

"I don't know," Donald whimpered.

"I'll ask you again. What do you want?" AK asked.

Donald paused and breathed slowly. The throbbing in his head died down and the storm eased off a little. The skies remained dark with few flashes of lightning and mild claps of thunder. The waves only rose up to ten feet. Donald sat up and continued to breathe more slowly, visiting more calm unto his psyche. He smiled weakly and nodded.

"I see what's happenin' here," he said almost to himself. "This place, whatever it is, is linked to me somehow."

"You still haven't answered my question," AK reminded him.

"I know, my little friend," Donald replied.

Donald stared blankly into the horizon. His breathing was steady and slow until he focused, freeing his mind of compulsive thinking. In that instant, he achieved stillness. Suddenly, everything around him mimicked his state of being and froze in absolute stillness as well. The trees, the waters, the air, everything stood still, as if someone hit the 'PAUSE' button on the remote control to everything within his perception. However, AK continued to juggle his soccer ball with his feet. Donald looked up to the sky and noticed, for the first time, that the brightness of the day was not from the sun because the sun was missing from the sky. He nodded with more understanding of the situation.

"I know I didn't answer your question, my little friend," Donald spoke calmly. "But I'll answer your question when you answer mine."

"You lost your mid-western accent," AK said.

"I know, my little friend," Donald smiled.

"Why do you keep calling me your 'little friend' and not AK?" AK asked.

"Why call you a name that isn't yours?" Donald retorted.

"Because it's the name I gave you," AK spat. "And I want you to use it. It's *MY* name, and I like it."

AK dropped his ball and folded his arms.

"Aren't you pouty all of a sudden," Donald stood up and walked towards AK.

"Stay away from me," AK ordered and picked up his ball. "And I won't share my ball with you anymore. You're mean."

AK raised his nose in the air and looked away.

"Because I'm now in control?" Donald asked calmly.

"Ha. You wish you were in control," AK snickered.

"I am, my little friend. And that's why you're so pouty," Donald replied. "But you don't have to be like that. I can be your friend," he smiled at A. K.

"No," AK replied and raised his nose further in the air.

Donald thought AK's gesture was cute and chuckled.

"Yes I can be your friend," Donald insisted. "You can be my little friend and I can be your big friend, no?"

"Well," AK hesitated. "How come you get to be the big one and I get to be the little one? Why can't I be the big one?"

"You can be the big one if you want to," Donald offered. "But you will have to start acting like a big boy first."

He took a knee behind AK while AK seemed to consider his proposal.

"And I think it's more fun when more people play soccer together instead of you playing alone," Donald added. "Won't you agree?"

"I guess," AK conceded.

"So, what d'ya say, pal? Let's kick some ball together. Cool with that?" Donald offered with a grin.

"Your accent returned," AK mumbled.

"Is that a yes?" Donald pressed.

"Yeah, I suppose we could," AK agreed.

AK turned around to face Donald.

Donald picked up the ball, juggled it a few times in the air with his feet and kicked it towards A. K., who passed it back to Donald with a head move. They played for a while until AK returned to the subject matter.

"You didn't answer my question," AK said as he kicked the ball to Donald.

"And I said I'll answer yours after you answer mine," Donald reminded AK.

He kicked the ball back to AK.

"And what question would that be?" AK asked, passing the ball to Donald once again.

"Well," Donald placed his foot on top of the ball, "I know this place is tied to me somehow. And that all of this-" he waved his hand in the air "- isn't real. The forest is uncharted territory, and I'm guessing I eventually gotta go there at some point."

"And what does that have to do with your question?" AK asked with a look of exasperation on his face.

"Patience, my little friend," he replied. "When I stilled my mind, everything became still. That is, everything except for you. Now why's that, I wonder?"

"Is that your question?" AK asked.

"No, it ain't. But at the same time, can't help but notice the significance of this," Donald replied.

Donald raised the ball in the air with his foot. When the ball was half way through its downward path, Donald kicked it towards AK. The ball landed on AK's chest. He slowed the ball to a stop on his chest by absorbing the momentum of the ball before he let the ball roll to the ground. AK placed his foot on the ball and placed his arms akimbo.

"I'm losing my patience, my friend," AK spoke in Donald's voice.

AK immediately realized what he had just done and cupped his mouth with both his hands.

"Need I explain myself any further?" Donald asked, raising an eyebrow.

"I don't know what you're talking about," AK averted his gaze to the ground.

"No more beating around the bush," Donald's tone of voice was sterner. "You didn't freeze with the rest of this scene for the simple reason that you and I are connected. You're me, and I am you. That's why I can play soccer so well even though I never played soccer my entire life. That's why I stopped calling you AK because that is not your name. Yes, AK is not my name. In here, whatever 'here' is, I can do whatever you can do. You are the part of me that eludes me, the part of me that I have to remember. And now, I will ask you the question I was supposed to ask you from the very start. Are you ready?"

"Go on," AK replied with a hint of pride in his voice.

"Who am I?" Donald asked.

AK met Donald's gaze and held it for a breath or two. He nodded slowly. The ball disappeared from underneath his foot and he took a step towards Donald.

"That is the question I've been hoping to hear from you for the longest time," AK said to Donald in Donald's voice. "I am the part of your subconscious you can access. I can only point you in the direction of what you're looking for, but you will have to do the digging for yourself. I am like the hand that points to the moon, but I am not the moon. Do you understand what I'm saying?"

"I do," Donald replied.

"Good. Do you see that?" AK pointed a finger at the forest.

"Yes, I do," Donald replied.

"Therein lies the answer to your question," AK replied and to Donald's surprise, AK looked like an eighteen-year-old version of Donald, only this time, his hair was braided in corn rows.

Cute, Donald thought.

"Thank you, my friend," Donald said.

He turned around and started walking towards the forest.

"Be careful out there, friend," eighteen-year-old Donald said in Donald's voice. "Let's just say, it's a jungle out there."

"You'll be my guardian angel, won't you?" Donald joked.

But suddenly, a blinding flash blazed across his vision and Donald leaped from his bed in his room. He hit the night stand. The mug and plate crashed on the floor, breaking into multiple pieces. He panted heavily and massaged his temples. He glanced at the broken pieces of the mug and plate on the floor and cursed.

What a dream. Or was it a dream? Either way, I'm either losing my mind or living in denial of something that is too insane to be real, and even more insane to be true.

A wave of claustrophobia slammed into him. He needed some air, desperately. Quickly, he picked up as many of the broken pieces from the floor as he could, grabbed his wallet and keys and headed downstairs. He dumped the broken pieces in the trash can, grabbed a jacket from the chair and dashed out of the house.

I need a drink and someone to talk to, he thought. *Hopefully, Sara can spare a moment of her time. Why her? Don't know, don't care. But I must talk to her now.*

He put the truck in reverse and backed out of Newman's compound with so much speed he left a trail of dust in his departure.

CHAPTER TWENTY-ONE

STAGE SETUP

JAMAEL WAS JUST another archangel. Correction. The guardian of the Spawn Sanctuary is not just another archangel. The Great Rebellion had left a large scar on Celestia and cycles later, that scar lingered still.

And am I glad I sided with Michael? Wings, yeah, Jamael smiled for the millionth time. *Hell. I do not envy those fools over there. Sometimes I pity them, but when I think about everything, I appreciate what I have all the more.*

Jamael summoned his wings and flapped them three times.

Guardian of the Spawn Sanctuary... I love the sound of that.

His promotion to archangel came as a huge surprise and when he received word of his promotion to guardian of the Spawn Sanctuary, his entire world had changed. However, with the exhilaration and pride that came with the promotion, confusion churn within his core.

I mean, I don't doubt my potentials and I did agree with Michael that all those who survived the rebellion deserved a promotion, he thought. *So, why do I feel like I don't merit this title?*

Perhaps the subconscious fear that the Spawn Sanctuary could be responsible for his predecessor, Maziel, joining the other side contributed to his confusion and feeling of inadequacy. His logic failed. Yet he held on to that failed logic. Or maybe the reason for his internal turmoil centered around something far simpler and less complicated: self-doubt and low self-esteem.

With Maziel, Michael himself had done the honors of promoting him, Jamael rubbed his chin and furrowed his eyebrows in thought. *But when it came to my turn, some random archangel, whom I've never even seen before, just approached me with the arrogance of seniority and spite and gave me the news.*

Jamael heaved his shoulders.

You'd think a position as important as this would be treated with a little more respect than what that archangel, I don't even know his name, demonstrated. But no. Absolutely no form of respect. Now why's that? What caused the change?

Jamael hovered back and forth a few times in front of the sanctuary's entrance.

I know what they were doing, what they ARE still doing, he pouted. *They just wanted to insult me by making me feel useful; like I matter. But I know them. I know their kind; a bunch of condescending, shiny-winged archies who think they're better than me because they came out of the spawn sanctuary before I did. 'Senior' my wings.*

Jamael summoned his wings and flapped them several times before he made them disappear. His boiling emotions calmed and ceased hovering back and forth.

Anyway, I am a guardian to the spawn sanctuary and my position is important to the realm and to me.

His resentment towards Michael and his inner council of senior archangels dominated his psyche every moment but he prided himself with loyalty and dedication to Celestia. Yet, when his predecessor, now Kazuk, the King of Hell Realm, had contacted him, he did not alert Celestia as per protocol.

Why? Jamael asked himself after Kazuk established contact the first time.

Kazuk reaching out to him was as bold as Luciel starting a rebellion, relatively speaking. Everyone in Celestia remained aware of Hell's spies dwelling among them as well as Hell Realm covertly building an army. Word on Celestia's streets was that Kazuk was doing a remarkable job turning Hell into a haven.

But that could just be propaganda from Hell realm sympathizers, Jamael shrugged.

Kazuk's non-corporeal voice reached his ears via a frequency slightly below that of Celestia, which bypassed Celestia's radar. Genius move on Kazuk's part. Against his every conscious effort, Jamael listened. Against the warning bells that went off in his head, Jamael paid attention to Public Enemy Number One. Against all logic, Jamael allowed a seed to be sowed into his subconscious, though his conscious mind pretended to riot against, and reject, whatever Kazuk had to say or was trying to say. Yet, against his own willpower, Jamael succumbed to the seduction that was Kazuk.

***

"Hello Jamael."

Jamael recoiled with shock and searched for the bearer of the voice.

"I apologize for startling you," the voice said. *"It is I, Kazuk."*

Anger flared within Jamael. However, he did not immediately alert Celestia.

I can't see him, Jamael thought. *But I'll lure him into a trap. Then I'll alert Celestia.*

"First of all, congratulations on your promotion," Kazuk said telepathically. *"You*

must feel honored to be the guardian of the spawn sanctuary."

Jamael did not say anything.

"So, I'm sure you went through the vigorous selection procedure with Michael, no?" Kazuk asked but without really expecting a reply.

"Oh wait. You didn't go through any selection process?" Kazuk asked. *"How odd. Allow me to share with you what I went through before I became guardian of the spawn sanctuary."*

Kazuk then proceeded to narrate the tests he went through with Michael and all the compliments he received from Michael with much detail. He made sure he focused a lot on his experiences *WITH* Michael, the highest-ranking archangel ever. Jamael could neither respond nor shut Kazuk out. Yet, Jamael still did not alert counter-intelligence.

I've only seen Michael from a distance and that was after the rebellion, the moment he promoted us all, the survivors, to archangels, Jamael thought.

"I can't help but wonder why you weren't tested the way I was," Kazuk said.

Now he's gloating, Jamael fumed.

"Well, I won't distract you any further now, Jamael," Kazuk added. *"But I shall return later. If you'd like, I'll teach you how to communicate with me through this undetectable frequency. But if you prefer not to learn, then alert Raphael when next I contact you."*

A moment of silence hung between the two of them.

"I'll talk to you later, Jamael," Kazuk said and ended the telepathic link.

Jamael chewed on Kazuk's words.

Was he lying? Most likely. After all, he is the King of Hell and should not be trusted for any reason. Yet, such details cannot be fabricated. Most importantly, what did he stand to gain by sharing his story with me? Clearly, he has ulterior motives, but what are they?

Jamael later arrived at a conclusion.

"Recruitment," he growled. "Maziel wanted to recruit me."

Jamael flared with anger.

"Who the flap does he think he is?" he raged. "Who does he take me for? I never should've entertained this madness in the first place. I must alert Raphael at once."

Yet, he did not alert Raphael. He could not alert Raphael.

Why? What's holding me back?

Jamael summoned his wings, flapped them once and dismissed them.

But what if Kazuk was telling the truth? It does seem odd that an assignment as important as being a guardian could be handed over with such nonchalance.

If what he had heard about Michael was true, then Kazuk's story was more likely to be the truth than to be a lie.

And if Kazuk's story was the truth, why did I not go through the same testing and selection process like Kazuk did? Was it because Michael didn't think I'm worthy, but someone had to guard the sanctuary? He pitied me, an archangel without use, without purpose? Was it even Michael who picked me or some random archy?

Jamael's low self-esteem rose like an avian monstrosity and clamored hard at his psyche.

How dare they. I may be lower in rank than they are but that doesn't give them the right. For Celestia's sake, I survived the flapping rebellion.

The self-loathe and anger at Michael and his inner council grew alongside his envy for Kazuk. Despite Kazuk joining Hell, Kazuk knew how to take a stand and make something for himself. He was even tough enough to last a few moves with Michael. He had been tested *AND* selected by Michael. Worst of all, Kazuk was certainly a better archangel than he, Jamael, was. So, why had Kazuk initiated contact with him? To taunt him? To mock him? To gloat?

I'm going to alert Raphael, but not until I've had words with that disdainful piece of scum from Hell, Jamael promised himself. *For now, I'll play along; long enough to lure him in for an eventual capture. Once Kazuk is out of the way, I'll seek audience with Michael. Seeking an audience with Michael will be a much tougher feat to accomplish, but I shall find a way.*

Thus, Jamael waited for Kazuk to initiate contact again. The waiting period saw a gradual growth in his fury, as well as his desire for payback. His hurt ego suffered more damage and demanded retribution.

This is blasphemy, he thought.

He did not know how he would get retribution, though. All Jamael knew was that, by his wings, retribution was his to serve, even if it meant burning down Hell and Celestia.

"Hello, Jamael," Kazuk's voice called telepathically from nowhere. *"Have you considered my offer?"*

Jamael maintained his position.

"I take it since the alarms haven't gone off," Kazuk continued, *"that you have decided to at least let me teach you how to communicate on this sub-Celestial vibrational frequency? I'll wait for a moment and, if nothing happens, then I'll take it as a yes."*

No alarms went off in Celestia.

"Great. Someone will come to you shortly and teach you," Kazuk said, with a little more excitement than warranted. *"Hold on, please."*

Jamael's eyes darted around nervously at the mention of 'someone' coming over to teach him.

Show no fear, he reminded himself with the resolve of a true soldier.

"He's all yours, Scribe," Kazuk said.

"My, my, my. He is a feisty one indeed, my king," The Scribe said.

Jamael was startled by the other voice. Someone called Scribe?

"Just get on with it, Scribe," Kazuk ordered.

"Of course, my king."

"This may sting a little, but you'll be fine," The Scribe said to Jamael.

Before Jamael could process what The Scribe said, a sharp pain radiated from the base of his neck to the left side of his head. He winced but tried not to make any sudden moves, lest Michael or one of those conceited creatures was watching him. He squeezed his eyes shut as the pain increased a little and when he opened them, everything around him looked crisper, more vibrant, brighter, finer and more colorful. Celestia never looked this beautiful before. He smiled and regarded his hands. He touched his face. His sensory perceptions were sharper than before and evoked a more vibrant sense of being. He turned around to look behind him and when he saw a stranger standing behind him, he stifled a scream and made to summon his spear. The Scribe raised both his hands in the air.

"You don't want to attract any attention now, do you?" The Scribe asked.

The Scribe slowly lowered his hands and approached Jamael, who took a step back, with his spear partially materialized in his right hand.

"I am The Scribe," he said. *"Though you can see me, no one else can. And no, don't worry, the alarms have not been triggered, in case you didn't realize. Now, try to say something."*

Jamael dismissed his partially summoned spear and opened his mouth but The Scribe shook his head.

"Without using your mouth, Jamael."

Jamael tried again and still opened his mouth. He closed it quickly before The Scribe could say anything. After two more attempts, Jamael still failed.

"Try to THINK of what you want to say and then mentally vocalize those words," The Scribe encouraged.

Jamael failed again. The Scribe shook his head in disappointment and turned to walk away.

"I told you, my king," he said. *"He's no good."*

"And who are you to tell me I'm no good?!" Jamael screamed with his mind.

Jamael's eyes popped in surprise when he realized that he was able to speak like they did. His anger quickly gave way to excitement.

"Ah, the power of persuasion," The Scribe said smiling.

The Scribe then turned and addressed Kazuk.

"My work here is done, my king,"

The Scribe vanished from sight without waiting for any reply.

"I'm glad you're able to communicate with us now, Jamael," Kazuk spoke cordially. *"I believe you have many questions for me. So, please, ask away."*

"First of all, why did you tell me your story?" Jamael asked, trying to keep his feeling of shame and humiliation under control.

"Because I wanted to share my story with you," Kazuk replied.

"Nonsense. You wanted to gloat, did you not?" Jamael spat in anger. *"You wanted to make me jealous, to make me know that you're so much better than I am, did you not?"*

"Are you assuming that I was already fully aware of the fact that you did not go through any form of testing before selection?" Kazuk asked calmly.

"Yes," Jamael replied. *"But now the real question is, how did you know already?"*

"I will be completely honest with you, Jamael," Kazuk's tone was loaded with sincerity and empathy. *"I did not tell you my story to gloat, or taunt you or to make you jealous, though I was fully aware of how you got your assignment."*

"Then why did you tell me your story?" Jamael asked.

"I did tell you a story, Jamael," Kazuk spoke with calm and control, a strategy which helped to quell Jamael's tantrum. *"But my story was not what I was trying to communicate to you. The real story is felt, not heard."*

Kazuk paused.

"I don't follow," Jamael's anger gradually gave way confusion.

"The reason I already know of your story is because I have brothers and sisters here and they apprise us of certain matters of utmost importance and purpose," Kazuk explained.

His words worked their way into Jamael's mind.

"You mean spies," Jamael's sense of loyalty to Celestia kicked in.

"I'll never use the term 'spies' to replace 'brothers' and 'sisters,'" Kazuk rebutted.

"But that's what they are," Jamael retorted. *"They ARE spies."*

"To you, they are, Jamael," Kazuk fired back. *"But to me, they are MY brothers and MY sisters. DO YOU UNDERSTAND THAT?"*

Something about his sudden outburst shocked Jamael psychologically. His resolve weakened in the wake of Kazuk's outburst. Maybe it was the authority, or the sense of loyalty, conviction and determination Kazuk portrayed as he spat out the words.

"And I will strike down anyone who tries to harm a feather on their wings," Kazuk promised. *"Do you understand me, Jamael?"*

"Yes," Jamael replied as if he were under some kind of trance.

"Good. Now, do you understand the story I was trying to tell you?" Kazuk asked, feeling satisfied that Jamael was already a little broken inside.

"I'm not sure," Jamael answered.

"How did you feel when you learned that I went through a selection and testing process, but you did not?" Kazuk asked.

"Foolish, disrespected, humiliated, insulted," Jamael said.

"Angry?".

"Yes."

"Furious?"

"Yes."

"Used?"

"Yes."

"Now you understand how I felt then," Kazuk let his tone reflect his sentiments.

"How so?" Jamael asked. *"Did you not get to meet with Michael in person? Did you not duel with him and last three moves? Did he not give you many compliments? How then could you possibly have felt what I felt?"*

"Because it was all a lie," Kazuk erupted. *"A flapping sham. Michael staged everything to make me feel good about myself. He wanted to make me feel important. That's what I learned later. That is what Luciel told me; that is what she confided in me."*

"Are you sure?" Jamael asked. *"Because if it is the Michael that I have heard of, he would not go to such lengths just to make someone feel important. All he would have had to do would have been just to shake your hand and congratulate you on the new assignment and before you know it, you're flapping your wings over the amazing person he is."*

"And you are absolutely correct," Kazuk agreed. *"But it's more than that. It's not about the assignment. It's about the most important thing that lies within the walls of that sanctuary. In fact, it's so important that it terrifies him, but he won't let anyone else know about it."*

"Anyone else?" Jamael asked.

"Yes, anyone else," Kazuk agreed. *"Because there are some who know, and one of those is Malichiel."*

"Is it true that he now goes by Metatron?" Jamael asked with more excitement in his voice than Kazuk expected.

"Yes," Kazuk replied dismissively. *"But that's not important right now. What is important is the question that I want to ask you."*

"What's that?" Jamael asked.

"Can I call you my brother?"

"That's a loaded question."

Kazuk did not reply. Jamael averted his gaze to the ground as he considered his options. Then he raised his head and met Kazuk's gaze.

"What is in it for me?" Jamael asked.

"A shot at payback to the one who insulted us both," Kazuk replied.

"That is quite a feat you hope to accomplish," Jamael said. *"Need I remind you that you are now in Hell because she had the same intention as you do now?"*

"I don't need a reminder, thank you," Kazuk retorted. *"I live it every moment in Hell. But I am not here in Celestia and I am not going to cause another rebellion. My goal is simply to eliminate the head, and the rest will follow. She failed to see and do this and that's why the rebellion was bound to fail from the onset. As long as Michael is around and as long as he lives, Celestia will thrive and remain strong. But remove him from the picture…."*

Kazuk left the sentence hanging.

"I appreciate you trying to avoid another slaughter," Jamael said. *"Another senseless war*

is pointless and a total waste. However, I'm unsure how you'll achieve this, Kazuk."

This was the first instant Jamael used Kazuk's Hell-Realm name.

"And your wisdom is most inspiring, Jamael," Kazuk smiled and approached him. *"Your questions reflect the mindset of one who is analytical, smart and wise. I could certainly use your skills in my council, should you be willing."*

"A most generous offer," Jamael stepped away from Kazuk. *"And thanks. Two things though; the first is that I have not yet agreed to join you and the second is that you have not yet answered my question."*

"I apologize, Jamael," Kazuk said. *"I did not mean to ignore your question. I was a little too confident that you would be a part of our team. But to answer your question, we plan on achieving this feat with your help. You see, you, Jamael, hold a very, very vital key to the success of our mission. And, without your help, there will be no way we could eliminate Michael, without the high possibility of another all-out war."*

Kazuk values me, Jamael thought. *He sees in me what no one else does. I am important. I have purpose. I am the key to Michael's demise.*

Jamael rejoiced in his mind.

By Celestia, I will have my vengeance on Michael. I will have his wings… and his head.

"So, what do you say, Jamael?" Kazuk asked.

"I'm in," Jamael replied.

"Thank you so much and welcome to the team… brother," Kazuk exploded with exaggerated elation.

"So, what is my mission?" Jamael asked, trying hard to conceal his excitement.

"Your mission is simple," Kazuk replied. *"When the moment is right, we will give you a set of instructions and then, you will retrieve the Zarark for us."*

CHAPTER TWENTY-TWO

A GOOD DEED

DONALD ZIGZAGGED ON the road like an arrogant, reckless, entitled, teenage son of a billionaire would, until strings of normalcy yanked at his psyche. He applied some pressure on the brakes and slowed the truck's speed to 5 miles per hour below the speed limit. Sunset was nigh but hitting Sara's bar right now was a little too early, by his drinking standards, anyway. As such, he took a detour to the only park in town. He parked his truck, picked out a bench and perched on it. The main road was visible through a small group of pine trees. The air lacked its usual trace of rancid smell from the sewage disposal factory located six miles away. He breathed in and out slowly to still the raging storm in his mind. He learned about controlled breathing from watching a show on TV about meditation and yoga. In the past, he temporarily attained calmness of spirit simply by breathing. However, right now, controlled breathing failed to tame the beast that was his raging thoughts.

The trees were his only companions. At times, children played hide-and-seek in the thicker group of trees on the opposite side of the park, away from the main road. Again, he tried to soothe his compulsive thoughts by turning his attention towards the calmness of the park. All was quiet indeed, except for the millions of insects chirruping their desperation to get laid as it got darker with the setting of the sun. At last, the sun took its leave behind the horizon and Donald had a dark, moonless and starless night for a sole companion. He returned to the solitary promenade of his mind, rendering himself oblivious to his surroundings.

The darkness of the night beseeched him to close his eyes. His heart pounded against his ribcage, transferring the sound of every beat across his body. Air whooshed in and out of his lungs like miniature gusts of winds in a storm. Blood flowed through vessels with the sound of ocean waves lashing on a seashore and many other sounds and sensory perceptions within his body heightened to levels he had never experienced in the life he remembered. Donald swayed to the sweet symphony that serenaded his psyche and brought peace to his punished person. Slowly, he opened his eyes. The hardness of the bench felt uncomfortable against his buttocks. He stood up, stiffly, and stretched. He glanced at his watch.

And where did two hours of my time go? he wondered with a smile.

He scanned his surroundings for no reason.

"Not ready to head home yet and it's still not time to hit Sara's bar," he said to himself. "I'll just go wait by the truck."

Donald stretched again and yawned as he headed for his truck.

"Better start working out, young man," he advised himself. "You're starting to act like Mr. Weinberg."

For the first time in a few hours, he grinned. He took in a lungful of the warm air of the night and exhaled.

Sweet, he thought.

Hands in his pockets, he took very slow steps around the truck.

Be mindful in everything you think, say or do, he recalled from a book he read on Buddhist teachings. *From walking, to doing the dishes, driving, everything.*

"Well," he said out loud. "No time like the present, right?"

More calm, peace and serenity radiated across his person in ways he had never experienced before. Nothing existed beyond the present and that present was all-encompassing. For a moment, the concept of his individualism became immersed in the boundlessness of Creation. His identity dissolved into a oneness that only one word could probably describe: life. His being experienced existence beyond the concept of who he thought he was until, alas, his individualism returned. Donald smiled and ceased his mindful walk. He leaned next to the front passenger door of his truck, closed his eyes and smiled from his heart. Unfortunately, he was so focused on his mindful walking that he never noticed the other presence nearby, blending perfectly with the shadows; a presence that waited for him as patiently as a predator stalking its prey would. The presence emerged from the shadows and glided towards Donald.

"Donald Smith," it called out to Donald in an evil, otherworldly baritone.

Donald stumbled to the ground from fright. The dark presence loomed over him blocking out the moon and stars with its thick, murky, shadowy form. Lips shivering with unsullied fear, Donald crawled until his back hit his truck. To worsen the situation, two orbs suddenly flashed where the evil creature's eyes were supposed to be, and light coalesced in its right hand into a huge, four-foot long sword.

"Your time has come."

And then, the creature attacked.

***

Patrick shielded himself in invisibility and kept a watchful eye on Newman's house in case the old man tried to act stupid or do something even more stupid. He knew no one could detect his presence, not even his agents

Well, maybe Sara or someone like her, he said to himself.

The agents assumed he had left town to handle some other business. Still, Patrick had ordered them to promptly keep him apprised of anything usual.

"Something's about to go down," he chewed on his gum. "Don't know what it is, but it's going down. My gut tells me so."

He sighed.

Well, whatever it is, this fallen angel has to return whence he came.

Patrick managed a chuckle.

"Whence... good old English."

He laughed harder before his expression turned grim.

He must return, Patrick reiterated. *To return, he must remember and he needs help to remember. But what kind of help would the angel need? I sure as hell don't know and neither does Father.*

"'Figure it out' he said," Patrick snorted. "Thanks, boss. The fate of heaven, hell and earth lies on my tiny shoulders now. Yeah, no pressure."

Patrick let out an expletive and sighed. More expletives followed.

This makes no sense at all. Father even tried to access Eliel's file in the Akashic Records but everything about Eliel was off limits. Nothing was erased; just shielded. Now that's some next level stuff. Some big boxer-wearing blokes are up there pulling strings on this fallen angel. But why? That's the million-dollar question. Well, with the fate of the realm involved, it's more like a seven-plus-billion-dollar question.

"I need to find a way to jog his memory," Patrick spoke out loud. "And when he remembers, will it be 'peace on earth' or 'doom for all mankind'? First things first, what can I do to make him remember?"

Several minutes later, Patrick had his epiphany.

Once, he was on a mission in Serbia. Four days of nonstop heavy rain had caused an overflow of the River Danube in biblical proportions. Massive floods, mudslides, landslides and everything else that could possibly happen when Mother Nature took such a long pissed happened. Amidst the terrible flooding in every city along the river, a desperate mother tried to reach higher ground with her toddler hanging on her back as the river dangerously eroded the ground beneath what remained of the concrete floor of a destroyed house the mother was standing on. Brave souls wanted to reach out to her and help her but could not. All they could do was shout words of encouragement to her.

Suddenly, a powerful current swept in and knocked her off her feet. Both mother and child were at the mercy of the raging current but, as if by a miracle, the child still clung to its mother's back. Well, the 'sudden powerful current' happened to be Patrick's assignment; a thirty-nine-foot long, six-foot broad serpent that had made its way to Earth Realm through a portal a black magician had unknowingly opened. The serpent was using the flood as cover to swim its way to the ocean, to freedom. Patrick had to make a choice, given his tiny window of opportunity: to save the mother and child, or to fulfill his mission and register his first failure.

Easy choice, Patrick thought.

However, when he was about to teleport to rescue the mother and child, the unexpected happened. The mother rose to the surface of the river and sprinted at half the speed of sound on top of the river as if she was on dry land. She continued sprinting until she reached safety.

But her esoteric signature indicates she's just a regular human, Patrick wondered. *Oh crap. Must complete assignment.*

Later, when she was interviewed, the mother said she had no recollection of doing what people said she did. All she remembered was that she was fighting for their lives and next thing she knew was that she and her son were safe.

Patrick thought her display of superhero tendencies certainly beat that of the nine-year-old girl who flipped over a car that was crushing her father, while he was doing some repairs under the car. Her father had ended up with a few broken ribs, but he was alive. The little girl had said that the only thing on her mind then was saving her father and that she had done the first thing that had come to her mind. Needless to say, school bullies stayed away from her from then on.

So, apparently, an overdose of adrenaline and something else seemed to be possible reasons why there are reports all over the realm of displays of 'impossible acts' of bravado, Patrick caressed his goatee. *Maybe Donald also needs a sudden boost of adrenaline and something else to remember he's Eliel.*

The thought of running this idea by Father Supreme crossed his mind.

Figure it out, he said, Patrick snorted again. *And that's exactly what I'm doing. Sounds ridiculous but I'm running out of options here.*

A moment of silence filled the car briefly.

Screw this, Patrick steeled his shaking resolve. *I'll do it and I won't consult Father.*

He glanced at his expensive watch.

"And time is of the essence," he said out loud.

He exited his car, still cloaked in a veil of invisibility.

"Don't know how I'll pull this off, but, like Father ordered, I'll figure it out."

Suddenly, Donald emerged from the house and hurried to his truck.

Patrick's clairvoyance showed Donald's aura changing rapidly between various colors of red and yellow. Clairaudience granted access to the chaos that was his compulsive thoughts. Patrick did not bother to turn on his clairsentience.

It's about to go down, he thought and teleported to the back of Donald's truck. *Take me to your crazy world, fallen angel.*

Donald pulled into a playground. Later, he started doing mindful walking.

Fallen angels and Buddhism, an invisible Patrick cocked an eyebrow. *Who would've thought? These are truly end times.*

Suddenly, Donald's aura changed from reddish gold to almost white.

A transformation? Patrick sprang with excitement. *An awakening? Is it happening?*

A few seconds went by, which felt like an eternity to Patrick.

Come on, come on, he clenched his jaws with excitement. *Where are the wings?*

A minute later, nothing happened.

What a major disappointment, he sank back into the rear seat of the truck. *So close.*

Minutes rolled by and Donald's aura still glowed white until the whiteness slowly changed into a violet green. Patrick grew with impatience and uncertainty with each ticking second. Finally, he heaved a heavy sigh.

Here goes nothing, he said to himself.

He teleported out of Donald's truck, still cloaked in invisibility. He sparked a thick, murky, shadowy field around his body and glided towards Donald.

"Donald Smith," he called out in an evil, otherworldly baritone. "Your time has come."

Then, he sparked the ethers into a sword and made his eyes glow with a fiery bright yellow.

This better work, he said to himself. *If not... well... I tried.*

Patrick brought down the sword towards Donald's neck.

The world moved extremely slowly and brightened as clear as day. However, Donald remained unbothered by the sudden change, which felt all too natural and familiar to him. The fear was gone, the instinct to survive gave way to a status quo he remembered with every cell of his body, but not his psyche. His attacker's sword had covered about one-fifth of the distance to his neck. A glow on each of his wrists caught his attention and he looked down at them. A golden bracelet appeared on each wrist. His attacker's sword was now halfway to his neck. Donald stood up and stepped aside, clearing himself out of the path of the sword. He leaned forward and regarded his attacker's glowing eyes as golden-yellow flames danced around his eyes.

It moves much faster than the humans do, Donald 2.0 thought.

Then, Donald balled his right hand into a fist and planted it into his attacker's solar plexus.

Patrick planned to halt his attack just before the sword touched Donald's neck. Instead, something slammed into his solar plexus with the speed of a small sedan. His diaphragm stiffened, the air fled from his lungs, his throat shut and the yellow glow of his eyes vanished instantly, even before his body crashed into a tree twenty-six feet away. His sword clanged to the ground and vanished in a puff of smoke. Patrick gasped for air as he writhed on the ground until he settled in a fetal position with his hands cradling his stomach.

Note to self, never EVER mess with an angel, he groaned from the pain that pulsed across his body. *Don't know what he hit me with, but God, it hurts so, so bad.*

After several coughs, he sensed a presence barely six feet away from him. He raised his gaze skyward. Above him towered a creature with a glowing, golden bracelet on each wrist, yellow flames where eyes should have been and a pair of flaming wings spread from each scapula.

Oh… my… God, Patrick's sudden exhilaration completely overrode his pain. *Wings. Wings of fire, of light. Pure, golden fire and light.*

Donald 2.0 flapped his wings twice before letting them hang idly. The flames neither singed nor burned his clothes.

He propped himself on his elbows and stared in total reverence at Donald.

I have seen an angel in the flesh, he thought with awe. *Dear God.*

Donald 2.0 stooped over him. He stared right back at Donald 2.0 without fear or reservation. Then, the flaming wings disappeared, as well as the bracelets. However, the flaming eyes remained and Donald 2.0 leaned menacingly closer to Patrick and glared fire at Patrick, literally.

"Whatever you are," Donald said, "return whence you came."

Whence, Patrick stifled a chuckle. *Whence.*

"The only reason you're alive is because I don't sense any evil in you," Donald 2.0 continued. "Do you understand me?"

"Yes, I do," Patrick replied with the same evil baritone.

"You will harm no one in this town," Donald continued. "Understood?"

"Yes," Patrick replied.

"Now begone before I change my mind," Donald's voice was changing into something else.

"So, you *ARE* a protector after all," Patrick rose to his feet.

And I'm glad you still didn't recognize me, he thought.

"You are the town's guardian angel."

Suddenly, the flames in Donald's eyes vanished and the same confusion and anxiety that plagued him hours earlier returned.

Patrick let out a few expletives.

I succeeded only to ruin everything again, he wanted to punch himself in the face.

Father is gonna kill me.

Donald's auric colors returned to the chaotic mix of red and yellow and his thoughts raged even more than before. He hurried to his truck and slid into it. Seconds later, the engine revved, the tires spun wildly and the truck left the park like a bat out of hell.

Patrick dismissed his murky costume.

"Tried my best but seems like only Donald can get himself out of amnesia and become Eliel," Patrick dusted his outfit. "I can scare him all I want, but all I'll see is another version of Donald. Never Eliel."

He teleported back to his car.

It's up to you now, Donald, he thought as he revved the engine. *I'll just go grab me a drink at Sara's and stick around until you remember. Hopefully, soon.*

Donald pulled up at Sara's bar and waited for a few minutes before stepping in. He ignored his healthy, clean-shaven zombie look. Patrick emerged from the restroom and headed towards Donald, who sat hunched over a glass of whiskey. He tapped Donald on the shoulder, startling Donald a little.

"You know it's rude to stare at a drink like that and not do it justice," he said.

"Hey man," Donald met his gaze briefly before averting his gaze.

"What da hell happened to you?" Patrick faked shock and slid into an open seat next to Donald. "You look like you just saw a ghost."

"Long day, that's all," Donald lied.

"You're a bad liar, my friend," Patrick signaled Sara. "Was fixing to head home but I won't be a good friend if I don't keep you company now, would I?"

"Thanks, man, but it's really okay," Donald lied again.

"Is that why you're still nursing that glass of holy water?" Patrick tried to lighten the atmosphere. "Come on now. It's holy water. Supposed to cast away all demons, including 'tiredness'," he traced his middle and index fingers of both hands in the air to indicate the irony of the situation.

Donald smiled and took a swig from his glass. He smacked his lips together.

"Better?" Patrick asked lifting an eyebrow.

"Yeah, man. Thanks," Donald smiled and raised his glass.

"Shoulda just gone to bed," Patrick joked. "Now we gotta finish this bottle."

"You chocolate boys behavin' yaselves?" Sara asked.

"It's his fault," Patrick complained. "I was fixing to get outta here and then he starts waving his glass in the air and all that crap."

Donald burst out laughing.

"Like I whooped your butt to stay" Donald countered.

"He did whoop my butt, Sara," Patrick said telepathically. *"With one punch."*

"I knew something was up," Sara replied.

"Tell you about it later, okay?" Patrick laughed at Donald's weak attempt at cracking a joke. *"But our boy here is very special."*

"You don't say," she replied as she waited on a couple.

"My place later?" he asked.

"Thought you'd never ask," she replied and from the corner of his eyes, he saw Sara grin at nothing and no one.

God, she's hot. 26,000 years old and she's still so freaking hot.

Patrick hoped crossing his legs would hide the hardness in his pants.

Patrick and Donald drank and chatted the night away. Donald's psyche fought back a yearning that stemmed from something beyond his psyche; a yearning to awaken to something much greater than what constituted the individualism he had cultivated over the past year; the only notion of time his memory could reach. Around eleven p.m., the two men parted ways.

Donald headed home and Patrick decided to use a little distraction before Sara came over. Newman was already asleep by the time Donald returned home.

Exhaustion weighed so heavily on Donald that he did not even remove his shoes before he fell on his bed. How he made it home safely with his level of alcoholic intoxication remained a mystery to him. But he was grateful nonetheless that no one, including himself, got hurt during his return home.

While Patrick was busy with his entertainment for the night, an idea so simple struck him.

How did I not think of this before? he wondered.

He wanted to smack himself across the face but he changed his mind and smacked his entertainment for the night's butt instead.

"Harder. Harder," she screamed and begged for more.

Patrick obliged, yanking her hair at the same time. They both climaxed together, which did not happen so often. He filled three-quarters of the condom.

Damn, player, He complimented himself. *What are you becoming?*

About an hour-and-a-half later, Patrick dropped off his one-night stand partner, returned to his room, showered and waited for Sara. Sara walked into the motel room a few minutes later and closed the door behind her. Her eyes flashed violet and the violet radiance from her body cast a hypnotic, beautiful violet glow in the dark motel room. Patrick was already weak in the knees even before Sara slid on the bed and united her naked body with his. Tonight was going to be another night of intense electricity, exhilarating energy and exulting ecstasy.

CHAPTER TWENTY-THREE

ON ENEMY TERRAIN

A SECTION OF Hell under construction buzzed in the horizon with a life of its own. Kazuk heaved his shoulders and folded his arms across his chest. Creatures of the realm scurried about in preparation of what was about to happen. He summoned and flapped his wings a few times. The exposed flesh of Lithilia's body pressed against his back. He dismissed his wings and stripped his gaze from the open space of the window. Lithilia pressed harder into him, but only as far as her voluptuous bosom would allow. She reached around his waist, took hold of his phallus and gently stroke it. Kazuk heaved his shoulders as he hardened before he turned around to face Lithilia. His bodied glowed in arousal. His hardness dug into her tummy. She pushed it down before she wrapped her arms around his neck and wrapped her legs around his hips.

In a smooth, expert hip movement, she took him into her warm wetness as if by a magic trick. Kazuk held her waist against his while she adjusted her internal design to perfectly accommodate him for maximum satisfaction. A soft moan left his lips and his eyelids fell halfway across his eyes. His wings spread out from his scapulae. He carried her to the ceiling, where they remained for several ravenous and passionate moments, before several squirts of angel light escaped his phallus and Lithilia spasmed before she stiffened and screamed in ecstasy. The couple freefell towards the floor and a bed burst out of the floor to absorb their fall.

He's great in bed, Lithilia admitted. *Too bad I feel nothing for him. Yet, I must continue dealing with this insanity as long as it gets me what I want. Then, I'll kick his sorry wings to the curb. Not much longer now…Not much longer.*

"I must see Metatron before I leave for Celestia," Kazuk said.

"Are you sure you're ready for this?" Lithilia asked.

Kazuk did not reply.

"I didn't mean it like that. I'm just worried if they try to end you on sight..."

"They won't," Kazuk stared blankly at the ceiling. "They have too much honor and scruples for that. Can't say anyone else from here would receive the same treatment."

"Because you are the King of Hell Realm," Lithilia interjected. "They will know your presence is for a serious cause."

"Exactly," Kazuk concurred.

"And what if Michael doesn't show up? What if Raphael shows up instead? What will you do?"

"It does not matter who shows up," Kazuk replied calmly. "The end result will be the same. Before they realize what's going on, it would already be too late."

Lithilia squeezed herself against Kazuk in a silent declaration that she was concerned for his safety. She wordlessly communicated to her husband that she would prefer he did not go because she feared the worst might befall him. But she understood it had to be done. He had been working on this plan for a few cycles and the moment of truth was nigh. Kazuk turned her face towards his. Tears streaming down her eyes. He kissed both eyes in a gesture of reassurance that all will be well. She kissed him on the lips, long and hard, until he had to peel himself away from her gently. But Lithilia sobbed and would not let go. Her clairsentience revealed his heart ached from her worrying about him.

Kazuk stripped himself from her and pushed himself away from the bed. He bathed his body with angelic light, returning his body to the splendor of an archangel. A white robe covered his body. He turned around and met his wife's teary gaze. She sat up on the bed, her nude form pulling on to him like a powerful magnet of seduction.

"See you soon," he said before he teleported away.

Lithilia counted to five before she grinned from ear-to-ear.

"Good job, girl," she summoned a gown over her body. "Your award awaits."

***

Kazuk appeared outside Metatron's domain and knocked on the door.

"Come in," said Metatron.

Kazuk walked through the door. Metatron was kneeling on the floor with his back to the door. Torso exposed, the mark of the seven-faceted crystal glowed between his shoulder blades.

"Hello Metatron."

"Hello, my king," Metatron replied in a monotone.

"You know why I am here, don't you?" Kazuk asked.

"Yes, my king," Metatron replied with the same monotone.

"Good," Kazuk said. "I won't insult you by asking if you're ready. I'm just trying to make sure that every piece is in place before I proceed."

"His majesty owes me no explanation whatsoever," Metatron replied.

Kazuk could not discern if Metatron was being sarcastic or not; not that it mattered, anyway.

I'll deal with him later, Kazuk promised. *I must focus on the task at hand.*

"Very well, then," Kazuk conceded. "I must say I appreciate the fact that you are willing to work with us for our common good. Our moment is almost finally upon us. We could finally regain our respect, honor, and glory."

"I could not have said it any better," Metatron replied. "My king…"

Kazuk shook his head. If Metatron did not hold such high importance to the plan, he would have ended Metatron right that very moment.

"Once you get the signal, act instantly," Kazuk ordered. "Everything has to be flawless."

"Everything will be perfect from my end, my king," Metatron reminded him. "Respectfully, you have nothing to worry about, as far as I am concerned. If I recall correctly, I was the one who told you about the artifact and the prophecies. Was I not, my king?"

"Indeed," Kazuk winced slightly from the sting of Metatron's words.

I beat him in combat and he slaps me in the face with a reminder of his importance, Kazuk fumed. *Enjoy it while it lasts Metatron.*

Kazuk made to teleport.

"Good luck, my king," Metatron said.

"Thank you," Kazuk replied and teleported away.

Metatron allowed a brief moment to elapse before he opened his eyes. Blood-red flames spewed from them and, when he smiled, blood-red flames seethed through his teeth. His smile was forged out of the fury that flared within; fury for the humiliation he suffered from being forced to address Maziel as 'king'.

My plan is coming together, Metatron fumed. *Let him obtain the artifact, but if he thinks she will bow to him just because he set her free…*

Metatron guffawed so hard that his domain shook like a violent earthquake in one of the lower realms.

Kazuk appeared in a neutral zone in Lemuria that was close to the border of Celestia. He allowed himself a moment of contemplation. Celestia, his former home, hung in the distance like a spherical teardrop in this part of Creation. A wave of nostalgia swept over him, which he quickly shrugged off.

The past is the past and now, a new future begins.

He switched to sub-Celestial frequency.

"Jamael, are you ready?"

"I am, brother," Jamael replied in like manner.

"Now is your last chance to back out," Kazuk added. *"No one will blame or judge you if you do."*

"Thanks for the offer, Kazuk," Jamael replied. *"My mind is made up. I'm all-in."*

"Okay, brother," Kazuk affirmed. *"It gives me great comfort and joy when you reassure me like this. Like I told you before, our mission cannot succeed without your help."*

"Then I must ensure my success," Jamael reaffirmed.

"And I trust that you, no WE, will succeed, brother," Kazuk chimed in. *"Be on the alert. It is about to happen."*

Kazuk teleported into Celestia. The moment his form crossed the border of Celestia, alarms blared all over the realm. He dropped to his knees and raised his hands in the air as hundreds of angels and archangels converged around him, weapons drawn and aimed at him. Kazuk remained motionless. Other angels and archangels positioned themselves at various corners of Celestia in preparation for any attack that may ensue. An archangel walked through the wall of angels and archangels that had formed around Kazuk and stood in front of him.

"I'll be wingless," the archangel exclaimed. "The King of Hell Realm himself."

"Good to see you too, Palubiel," Kazuk replied.

"The feeling is not mutual, Maziel," Palubiel retorted. "Or would you prefer I call you Kazuk?"

"I'd love to entertain your childishness," Kazuk spoke calmly. "But I am here for more important business; like meeting with your superior."

"The only thing you will meet here is your end," Palubiel spat.

"And risk an instant war?" Kazuk cocked an eyebrow. "I am very sure you do not want to go down in history as the one who started another slaughter because your emotions were completely devoid of any intellect."

Palubiel glared and sparked the ethers into a spiked club.

"Stand down, everyone," the unmistakable commanding voice of Raphael boomed through the crowd.

Everyone executed the order except for Palubiel.

"Palubiel?" Raphael glared at her.

"Yes, sir," Palubiel answered and dismissed her weapon.

Raphael approached Kazuk, wristband glowing with the brilliance of combat.

'Try anything stupid, and you and Hell Realm will be decimated with extreme prejudice,' was the unspoken message, and Kazuk heard the message loud and clear.

"Why are you here?" Raphael asked with fire in his voice.

"To speak to Michael," Kazuk replied.

"Really?" Raphael scoffed. "You want to see Michael."

"Yes," Kazuk replied.

"Whatever message you have for Michael, you can pass it onto me. I will see to it that he receives it."

"If you will not allow me to speak to your superior," Kazuk said. "Then my purpose here is done, and I should return to my realm."

"And who said I was going to allow you return to Hell?" Raphael asked.

Kazuk smiled before replying.

"I don't recall saying that I needed your permission to return to my realm, Raphael," Kazuk said.

Then, in the sub-Celestial frequency, he uttered one word.

"NOW."

Metatron's eyes flared and the mark between his shoulder blades glowed with a bright, blood-red hue. It burned his skin and pain possessed his body. He sparked the ethers into a dagger in his left hand and he lifted it over his head. He closed his eyes, gritted his teeth and drove the dagger into the mark. A beam of blood-red light shot out from his mouth as he screamed from the pain that pulsated with exponential intensity through every ether of his being. His eyes threatened to pop out of his head and his body spasmed and stiffened repeatedly. The connection became stronger until he could no longer take it. He retrieved the dagger from the mark and collapsed to the floor. Blood-red light beamed from the cut until, gradually, it closed up and sweet relief washed over his body.

"Your turn now, Maziel," he murmured. "My role is done."

***

Michael watched Kazuk teleport into Celestia. Raphael's squad leaped into action immediately. He nodded his approval and satisfaction at the efficiency of the response against Kazuk's sudden entry. Raphael seemed to interrogate Kazuk.

"Why are you here, Maziel?" Michael asked himself. "What's your goal?"

Michael summoned a chair and relaxed into it. He tapped the left armrest of his seat with his index finger absentmindedly and repeatedly, while his mind explored various possible reasons for Kazuk's unexpected visit.

"By Celestia," Michael exclaimed. "It's a decoy."

He leaped from his chair and summoned his battle outfit.

"Ra-"

Pain beyond his imagination seared through every iota of his body, preventing him from alerting Raphael. He crashed on the floor with a wing-clipping scream of pain. The mark between his shoulder blades glowed and burned through his war garment and he screamed again. The pain pummeled from everywhere and nowhere at once and his very existence withered away, as if drained through a portal created by an unseen power in the mark between his shoulder blades. He writhed, thrashed and wailed on the floor. Even summoning any of his inner council members proved an impossible feat. Finally, the pain dissipated and relief flooded his body. Michael lay on the floor and stared blankly at the ceiling until his vision cleared.

"What just happened?" he wondered. "Why the pain? Why the mark? What or who could-"

Michael sprang up from the floor.

"The mark," he exclaimed. "Malichiel. By Celestia."

Michael immediately teleported to the spawn sanctuary. Jamael was nowhere to be found. He cursed and teleported into the sanctuary, hoping for the best but fearing the worst. He glided towards the containment of the Zarark and opened it. Then, a barrage of expletives escaped his lips followed by a rageful scream.

***

Jamael boiled with nervous excitement after his brief chat with Kazuk. Shortly afterwards, the alarms went off and Celestia careened into commotion.

Stay put now, he told himself. *That is not the signal.*

He straightened his shoulders, puffed his chest and raised his chin.

"I am the guardian of the spawn sanctuary," he said out loud. "It is my duty to protect and defend this sacred location."

He summoned his wings, flapped them twice and closed his eyes before he dismissed his wings. When he opened them, an archangel stood in front of him.

"By Celestia," he exclaimed and summoned his spear. "Identify yourself."

"We're on the same side, brother," the archangel raised his hands in the air. "Kazuk sent me. I'm to retrieve the artifact and affirm your non-association with the plan."

Jamael lowered his spear and eyed the archangel suspiciously.

What is the meaning of this? he wondered. *Is this a test?*

"We must hurry, brother," the archangel pleaded, glancing over his shoulders, "Our window of opportunity is closing. Michael will be upon us if we delay."

In an appreciation for the urgency of the situation, Jamael dismissed his spear.

"No, keep your spear," someone ordered via sub-Celestial frequency.

Jamael recognized the voice.

"Scribe?" he asked in sub-Celestial frequency and re-summoned his spear.

"Yes," The Scribe replied dismissively. *"Now, look up the wall behind you and*

identify a mark."

"I see it," Jamael replied. *"It was never there before."*

"Strike it with the tip of your spear," The Scribe ignored Jamael's distracting curiosity. *"Now."*

A door appeared in the wall as he cocked his spear. When he struck the mark, the door shattered revealing the inside of the spawn sanctuary. Mouth agape with shock, Jamael regarded his spear as if he had never seen anything like it before.

"But... how?"

"Stay focused," The Scribe yelled at him.

"Sorry," Jamael jerked back to the situation at hand.

"Go straight and then make a sharp left," The Scribe instructed. *"After the sharp left, you will find an altar straight ahead with the statue of two angels on either side holding what looks like flaming swords. On the altar, you will find a tablet with the same mark you saw on the door just a moment ago. Retrieve this tablet and leave the sanctuary!"*

Jamael followed the instructions of The Scribe to the letter and found what he was looking for. He picked it up and teleported out of the sanctuary. When he emerged out of teleportation, the other archangel summoned a sword, burning with archangel battle flame, and took his head off in a single horizontal strike. Bright, golden light spewed from the exposed stump of Jamael's neck where his head used to sit. The other archangel retrieved the tablet from Jamael's hands before Jamael's headless and lifeless body collapsed to the ground and burned away without a trace.

The archangel immediately teleported to a neutral zone in the dimension, where he handed the artifact over to a stranger. The stranger accepted the artifact and as the archangel defected to Hell Realm, his new home, the stranger teleported to Keerim. The stranger, The Scribe, handed Celestia's artifact over to Keerim, who promptly shielded it from any form of detection from any creature in dimensions lower than the Dimension of Mueba. Slowly, Keerim's sanity returned to normal, as well as a temporary feeling of peace.

"You finally came through, Scribe," Keerim said. *"I'm impressed."*

"It's always great to see how you hold such high expectations of me," The Scribe retorted with heavy sarcasm. *"You just uphold your end of our arrangement."*

"You do not have to worry about me now, Scribe," Keerim replied.

"Oh, I'm not worried about you at all, Keerim," The Scribe remarked. *"I'm just worried about what you'll do when she returns, which may be a lot sooner than you expect."*

The Scribe smiled and gradually faded into sub-etheric levels.

"You know, given the most recent turn of events, that is..."

Keerim knew The Scribe was correct and with this notion, his temporary feeling of peace disappeared without leaving a trace, just like The Scribe.

The archangel did not lie when he said Kazuk sent him to affirm Jamael's non-association with Kazuk. It was not his fault that Jamael had been deemed too stupid and too high of a risk to keep around after stealing the artifact. Jamael had played his role, and that was it.

Just another loose end to get rid of. Nothing personal.

The archangel appeared before Kazuk's inner council.

"Greetings, brothers and sisters," he said. "I am Samael, a recent defector and former member of Michael's inner council."

"Welcome, brother," Kazuk's inner council hailed.

"It is customary to have a new name," a member said. "What's yours?"

"Devilus," he replied.

***

Raphael searched around as a second set of alarms blasted across the realm. He gave a series of quick orders. Then, he picked up Kazuk with his left hand and lifted Kazuk off the ground as a foot-long dagger appeared in his right hand.

"Bring him over," Michael ordered telepathically.

"But Michael-" Raphael tried to protest telepathically.

"Now, Raphael," Michael insisted. *"We have a much bigger problem."*

Raphael teleported Kazuk to Michael's domain. Michael approached Kazuk, who regarded him with an expressionless face. Without any warning, Michael punch Kazuk in the stomach and Kazuk doubled over, collapsing to the floor with a grunt of discomfort. He picked up Kazuk with his right hand, lifted Kazuk up in the air and slammed him on the floor. Kazuk's face contorted with pain but he did nothing to resist Michael's attacks. When Michael knelt beside him, Kazuk started laughing hysterically.

"Where is it?" Michael hissed through gritted teeth.

"Good to see you too, Michael," Kazuk healed his body with golden light he sparked with Celestia's vibrational frequency.

"I will ask you one more time, where is it?"

"And if I don't tell you, will you beat it out of me?" Kazuk mocked.

Raphael made his spiked hammer appear in his right hand.

"Let me finish him, Michael," Raphael begged.

"We need him alive," Michael hissed and stood up. "For now."

Kazuk also stood up, summoned his wings and flapped them twice before dismissing them.

"Why is that?" Raphael asked, but Michael did not say anything.

"Raphael dear, remember when I told you that I won't need your permission to return to my realm?" Kazuk mocked. "Your superior will tell you when I am gone. And as for you, archangel supreme," he added, shifting his attention to

Michael, "I will return shortly to discuss the terms of our negotiation. For now, I will let you big boys brush each other's wings. I have some celebration to do, if you don't mind."

Kazuk teleported out of Celestia.

"What the flap is going on, Michael?" Raphael demanded.

Michael peeled his stare from the nothingness where Kazuk occupied a-blink-of-an-eye ago and gazed at Raphael. The anger, humiliation, and powerlessness that churned in Michael's eyes and clenched jaws caused Raphael to narrow his eyes with concern. It had been many cycles since he last saw Michael in this state.

"Brother," he spoke softly. "What is going on?"

"Kazuk has the Zarark," Michael replied.

CHAPTER TWENTY-FOUR

THE ZARARK

THE ZARARK IS an artifact of Creation that resides in the central realm of every dimension. It is a physical representation of The Logos and bears the mark of The Logos; a glyph of a seven-faceted crystal. In certain realms, the Zarark is housed in special structures, while in others, it abides in the core of the realm. Word has it that the Zarark acts as a conduit for new vibrations of consciousness to impact a dimension. While the use of the Zarark includes the spawning of new creatures, its other uses remain a mystery to the vast majority of the creatures of Creation. Perhaps only multidimensional beings are aware of all the uses of the Zarark. For realms that have attained a certain level of evolution, a creature of that realm is chosen to become an overseer or guardian of the Zarark.

In Celestia, Michael was the original overseer of the Zarark by default, though that responsibility later shifted to Malichiel when the visions began and he became the transcriber of the messages from The Logos. However, after the rebellion, Michael resumed that responsibility until Maziel, now Kazuk, took over. So, when Malichiel, now Metatron, first proposed the plan to obtain the Zarark and move it to Hell Realm, Kazuk thought that Metatron's prolonged moments spent in solitude had cost the fallen archangel of great repute his mind. However, when The Scribe proposed a similar plan and explained how the plan could work, Kazuk realized Metatron, the Silent One, was far removed from losing his mind. Also, who else was better suited to be the overseer of the Zarark than one who was a previous overseer himself?

Well played, Metatron. Well played.

And why did Hell Realm need the Zarark in the first place? To increase their numbers by spawning new creatures, instead of relying on defectors from

Celestia and immigrants from other realms and dimensions within the cosmic cluster. As such, Hell Realm could now tip the scales of victory in their favor when the moment to attack Celestia arrived. Kazuk's inner council rallied behind this plan unanimously. Hell Realm would no longer cower because of their smaller numbers and Celestia would be unable to build their numbers without the Zarark. Celestia would become weaker, while Hell would become stronger, thus tipping the balance of power in Hell Realm's favor.

"And what about Michael?" the inner council had asked.

"You leave him to me," Kazuk had replied. "He may be the best of us all, but his best is not a preclusion of infallibility and I have something special for him."

"Care to share with us?" the inner council demanded.

"Best the plan remains a secret for now," Kazuk had replied.

Why would I want to share vital information with you, such as information related to the connection Michael and Metatron share through that glyph on their backs? Kazuk thought. *No other creature in Hell or Celestia knows about this, none but Lithilia and Metatron. Lithilia cares not for the affairs of Hell or Celestia but Metatron on the other hand...*

It was on this premise of secrecy that Kazuk had worked with Metatron to execute the flawless plan of weakening Celestia: Phase One of the grand plan. Kazuk, the King of Hell Realm, would serve as the ultimate distraction. While Raphael and Celestia focused on him, Metatron would give Michael something to think about. In his distraction, Michael would not notice that the Zarark had been stolen until it was already too late. Kazuk would then have immunity and complete bargaining power because he, and he alone, would know the location of the Zarark. This was another part of the plot that only Kazuk and The Scribe were aware of. It was best that way. Kazuk loved the power he wielded as ruler of the realm and preferred to keep it that way.

The knack for survival is always a good motivator. Poor Metatron. He must be livid in his domain. What did he expect? That I was just going to hand over the Zarark to him?

Phase Two of the plan was the elimination of Michael. The details of this part of the plan remained a secret as well.

Whoever takes out Michael immediately earns unsurpassable reputation, the kind that strikes fear in the cores of both allies and enemies, Kazuk thought. *Why hand over such a great opportunity to someone else?*

Kazuk's inner circle, Metatron and even Lithilia boiled with rage when they learned the Zarark was not going to come to Hell Realm right away.

"We demand an explanation," they chorused like a small, angry mob.

"Tell me something," Kazuk spoke calmly. "What would you do if the Zarark was brought here right away?"

"I was under the impression we have a means of keeping it safe, my king,"

Lithilia replied, careful not to let the rest of the council in on Metatron's role.

Kazuk's inner council erupted in agreement, while Metatron and Devilus eyed Kazuk with vile contempt.

"Be that as it may, my queen," Kazuk replied with polite sarcasm. "Have you thought about the implications of having the Zarark within our realm this very moment?"

"Other than superior advantage?" asked an inner council member from the Realm of Kremus.

The inner council member applauded his sarcasm.

"You ignorant buffoons," Kazuk spat. "Can't you fools see that having the Zarark here is an open invitation for war with Celestia?"

A deathly silence spread across the inner council as understanding dawned on everyone present.

"If you want, I can go retrieve it where I safely hid it and bring it right here, right now," Kazuk spat. "Tell me, are you stupid imbeciles ready for war with Celestia? Huh? Are you?"

Heads inclined and eyes averted away with the silence that ensued.

"I ask you all a question," Kazuk's voice echoed in the silence of the room, causing a few of the inner council members to jump slightly.

"I alone know where the Zarark is," Kazuk continued. "For the sake of the realm, and all your sakes, it is best that way. Until we execute Phase Two of the plan, eliminating Michael, the Zarark shall reside away from Hell."

"But what makes you so sure they won't attack us anyway?" an arachnoid creature from the Realm of Crappoxia asked.

"See anyone attacking us right now?" Kazuk asked in return.

"No. But that doesn't mean that they won't," the same creature rebutted.

Murmurs of agreement with the arachnoid creature crawled from the council. Kazuk leaned forward and stared the council down to silence.

"You really think that an artifact as important as the Zarark gets stolen and Michael will just sit back and do absolutely nothing?" Kazuk asked calmly.

Their features soften with the understanding of the implications of Kazuk's words. Celestia was going to react, but not necessarily in an all-out war manner. Locating and retrieving the Zarark was of utmost priority.

"When I say there is a plan and it has to be kept secret, for now, I mean just that," his toned of voice edged towards impatience and annoyance. "I cannot risk having you empty-headed fools running around jeopardizing a plan that is already working so well. Secrecy greatly minimizes the risk of failure and I am not one who fancies failure. I will not make the same mistake she made."

Metatron winced and suppressed the red flames that threatened to spill from his eyes and mouth, much to Kazuk's concealed pleasure.

"Do you understand?"

"Yes, my king," they chorused.

"Good," Kazuk said. "Now, on to other important matters. I'm pleased to announce the newest member to our circle, Samael. He was most instrumental in our recent victory. Everyone, give Samael a very warm welcome."

The council welcomed Samael.

"Thank you, my king," Samael said. "Respectfully, it is now Devilus."

"Excellent. So quick to adjust. Welcome amongst us, Devilus," Kazuk said.

"Thank you, my king," Samael replied.

"Do you have anything to say?" Kazuk asked.

"Not this moment, my king," Devilus replied.

"Very well. You're all dismissed."

Everyone left, safe for Lithilia and Metatron.

"Do you have anything to say, Metatron?" Kazuk asked.

"You have your reasons for hiding the Zarark, my king," Metatron replied. "If I can't sense it, then neither can Michael. My guess is that you hid the Zarark in a higher dimension."

"I do not care for your guesses," Kazuk replied dismissively. "I was not lying when I said my plan will remain a secret for security reasons."

"And by 'security', do you mean the security of Hell Realm or your personal security, my king?" Metatron asked.

"Security is security. The rest is perspective," Kazuk replied.

"I trust my king is making the perfect decision then," Metatron stood up from his chair. "For the ultimate good of us all…"

He teleported away, leaving Kazuk and Lithilia to themselves.

"I take it you won't tell me where you hid the Zarark either?" Lithilia asked, desperately trying to conceal her anger.

"No," Kazuk replied flatly.

"As you wish, my king," she reached out and held his hand in hers. "I must say I am very proud of what you're doing keeping us all in the dark. It is a real display of wisdom and strength"

"Or common sense," Kazuk interjected, sliding his hand away from hers.

"Anyway, well-played, my love," she rebutted and stood up.

Kazuk kept his gaze away from her. He stared blankly into space as if his mind was somewhere else. Lithilia nodded.

"I'll be at our domain whenever you're ready," she teleported away.

"I think your number of fans just reached a record high," The Scribe said as he manifested from nothingness. "Where do I start? Raphael, Michael, Malichiel, Lilith and the list goes on and on."

The Scribe applauded.

"Bravo, Kazuk. Bravo!"

"Is the Zarark safe?" Kazuk asked, ignoring The Scribe's words.

"Oh, so you don't trust me as well? I'm a little offended, I must say," The Scribe joked.

"My trust in you is matched only by my loyalty to Michael," Kazuk scoffed.

"The only reason you trusted me with the Zarark was that the hiding location is as important to my plan as it is to yours, right?" The Scribe asked.

Kazuk did not bother to reply. The Scribe stared at Kazuk for a moment and then smiled.

A law of Creation forbade a being from another dimension to procure and/or keep the Zarark of another dimension. This law prevented multidimensional creatures, like The Scribe, from obtaining the Zarark by themselves. However, a loophole existed in this law. It did not forbid a creature from accepting a Zarark willingly offered to them by a creature from the Zarark's home dimension. Hence, The Scribe had to get a creature from the Dimension of Lemuria to obtain the Zarark from Celestia. This was where Jamael and Kazuk came into play.

Certain creatures in dimensions of higher vibrational frequency could contain the Zarark of dimensions of lower vibrational frequency within their form. The Zarark releases pure vibrations of consciousness in small, continuous pulses while in an idle state. These pulses of pure consciousness from the Zarark help to bring balance to the psyche of the creature housing the Zarark within its form. The Scribe was aware of this, hence why he gave Keerim the Zarark for housing. The transition to new cycles, be it of the dimension or cosmic cluster, caused much instability to the psyche of Paradins. During such instability, their Paradin essence becomes exposed, making them more susceptible to polarization, which is identification with either the vibration of good or evil.

The transition in cycles was monumental because it involved not just the Dimension of Mueba or the cosmic cluster. Creation was about to go through a new perfect cycle and a Great Reset marked the end of the current perfect cycle. Keerim, as well as many other Paradins, had experienced destabilizations of their psyches before; but this was different for all of them and Keerim suffered the most because he had become highly polarized, even before his comrades started going through the phase. His exposed, unstable essence neared a tipping point, which threatened to offset The Scribe's grand plan. Finding a polarized Paradin was infinitely harder than finding a polarized archangel. The only remedy for a Paradin with an unstable essence was a Zarark from lower dimension, which he obtained. Keerim returned to his normal self and all was right again with The Scribe's plan. Also, in housing the Zarark within his form,

Keerim also rendered it undetectable to Michael and Metatron.

And with that, Kazuk had leverage over both archangels.

"You're finally starting to look at things from a broader perspective, Kazuk," The Scribe said with a hint of admiration. "And you're learning the basics of power and control. Bravo."

Kazuk still did not reply. The Scribe nodded imperceptibly and gradually vanished into nothingness.

Lithilia lay on the bed and stared at the ceiling. Kazuk's shrewdness mocked her ego. She gritted her teeth. Granted, she had no interest in the Zarark.

That smug look, she thought. *The derision and condescension in his voice.*

A new version of Kazuk was present during the meeting.

It's as if his trip to Celestia brought out his true personality, she rationalized. *A cold, calculative, conniving, conceitful cynic.*

Lithilia sat up and stretched.

"I wonder who or what he'll become if he succeeds in taking out Michael," she chuckled. "This is going to be a very interesting situation. Well played, dear husband of mine. Well played."

Lithilia's eyes flashed orange.

"I believe it's time to revisit my plan."

An evil grin spread across her face.

"Let's begin, shall we?"

Metatron sat on his heels in silence. The fire in the pit of his core burned still, only with less intensity. Like Michael, he too preferred to be in control and the Zarark in his hands was supposed to give him the control he sought.

"My plan must be revised," he seethed. "Kazuk has an ally, a very powerful one. I must find out who that ally is."

He closed his eyes and tried to quiet the rage that still burned within his core.

He should be reaching out any moment soon, he thought. *Phase Two begins shortly.*

"I'm heading out now," Kazuk's voice called in his head. *"Be prepared."*

"Yes, my king," Metatron affirmed and prayed, yet again, that it was the last time he would ever address Kazuk as such.

***

"So, what now?" Raphael asked Michael.

"We wait," Michael replied. "Hell hasn't attacked yet and Kazuk obviously wanted to have leverage for something bigger."

"Well, he has more than enough leverage now actually," Raphael corrected. "I wonder what his grand plan is."

"We'll know soon enough," Michael said.

The other senior archangels appeared one-by-one in his domain. Samael was still to join them. Deliberations began immediately, which quickly turned into a disorganized meeting until Michael stood up.

"We've run every possible simulation except for the most likely one," he started. "What if Kazuk stole the Zarark because he wanted to use it against me? And what if he does?"

"Stop this madness," Gabriel said. "It's not going to happen."

"Maybe," Michael replied quickly. "But we must entertain that possibility as well. What if I am no longer around? Who among you should take my place?"

Without the slightest hesitation, everyone but Raphael chose Raphael. Raphael chose Uriel and Uriel burst out laughing.

"You're so sweet, Raph," Uriel blew him a kiss.

"You're all too kind," Raphael spoke with appreciation. "If I didn't know any better, I'd say you winged fools planned this in advance."

"And what a wonderful plan that would have been," Michael said. "You are the strongest and toughest of all of us-"

"Really, Michael?" Gabriel said.

"Okay. Apart from me. How does that sound?" Michael smiled.

"Go on…" Gabriel said and Drusiliel smacked his occiput.

"Where's Samael, by the way?" Michael asked.

"He's not in his domain and he is not responding to my calls," Uriel said with a worried look on her face.

"Or mine," Gabriel chimed in.

"I guess it was him then," Raphael spoke sadly. "Our systems detected an archangel heading towards a neutral zone. The archangel never returned."

"We've lost another to Hell," Drusiliel's voice was heavy with rage. "Damn Kazuk. And I'm going to call it first. Samael is mine."

The rest of the inner council nodded in agreement.

"And to think that we were best friends," Drusiliel clenched her jaw in anger.

"You'll get your chance soon, with the way things are going," Uriel said.

"Anyway, back to more pressing issues," Michael sat down. "I know you will take care of Celestia like you always have, Raph."

"You're not gone yet, Michael," Raphael cut him short. "Save the speech for later, because we all know that no matter what happens, you'll be back."

Everyone chorused their agreement.

No need arguing with them, Michael thought.

The alarms went off again and Raphael teleported away immediately. He reappeared a short while later and tossed Kazuk to the floor. Kazuk stood up and straightened his outfit.

"Hello everyone," Kazuk said casually.

If glares could end existences, then Kazuk's existence would end in a way that his very name would be erased from the walls of Akasha.

"What do you want?" Raphael asked.

"To return the Zarark on one condition," he replied.

"And what would that be?" Raphael asked.

"That he comes to get it," Kazuk replied pointing at Michael.

"Forget it," Gabriel said.

"He can speak for himself, Gabriel," Kazuk stared Gabriel down.

Kazuk's lips curved in an evil smile while scoffs and snickers popped out from the inner council members. Michael raised his hand for silence.

"And if I go with you, what happens?" Michael asked.

"You can't be seriously thinking about-" Gabriel started, but Michael raised a hand in the air silencing Gabriel.

"If I go with you, what happens?" Michael repeated his question.

"Then I return the Zarark, as a measure of good faith," Kazuk replied.

"Good faith of what?" Raphael asked.

"Peace."

"Broken wings. He must take us for fools," Gabriel exclaimed. "Peace? Like that will ever come to pass."

"And you wonder why I would rather speak with Michael," Kazuk shot back at Gabriel. "Obviously, he is the only one here who seems to want peace as much as I do."

Kazuk returned his attention to the inner circle.

"We all agree that too many of our brothers' and sisters' existences ended because of her. I don't want another foolish war. I don't want another senseless massacre. I apologize for stealing the Zarark, but I needed to get your attention somehow. Imagine that I walked in here and started negotiating peace talks. What are the odds of us having a sit-down, without the right amount of motivation, like stealing the Zarark?"

Kazuk studied the faces of the inner council members. The stiffness in their features borne out of agitation and tension softened as they appeared to consider his words.

"Look, I'm not asking that we all be friends again," he continued. "I'm only asking that we enjoy our existences in our separate realms without ever worrying about attacking one another. We don't have to like one another. We just have to agree to coexist peacefully. That's all I'm asking for."

"And if you're so forthcoming all of a sudden," Uriel said, "why do you insist on Michael coming alone?"

"Michael is the overseer to the Zarark," Kazuk explained. "I came to your realm alone. All I ask, from one leader to another, is that you accord me the same intent at peace by letting your leader come with me to the location of the Zarark. I assure you, it is not in Hell."

"I don't trust your talk on wanting peace, Kazuk," Raphael said.

"It is your prerogative not to trust anyone, Raphael," Kazuk rebutted. "But these are my terms. So, it's up to you."

"I'll come with you," Michael replied without giving any of the inner council members a chance to respond.

"In case you have forgotten," Kazuk gestured towards Michael. "I don't stand a chance in a fight against Michael, or any of you for that matter. You are, after all, the finest Celestia has to offer, no?"

Michael stood up and leveled a stern gaze at his inner council. His silent message was clear.

If I do not return, decimate Hell with extreme prejudice.

His gaze lingered a little longer at Uriel. In their connected stare was the hope that all was not lost; that everything would fall into place at the perfect moment. In their connected stare was the hope that the prophecy would indeed come true, even if it meant the final fall of a once fallen angel.

"Shall we?" Kazuk gestured towards Michael.

Michael closed his eyes, heaved his shoulders and bid a silent farewell to his friends, his brothers, his sisters and his family, with a curt nod.

This is the last time I shall lay eyes on Celestia again, he thought.

Kazuk teleported away, leaving his teleportation trail for Michael to follow. They appeared in a barren realm somewhere in Lemuria. Michael no longer felt any connection to Celestia. He scanned his environs. Somber and lonely. Not a single lifeform came within their perception. Their angelic glows provided the only sources of illumination where they stood. Michael's glowed bright- golden while Kazuk's glowed red.

"Where are we?" Michael asked.

His caution and alertness spiked.

"Right this way, Michael," Kazuk walked ahead of Michael.

Michael hesitated before he followed his red-glowing enemy. A few paces later, a chest floating in midair reflected Kazuk's red glow.

"Therein lies your artifact," Kazuk gestured towards the chest.

"And how can I be sure you're not playing a trick on me?" Michael asked.

"You're welcome to strike me down if I am," Kazuk replied. "After all, you trusted me enough to follow me here, so far away from home, no?"

Michael glared at Kazuk, but Kazuk pointed towards the chest. Michael turned and approached the chest with extreme caution.

May Celestia damn me if I go down without a fight, he said to himself.

The dimensions of the chest were slightly larger than those of the Zarark.

Good sign so far, Michael thought.

He reached for the chest and undid the two locks. His hands hovered in front of the chest, hesitation and uncertainty weighing hard on them.

I have come thus far already, he thought. *I might as well see it through.*

He lifted the lid of the chest and the moment he did, every ether of his being screamed for him to flee.

"NOW METATRON," Kazuk ordered telepathically.

Michael tried to teleport away from the chest, but it was too late. His mark glowed and burned, and paralyzing pain pulsed across his body. He collapsed to the ground and cursed at Metatron with his scream of agony. An egg-shaped piece of milky-white crystal lay at the bottom of the chest. However, this crystal was capable of far more than what its beauty portrayed. The crystal created an energy field of imprisonment around any creature it became exposed to. It copied the esoteric signature of its prisoner and customized the imprisoning energy field to neutralize its prisoner's powers and abilities before it slowly drained the life out of its prisoner without killing the prisoner. This crystal of incarceration was the worst form of torture known to any creature within the manuscript of this part of Creation The Scribe labeled *The Soulless Ones.*

Michael raged against the energy barrier that was now his cage. He punched, he kicked, he stabbed and yelled, but nothing happened. Kazuk glided towards Michael, hands clasped behind his back.

"Looks familiar?" Kazuk tapped on the field. "The Prisoner's Yoke; I love the name of this crystal."

Michael glared and let out a barrage of curses at Kazuk.

"I know, I know," Kazuk giggled. "Same thing you used against her, no? I'm curious. How did you come across this? I know you did not obtain it from The Scribe. You're too..." Kazuk searched for the word. "Tainted. Yes, you're too tainted for The Scribe; and by that, I mean you two can't share a common goal."

"Why not just kill me?" Michael asked through clenched teeth.

"Because, Michael, you're far too important to me alive than dead," Kazuk replied tauntingly. "Don't you see?"

Michael punched harder into the energy field out of frustration, though he knew his actions were pointless.

"You're wasting your precious moments," Michael said.

"And precious moments are all I have to spare," Kazuk replied.

"Celestia will decimate Hell if I do not return," Michael assured Kazuk.

"And you think I don't know you gave the orders already? Come on now, Michael, even you have to know that I did not rise to my ranks simply because of my good looks."

Kazuk shook his head in disgust.

"You, on the other hand, are not in a good place right now, and I mean that literally," Kazuk added.

"When I get out of here-"

"*If* you get out of here," Kazuk corrected him. "But enough with all this moment-wasting. I'll ask you one simple question and I'd strongly suggest you cooperate. Where is she?"

Michael stared at Kazuk for a moment as if Kazuk had lost his mind. Then he erupted into the most derisive laughter Kazuk had ever heard. Suddenly, the insignia in between his shoulder blades flared and excruciating pain possessed his body. Michael writhed on the floor of his incarceration and screamed like he had never screamed before.

"Do not stop until he starts talking," Kazuk ordered telepathically.

"But it could end him," Metatron protested telepathically.

"Then so be it. Keep going," Kazuk yelled.

Michael had never felt pain like this before. The prisoner's yoke increased the pain exponentially. He fought the pain with all his might and will, and even those were insufficient. His mind started slipping away, but the prisoner's yoke would not let him expire just yet. It still had many torturous plans for Michael. Nothing personal. His resolve slowly withered. His identity as archangel supreme... as archangel... as a creature... as... as....

"Where is she?" Kazuk asked calmly.

"Where... is... who?" Michael asked weakly, as if in a trance.

"He's about to end, Kazuk," Metatron gritted his teeth as he, too, fought to resist the pain that flared through his being.

"Keep pushing," Kazuk commanded.

Kazuk knelt down and brought his lips as close to Michael's head as the energy barrier would allow. Michael's eyes had rolled backward and his life force grew weaker by the moment. Kazuk knew Michael did not have much longer.

"Where is Luciel?" Kazuk asked softly. "Where is your lover?"

Michael whispered a few words and Kazuk inched closer to make sure he heard correctly. Michael repeated the words like a mantra as his mind and life force ebbed away irreversibly, even though Kazuk had already teleported to the location and Metatron had pulled out the dagger from the mark between his shoulder blades.

CHAPTER TWENTY-FIVE

DESPIERTA

TIMELESS

I beheld eternity
A blessing to infinity
When care-freedom was my mark
Creeping, my means of mobility
Crying, my channel of communication.

I saw eternity
A timeless serenity
Despising the distractions of this dungeon
Watching the bonds of eons past
Break off like fetters of straw.

I walk towards eternity
Gaze glued to my destiny
Slowly, steadily and in total humility
Surrendering all I am and will be
To that surreal beckon in reality.

I step into eternity
Accepting my identity
Finally free from illusion's tragedies

Becoming who I have always been
And never knew, but now know.

I dwell in eternity
Dining with divinity
Melting to that melody
Swaying to that symphony
Finally free, finally me.　　　　*Leo E. Ndelle.*

THE FACT THAT Donald made it safely back home was a miracle by itself. The events of the past few hours taxed his body, mind and psyche in ways he had never before experienced. Raising elbows with Patrick provided temporary relief via the state of being tipsy. Drunkenness beckoned though, given the pace at which Patrick downed his drinks, a pace Donald could not match.

How can anyone handle that much booze? Donald wondered. *Nice of him to offer to drive me home. Although, I didn't trust him behind the steering wheel after all that drinking. Liquor shark… I should probably call him that.*

Donald jerked awake when his head banged against the steering wheel.

"I thought…" he started saying.

He shook his head and rubbed his eyes.

Could've sworn I was in my room, he thought.

The truck engine was still running, the headlights beamed on the front of the house and that journey to his bedroom had only taken place in his imagination. Using the last bit of energy he had left in him, Donald killed the engine, turned the headlights out and opened the driver side door. Or so he thought. He grunted like an old bull before he let his left leg land freely onto the ground; but when his right leg followed, the last thing he remembered before everything went black was the ground rushing towards his face and a drape of darkness smothering his consciousness, creating a feeling that was both alien and subconsciously real to him at the same time; death.

***

Donald awoke with the sun's heat hitting one-half of his face and the other half buried in sand. He expected a splitting headache and sore muscles, but none of those greeted him. He pulled his hand close to his ribs and pushed himself slowly to his knees. He, surprisingly, felt strong and rejuvenated.

What happened to the hangover? he wondered.

Donald wiped the sand off his face and his bare torso.

Sand, bare torso, flowery pair of shorts…

He surveyed his environment and smiled.

"I remember you," he said to himself. "And where's my little friend?"

He searched as far as his eyes could see.

"A.K.," he called out. "A.K?"

He jogged along the beach, calling out to A.K. and got no response.

"Bummer," he sighed with slight disappointment.

But he never left, he recalled. *He's here. Always has been here. I am him and he is I.*

Donald turned his gaze towards the forest.

I guess it's time to pay you a visit, he thought. *You have what I'm looking for: answers. I don't know what to expect. I only know what I'm searching for.*

Come to me.

The forest beckoned to him. It tugged on his being within like the promise of paradise in the touch of a temptress: seductive and irresistible.

Come to me.

The stirring in his being intensified and his features softened.

Come to me.

He closed his eyes and took one step.

Come to me.

Donald opened his eyes and his instinct for survival kicked in.

Could be a trap, he thought.

Come to me.

"I know I'm not human," he said to himself. "If I must know who I am, then I must go in there."

He lifted a finger towards the forest.

"I seek answers," he spoke firmly. "I seek liberation."

Then, come to me.

His resolved turned harder than titanium and he marched towards the forest.

Signs, he thought. *I need signs.*

He searched around and found nothing. Some shrubbery separated the beach from the forest and a clear footpath appeared across the shrubbery.

There's my sign.

He took steady strides towards the forest but he never neared the forest. He broke into a jog and yet, he appeared to jog on the same spot. He stopped, turned around and looked towards the sea. Nothing had changed, distance-wise. He still remained on the same spot where he stood before his walk towards the forest.

What am I not doing? he wondered. *What should I do?*

He broke into a sprint and even that changed nothing. His position relative to the beach and the forest remained the same. He stopped running and studied the path. It phased in and out repeatedly.

An illusion. But why? What do I have to do?

Suddenly, an instant of clarity hit him.

"I'm only doing what I'd logically do in the real world," he said out loud. "But this is something else. This is the entrance to my subconscious. The forest is my subconscious. To fully access my subconscious, I must let go of linear thinking and the logic of the intellect."

Donald straightened his shoulders and stared at the forest.

"How do I get to you?"

By willing yourself here.

Donald closed his eyes. When he opened them, a smile spread across his face. Trees of various species, shapes and sizes stretched as far as his eyes could see. Sunlight sliced through their canopy of leaves in golden streaks. Flowers, insects, birds and many other small creatures adorned the forest with benevolent beauty. Donald's core surged with respect and appreciation for what he beheld, as well as the impermanence they held.

"As heart-touching as you are, you're not real," he spoke out loud.

"That is because you have not stopped to smell the roses, Donald," said a young lady who appeared from nowhere.

Donald whipped his head to his left, startled by the sudden intrusion. The smile from a most stunning-looking beauty greeted him. A pale green, flowery, transparent, lace-like gown flowed over her physique, accentuating her feminine form, built in perfect proportion. Her hard nipples pressed against the dress and the lacy-nature of her outfit partially exposed her nudity underneath. She held a red rose in front of her so that its petals rested in between her breasts.

"I apologize, miss," Donald straightened his gait. "Didn't expect company."

"It is I who must apologize for startling you," her smile brightened.

"And who do I have the pleasure of talking to?" Donald asked.

"You can call me whatever you like."

Her voice bounced off his eardrums like a distant echo. A few strands of her long, black hair fell over part of her left eye and her lips thickened slightly and parted just enough to reveal the tip of her tongue. Her smile never left her face. Donald's gaze zoomed in on her chest area and the more he focused, the more her already transparent outfit became more transparent.

"You seemed lost in thought when I first spoke to you," she said casually. "May I ask what it was, please?"

"I just got here, miss," Donald replied and swallowed.

He forced himself to look away from her chest area.

"I was just appreciating this place."

"And whatever you focus on eventually manifests," she said. "Come. Smell the rose."

The lady held the rose away from her chest and towards Donald.

Donald approached her and brought his nose to the rose. He inhaled. Its scent filled his nostrils with a sweet, savory scent. The lady brought the rose to her nose, closed her eyes and inhaled as well. She kept the rose in front of her nose and opened her eyes. Donald felt the tug in his core once again; this time, it came from her eyes. Donald stepped closer, drawn to the sweet seduction in her eyes.

Come to me.

Donald accepted the invitation and inched closer. She closed her eyes once again and so did he. Together, they savored the scent of the rose and opened their eyes in unison.

Come to me.

Many glowing specks of light flowed from the rose and engulfed the two of them in a sparkling radiance.

Come to me.

His right hand slid around her waist. His left hand caressed her back and settled on the back of her neck. She let the rose fall to the ground. It disintegrated into more glowing specks of light and dispersed into the other specks of light.

Come to me.

She wrapped her arms around his neck, drew his body into hers and pressed her lips against his.

Take me…

Their clothes disappeared. Two naked bodies pressed against each other. Lips parted and met in a fiery, passionate, tongue-filled kissed. She wrapped her legs around his waist, granting him access to everything she was. Donald pressed her against a tree behind her and readied to take her.

"And whatever you focus on eventually manifests," he remembered her saying.

Donald pulled his lips from hers and kissed her neck, working his way up to her left ear as she moaned, squirmed and gyrated her hips against his, begging him to take her wholly and unreservedly.

"I must go now," Donald whispered in her ear. "I'm sorry. I have something very important I must attend to."

When he opened his eyes, he was alone; bare torso, flowery shorts and alone.

"Thank you, mystery lady," he murmured.

He resumed his walk deeper into the forest.

She must have been some kind of test, he thought. *Well, since she was here, it means she was neither a friend nor an enemy. Just another part of me, because this is my subconscious.*

"Help me. Help me," a child called out from a distance.

He immediately willed himself towards the sound of the child's call for help. He arrived to find a lad, no more than eight years old, struggling desperately to free his right foot, which was stuck in the ground. However, the child screamed with heart-rending fright because an eagle with a wingspan of over twelve feet kept swooping menacingly towards him. Donald placed himself between the boy and the avian monster and readied himself for an attack.

The creature screeched and dove for the much larger prey that was Donald. Its claws snapped at the empty space where Donald once stood as he evaded the attack with a forward roll. It soared upwards again and gathered more momentum for another attack. With a skin-crawling shriek, it whizzed towards him once again. He waited until the creature was close enough before he ran for a tree to his left. He took three steps up the tree and propelled himself sideways with all the leg strength he could muster. His shoulder crashed between the monster's wings, and Donald caught the base of the bird's left wing to prevent himself from rolling off the bird.

The giant, winged monster shrieked with rage and soared upwards. Donald clung onto its back regardless of how much the bird turned and twisted around during flight. Unsure of what to do next, he clung to the creature. Fear had no place in his heart.

The boy must be protected at all cost, he reminded himself.

The eagle dove for the ground. When it was close enough to the ground, Donald leaped off its back and absorbed his fall with three forward rolls.

I need a weapon, he thought.

"Look. Over there," the boy cried and pointed at something.

Donald followed the boy's finger and saw a metallic spear lying on the ground, ten feet from him.

How could I have missed that? he wondered. *Maybe because I was too focused on protecting the boy?*

He evaded the creature's attack with another forward roll in the direction of the spear. He fended the creature off. The flapping of its wings sounded like gusts of wind as it soared higher in the air. Then, it spread its wings and, in a shriek of defiance and death, it swooped towards Donald for the kill. It tore through the air like a majestic, aerodynamic work of Mother Nature. Donald tightened his grip around the spear, closed he left eye and cocked the spear. The creature whooshed steadily and rapidly towards him. He slowed his breathing, stilled his mind and waited for the perfect moment. The perfect moment did come, but instead of throwing the spear at the creature, Donald's features softened and he regarded the creature with compassion and loving kindness.

Gone was his aggression and the need to protect the boy. The creature, however dangerous and imposing it appeared to be, no longer posed a threat.

Not an enemy. Not a friend, he lowered the spear. *You're a part of this forest, a part of me. You represent my pride, my aggressive side,* the part of him that always sought to justify what was right and what was wrong.

He turned his attention towards the boy, who sat on the fallen tree; leg free of the ground and no longer mortified with fear.

You are my innocence and purity trapped in my basal and carnal instincts.

A wave of peace and unburdening flooded his being with this realization. Eyes closed, he waited for his next test. When nothing happened, he opened his eyes. The beastly bird and the boy were both gone as if they were never there before.

"Thank you," he said barely above a whisper.

An overpowering presence loomed dangerously close from behind. Warm breath brushed the back of his neck with each exhalation. Still, Donald remained calm and unafraid, though he did not turn around to face the origin of the presence yet.

"Why are you here, human?" asked the presence in the deepest voice Donald had ever heard.

"I don't know," Donald replied and turned around.

A pair of eyes from a lion far larger than those he had seen on TV stared at him. A shiver shimmied across his body. On its four legs, it stood at Donald's height. Its face and mane were so large that it obscured the rest of its body from Donald's view. Donald took two steps back and the lion's body came into view. He walked around the lion, letting his hand glide across its velvety skin.

What a creature, he thought. *So full of power, strength and majesty.*

His being tingled with the energy radiated by the lion.

Incredible..

It walked six feet away from Donald.

"Why are you here, human?" it asked again.

"I honestly do not know, sir," Donald replied.

"You seek something, human," the lion said. "You just have to be truthful about what you seek and be true to yourself."

"I do seek something, sir," he agreed. "But I don't know what I seek because, in fact, I seek myself and I don't know who I am. I don't remember who I am."

Donald saw a gentleman, around his late seventies, walking about sixty yards away from him, struggling with a bag that appeared too heavy for his head to balance. Without any hesitation, he bounded off to help the elderly gentleman.

"How rude of you to walk away from me like that," the lion roared. "Do you know who I am?"

"I'm sorry, sir, but I'll be right back," Donald broke into a jog. "I must help this gentleman."

Donald approached the gentleman.

"Sir," Donald called out.

But the gentleman did not respond. He kept walking on with his heavy load.

"Sir," Donald called out again. "Please wait."

The gentleman stopped and turned around.

"Would you like some help with your baggage?" Donald asked.

The gentleman studied Donald.

"Thank you, young man," the gentleman replied. "But how do you propose to lend a hand with my baggage when you have baggage of your own?"

Before Donald could even begin to process the gentleman's words, his knees buckled and he staggered for support from some baggage that pressed heavily upon his shoulders. The baggage grew heavier with every breath he took and he fought with all his might for support. Still, the baggage only grew heavier until he collapsed to a knee.

"This is too heavy for me," Donald cried.

"Then why carry it?" asked the elderly gentleman.

The elderly gentleman dropped his own baggage to the ground.

Donald's moment of realization struck him like a bolt of lightning and he dropped his own burden as well. His being soared with a feeling of letting go, peace and more self-awareness. He closed his eyes and savored the feeling. When Donald opened his eyes, the scene had changed. He was still in the forest, but this time, the elderly gentleman sat on a marble, throne-like seat. A marble sphere with intersecting circular markings all over it rested in his right hand. Gone were the wrinkles, frail look and weakness. Strength, power and majesty pulsed from his being. When Donald realized what this elderly gentleman symbolized, the elderly gentleman morphed into the giant lion he had just met, and the marble sphere rested beneath its front right paw. The throne-like seat morphed into what looked like an altar.

"What do you want, human?" the lion asked.

"To remember," Donald replied.

"What do you want to remember?" the lion asked.

"I want to remember who I am," Donald replied.

"The one who speaks the truth will also see the truth," the lion said. "Do you understand me, human?"

"I mean no disrespect, sir," Donald said. "But I am not human."

The lion's fiery gaze burned into his core for a moment. Donald held its gaze, unfazed and unafraid of anyone and any creature. The lion nodded.

"Come," it ordered.

Donald approached the altar.

"Kneel."

Donald knelt in front of the lion and closed his eyes.

"This platform is symbolic of your impending death and rebirth into a new life. A yearning, a desire, an ache burns deeply inside of you. This ache is so strong that it surpasses that of an angel. It is an archangel's ache. On this platform, you will die a fallen angel, and on this same platform, you will rise as an archangel, the first of its kind."

As the lion spoke, a pair of green, glassy, serpentine eyes of light formed above Donald's head. Then, the rest of the serpent coalesced into a body of light and wrapped itself three-and-a-half times around Donald. The lion raised its right paw from the marble sphere and placed it on Donald's forehead, between his eyes.

"And now, behold the truth of which you speak," the lion said. "The truth which you seek."

With these words, the lion gave the loudest roar Donald had ever heard. The entire forest resonated to the roar. The very earth beneath his feet trembled and affirmed. His essence resonated with the roar and gave its answer. The roar tore down the walls of his mind and memory flooded his essence with light and the truth he sought.

Donald opened his eyes. A human hand retreated from his head and hung freely beside a human form. A golden bracelet glowed on its wrist. On instinct, guided by a part of his newfound memory, he searched for the other hand. A golden bracelet glowed on the other hand as well. His gaze traced upwards towards the rest of the body. Wings of fire spread from the archangel's shoulder blades and a pair of flaming eyes stared straight back at him. Donald stared into the face of himself. He rose slowly to his feet until he stood face-to-face with himself. His new self reached around and took hold of the marble sphere in his right hand. He held it in front of Donald and Donald placed his right hand on the sphere as well.

"Who are you?" his new self asked.

"I am Eliel. I am The One."

Light of tremendous brilliance beamed from the sphere and enveloped both of them. The light continued to spread throughout the forest, which represented Eliel's subconscious, until the two Eliels merged into one.

Once upon a moment, Eliel was a lowly angel. This lowly angel fell to a lower realm called Earth, out of his own volition. He lived amongst humans and was a part of them, with amnesia of his origins, until the archangel's ache initiated his awakening. Once upon a time, he died. Yet, in his death to the old self, he was born into a new self as the first of his kind; the first creature from the Realm of Celestia to experience an archangel's ache.

***

Newman was still awake when the truck pulled up the driveway. The maze of his racing thoughts warped his perception of time. Too many hours had gone by since his conversation with Donald.

When did he even leave the house? Newman wondered.

Over half an hour later, the engine still ran.

"What's goin' on out there?" Newman sat up. "I hope he's okay."

Then, his mind entertained his worst fear.

"No, no, no," Newman sprang from the bed and headed for the stairs. "No, no, no. Please, God. No."

With a surge of adrenaline, Newman bolted down the stairs faster than he ever had in the three decades of living in his house.

Did those things in the video finally get him? Oh God, please no.

He yanked the front door open. Donald lay on the ground, motionless, just below the open driver door. A lump gathered in his throat, mortared by the morbid dread of his worst fears finding their way to the surface. Heart scattered asunder from instant pain and grief, Newman fell to his knees in the glare of the truck's headlights. The lump in his throat turned into a mournful whimper, which slowly eased out of his mouth.

Silent tears of pain and sorrow graced his cheeks. He remained kneeling on his front porch, not knowing how to proceed or what to do. A thousand and one thoughts raced through his mind; thoughts of regret for not telling Donald much sooner who Donald really was, thoughts of guilt for being too selfish and getting too attached to Donald, because he had been too ashamed to admit that he was a very lonely man. Newman buried his face in his hands and let out a soul-scathing scream of pain. Suddenly, the engine died and the headlights of the truck went out. Peering through the open spaces between his fingers, his body stiffened with shock. His jaw dropped as if it had a separate mind of its own and his sobbing stopped immediately. Pain and grief gave way to unrivaled elation and awe.

"DEAR GOD," Newman exclaimed.

***

Patrick and Sara lay on the bed, basking in the moment of shared ecstasies and catching their breaths in preparation for another bout of erotic escapades. Suddenly, Sara sat up ramrod stiff on the bed and fidgeted with restlessness and excitement at once. She jumped off the bed, reached for her clothes and dressed up faster than Patrick's zip speed. Patrick stared at her in confusion.

"Hey," he asked calmly. "What's going on?"

She ignored putting on her shoes as she dashed for the door.

"Something big is about to happen," Sara replied.

She reached for her keys, hesitated and dropped them back on the desk.

"I can feel it in my being," she added.

"Maybe it's Donald," Patrick bolted from the bed as well. "Maybe this is it."

A zip around the room later, he was fully clothed. He joined Sara at the door.

"Can you teleport us-" he started saying.

But Sara had already teleported them close to Newman's house.

"-to… Never mind," Patrick finished his sentence

Patrick sparked the ethers and cloaked both Sara and himself in invisibility. The pair arrived just in time to witness a most amazing and beautiful unfolding of a once-in-only-a-fantasy phenomenon. Donald's body lay on the ground, unmoving and seemingly lifeless. The head and tail lights of the truck shone brightly in the darkness of the night and the engine still hummed in its idle state. Suddenly, the truck's engine died and the lights went out, casting Newman's house in near-pitch-blackness. Then, bright, golden light engulfed Donald's body before the light exploded with a brilliance that made the brightness of the midday sun look like pitch-blackness.

When the brightness diminished, Donald's lifeless body no longer lay on the ground. Instead, a magnificent creature of bright, golden light stood in its stead. Two golden bracelets glowed on each wrist and a pair of wings, ablaze with golden-yellow, heatless flames, spread out from his shoulder blades. Archangel Eliel flapped his wings thrice and walked up to the porch, where Newman knelt, mouth open wide and eyes bulging with awe and reverence.

"It's okay," Eliel said telepathically to Sara and Patrick. *"You two can stop gawking and join us now."*

Patrick and Sara teleported next to Eliel and Newman. Eliel helped Newman to his feet. Newman stared speechlessly and reverently at Eliel. Then he turned his gaze towards Patrick and Sara, who had just suddenly appeared next to them.

Think he's gonna have a heart attack? Patrick asked Sara via telepathy.

He'll be fine, Eliel smiled.

Just making sure, Patrick said. *Although he looks like he's about to crap his pants.*

Sara nudged him in the rib.

Pictures did so much injustice to these creatures, Patrick thought. *I mean, look at him. I knew he was an angel, but I never expected this. Oh my God. Wait until I tell Father.*

You know we can hear you, right? Sara asked via telepathy.

I'll sign your autograph later, Eliel chimed in.

Sara snickered. When Patrick reached out to touch Eliel's wing, Eliel flapped his wings twice. Patrick quickly withdrew his hand, evoking a snicker from Sara.

You don't get to do the honors, Eliel said coldly. *Not after your disrespectful comments.*

Patrick swallowed nervously. He opened his mouth to say something but Sara nudged him harder in the ribs.

"It's okay, Mr. Weinberg," Eliel said. "You can touch them. The flames won't burn unless I want them to."

Cautiously, Newman reached out and gently placed a finger on Eliel's left wing. Feeling more confident, he held it with his hand. The flames crept over his hands and not even a hair on his hand was singed. He fell back to his knees and bowed at Eliel's feet.

"No, Mr. Weinberg," Eliel reached down and gently took Newman by the shoulder. "Even if I was to be worshipped, you will be exempt. I will never forget what you did for me since I arrived here. Rest assured, you will always have me by your side from this day forth."

"I..." Newman stammered. "You...I..."

Eliel smiled and gathered Newman in his arms. His archangel battle flame engulfed Newman's body. Newman trembled with joy before the tears of joy flowed freely down his cheeks. Sara shed a tear. Patrick smiled and sighed.

Beautiful, Patrick said to Sara via telepathy. *Just... beautiful. I lack the right words to describe this scene. Now, I kinda feel bad I gave the old man a hard time.*

You what? Sara glared at him.

Talk about it later, Patrick straightened his shoulder and puffed his chest.

Eliel removed himself from Newman and turned so that he had Newman, Sara and Patrick within his view.

"Well, my friends," Eliel said. "I understand you have a lot of questions and I assure you that I will answer them in due time. Unfortunately, I must return to Celestia, my home, immediately before all Hell breaks loose; and I mean that in a very literal sense. I'll explain later. And now, a brief introduction. My name is Eliel, and I am, or was, a fallen angel. Now I have awoken as the highest-ranking archangel, the first of my kind.

"Right now, my home, Celestia, not heaven," Eliel smiled, "is having a celestial crisis, literally. If I don't return and defuse the situation, then another war between Celestia and Hell will break out. Worst still, this crisis may spread beyond our dimension, and I can't let that happen. When everything is over, I will return, and we will all catch up. But for now, uh 'time' is of utmost importance. Alright?"

Patrick, Sara, and Newman nodded like mindless zombies. Eliel chuckled.

"I understand it's too much," Eliel said. "But like I said, we'll catch up later."
He then turned his attention to Sara.

"You really don't know who and what you are, do you, Sara?" Eliel asked telepathically and only Sara could hear him speak to her.

Sara said nothing. Eliel nodded.

"Soon, very soon, you will know. I promise you," Eliel assured her.

Eliel then turned his attention to the rest of the group.

"Good bye, my friends. I'll see y'all soon." he said.

And with these words, Eliel turned his gaze towards the sky before he teleported upwards in a beam of golden light. Newman, Patrick and Sara gawked in awe and wonder for a very, very long time.

CHAPTER TWENTY-SIX

SOUND THE ALARM

PATRICK, SARA, AND Newman held several minutes of awe-filled silence on Newman's front porch after Eliel's departure, until Patrick broke the silence.

"You gonna be alright, old man?"

"May take a while, but I think I'll be fine," Newman replied weakly.

He took a step back and leaned against the door, shoulders slumped and head bowed slightly from an overload of a myriad of emotions ranging from elation, reverence and a deep sense of loss.

"It's gon' be alright, Newman," Sara stepped forward and took Newman's right hand in her left hand. "You've got an angel looking out for ya; and not just any kinda angel, right? What was that he said again, Patrick?"

"The highest-ranking *ARCHANGEL* there ever was," Patrick replied with a broad smile. "How cool is that, old man?"

Newman smiled and met Sara's gaze.

"Thanks, you two," Newman also glanced in Patrick's direction.

"Of course," Sara replied. "And hey, I'm still around, right?"

"Yeah, you're still here," Newman agreed. "You've always been good to me and for that, I thank ya."

"As you have been to me," Sara kissed him on the cheek and let go of his left hand. "You get some rest now. Patrick and I will head back ourselves."

"Where's your car?" Newman asked.

"Parked up the street," Patrick lied.

"Lemme drop you kids off-" Newman offered, but Patrick waved him off.

"No need to, old man. You just go on and get some rest. You could use some right about now."

"Yes, Newman, you do need some rest," Sara insisted. "Please?"

"Okay, okay," Newman conceded. "You kids making me feel old."

"I'm a lot older than I look, Newman," Sara winked at him.

"And you still don't wanna share your secret."

He reached for the door knob.

"I'll see you around, Sara," Newman said. "As for you, young man, I take it I won't be seeing ya in these parts for a while, huh?"

"Maybe under better circumstances," Patrick replied. "And speaking of 'better circumstances', I trust you'll keep all this to yourself?"

"Really?" Newman stared at Patrick in utter disbelief.

"I need an answer, old man," Patrick's expression turned cold.

"No, I won't tell nobody nothin'," Newman growled.

"And by nothin' you do mean NOTHIN', right?" Patrick insisted.

Sara wanted to glare at Patrick but she opted for a sigh instead.

"Absolutely," Newman replied. "I'm just an old man with occasional memory loss. Hate being senile."

"Good to know, old man," Patrick winked at Newman. "Good to know."

"Don't take this the wrong way," Newman opened the front door.. "But I hope I never see you again."

"No offense taken, old man," Patrick said. "Your wish is my command."

Patrick bowed in Newman's direction.

Really? Sara asked via telepathy.

You don't understand, he replied. *Better I take him at his word than erasing his memory.*

I was referring to the bowing, she said.

Oh, Patrick said.

"Yeah right," Newman scoffed and shook his head. "You two be careful."

Newman disappeared into his house and locked the door behind him.

"Did you really have to be that hard on him?" Sara frowned at him.

"Had to make sure he understands how serious this is," Patrick replied.

"Still," she hesitated. "Anyway, Imma just let it be."

"Good," Patrick offered his elbow. "Care to join me for a walk?"

Sara's lips peeled back in a most beautiful smile.

"Sure," she took his elbow.

They walked slowly away from Newman's house. A few paces later, Patrick dropped his arm and Sara intertwined her fingers with his.

"You know I still woulda asked if Newman wasn't spying on us, right?"

"I know, Patrick," Sara gave his hand a gentle squeeze. "I appreciate it."

Patrick reached in to his pant pocket to retrieve his cell phone, but Sara spun around and placed her free hand on his wrist. Her facial features softened and her pupils glowed violet. Patrick smiled, even before she closed her eyes, inclined her head and touched her lips to his. He closed his eyes and kissed her sensually. Several seconds later, they separated their lips from each other's kiss.

"You may make your call now," Sara said.

"Yes, ma'am."

He retrieved his cell phone, dialed a number and placed the call on speaker.

"Yes, sir," a voice said over the phone.

"Mission accomplished," Patrick spoke with authority. "Return to Rome at once. I expect your reports within 48 hours."

"Aye, sir," a chorus of agents affirmed.

Patrick ended the call.

"Look at you, boss man," Sara cooed and snuggled against his body.

Suddenly, she jerked away from him and let out an expletive.

"Oh no, did they see Eliel? Did they see us?" she almost panicked. "I'm sorry if I caused you any trouble, Patrick. So sorry-"

"Relax, sweetie," Patrick took her gently by the shoulders. "If they saw Eliel, my phone woulda been blown up with calls and messages a long time ago. Eliel cloaked us and himself. So all my agents saw was a quiet house with no activity."

"And what about us just now?" Sara asked before she relaxed her features. "You cloaked us already."

Patrick smiled at her cuteness and kissed her on the forehead. She kissed him on the lips and snuggled against his arm.

"Let's get outta here," she said.

They walked until they were out of sight from Newman's house. Then, they teleported to Patrick's motel room. About ninety minutes later, they lay in bed, spent, satisfied and... happy.

"I, uh... I gotta head back to Rome now," Patrick said after a while. "Gotta be debriefed."

"I understand," Sara nuzzled against his chest. "Duty calls."

"Good thing I'm just a hop away, huh," Patrick scratched the back of his head.

"Yeah, I guess," she replied sadly.

She gently peeled herself away from him and propped herself on an elbow.

"And... uh... If I never see you again... well, I'll understand," she started sliding off the bed.

Patrick sat up and took her by the shoulders. Sara sat at the edge of the bed, eyes averted towards the floor.

"Hey, now," Patrick said softly.

"Hey, look at me," he urged gently.

Sara's eyes remained averted to the floor. She could not muster the courage to face Patrick. She was not angry at Patrick or herself. She regretted nothing and if she could rewind time and have the chance to do this all over again, she would not hesitate to repeat this aspect of her history and million times over.

So why can't I face him? she asked herself. *Why can't I look at him in the eye?*

The bed depressed as Patrick inched closer to her back.

As powerful a creature as she was, Sara felt powerless to the inevitability that was about to come to pass. She had said 'goodbye' to too many humans to remember in 26,000 years. But all those millennia of practice summed up to naught when it came to Patrick.

Why? What about him makes it so hard for me to say goodbye?

Patrick kissed the back of her neck.

During the short span of time she had spent with Patrick, Sara had developed deep feelings for him. The last twenty-six millennia had been replete with lovers, acquaintances and bed partners too many to count. However, Patrick proved to be different. Her feelings for him hailed not from a release borne out of the carnality that came from eroticism. Her level of maturity protected her from being smitten by intense sex sessions. The deep feelings stirring within her bore no kinship to the imaginations of a naïve girl with a grandiose fantasy of perfect, eternal love. By Creation, these sentiments were expected human tendencies and she was not even human. She had lived longer than any other human she knew. Yet, she could not explain how she had fallen madly and hopelessly in love with one and now, her heart beat in the form of many millions of shattered pieces she was desperately trying to glue together with nothing more than a willpower she could not even hold on to.

"I'm sorry, Patrick," a lump bubbled in her throat. "I shouldn't have become so attached so shortly. Don't worry about me. I'm a big girl. I'll be fine."

"Look at me, Sara," Patrick urged her.

Sara sniveled. Summoning some strength, she turned towards Patrick, but she could not bring herself to look at him in the eye. He placed a finger under her chin and raised her head until she faced him. Still, her eyes remained shut.

"Look at me," Patrick urged again. "Please."

Sara opened her eyes, a tearing pair of magnificent, but sad, violet-glowing orbs. He kissed each cheek.

"I just gotta be debriefed and I'm just a hop away," Patrick said. "And just so you know, you're not the only one in this dump of a motel who's become a little too attached. Alright?"

The brightness in her eyes intensified. He smiled and she smiled back at him.

His words bore no promise, though they provided a panacea to the pain that possessed her psyche. She sobbed, sniveled and chuckled as more tears flowed down her cheeks. The tears that flowed from her eyes now glowed with the joy and relief that resonated through her being.

"Alright," Sara replied softly and sniveled again.

She inadvertently turned on her clairsentience when Patrick smiled. His smile communicated something deep and lovely in his heart, which infected hers. Her chest area glowed violet. Patrick gently placed a hand over her glowing chest.

"I'm never gonna get used to this," he said.

Did he just insinuate… she held her breath as her mind processed his words.

"This could be the start of something very strange but even more beautiful than you and I can imagine, don't you think?"

Patrick kissed her softly on the lips.

"Never took ya for a poet" Sara returned his kiss.

"Stop plagiarizing, woman," Patrick teased. "That's my line."

They kissed passionately again.

"I really gotta go now," he said and peeled away from her.

Sara nodded.

They got dressed and left the room. Patrick checked out of the motel and got into the car with Sara.

"You know you can always visit, right?" Patrick said.

"When you send me your address," Sara replied.

"Home address? Really?" Patrick said, shaking his head. "You mean to tell me you can't track our telepathic link?"

"Oh yeah, I can do that," Sara flashed a sheepish grin. "In my defense, it's been a while."

Then, she averted her eyes.

"Does that mean… I can…." she hesitated.

"Yes, silly. You can have access to my link," he said. "But no mind reading, okay? Just link access. We still have to respect each other's privacy."

"It's really happening," Sara spoke as if she was in a daze. "We're really doing this? I am yours and you are mine?"

"In this day and age, we say we're dating" Patrick rolled his eyes playfully.

"Where I'm from, we declare ourselves as an offering to each other," Sara seemed to be lost in some fog in her memory.

"Remembering anything?" Patrick narrowed his eyes in hope.

"No. I'm sorry," Sara replied, a grimace of embarrassment graced her face. "Thought I was for a sec."

"Don't sweat it, babe," Patrick said. "It'll all come back eventually."

Patrick reached for his cellphone in his left, jacket pocket. He sent Sara a text message. Her phone vibrated and she retrieved it from her purse. She entered her pin and clicked on the message app.

"What's this?" Sara asked.

"My home address, in case you prefer to catch a flight," Patrick said with playful sarcasm.

Sara punched him in the arm and the couple laughed a little.

"I'll see you later, Sara.".

"See you later… babe…" Sara replied.

Patrick smiled and nodded.

It's really happening, he thought.

Decades of living the life of a kite in the wind were about to be blown away by the firestorm of a vivacious, violet-electric-spark vixen.

I'm so screwed, he joked at himself.

He kissed her lightly on the lips again, removed his fedora and placed it on her head before he teleported away. She grinned like a school girl, adjusted his fedora on her head and check herself out in the mirror.

"I do look cool in this," she admitted. "Gonna add this to my style now."

Sara started the car and headed home. She had to get ready for another day of running a business.

"They're gonna gossip about ma new style," she chuckled. "These folks. Well, let them talk. I ain't got no problems showing off ma man's hat. Might even keep some of them horny fools away from me too."

A second later, Sara shook her head.

"Nah, ain't gon' stop them," she laughed a little.

Patrick appeared in his rental. He could not drive quickly enough to the car rental return forty-six miles away. After topping the tank and returning the rental, he caught a shuttle to the terminal and headed for the nearest restroom. The last person to subconsciously notice Patrick before he teleported to Rome was the shuttle bus driver and even her subconscious memory of Patrick would become suppressed within the hour, thanks to Patrick sparking the ethers around her when he was close to her. He appeared in Shi'mon's private chamber. Shi'mon sat in his favorite armchair of all time.

"Fantastic work out there, son," Shi'mon said, staring out the window.

"Thank you, Father," Patrick replied. "We lost too many of our own, though."

"I know," Shi'mon replied flatly and turned around to face Patrick. "Now tell me again what happened out there. Leave nothing out."

Patrick narrated everything with as much detail as he could. He skillfully omitted the parts that had to do with Sara as an extradimensional creature though. He had to protect her until he learned more about who and what she was. About half an hour later, Patrick was done with his narration.

"And lo, I beheld an archangel in the flesh, boss," Patrick said with the flair of a theater performer.

Then, he narrowed his eyes and leaned towards Shi'mon.

"Have *YOU* ever seen an angel, let alone an archangel, boss?" Patrick grinned with playful pride.

Shi'mon leveled a poker expression at Patrick.

"I am surprised you are not bouncing off the walls," Shi'mon replied flatly.

"Let the record reflect I said I have seen an archangel, NOT angel. He was far beyond cool. I have never seen anything more beautiful."

Not even Sara, he wanted to add but knew better.

"Good for you," Shi'mon said dismissively. "Are you absolutely certain that is all you have to tell me?"

"Yes, Father," he lied. "Unless you wanna hear about my indiscretions with the local distractions..." he added.

"No fedora today?" Shi'mon asked passively.

Damn it. Damn it. Damn it, he cursed in his mind. *Should've kept it.*

"Lost it when I gave Lilith a beating, boss," he lied with grace.

Shi'mon eyed him keenly and slowly nodded.

"Very well," Shi'mon said. "At least, the angel has returned whence he came."

Patrick desperately wanted to correct his boss. *Eliel is an archangel, not just an angel.* But he reminded himself that, at the end of the day, Shi'mon was his boss, not his drinking buddy.

"I fear this is not the end of it, though," Shi'mon said. "You said the angel mentioned something about a celestial crisis, right?"

"Yes, Father Supreme," Patrick answered.

"Then this is far from over," Shi'mon said, rising from his chair and walking towards the window. "If he really is above Michael, then part of his purpose is to avert something so big that maybe Michael and his host would not have been able to handle on their own."

"What would that be, Father?" Patrick asked.

Shi'mon heaved a heavy sigh.

"Something extremely... evil is coming," Shi'mon replied. "And I pray that Eliel is not too late."

***

"He's not coming back," Gabriel said.

"We must wait," Raphael insisted.

"He knew it was a one-way trip, Raphael," Gabriel added. "Don't you see? He already got us to nominate you as our next archangel supreme because he knew he wasn't coming back."

"He's right, Raph," Uriel said and the inner council chorused their agreement.

Raphael clenched his jaw in frustration.

"We all wish he was coming back," Uriel said. "But that won't happen. We all know what is coming next and you know what must be done."

"We don't want another slaughter, but these are desperate times," Gabriel said. "They slashed the first wing and we cannot let them slash the other wing. Our best and most advantageous option now is a preemptive strike."

"You think I do not know that?" Raphael barked at Gabriel.

"We are ready, Raphael," Norael chimed in. "We'll follow you, just like we did with Michael."

The rest of the council chorused their agreement.

"We've been ready since the rebellion. History must not repeat itself."

Raphael rapped his fingers repeatedly on the table.

My first order as the new archangel supreme is to wage war against Hell, he thought. *Another massacre. Another slaughter. There has to be another way.*

But he could not think of another way. Raphael, The Ruthless, stood up and his inner council stood up as well.

I was a general even before I became archangel supreme, he thought. *This is what I do best. This is what I have trained many for.*

Raphael, The Ruthless, opened his right hand and summoned his battle hammer. He lifted his battle hammer in the air and brought it down into the marble-like floor. The force of the hammer striking the floor reverberated across Celestia and, across Celestia, the bells of war rang. Angels and archangels took up formation like they had rehearsed on countless occasions, but this was not a drill and they knew it. Every angel and archangel summoned their weapons and were ready. No need for questions. No need for validation. They only had to follow orders and the bells of war was their order.

"Hell just made a mistake they will never recover from," Raphael bellowed. "Hell will know why the call me The Ruthless and they will pay the ultimate price for their blasphemy."

Raphael stretched out his hammer. The inner council members summoned their weapons and stretched them out to touch Raphael's.

"Let's make them pay. FOR MICHAEL AND CELESTIA." Raphael, The Ruthless, roared.

"FOR MICHAEL AND CELESTIA," the inner council chorused.

As the members of Raphael's inner council teleported away to their respective battle locations, Uriel's core ached with hope.

Where are you, Eliel? she asked herself. *We need you now.*

***

Kazuk glided towards the dark, ball of energy that was a realm hovering on the edge of the dimension. He maintained a telepathic link with Metatron to avoid getting lost.

"I see why Michael chose you," Kazuk addressed the realm

An invisible energy field around the realm prevented him from gliding in. But he forced his way through, with the invisible barrier pressing against his body throughout. When he broke through the barrier, his telepathic link grew fainter.

"I must hurry before I, too, get lost," he said to himself.

Kazuk hovered above the realm, with its features carved out into various shades of dark, murky energy. He summoned his archangelic glow, but the forces of the realm dissolved his glow.

"The Realm of Hadesina," Kazuk spoke with admiration. "The most heinous and perfect prison for any creature. No wonder they nicknamed this place 'The Abyss'. I wonder if there are other realms like this in other dimensions?"

He reached into his garment and pulled out a black, oval-shaped, smooth piece of rock. He glided to the right, guided by a force that pulled on the piece of rock in his hand. His telepathic link grew dimmer the closer he approached the floor of the realm.

"I am losing you, my king," Metatron's telepathic voice sounded faint.

"I know," Kazuk replied. "I am almost done."

You would love for me to get stuck here, would you not, Metatron? he thought.

Kazuk stopped, as dictated by the rock. In the center of the blackness, a tiny hole appeared and started spinning into a whirlpool of darker energy. A portal emerged and grew larger until it was large enough for a creature the size of an angel to easily walk through. Kazuk continued holding the rock in front of his body to keep the portal open. A hand emerged and grabbed the edge of the portal. Another hand appeared and did the same. Both hands pulled along the edge of the portal until a head emerged. Long, black hair covered the face. Shoulders followed until the body of a naked, female angel slid out of the portal. Kazuk dropped his hand to his side, closing the portal. He stowed the rock away. The female angel glided towards him and parted her hair from her face. Then she summoned her wings, flapped them several times before she dismissed them.

As beautiful as ever, Kazuk thought.

"Hello, Luciel," he smiled.

"Maziel?" Luciel's voice revealed her shock. "How come?"

"A lot has happened since you, um… were gone," he hesitated.

"How long has it been?" she asked.

"Too many cycles," he replied flatly.

He imagined her shaking her head in the darkness.

"So, who has been leading the following then?" Luciel asked.

"Me," Kazuk replied.

"You?" Luciel exclaimed. "How come? Where is Zukael?"

"I cast him out," Kazuk replied casually. "Well, I 'cursed' him BEFORE I cast him out. Your top generals have been ended as well."

A maniacal cry of rage escaped Luciel's throat. She summoned her archangel battle flame. A flaming sword appeared in her right hand before she grabbed Kazuk by the throat with her right hand and lifted him up in the air.

How can she summon her battle flame in this realm and I can't? Kazuk wondered. *Can Michael also do that, as archangel supreme?*

"How dare you, Maziel," Luciel screamed and glared golden, yellow flames at him. "Give me one reason why I should not end you right now."

"I'll give you three, actually," Kazuk replied, calmly. "But first, you'll have to let me go so we could have a less agitated conversation."

Luciel pressed her sword deeper into his neck, breaking flesh and drawing angel light, which disappeared quickly thanks to the unknown forces in the realm. The cut in his neck remained open and unhealed.

"Do not test me, Maziel," Luciel barked.

"Very well," Kazuk said calmly, when he realized the realm prevented his body from healing. "First, you will not be able to find you way back without my help. I assume you know that already. Second, Hell Realm, our new home, could very well be under attack from our brethren on the other side as we speak."

Luciel's shock extinguished her archangel battle flame.

"What do you mean we could be under attack?" Luciel asked.

She dismissed her sword and let go of his neck. Kazuk tried to heal himself without success.

Damn this realm, he cursed in his mind.

"And how come that dump of a realm is our new home?" Luciel seethed with anger. "What have you done, Maziel? In the name of Celestia, WHAT HAVE YOU DONE?"

Her outburst of fury both intimidated Kazuk and stirred his loins.

All those cycles in incarceration and she has not lost an iota of her intoxicating personality, he thought with deep admiration. *You will serve me well, Luciel.*

"I can take you home and show you?" Kazuk offered.

Luciel eyed him with intense suspicion.

"The longer we delay, well..." Kazuk left the statement hanging.

If he tries anything stupid, I shall end him without reservation, she promised herself.

"Lead the way," Luciel finally said.

She summoned garments over her nudity, locked on to Kazuk's telepathic trail and followed him to Hell. Word of her arrival spread throughout Hell faster than a summoned archangel battle flame. Creatures of Hell, from those who fought for and against her, to those who had only heard of her, congregated around her, chanting her praise in a glorious welcome. Luciel's heart soared with appreciation.

"Lucie?" a voice called from behind her.

Luciel turned around and her jaw dropped.

"Is that really you?"

"Malichiel," Luciel cried out and rushed into his arms.

Cycles spent apart, with nothing but hope to keep them going, paid off in that perfect moment of warm, loving embrace.

"Maziel said you were all dead," Luciel spoke into his ear.

"They all are, Lucie," Metatron replied. "I am the last one left."

"No, brother," she withdrew herself and took his face in her hands. "I am here now. We are here. Together again. Just like old times."

Metatron smiled and his heart overflowed with joy.

"Just like old times, my dear sister," Metatron agreed.

Hell Realm continued chanting Luciel's name non-stop.

"Just say the word, and I will end this fool," Metatron hissed.

"I promise you, my friend, he will be yours to take care of," Luciel whispered her assurance. "But not now. We must be certain of what he is really up to first."

"I have truly missed you, Lucie," Metatron said with admiration. "You have not lost your wit and wisdom even after all these cycles."

"And I have missed you too, my dear friend," Luciel replied. "Let us get onto business now, shall we?"

Metatron nodded.

Luciel turned towards Kazuk and whispered in his ear.

"So, what stops me from ending you right here? You have seen for yourself where their loyalties lie, have you not?"

Luciel gestured at the crowd that was still chanting her name and praises.

"I never gave you the third reason, did I?" Kazuk replied, masking his burning jealousy behind a calm persona.

"Okay, let us hear it," Luciel said with exasperation.

"Michael is no longer around," Kazuk spoke quietly.

Paralysis borne out of shock seized Luciel. Disbelief rendered her speechless until that disbelief morphed into red, hot anger.

"You never should have," she glared at him. "Michael was mine to kill."

She inched towards him, mouth and eyes burning with her archangelic flames.

"What you have done is unforgivable," she reached for his throat. "For this, you must die a slow and very, very agonizing death."

Warning bells blared across Hell Realm.

"And, I was just about to add that Michael's war-crazed, top general, Raphael, The Ruthless, is now the supreme leader of Celestia," Kazuk grinned. "I suppose you know the meaning of those alarms, no?"

Luciel gritted her teeth and clenched her fists. Flames flared from her eyes and mouth as she glared at Kazuk once more. The corner of Kazuk's mouth stretched in a mischievous and satisfied smile of victory.

"I believe Raphael, The Ruthless, has a wing to pick with you, Luciel," Kazuk added and glared at Luciel with disdainful spite. "Welcome to the new order. MY new order."

"I will make sure you die slowly and painfully, Maziel," Luciel promised.

"Let us not restate the obvious, Luciel," Kazuk said dismissively. "And here, you will address me as Kazuk, YOUR king."

Kazuk walked away from Luciel to face the crowd, leaving Luciel to mire in her shock, fury, and confusion. He summoned his spear and raised it in the air. A deathly silence smothered Hell Realm.

"My brothers and sisters," Kazuk began his speech. "You have all heard the alarms. You know what this means. Celestia has declared war on us, just like we expected. They are weaker because Michael is gone."

A ripple of happy murmurs spread across the realm.

"And we are stronger because they do not know that our general, the great and mighty Luciel, is back."

Hell Realm chanted Luciel's praise.

"She will lead us again, but we will win this go-round. We will crush Celestia and take our rightful place in this dimension."

Kazuk then turned towards Luciel, who fought to maintain a calm demeanor despite Kazuk's overload of surprises.

"If our general could come forward, please," Kazuk asked politely.

Luciel obliged. Kazuk smiled at her and spoke out.

"When we turned our backs on Celestia under your leadership, we also let go of our past identities and names," he said. "We all have new names to symbolize our new lives and identities. So, we ask you, what would your new name be?"

Luciel thought for a few moments. During her cycles in Celestia, she was nicknamed, 'Lucifer', meaning 'Light Bearer,' because of her exceeding wisdom and charisma.

I do not want to let go of my identity as an archangel yet, but I must not disappoint these creatures, my followers, she thought.

"From this moment on," Luciel bellowed, "I shall be called Luceefa."

Hell Realm chanted her new name over and over. Her weapon, her sword, formed in her left hand and she raised it. Hell Realm followed suit.

"Who is ready for war?" Luceefa roared.

Hell Realm roared their answer.

"Let us reclaim our rightful place," she bellowed.

She's really good, Kazuk nodded with admiration.

He glanced in Metatron's direction and smiled.

He stands besides her like the loyal pet he is, he thought. *This will be fun.*

And as Hell Realm flew out for war, Lithilia watched from her quarters.

"Finally," her heart pounded hard against her chest with elation. "My plan comes together. Hell will suffer, starting with that bitch from The Abyss."

CHAPTER TWENTY-SEVEN

A NEW ORDER

ONCE AGAIN, IN the Dimension of Lemuria, history was about to be made. And while this history was going to be written in the ink of death and destruction, the Realm of Celestia refused to be the tablet upon which this history of violence would be written. Never again, like it did during the Great Rebellion cycles ago. A neutral zone in the space between Celestia and Hell became the designated battleground. Celestia and Hell faced each other, burning with the fire for conquest and desire for survival. Celestia outnumbered Hell by six-to-one, but Michael's absence was a blow below the belt. Hell, though highly outnumbered, had a surprise for Celestia.

Raphael, Uriel, and Gabriel flew to meet Kazuk and Metatron in the middle.

"Hello, Archangel Supreme," Kazuk bowed slightly in Raphael's direction. "And to the rest of you."

"Let us not stand on ceremony," Raphael scoffed. "I give you my word that if you stand down, we will let you all live. No need for another slaughter."

"I extend you the same courtesy, archangel supreme," Kazuk countered.

"You know we greatly outnumber you, right?" Gabriel asked.

"We can count, thank you," Kazuk mocked. "Wouldn't you agree?"

Kazuk turned to face Metatron, who stared blankly at his once-upon-a-moment brethren.

"Perhaps you could talk some sense to Maziel," Uriel addressed Metatron. "His pride will only lead to his quick demise and yours."

"Why are you even addressing him, Uriel?" Gabriel asked. "He is responsible for Michael's demise. His head is mine."

"A most unfortunate demise indeed, boys… and girl," Kazuk taunted and broke into a derisive laughter.

Gabriel's eyes flamed up and Raphael raised a hand towards Gabriel. With a puff, Gabriel extinguished his flames.

"It is never too late to return, Malichiel," Raphael said.

Metatron staggered a tinge with shock.

"But not as a member of the inner circle."

"Too late, Raph," Metatron shook his head. "There's no going back for me."

Raphael nodded and walked past Kazuk to face the creatures of Hell. As the new archangel supreme of the commanding realm of the dimension, Raphael resonated his vocal frequency with Lemuria's vibrational frequency. Every creature within half of Lemuria's radius could hear him clearly.

"You already know by how much we outnumber you," Raphael said. "I will make this offer once only. Lay down your weapons and I guarantee you, on my honor as archangel supreme of the Realm of Celestia, you will live."

He waited for a response from the crowd. Silence.

"Take my offer," Raphael continued. "You will not get a second chance. Why not listen to the voice of reason?"

"Because mine is the only voice they listen to," a familiar voice replied.

Raphael burned red hot with anger Uriel had only witnessed from him during the first rebellion. She cursed and immediately flew towards him. Even before his body burned with his archangel battle flame, Uriel was upon him, trapping his arms to his body with her arms around him and pinning him to her body.

"No, Raph," she grunted into his ears. "Not now."

The crowd parted and Luceefa glided towards Raphael and Uriel, wearing a smile of derision, evil and vileness on her face.

"Gabriel, help," Uriel called out.

Gasps and murmurs of shock, anger and awe waved through Celestia as Uriel and Gabriel used all their strength to subdue and drag Raphael back to their camp.

"Not now, brother," Gabriel pleaded. "I, too, want her head so badly. But not like this. Please, brother."

Raphael's body relaxed slightly, but Uriel and Gabriel did not let him go yet.

"You will have your chance," Uriel growled. "I promise you. We'll see to it."

"I swear on my wings, brother," Gabriel concurred.

Raphael heaved his shoulders and nodded. The tension in his body vanished. Uriel and Gabriel let go of him. He flexed his shoulders and straightened his gait.

"Luciel," Raphael glared hatred untarnished at her.

"Hello, brother," Luceefa returned his glare with a smug condescension.

Uriel stood so close to Raphael her shoulders touched his.

"Raph, control yourself," she spoke via telepathy only to his hearing. *"We have younglings who look up to us for leadership and guidance. We must send them the right message and practice what we teach. We must show them that we can actually do battle without letting our emotions getting the better of us."*

"You are right, sister," Raphael replied in kind. *"Thank you."*

"Thank me after you take off her head."

Raphael smiled and shot Uriel a sideways glance. She too smiled.

Why are they smiling? Luceefa wondered. *They're about to die and yet, they smile? Brave of them. They know they can never beat me and with Michael gone, their hopes just got squashed even more.*

Luceefa chuckled.

Desperation… hopelessness… they know their end is inevitable.

"Michael is not here," Raphael smirked at her. "You know what that means, do you not?"

"Indulge me," she spoke with exasperation.

"No one will stop me from taking off your head," he replied.

"Perhaps," Luceefa shrugged. "Believe it or not, that was the only reason why I didn't end him when I had the chance. I owed him; a debt which I paid for in kind. Still, he was supposed to die by my hands."

She turned and leveled a pair of flaming eyes in Kazuk's direction.

"What?" Kazuk shrugged and grinned sheepishly.

"They listen to you, Luciel," Uriel called out.

The flames in her eyes vanished and she returned her gaze towards Raphael. Uriel stepped in front of Raphael and Gabriel took Raphael by the arm.

"I'll handle this, Raph," Uriel said via telepathy. *"Your anger is flaring up again."*

"Please, we don't need another slaughter. You will lose again," Uriel urged.

"You were soft then and, with Michael gone, you're softer now," Luceefa spat. "Look at them."

She turned and waved at the creatures from Hell.

"They know why they are here. They know what they want. And nothing will stop them."

"A terrible mistake," Uriel said.

"A risk we are willing to take," Luceefa rebutted. "Against all hope, we have grown in our numbers. Against all expectations, you lost your Michael. Against all logic, I am back and against all odds, we will take Celestia, with or without your consent. And if our path to victory will be paved with the end of the existences of many on both sides, then so be it. But I will be damned for an eternity of cycles if I do not see my vision come to pass."

"Wings, Luciel. Your ego hasn't changed one bit after all these cycles," Uriel remarked, shaking her head. "If anything, it has grown even bigger and will be a detriment to you and Hell. I feel bad for your followers, though. They don't know who you are. They don't know WHAT you are. They follow you blindly because all they see is your charisma. But they know nothing about your true agenda, do they? Not even Malichiel."

Luceefa's eyes flashed. She bared brilliant, white teeth and glared at Uriel. Kazuk placed a hand on her shoulder.

"Yes, Luciel," Uriel smiled with satisfaction. "You know exactly what I'm talking about. You think you're so wise and full of wit. Well, I have news for you, you pathetic excuse for an archangel. The only reason you were ever the 'wisest and smartest' was because I, Uriel, made you feel that way. I, Uriel, knew of your every intention and your every move. I, Uriel, know what you really are."

She flamed up in Hadesina but I couldn't, Kazuk recalled. *And I'm an archangel. Is that because she's different from us? Is Michael also different from us? What does Uriel know about her, and possibly Michael, that we all don't?*

"Then why didn't you stop me then, if you speak truly?" Luceefa asked.

"Michael wouldn't believe me," Uriel replied. "And I didn't have proof. But I knew. The insanity you two called love blinded his judgement."

"He was honorable," Luceefa retorted. "He had the chance to end me, but he offered me another solution, which I refused. As such, he chose to end me in battle and after the rebellion, he promised to end me when next he saw me."

Luceefa's voice softened as she spoke but she quickly regained her composure.

"Well, he's not here but Raph will take immense pleasure in doing just that," Uriel spat.

Raphael, Gabriel, Kazuk, and Metatron followed the exchange between Uriel and Luceefa with faces contorted with looks of confusion. Raphael's confusion, however, turned to admiration when he appreciated Uriel establishing intellectual superiority over Luceefa, whom Celestia used to consider the wisest of them all. The more Uriel spoke, the more he realized that Uriel may have been the greatest mastermind Celestia had ever known.

And if that is the case, how much of an influence has she been? he asked himself. *And how much of a covert influence is she right now?*

"Hear my words, Luciel," Uriel growled and stepped closer to Luceefa. "I swear, on the light of my fallen brothers and sisters of the first war, that if Raphael does not make you pay, I, Uriel, will cleave your head from your neck."

Uriel summoned a dagger in her right hand. She raised her left hand and slashed her palm with the dagger. Angel light oozed from the gash. She closed her left hand into a fist and squeezed as she dismissed the dagger.

"And I seal my promise with my angel light," Uriel added fiercely.

What gesture is that? Gabriel wondered. *This is not of Celestia, or Hell.*

"Well, since none of us is willing to surrender," Kazuk jumped in with misplaced sarcasm, "let's go to war then. Enjoy your final moments, archangels."

Each group returned to its respective side.

"I forgot to tell you," Uriel said telepathically to Luceefa. *"I was bedding Michael long before he started bedding you."*

"And he dumped your sorry wings for me," Luceefa rebuffed.

"Oh no, you misunderstand, you whore of a creature," Uriel countered. *"It was I who dumped him. You were just a tool of solace for him. I guarantee you that whenever you two were humping hips together, he was thinking of me."*

Uriel turned around at the perfect moment to catch Luceefa's hateful glare, which she matched with a grin of victory.

"Don't worry, Luciel," Uriel added telepathically. *"Very soon, I'll put you right back in the hole Maziel dug you out of. Then, I shall pull you out of that hole and cut off your head."*

"And I just made you my personal mission, Uriel," Luceefa promised. *"I will make you suffer long before I end you."*

Hope for the miracle that was Eliel's return dwindled with the widening of the gap between Raphael's group and Kazuk's group. Uriel had stalled as long as she could and had even revealed more than what she intended to. The questions will come after the war, but she will worry about that later. She really did not want another war because the death toll never justified the reason for war. Instead, it served as a sour reminder, a scar to the psyche, that war must be avoided at all cost. Only Michael and an awakened Eliel had that power to put a stop to this insanity; neither of whom were around when they were needed. Raphael was a worthy leader, but he was no Michael, yet.

While Raphael and Luceefa gave their war speeches, Uriel's core ached for the many younglings who masked their fear with looks of courage. In the frontlines, the senior archangels stood in all their glory, strength and fearlessness. Smiles of excitement stretched across their faces, causing her to smile as well. The bravest creatures in Lemuria will whoosh over Hell with extreme prejudice. They were going to break their number one rule of fighting, which was never to let their emotions get the better of them. Unfortunately, Hell had taken Michael, their most revered leader, away from them and for that, Hell realm will only exist as an uninhabited, barren, lifeless realm when the war was over.

Uriel's bracelet glowed on her left wrist and a sword formed in each of her hands as flames spewed from her eyes and mouth. No need for shields when one was that great a fighter. A helmet appeared on her head. She glanced to her left and nodded at her archangel compatriots. They returned her nod. She did the same to those on her right. A fluttering of wings behind her caught her attention.

Which angel is foolish enough- she started thinking as she turned around.

"What are you doing, Beliel?" Uriel scolded her. "Return to the back lines."

"No disrespect, madam," Beliel said firmly. "But after everything you've done for me, may I be damned if I don't fight by your side. I am willing to lay down my existence for you, madam."

Uriel's features soften and the protective elder sister side of her took over.

"I admire your courage, my dear," Uriel spoke softly. "But you will not fight by my side yet."

"But madam," Beliel's eyes drooped with disappointment.

"You can be the eyes behind my back. The front line is for generals and you are not yet a general. Okay?"

"Yes, madam," Beliel beamed with delight. "I won't fail you."

"I know you won't," Uriel chuckled. "Now, just stay alive."

"Celestia is much bigger than my existence, madam," Beliel said firmly. "I fight for her and for Michael."

She gestured towards Hell's camp.

"It is they I feel sorry for," she added.

"What have I done?" Uriel smiled with admiration.

She smacked Beliel lightly on the helmet and turned to face Raphael.

Your head will earn me a seat at Kazuk's inner council, Beliel smiled evilly.

With a mighty war cry, Hell charged. Raphael raised his right fist. Celestia waited as Hell continued its charge. Raphael still held up his fist, his weapon not yet summoned. Hell charged closer and Raphael still held up his fist. Celestia stared at a mixture of creatures from other realms and dimensions within the cosmic cluster that constituted Hell's army. Luceefa led the charge in her flaming, archangelic glory, while the other fallen archangels burned with different colors other than golden yellow. Raphael held her stare and summoned his hammer. Finally, he brought his fist down and, with a mighty war cry, Celestia charged.

Suddenly, an object of intense brilliance appeared and streaked from above and crashed between the two camps that was about to go to war. Both camps immediately halted their charge and focused on the object as the intensity of the brightness diminished. An archangel emerged from the brilliance burning with archangelic battle flames. A golden bracelet glowed brightly on each wrist. Uriel's core screamed with joy. Kazuk screamed with rage. Raphael and Luceefa stared with uncertainty at each other. However, Metatron smiled. Eliel tuned into the frequency of Lemuria and resonated his vocal cords with that frequency, which was something only an archangel supreme could do.

"There will be no war," Eliel said for everyone present to hear. "Return to your respective realms at once."

"And who do you think you are?" a general from Hell asked.

Eliel turned his attention towards the general. A pair of serpentine eyes manifested above his head. Every creature present cowered in fear and awe at the sight. Then, flames shot out of Eliel's eyes. In a flash, nothing remained of the general from Hell who dared to defy him.

"Do I need to repeat myself?" Eliel asked.

Raphael and Luceefa hesitated, neither one of them wanting to be the first to leave and look more of a coward than the other. Eliel understood and turned towards Hell camp.

"Off you go now," Eliel commanded.

He chose Celestia, Kazuk pouted.

Luceefa hesitated, wrestling between defiance, which will lead to the same outcome as her general, and her pride, which she would still be alive if her pride got hurt. With a shoulder heave, she made her decision.

"Return to Hell," she ordered.

Hell Realm followed her order.

"Return to Celestia," Raphael ordered.

Within a moment, the space between Celestia and Hell, on which the story of another war was going to be written in the ink of death, pulsed with silence and emptiness, except for two archangels. Uriel glided towards Eliel until she hovered about three feet away from him. She switched her battle outfit into a long, white, ankle-length gown. He, too, replaced his outfit with a similar-styled gown. Then, she grinned, closed the gap between them rapidly and hugged him tightly. His hands gently rested on her back and held her closer to his body.

"I'm so glad you're here," Uriel exclaimed. "I'm so proud of you. You made it, Eliel. You made it."

"Yeah, I did," Eliel replied. "Perfect timing too, it seems."

"By flaming wings, yes," Uriel agreed.

Uriel peeled her body away from his but lingered close to him.

"Welcome back. I'm so glad you're here. Wait. I said that already."

Uriel averted her gaze to her toes to hide her embarrassment. Eliel's hand took her chin and tilted her head upwards. She did not resist his touch. Her eyes met his. They burned with a fire that Michael never had. The confused angel who fell was no longer there. An archangel exuding traits she had never witnessed in anyone smiled at her.

Everything will be alright, she thought. *Whatever 'everything' constitutes. He's here, our new leader… my new leader.*

Uriel placed her left hand on his cheek. She ran a finger along his cheek. Her hand slid down to his chest and rested there. Her gaze followed her hand before it returned to his eyes, the eyes that belonged to the lowly angel she had fallen in love with from the very first moment she had laid eyes on him.

"Eliel," she spoke softly. "There's… There's something I must tell you."

His lips found hers even before she mustered the courage to confess her love for him. Her core melted to the feeling of his lips on hers, to his body pressed against hers and to the knowledge that he, too, felt the same for her. He gently peeled his lips from hers.

"Let's go home now," Eliel said.

Even his voice seems to have changed, she thought. *Or maybe it's just the authority that comes with it.*

"We have a new order to establish."

We? I like the sound of that, she thought.

***

Lithilia watched Camp Hell's return.

"Looks like things didn't turn out as planned," she scoffed. "Wait a minute, they actually didn't. They're back here and they're not celebrating. What could've happened? Anyway, I'll deal with this later."

She leaned against the window sill of her domain.

"You with the violet theatrics," she frowned. "What are you?"

She pulled the outfit she wore the night she traded punches with Patrick towards her using telekinesis. She held it in her hands and examined it.

"This is the only link I have to her," she scowled. "Time to hunt you down."

Teleportation brought her to a domain that appeared empty. She took a knee, placed the outfit on the floor and waited. Two bright red orbs appeared and hovered close to the outfit. Lithilia reached around the red eyes as the body of a hound with thick, dark-gray fur formed around the eyes.

"Hello, Chiram," Lithilia gently rubbed the hound behind her ears.

Chiram bent down and sniffed the outfit.

"I can pick up something," she said, ignoring Lithilia's greeting.

"Wow, not even a 'hello,'?" Lithilia tried to sound friendly.

"Let's be clear about something, you bitch," Chiram retorted. "You and I are not friends. Obviously, you're here for something. So, start talking."

"Can't say I blame you for your hostility towards me," she retorted.

Chiram bared her fangs and growled menacingly at Lithilia.

"Okay, okay," Lithilia raised both hands in the air. "Could you please find this creature for me?" she gestured towards the outfit on the floor.

"Of course, I can," Chiram spat.

"Good. And when you find the creature, could you please contain it till I get there?" Lithilia asked.

"That will depend," Chiram said sarcastically.

"On?" Lithilia asked.

"My mood at the time," Chiram replied with more sarcasm.

"I'll ignore the attitude, Chiram," Lithilia almost lost her patience. "If you can't forgive me, that's fine. I accept that."

She stood up.

"Thank you again," she added. "And, for what it's worth, I'm truly sorry."

Lithilia teleported away.

Chiram stared blankly ahead for a few moments.

"Hounds," she called out.

Six red pairs of eyes appeared behind her.

"We are going hunting," she said.

Howls of excitement echoed across the domain.

***

4 a.m., barely two hours after she closed the bar. Sara slept deeply after another busy night at the bar. Suddenly, her eyes snapped open and glowed bright violet. She remained motionless in her bed, sensing a familiar presence in her room. Then, an avalanche of memories came crashing down from her subconscious. A smile spread across her face and she attached a name to the familiar presence in her room.

"Hello, Ashram," Sara said.

Ashram manifested from the shadows and walked around the bed towards her. His thick white fur glowed beautifully in the glare of the moonlight that pierced through the curtain-less windows of her bedroom. He licked her face, and she brushed the fur around his ears.

"It has been a while, my friend," he said. "You know why I am here."

"I know, my dear friend," Sara replied.

Seven pairs of red orbs appeared in the darkness in front of them.

Sara's eyes glowed brighter and Ashram's glowed in a bright, white radiance before Sara spoke again.

"I know, and I remember."

CHAPTER TWENTY-EIGHT

COUNTER MEASURES

THE ONE HAS *returned. So what? Who gives an esoteric crap. You think this is over? You think a new big boss changes anything? You poor fools. There's more to come, creatures of Lemuria; you all wait and see. A lot more. You haven't even seen my catalyst, my agent of chaos, in full blossom yet. The inevitable will always remain inevitable. It can only be postponed. Everything will come to pass according to MY will. I know, because I've seen it. I know because I designed it. I know because I am a purveyor of purpose. I know because I am The Scribe. I am Chaos and I am perfect.*

Celestia was never part of the initial manuscript, The Soulless Ones. *However, when the first batch of angels were spawned, I realized how much Michael and Luciel reacted to polarization, how much they struggled with identifying with the vibrations of good and evil. I couldn't pass up on such an opportunity even if I wanted to. On Earth, I had to engineer the Bright Eyes. What a waste of my precious moments and talents. Absolute failures, those pathetic creatures. However, in Celestia, every angel and archangel was physically and esoterically ready to receive the vibration of chaos at the Great Reset from the moment they emerged from the spawn sanctuary, thanks to their makers. However, Michael and Luciel were the best candidates to serve as my catalyst. All I need is one and I already made my decision.*

The Scribe accessed the Dimension of Time by extending his consciousness past the self-created boundaries of his limited form. The history and future of Creation revealed itself to him in the ever-present. He chose a point in the ever-present, before the Great Reset, which marked the birth of Celestia.

The Shemsus, he thought. *So you're the ones who created the angels.*

The etheric video of Celestia's creation and population play within his near-boundless being.

This explains their penchant for violence and self-annihilation, The Scribe nodded. *So that's why Michael and Luciel are different from their peers. This explains a lot actually.*

The etheric video came to a pause upon his telepathic command. A moment of silence elapsed before he resumed the video.

I need a much better, more powerful catalyst for Earth Realm, The Scribe concluded. *A creature far too powerful for the humans to handle, in case Maduk and Beelzebub turn out to be disappointments, like the Bright Eyes were.*

The Scribe considered importing possible candidates from one of the many manuscripts he had written for many portions of Creation.

I shall stick to The Soulless Ones, he decided. *I'll find something within this manuscript.*

The Scribe extended his consciousness and accessed the Dimensions of Time, Space, Energy and Ether at once, with concentration on *The Soulless Ones.* An instant later, the warm feeling of a smile spread across his etheric being.

There you are... my ultimate catalyst, the feeling of satisfaction that can only result from a resounding success washed over his etheric being. *And now, I rewrite* The Soulless Ones *manuscript.*

A golden pen and a golden manuscript titled *The Soulless Ones,* formed within the cosmoscape. Using telekinesis, The Scribe willed the pen to trace golden glyphs within the cosmoscape. The manuscript opened to the first page. When he finished tracing the glyphs, they disintegrated into etheric pieces and flowed towards the manuscript. The pages of the manuscript turned under his power of telekinesis and the etheric pieces of the glyphs buried themselves in the pages of the manuscript. The new version of *The Soulless Ones* closed and disintegrated in to the cosmoscape.

Excellent, he complimented himself.

A virtual, copied aspect of Creation projected itself unto a virtual cosmoscape he generated within his psyche.

Initiating simulation of the new manuscript, he said to himself.

Within the virtual Creation, the cosmic clock counted down to the end of the perfect cycle. The Great Reset started and the vibration of chaos began pulsing from the Core of Creation.

Perfect, The Scribe exclaimed with satisfaction. *The inevitable remains the inevitable. Not that it comes as any surprise, anyway. Nothing new. I am Chaos. I am THE purveyor of purpose and I am perf-*

A wave of shock rocked his etheric form.

Impossible, he thought. *It was there, a tinge of something... familiar.*

Another wave of shock rocked his etheric form.

This cannot be, he exclaimed.

He returned to his virtual simulation expecting that what he perceived and concluded from that perception were mere errors.

Which itself was impossible because I am The Scribe and I don't make mistakes.

Yet, his perception of the familiar was not an error and the conclusion was on point. The undoing of Creation in his simulation was being reversed by something or someone with similar abilities as his. Shock slowly turned to fury and fury slowly morphed to something beyond fury as he watched the simulation of a partially undone Creation return to normal. With extreme annoyance, The Scribe gently exited the Dimensions of Space, Time, Energy and Ether because if he remained furious while in that state of rage, the vast majority of Creation would have been affected and Akasha and maybe even The Logos would have stepped him and destroyed him completely.

I want to undo all of Creation, not most of it, he pouted as he slowly returned to his default form. *Kundalini and The Core don't care about what I do and neither does The Logos. It's not Akasha either. I'd know if it was her.*

His default form returned. He hovered in a portion of Creation that was uninhabited for billions of cosmic clusters.

This can only mean one thing, The Scribe thought. *Someone is rewriting my manuscripts. Not just one or a few, but all of them. Someone is giving Creation a fighting chance.*

The cosmic power of a multidimensional being, fueled by something beyond rage and hatred, seeped into this part of Creation where The Scribe hovered. Trillions of realms seized with seismic activities of the apocalyptic kind because of their inability to resonate to cosmic vibrations unthinkably far beyond their levels of consciousness.

I have a new archnemesis, The Scribe fumed with frustration. *Who are you?*

Unable to hold his feelings back any longer, The Scribe let out a scream of rage so pure and intense that pure vibrations of chaos pulsed across this part of Creation. Nothing remained of the billions of cosmic clusters. Not even an ether.

Balim and Synath, the Paradins overseeing the area of Creation The Scribe recently destroyed, detected a massive spike in energy unlike anything they had ever seen before. Then, nothing remained.

"What was that?" Balim asked.

"I do not know," Synath replied. "We must inform our superiors at once."

The Paradins did report to their supervisors, not that The Scribe cared.

You can hide for now, but you won't hide from my wrath forever, The Scribe promised his unknown archnemesis.

***

The multidimensional being resonated to the most subliminal vibrational frequency it could summon.

Practice, practice, practice, it said to itself.

It could easily access the Dimensions of Space and Ether. But accessing those of Time and Energy still required more practice.

I can go through the cosmoscape with Space and Ether, but I need Time and Energy to complete my mission, it reminded itself. *Come on. Come on.*

Frustration clawed at its being and it paused for a moment.

Calm down now, it said to itself. *Just... calm down.*

Gradually, the claws of frustration let go of its etheric being. It extended its consciousness past its self-created boundaries. Its being tingled with pure energy and the ever-present revealed itself.

Energy and Time, it thought.

A warm feeling washed over its etheric being.

The multidimensional being peeked into an instant in the ever-present, before the Great Reset, to represent the past. Everything looked undisturbed. However, when it searched for a point in the ever-present, beyond the point of reference of the Great Reset that represented the future, a dark, empty, lifeless void gaped at him. No life, no energy, absolute nothingness. Sadness seized its etheric being.

I'm too late, it thought. *Why am I even a multidimensional being if I can't do anything?*

Despair and disappointment draped over its thoughts. Suddenly, its etheric being flooded with clarity.

The future I see is based on a series of events The Scribe has set into motion across Creation. I know what I must do.

With hope and excitement firing through its etheric being, it scanned across Creation using its consciousness. One-by-one, it accessed every single manuscript The Scribe had written. It studied each manuscript carefully. When it finished, it returned the manuscripts.

You don't know who I am, Scribe, it said with determination. *But when the moment is perfect, you and I will have words.*

Yeshua sparked a golden pen and several manuscripts from the ethers. Using telekinesis, he wrote several glyphs, which dissipated into many etheric specks and buried themselves into the pages of the manuscripts. The manuscripts closed and dissipated into the Dimensions of Space, Time, Energy and Ether. Yeshua chose a subliminal form for himself. A seat formed to accommodate his form. He relaxed into the seat, closed his eyes and smiled.

"And now, we wait."

THE END OF PART THREE

AUTHOR NOTES AND CONTACT INFORMATION

Thank you so much for reading *An Archangel's Ache,* Book Two of *The Soulless Ones.* I hope you enjoyed reading it. Follow me on social media.

Follow me on social media:

Facebook Page: *Leo E. Ndelle*

Instagram, Snapchat, Twitter: *@elonendelle*

www.eloverse.com

Leave a rating and review.

Please take a moment to read a sample of Book Three of the series titled *Baiting The Beast.* Enjoy!

BOOK THREE

BAITING THE BEAST

A LIFELESS PITCH blackness smothered the land from horizon to horizon. The earth was parched, rock-hard and cracked in a myriad of erratic patterns. The land reeked of loneliness and emptiness.. And except for a single soul that sat cross-legged on the ground, eyes closed and in deep meditation, the land was encased in an aura of death.

Marissa blended with this stillness, becoming one with it. She felt the anima of the barrenness, desolation and death of the land using clairsentience. Her anima resonated with the anima of this plane of existence. Marissa savored this resonance and unity. Then she breathed in slowly and deeply, and a zephyr blew across the land. She slowly exhaled and the zephyr continued to blow across the land. Marissa continued breathing slowly until her breathing synced with the zephyr. Her eyes remained closed. But in her mind, she formed an image of an all-engulfing brightness.

"Let there be light," she commanded in a quiet voice.

Immediately, the darkness was chased away by the light, revealing the dire nature of the land. Marissa opened her eyes and appreciated what she saw. She assigned no labels or judgement.

I'm getting better, she thought.

However, her logical mind started doing what it did best; run in every direction of the world it had created for itself during her millennia of existence in the realm.

Not right now. She thought, and her mind stilled.

Marissa let it all be. She embraced and accepted it all for what it was. She smiled and felt Mother smiling back at her. At least, her clairsentience indicated that this was the case. All was peaceful; all was serene until the ruckus began.

It started with a violent earthquake that shook the realm like a rag doll. But after a countless number of reruns, Marissa was unbothered by it. She had been petrified the first few times, though, and many mistakes had resulted from that initial fear. But just as practice precedes perfection, she had gotten better. And now, she remained as calm as a mountain in the storm that was the earthquake, as the earth rocked and split under the sheer force of geological spasms. Then, seven hills of equal sizes broke out of the ground in succession and equidistant from one another. From an aerial perspective, if the tops of these hills were connected, they would form a heptagon or an outline of a seven-faceted crystal. Marissa waited for what she already knew was about to unfold.

A ball of fire streaked across the sky like a falling star, leaving a trail of white sparkles in its wake. It streaked and burned across the skies like a cosmic torch and headed straight for the seven hills. It burned brighter as it entered the realm's atmosphere and its acceleration was beyond that of the realm's gravitational pull. The falling star provided more illumination for the already lit, barren realm. Its downward path heralded a promise of apocalyptic obliteration for anything it impacted. One of the newly-formed seven hills suddenly became so big and tall that Mt. Everest would look like a mole hill next to it, and its sudden increase in size was perfectly timed with the collision from the falling star.

A mega explosion more brilliant than those from a hundred Solaras combined followed the impact and half of the mountain was destroyed by the fallen cosmic object. However, the cosmic object, a twenty-four-foot-diameter ball of red-hot, magma-burning fury, remained intact and settled at the bottom of a ten-mile wide and one-mile deep caldera that had just been created in what remained of the mountain. Slowly, as if it had a mind of its own, the ball of fire started rolling up the caldera. It paused at the edge. Marissa was facing this cosmic body of mass destruction and this cosmic body seemed to stare down at her. And then, as if guided by an unseen, malicious force, it slowly tipped over the lip. Once its center of gravity crossed over the edge, it accelerated towards her.

Marissa remained still. The gigantic, blazing ball of fire incinerated everything in its path. Six leagues… Marissa remained still. One league… Half a league… Four hundred fathoms… Three hundred… Marissa did not even blink. She was still; in mind, in body and in her being. She was still by her own nature. When the ball of fire was two hundred yards away, it burst open and a nine-foot-tall creature leaped from its bowels, leaving a trail of fire and smoke as it sailed through the air. The creature landed ten feet away from Marissa in a crouched position before slowly rising to its feet.

The creature appeared mostly human, all nine feet of its smoldering, muscular body, with claws for fingers and toes. It sparked the ethers and a twelve-foot long, smoldering trident coalesced in its right hand. A bright yellow-red flame blazed around its body like a smoldering silhouette. The creature focused blazing yellow-red eyes on Marissa, whose real name was Sarael, and when it opened its mouth to speak, yellow-red flames spewed from its mouth. The creature lifted its trident and crashed the hilt of the trident three times on the ground. A violent earthquake followed each crash and each earthquake was more violent than the previous one. On the third crash, the earth ruptured and fissured towards Marissa in erratic patterns. When the fissure was close to her, it forked on either side of her as if it was forced to do so by an unseen force. Marissa remained still.

"You are getting better," the creature complimented her.

"You bore me," Sarael replied.

"Oh, Sarael," The Beast smirked. "You should learn to lighten up."

"I won't fail this time," Sarael reassured herself and The Beast before levitating in the air.

Sarael sparked the ethers. A golden sword formed in her left hand and a golden shield appeared in her right. She uncrossed her legs and let her feet touch the ground as shoes of gold formed over them. Then she pulled the shield in front of her and placed her sword next to the shield in a battle stance as an armor of gold formed across her torso. A golden hair band appeared behind her head and tied her long, black hair in a tight bun. Green flames then erupted from her eyes and mouth at the same time.

"Today you fall," Sarael promised and lunged towards The Beast.